Black Walls Turn Gray

Black Walls Turn Gray

Brad Jones

Cincinnati Book Publishing

Cincinnati 2014

But how is it
That this lives in thy mind? What seest thou else
In the dark backward and abysm of time?

William Shakespeare
The Tempest

BLACK WALLS TURN GRAY

BY BRAD JONES

Published by Cincinnati Book Publishing
Cincinnati, Ohio

Anthony W. Brunsman, President and CEO
Sue Ann Painter, Vice president and Executive Editor
Mark P. Painter, Copy editor and interior design
Karen Bullock, Public relations manager
Amelia Stulz, Web and electronic media manager
Rebecca Goodman, Copy editor
Cover design by Brent Beck
Photographs by Brad Jones

www.cincybooks.com

Black Walls Turn Gray BOOK 978-0-9910077-5-2
Black Walls Turn Gray EBOOK 978-0-9910077-6-9
Library of Congress Control Number: 2014935615

Printed in the United States of America
First Edition, 2014

To purchase additional copies online, visit
www.cincybooks.com

Discounts available on quantity orders. Email: info@cincybooks.com or call 513-382-4315.

To arrange appearances by the author, contact him directly at
blackwallsturngray@gmail.com

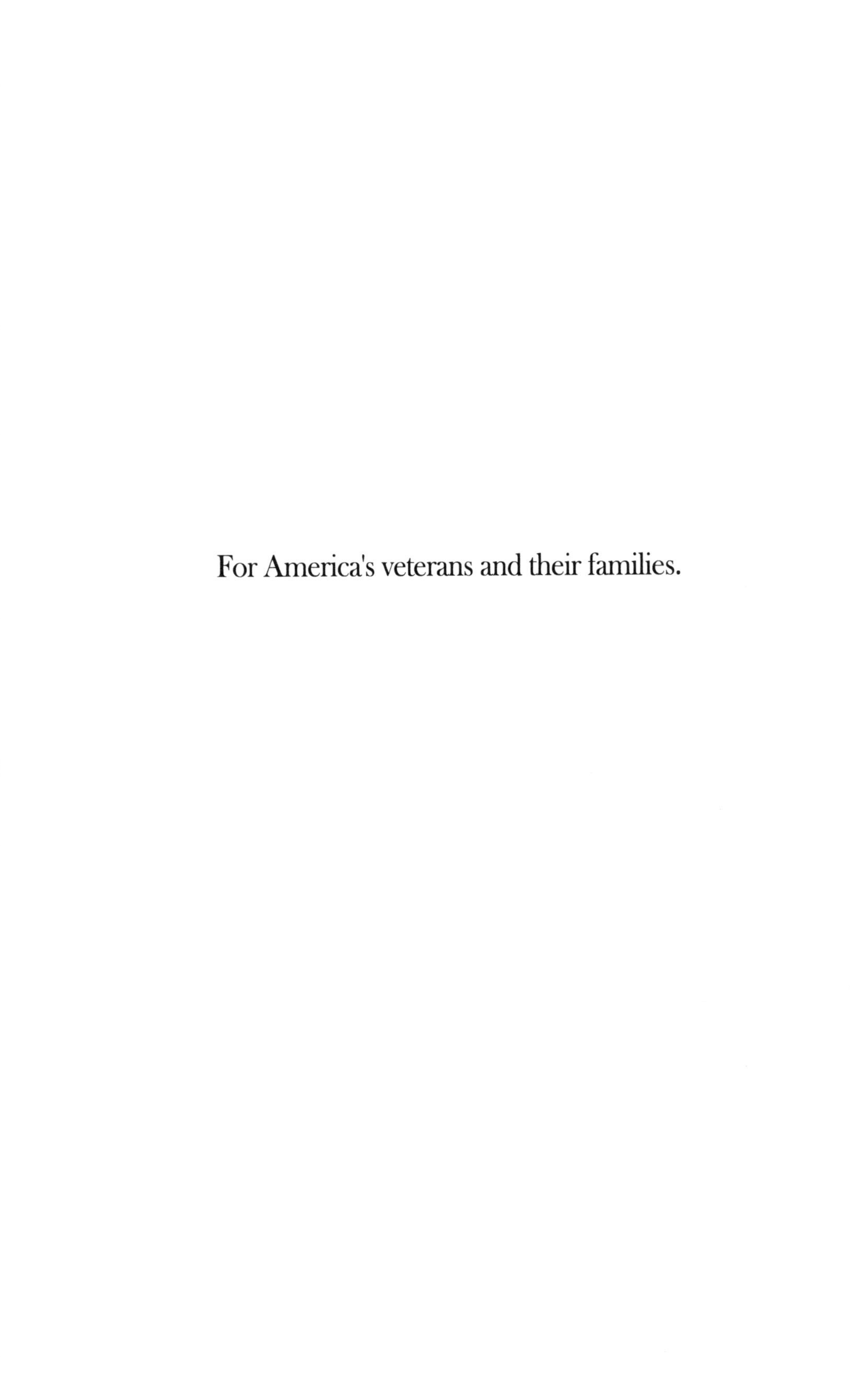

For America's veterans and their families.

Chapter 1
≈ Campus: Fall 1998 ≈

Themistocles wore a fierce stare. His marble bust sat aloft on a table, and gazed over the room between bookshelves, as if they were peaks near the shores of Salamis. David, sword unsheathed, postured above Goliath's decapitated head. A vent hummed, making sounds like a cicada crying in a summer tree. Jade plants grew in pots beneath a window. Shadows filled the room. Shelves sagged with aging books. Yellowing pages excreted a stale, pungent odor.

Quince sat alone at a small corner table among the sculptures and plants. It was the week of mid-term exams, and the room was his favorite study area. He found focus there among the shadows and tranquil sounds. And when he grew weary, the statues inspired him, mending his frayed concentration. It was Friday. Only one exam remained, but exhaustion now weakened his discipline. There was a futility about his studies that afternoon. He sat over a book and struggled to read the barren words. His head rocked in swaying motions; tired eyes rose and fell until they finally dropped like sashes, and his face tumbled into the book. His breathing took on rhythms of sleep. Slobber moistened the pages below his mouth. A vent chirped somewhere. Must hung like perfume in the air. Shadows grew. Sculptures stood guard.

Later, as he slept, a door slammed; the clap so loud and sudden that David's bronze flesh seemed to flinch. Startled, Quince awoke. His groggy face swiftly rose from the pages. His eyes swept over the room, but were unable to locate the elusive whispers that mingled among the books. In minutes, Quince's pulse accelerated from the soft rhythm of sleep to sudden excitement. Blood rushed to his brain, and he felt light-headed. As whispers drew close, he watched Themistocles, and in his temporary delirium, swore the general's lips poised and called down fleets of triremes. Turning, he saw David's biceps tense as he gripped the sword, staring down an aisle, between shelves, as if it were the Valley of Elah.

Soon, tense moments faded. Whispers fell silent. Quince drew a deep breath. His pulse idled. The delirium passed, and a grin lifted his cheeks. He surveyed the room, and found David standing proud, but quiet, above the slain. And, high on a shelf rested a forgotten bust. Quince's eyes fluttered, and closed. His head slowly fell onto the pages, moist with slobber. His breath took on rhythms of sleep. The library was quiet.

"Wake up, Boss!" a voice suddenly shouted.

Quince's sleepy face rose from the pages.

"Get up! You done missed it! Done missed the final exam!"

Quince's eyes swelled with confusion, and swept over the room; a deep, red mark, a sleep scar, was indented along his temple.

The shouting soon melted into laughter. A young, stocky man cradled his belly, laughed, and pointed at the student's surprised face. Slobber dribbled from Quince's lip, and the sleep scar resembled a lethal wound.

"Boss," taunted the stocky man. "You were ready to hump that book. Climb her like a prom date!" The man burst into laughter, still cradling his belly.

Quince sighed. His face was pinched as he cursed, "Bastard!"

"Why are you doing this to yourself?" said the stout man.

Quince massaged sleep from his face, rubbing his cheeks and drying dribble from his lip. "What are you saying, Baxter?"

"Saying you can't keep it up."

"Keep what up?"

"What?" chuckled Baxter disbelievingly, "Burning the candle at both ends. Man, that's what! You do too much!"

Quince rubbed his cheeks, and defiantly proclaimed, "Watch me."

Baxter's thick head shook. Quince's serious tone had wiped a smile from the man's face. "Two-a-day practices? Classes? And, each weekend, you run home to help your old man farm?"

Quince stood, closed the book, tucked it away in the pack, and zipped the bag. He slid the pack over his shoulder, and boasted, "A lesser man would crack!"

"Why do it?" Baxter worried, pursuing Quince across the room, passing through David's shadow, turning right at the shelf holding a bust of the mighty Greek General Themistocles, and moving through a hall and down marble steps.

"What choice do I have?"

"I know why. Cause you are the first Magowan to attend college. First to leave the farm. Honorable, man! Noble. Real noble shit."

Quince walked, and tersely answered, "I reckon."

"A country boy from Lemonsburg making it big."

Quince retorted, laughing, “It’s Flemingsburg, you idiot!”

“Except you never left the farm. You’re there every weekend. Working dawn ‘til dusk and what does it get you? Nothing. A sore back and a boot full of cow shit!” Baxter let loose a condescending chuckle.

A smile lifted Quince’s cheeks. “No one spreads bullshit like you. Not even a herd of Black Angus!”

“Nevertheless. Why? Why do it? You’re not majoring in Black Angus?”

“Baxter, we’ve been over this.”

Baxter’s thick head shook. “Cause your old man needs help. And, cause your grandfather farmed the land before him.”

Quince nodded.

“Real honorable stuff,” Baxter noted.

“I reckon,” Quince sighed.

Frustration bubbled from Baxter’s portly face as he exclaimed, “Man, you’re a senior for State. Fifteen thousand students strong. More than half are smoking hot co-eds.”

“Yeah. All smart enough to avoid you, Baxter.”

Baxter persisted, “Time you act like a senior! Enjoy it! Live!”

Quince ignored him, walking.

“How about it?” Baxter continued.

Quince shrugged, answering unenthusiastically, “Sure.”

Baxter’s face dropped, conceding, “Honorable. Real noble.”

Quince slowly descended the stairs while the soft clap of his feet echoed about. He walked quietly. The electric flame of a sconce threw light over his face. Groggy, the yokes of his eyes were webbed with lines, but the red scar over his temple had begun to fade. He tugged at the pack straps, and walked without speaking. Baxter walked alongside; his face was loud and busy even during those silent times. Together, they turned and crossed a wide landing beneath a window. Light poured over them as they descended the last flight into a foyer. “So, what’s next?” asked Baxter, turned to the taller man.

Quince sighed, “Early 20th Century History.”

“Booker?” Baxter asked, bursting into laughter. “Man,” shook his thick head, “his lectures are the worst. Bland stuff. Real theory-type shit!”

Quince nodded.

“Last semester he gave a lecture on the Eighteenth Amendment that would drive a Mormon to drink!”

Quince chuckled. Baxter walked alongside, shaking his thick head. Echoes softly clapped about. Walking slowly, they passed portraits of college presidents hung high above the steps. Baxter relentlessly shook his head. Quince's red-yoked eyes gazed ahead while faces from the last century smiled at the two students.

They soon descended into a foyer, a large room filled with dark paneling. A tall counter stood near the wall. Quince turned, but Baxter grabbed his arm before he could leave, hoisting a book near his chest, "Hold up! I need to return this."

Quince nodded, and said, "Outside." He then turned, opened a glass-paned door, took a step, and stopped flat, sunk in the moment as if wet, gooey, concrete had swallowed his feet. Standing near the library door, he stared across a lawn, smiling. His cheeks were leavened by something he saw. It was fall. Campus was busy. Students ambled along sidewalks. Nearby, large trees burned with autumn's color. Some students scaled a slope to the library, dodging the tall, wiry student, as they entered through a glass-paned door. Quince stood on the sidewalk, frozen, staring. Each time the door swung open, and lazily closed, his reflection colored the panes in an October sun; hair, thick and dark; eyes, focused; a jersey stretched over his shoulders; a red pack, filled with books, on his back. Along the street, students perched on a stone wall, talking and studying. Others squatted in lush grass, beneath stone buildings. The excitement of Friday sifted through a perfect afternoon.

Quince's stare slid down the hill, stopping near a maple that shook in a soft breeze. Leaves dropped from the old tree like red snowflakes, gently bouncing into the grass; a blanket of them, perfectly circular, lay around the maple. A book rested in the leaves, open, and the shadow of a young woman grayed the pages. She sat cross-legged, leaning over the book, occasionally lifting a page and slowly dropping it. Her eyes focused on the turning page as if she valued every word. Her thin, bare neck browned in a soft sun. Waves of hair fell over her face. She seemed tiny and alone below the huge tree, as if the large book would grab her finger, yank her into the bland text, and close.

Quince grinned, watching as she brushed leaves from the book. He sank in the moment. Lost to him was the breeze, tugging at this jersey, or students slipping past him and through the door. That was Quince. He stood his ground, and ignored life's pushes and taunts; stood against the flow, the grain. The needle of his compass didn't always point in that direction, but when it did, he wasn't afraid to turn, face the winds, and go.

Again, the door swung open, and lazily closed. A crimson jersey colored the panes. "So," Baxter shrugged, "What's up? What's this?"

"What?"

"Man."

"What?"

Baxter chuckled, "I come out of the library and you're standing here like the statue of a dead dean."

Breath escaped through Quince's nostrils as he laughed.

"That's it. Like you were cast in bronze. Dropped right here, in the way, for everyone to see. Freaking dead dean, Magowan."

Quince shook his head, cursing, "Bastard."

Baxter grinned. "So? What's this?"

Quince paused, smiling, "Just admiring things."

"What?" asked Baxter.

"Scenery."

"Scenery?" he chortled. "You mean trees? Nature and shit?"

Quince shook his head, "Nope."

"What then?"

"Just things."

Baxter followed Quince's eyes to the maple, and the young woman reading in the grass. His brow rose. His chubby face spread to the point of breaking apart, and falling in pieces along the walk. "No!"

"What?"

"No!" laughed Baxter.

"What?"

"What?" Baxter worried, retreating again.

Quince turned and smiled, nodding his head.

"Sara Foster?" continued Baxter, lines furrowed along his brow. Students walked around the two men. Frustrated expressions taunted them. The door opened, and slowly closed. The October sun painted two crimson jerseys in the panes.

Quince nodded.

"Sara Foster?" asked Baxter.

Quince smiled, "It just sounds right, Sara Foster."

"It don't sound right. It sounds wrong, man."

Quince's lips pursed. He nodded.

"Man, you know her story."

"You're about to tell me."

Baxter advanced a few steps, "Trimble."

"Trimble?" Quince frowned, "I don't like him."

"Well, she did, once anyway. And he liked her."

"Once?"

"We're talking about the quarterback. QB. Ohio Valley Conference's Broadway Joe. She's Trimble's girl."

Quince's head shook. His face pinched as if Baxter's words had an odor, smelling of a sewer. "They went out?"

"Many times."

Quince flashed a look of skepticism.

Baxter shook his head.

"Besides, he doesn't need her. He has other girls."

Baxter paused, his face was open with disbelief, "Man, you're setting yourself up!"

Quince grinned. His cheeks rose, "Maybe."

Baxter's face opened, nearly breaking apart. He was easily excited. His nerves could rattle seismographs across states. Composure was utterly undetectable in the stocky young man. "You know what I mean? It's Trimble!"

Quince's face pinched, and he shrugged. "He's got nothing."

"He's got something for you if you take his girl."

"I'll fight Trimble."

Baxter advanced, trying to sway Quince, "I'm not talking about a fight. Trimble won't fight. He's a showboat. Pretty-boy type."

"What's he got?"

Baxter rolled his eyes, advancing, "He won't fight. He goes personal. Pride and shit."

Quince shook his head. "Nothing."

"He's the QB. Coach lets him run the option. He'll . . ."

Quince nodded, and finished the words Baxter began, "stop the pass."

"It's your record, man." Baxter's face was wide, nearly breaking apart. Seismographs rattled along the New Madrid fault.

Quince nodded.

"If I see Sara," Quince pointed at the young woman, "Trimble will go with the run next Friday night?"

"The ball will never see the air," Baxter answered confidently.

Quince grinned, his eyes focused on the young girl under the maple, reading. "He can try."

"You're on course to break the OVC record for single season receiving yards. Hell, you could break it sooner. One good game! That's all! We're talking receiving record, man! Your name goes in the books. Goes up on the wall of that tunnel. Hell, every player for the next hundred years will see the name Quince Magowan in giant-ass crimson letters as he walks out of the locker room, through that tunnel, onto the field. That right there. That's immortality. Real stuff!"

Quince shrugged, "Next Friday."

"Against the Dawgs?"

Quince nodded.

"Antigua Sherman? The best defensive back in conference?"

Quince's lips bunched. His shoulders shrugged.

Baxter's hands flew up in a fit of reason, as if he were surrendering. "Let's be honest. You're not getting those yards on Sherman! The guy's an animal. Man among boys. Truthfully, he scares the shit out of me!"

"I'll get it," bragged Quince.

Baxter shook his head. "You'll need Trimble to get those yards."

Quince frowned.

"Trimble is a real spiteful SOB. You make a pass at his ex, and he won't throw it. We're talking run the whole game. On the ground, round-and-round. Just me running scared from Antigua Sherman!"

Quince gazed down the hill.

Baxter shook his thick head, warning, "Don't do it!" But his words were never heard.

Tom Quincy Magowan walked down the hill, through the grass, green with autumn's moisture, toward the maple.

Chapter 2
≈ On the Field: One week later ≈

It was a Friday night ritual. Explosions inaugurated the evening. Heavy smoke scratched their lungs. Lights pierced the black sky as the team jogged across the field, and huddled around Coach Simpson. Coach gave a speech, telling them to play hard, and to respect the opponent. He spoke to them like men. When the huddle broke, they stood along the sideline with a hand placed on their chest. Around the stadium, speakers played the national anthem. It sounded like a scratchy old record. Bleachers, crowded with fans, rose in steep angles around the field. The air was cool. Everyone stood and sang. Quince sang. The helmet dangled from his left hand. His right palm lay across his chest. He loved this time. The crisp breeze and the patriotic feeling of the night lifted pimples along his arm.

Fans clapped as the scratchy sounds fell silent. Then, the sky exploded. Flares rocketed over the stadium, and explosions illuminated the evening sky, heralded by the cheers of thousands. Together, the team stood on the field as red and green flares showered down around them. Smoke fell across the stadium like fog.

Finally, a horn bellowed over the stadium. The team donned helmets and head-butted each other, smacking their shoulder pads. They growled. They jumped in place to warm the adrenaline. Behind the thin, silver bars of his facemask, a smile lifted Quince's cheeks. He loved this night. It was time to play.

The opponent was tough—a big team with experience. Quince knew the first half would be physical. He knew they had a chance if the game were close at halftime. But, thirty minutes later, as the horn sounded, and referees ran across the field, blowing whistles, his fears were realized. A bruising, brutal half was over. Already, their lungs had choked more smoke than a coal stove. Their legs ached. Fresh bruises dotted their arms and shins. Mud and grass stained their crimson jerseys. Together, they walked across the field with a defeated posture. Helmets dangled freely in one hand. Their faces hung low. No one spoke. As they disappeared into a tunnel between the bleachers, the team resembled teenagers who had just been whipped by bullies.

Baxter sat on a bench along the locker room wall. Sweat puddled between his feet. "Coach," whined the running back, "They're all over me. I can't get free. They have shallow coverage and their backs are cramming the box. Coach," he paused, his face contorted in frustration as he gulped water from a plastic bottle, "they're ready for it. Ready for our run game." His brow lifted in the middle. His eyes wore the look of fear. His arms were bruised and stained with grass and soil. Sweat and water dripped from his chin. The helmet's inner pads had temporarily scarred his forehead. His crimson pants were green along the knees. When he finished speaking, his head just sank. Everyone knew Baxter was an intrepid whiner. The shame of it just never bothered him. But there was something profoundly true about his words this evening. He wore the scars of battle.

Coach Simpson was a sympathetic old man. He became head coach during the Eisenhower administration. Generations had played for him. After all those years, students just referred to him as Coach; a surname wasn't necessary. But years of coaching left him mellow. Ambition faded decades ago when he accepted this position as his life's work. Age cooled his temper to a tepid Fahrenheit. During that moment, he approached the stocky running back, and patted the young man's shoulder. His face momentarily hung down, his thick jowls drooped, and loose skin covered much of his dim eyes. He slowly turned, and pulled the lid from a marker. Standing near a white board, he drew one line over the other, and did the same, again. Up higher, he drew several more. He closed the marker, and turned, slowly. With Coach Simpson, all things moved slowly. He walked slow, talked with a slow drawl, his arms moved as if they were bearing heavy weights. But his mind knew football.

Coach's head shook, slowly, "Men," he paused, "Baxter's right. They're playing tight. Loading the box. Anticipating the run. Trimble," his head fell and twisted, "I trust you with the option. Have all season, but tonight," his head twisted, slightly lower, "you've gone short every time. They're anticipating it." He walked a few steps and paused in front of the whiteboard. "We need a passing game. Extend them. Spread them out. Trimble," he paused, "We need Quince in the game."

The room was filled with men in crimson jerseys. Most were sitting, leaning forward, elbows resting on their knees. A few men stood around the walls, holding clipboards. Their faces were grim. Quince sat on a bench, in the corner. He gazed across the room at Trimble. Just the sight of him warmed Quince's adrenaline. His face drew in, pinched, as if he'd just bitten into a lemon.

Trimble leaned forward; his face appeared honest, concerned, "Coach," his voice broke, "I'm getting a feel for the defense."

"Trimble . . ." Coach interrupted in his deep, monotone voice.

Trimble glanced at Quince, stepping over Coach's words. "I'll throw it. Get in a few long ones. Mix it up. Spread them out."

"Coach," Quince interrupted, "Get me the ball. They're tight. Been ready for the run all game. Get me the ball. Throw it up. I'll get it. I can beat my man. Have most of the night."

A few players grunted, giving their approval. "We need Quince in the game," someone chanted.

"Coach," Trimble interrupted, his voice shaky with nerves, "I'll mix it up."

From the very first play, Quince knew Trimble had learned about him and Sara. He knew Trimble would go with the run; knew the pass would not happen. He knew the defense would collapse, and Antigua Sherman would eat them alive. Now, at halftime, he was angry. Quince had the temper of youth. His anger rose like a rocket and fell like a feather. Now, his head throbbed as he sat in the corner and seethed. Listening to Trimble's lie boiled his adrenaline. His fist closed. Bone bleached the skin around his knuckles. Blush colored his cheeks. "Get me the damn ball, Trimble!" he demanded. His green eyes lit up like flares rocketing over the stadium. He stood, leaping to his feet with enough velocity to propel him across the room, over his filthy, stinking, sweat-soaked teammates. Swinging a fist, he barely missed Trimble's chin.

"That's enough!" bellowed Coach's deep voice. "I won't have fighting amongst my team!" At that moment it happened. It wasn't easy, but it happened. It took fighting between his players to stir Coach's ancient anger. His stern reprimand was enough to silence Quince. Always respectful of Coach, the young man nodded and returned to his corner seat. But his jaw was still locked tight as he gazed at Trimble.

Coach nodded, slowly walking back to the whiteboard. He drew a circle below the X's, and then another. "Baxter," he turned, "run a pitch formation. Make them think we're still going short. Keep them honest. We'll move the defense to the left side. Trimble," he pointed with the marker. "Get Quince the ball on the post."

Quince grinned.

Trimble's face pinched in frustration. He stared at Quince, and a smirk lifted his cheeks.

Coach then turned, and asked an assistant to pray. The assistant, an old veteran of the staff, stepped forward, bowed his head, closed his eyes, and began to pray. Coach bowed his head. The team closed their eyes. Trimble smirked at Quince across the bowed heads of their teammates. The assistant prayed. Quince gazed at Trimble with disgust. His cheeks blushed with anger.

Afterwards, the team stood and exited the locker room, moping through the tunnel. Trimble walked ahead of them, alone. His chin, unlike his teammates', was high and distinguished, as if a cast of a heroic Greek bust stored on a forgotten shelf. His posture was stiff, proud as he pranced off the cement, onto the dewy grass. Fans in the nearest bleachers cheered as the team ran onto the field. Boos tumbled down from the opposite bleachers. Soon, whistles blew, echoing in the shadowy mountains above the stadium. The team donned helmets, and gathered around Trimble, who'd knelt beneath them. "Listen up!" he barked. "Coach wants it. We'll give it to him. Option left, nine twenty-four on two. Option left, nine twenty-four on two." Trimble then offered a hand to the group. One by one, the team dropped their hands in a pile, except for Quince. Behind the thin, silver bars of his facemask, Quince glowered at the quarterback.

"Ready," Trimble barked. "Break!" The team clapped, smacking together their callused hands before the huddle dispersed. Each took his position. Some stood. Some knelt, digging their knuckles into the soil. Trimble stood behind the center, hands cupped. Quickly, he turned, and smirked at Quince, who stood along the right sideline. Baxter, standing on Trimble's right side, watched the quarterback, and shook his head.

Quince tried to focus, and ignore the arrogant Trimble. His eyes surveyed the defense: their dispersion, posture and eyes. They were a veteran group. Suspicious stares watched him from their backfield. Just a few feet away, bent in a readied stance, was Antigua Sherman. Sherman was a defensive specialist, an all-conference player, known for shutting down the pass. That moment, his eyes were glued to Quince, locked on the tall receiver as if Quince were held in the grip of his powerful hands. Before the game, he was overheard bragging that no receiver was going to break a record against him. "Not on my watch," he taunted. "Hell no!" Now, standing just a few feet away, he repeated those words. From across the line, a bass-toned voice echoed, over and over, "Not on my watch!"

Trimble turned and slid his cupped hands under the center's fat ass. "Read-a-a-a-y," he yelled in a gravelly voice, "S-e-e-e-t-t-t, Hut." Anticipation grew. Quince's muscles tightened. Sherman's arms flexed. Baxter stared, nervous. "Hut." Suddenly, the ball snapped into Trimble's hands. The line jumped; pads crashed together, echoing across the field. Players grunted. Quince lunged. Gigantic defensive linemen surged forward, driving their cleats into the ground like bulls stomping their hooves. The offensive line sank onto its heels. The whole line wavered. Quince sprinted down the right side.

Trimble dropped several steps, and feigned left. Baxter moved in a linear motion behind him. The line wavered, surging left. Quince pumped his arms, and drove his cleats into the grass. He shot past Sherman, turned, and looked over his shoulder, expecting the ball.

Trimble faked a toss to Baxter, twisted, held the ball over his shoulder, and paused, staring downfield. Three-hundred-pound men tore through the line. The offense collapsed. Defensive backs poured in like water over a dam. Baxter was knocked onto his thick ass. Trimble stood there, staring down field.

Quince sprinted. Sherman chased him.

The defense chased Trimble. He ran, dodging, ducking, and slithering between their meaty hands. Their eyes were ablaze. They had the look of mad men. Just before they struck him, he paused, turned, reared, and slung the ball across the field. The ball sailed in a perfect spiral, over the outstretched arms of a linebacker. Quince saw the ball lift into the cool air. His pace slowed. Suddenly, he stopped, turned and sprinted up field, retracing his steps toward the line of scrimmage. Sherman ran alongside him. His powerful arms pumped like machines. His breathing shared the decibels of thunder.

The ball quickly sank. Quince ran, lifted his hands, and leapt over Antigua Sherman, letting loose an agonized grunt. Sherman jumped, reaching, but the ball sailed through his arms, slamming into Quince's hands. Quince pulled the ball into his chest just as he began to fall and careened over Sherman, tumbling to the ground. A thud echoed across the field. Defensive backs piled on the receiver, smothering Quince. "Not on my watch," Sherman bragged in a thundering voice. "Not on my watch." He stood and danced back to the defense's huddle.

Across the field, Baxter was dazed. He slowly rose to his feet and swayed around as he searched for balance. Jogging back to the huddle, his meandering gait resembled a drunk man running from police.

"Magowan for a ten-yard gain," echoed the loudspeaker.

Quince lay beneath a pile of defensive backs. One by one, they stood, unearthing the wiry receiver like layers of soil stripped from an ancient artifact. As the last back stood, Quince's eyes saw stars hovering above Appalachia. Offensive linemen strutted downfield, and pulled Quince to his feet before returning to the huddle. One lineman, a giant bull of a man, approached Trimble who'd knelt below the huddle. "What the hell, Trimble?" he cursed. His big, meaty face was bunched up under the helmet.

Trimble was silent.

"Why did you hold it?" persisted the big man.

Trimble ignored him.

"He had his man beat. Why go short?" blasted another angry lineman.

Quince walked across the field, shaking his head. His adrenaline boiled. His lips were thin, mashed so tight they nearly disappeared. Quince Magowan was not about to let the moment pass. The needle of his compass pointed across the dewy grass, directly at Trimble. He stormed across the field, through the huddle, grabbed Trimble's facemask, and pulled the quarterback to his feet. Quince's face was pinched. His eyes were ablaze. Trimble tried to push him away, free himself, but Quince gripped his mask like a vise. "You try that shit again and they'll carry you out of here!" he threatened.

"Let go of me," Trimble shouted, trying to break free. "Get him off me," he frantically pled. His eyes sought help around the huddle, but no one moved. The huddle was still, silent.

Quince jerked Trimble around, holding his mask. At times, his feet dangled like a puppet before Quince finally threw him to the ground. Trimble's eyes bulged. He flew backwards, across the huddle, landed on his ass, and slid across the wet grass. Offensive linemen let go deep, haughty laughs. Baxter laughed and clapped his hands. Quince stood there. His muscles tensed as he gazed at the rattled quarterback.

Trimble stood. His legs were shaky with nerves, but he managed to turn and face Coach Simpson. Coach gave instruction for the next play. His arms waved in different motions, up and down. He slowly moved them. Finally, he rested. Trimble knelt and turned to the linemen, "Spread them on the right. Make a hole. We're going for the run on three."

The huddle let out a singular gasp. Eyes focused on the kneeling man with disbelief.

"Bullshit," someone chimed.

"Coach called a pass," corrected Baxter.

"I'm calling the option to run."

"Coach called a pass."

Trimble paused. Blush colored his cheeks. His face looked as if it would explode.

"Fine," he cursed, "Gibson, you run the slant. Baxter, you stay back. I'll feign the throw and dump the pass to you on the sideline."

"Coach wants Quince in the game," argued Baxter.

Quince pushed his finger into Trimble's face, "Get me the ball!" His adrenaline warmed. His eyes were set afire.

"Dump pass on three," said Trimble, ignoring him. Quince had enough. He lunged at Trimble, but an offensive lineman grabbed his collar. His cleats tore through the wet grass, but he couldn't move the 300-pound man.

"Not now, Magowan," said the giant man.

Trimble offered a hand to the group but it lay awkwardly across the huddle, alone. His eyes darted around, desperately searching the face of each player. Unlike before, players stared with disbelief at the quarterback. One giant lineman shook his meaty head. Trimble seemed small, kneeling like a child below them. Finally, he gave up. His hand dropped, and he barked, "Ready, break!" No one clapped. The huddle dispersed, and each player took his position. Quince and Gibson stood near the side. The line knelt. Seconds ticked away on the scoreboard. Trimble turned, smirked at his receiver, and knelt over the center.

"Not on my watch," taunted Antigua Sherman.

Quince turned and faced the defense.

Sherman wanted inside the receiver's mind. He was experienced. Intimidation, he knew, was worth half-a-step. He stooped and flexed his thick arms. Tense eyes focused on Quince. He looked mad and acted insane. "Not here. Not tonight," spoke the bass-toned voice.

Somehow, Quince managed to cool the adrenaline, and focus on the play. Anger had temporarily dazed him, and Sherman's taunts were a smelling salt to his delirium. Quince stooped and gazed at Sherman, but he felt the weight of someone else's stare. He turned to find Baxter pointing at his cleats. A meaty grin filled Baxter's helmet.

Quince nodded and turned to face Sherman. Seconds ticked away.

"Read-a-a-a-y," yelled Trimble's gravelly voice, "S-e-e-e-t-t-t, Hut," He paused. "Hut." Sherman flexed his powerful arms.

Quince's muscles tightened. He stared at Sherman.

"Hut."

The ball smacked against Trimble's hands. The line jumped. Men crashed into each other. Echoes circled the field.

Quince lunged forward, ran right, and feigned downfield.

Offensive linemen gasped. The defense surged forward; their cleats dug deep into the grass, stomping like angry bulls.

Gibson ran downfield, and broke left, slanting at the forty. Baxter leaned forward, pumped his stout legs, and ran, abandoning his position.

Trimble retreated from the wavering line.

Quince darted forward, but crashed into Sherman, struck in the chest by his powerful arms. He stumbled. His lungs sank. His mouth gasped for air. Finally, he found footing, pumped his legs, and struck Sherman. The defensive specialist stumbled.

Trimble faked a deep throw to Gibson who was flying downfield. Trimble then turned right, reared, and tossed the ball to the spot where Baxter once stood.

The offensive line collapsed.

The ball sailed over the defense; a perfect spiral swiftly cut through the cool, autumn air. Quince ran up field and leapt. An agonized grunt rumbled from his throat. He stretched. His fingers nearly broke apart as he grabbed the ball, pulled it into his chest, and slowly sank to the ground. The crowd cheered. Air sucked threw his nostrils. Quince fell and it felt like forever. Sherman, he knew, was close. Visions of Sherman striking his legs, upending him and driving him into the grass, gave him panic. His body tensed, bracing for a blow. He waited, falling. Then, relief! His toes tapped the grass. His cleats submerged into the soft soil. Muscles tensed. Legs locked. He turned, dug his cleats deep into the grass, and sprinted downfield. The defense chased him. They ran downfield. They grunted. But they fell far behind. Some stooped, leaned against their knees, and gasped for air.

Quince ran. His cleats kicked dewy grass in the air. Baxter blocked for his friend. Sherman gave a determined chase. Thrusting, driving his thick, powerful arms, he overcame Baxter, pushed the stocky man aside, and darted downfield after Quince. Baxter tumbled forward. His arms swung like a windmill as he fell to the ground, and slid on his fat belly across the grass. Quince ran hard, but Sherman was faster. He followed in trace, and pushed hard, kicking grass from his cleats. Quince crossed the forty. Sherman pursued. He crossed the fifty, and Sherman was less than ten yards away. He crossed the forty. Thirty. Sherman was within five yards. He crossed the twenty, using everything he had. Wind sucked through his nostrils. His chest thumped. Sherman's heavy breath echoed in his ears. The crowd yelled. Quince darted past the bleachers. Fans jumped and clapped. They cheered. Sherman's labored breath echoed in his ears. Quince ran.

Sherman was fast. His powerful arms pumped; fists struck the air as if sparring with a phantom opponent. Quickly overcoming Quince, he lunged and drove his helmet against Quince's lower back. The collision echoed around the field. Fans gasped. Sherman wrapped his arms around the opponent's thighs. Quince jerked. Spasms shook his wiry frame. His cleats pawed at the wet grass. Sherman pulled. He grunted. His thick muscles flexed, as he wrestled the sturdy receiver. Quince ran. Sherman pulled. Their cleats kicked grass in the air. Grunts echoed.

Spasms shook Quince's body. He was wiry but strong, slippery. Hard to get a hold of, some said. He jerked. Sherman's grip, loosened. The echo of Sherman's taunts, Trimble's actions, boiled his adrenaline. "Not on my watch," spoke a voice from within. "Greatest receiver never to hold a record," taunted Trimble's voice. Quince was angry. He scowled as voices spoke to him. His cleats stabbed the wet grass. Sherman's grip loosened. His hands began to slip from Quince's thighs. Quince pumped his legs. Finally, Sherman fell and slid across the wet field, grunting.

Quince burst over the fifteen, crossing the ten, and into the end zone. Air sucked through his nostrils. His chest thumped, making thunderous noises in his ears. Fans cheered. Quince stood alone in the end zone. He held the ball over his head, and pointed a finger at Sherman, who lay on the field, already humbled. He shook a finger at Trimble whose mouth was agape, before he reared, and slammed the ball to the ground. Teammates ran downfield, and tackled the winded receiver. Baxter leapt on the pile. Wind sucked through Quince's nostrils. Thunderous breaths echoed in his ears.

The crowd cheered. A scratchy voice bellowed from a speaker, "Folks, that's a new Ohio Valley Conference record for most receiving yards in a season. Let's hear it for Quince Magowan." Fans cheered. Quince lay beneath his own teammates. One by one, they stood; an ancient artifact unearthed a second time that evening. As the last player stood, Quince, lying on his back, turned his head toward the bleachers. His eyes sifted over cheering fans until they found a petite brunette. She was smiling.

Chapter 3
≈ Summer 1999 ≈

Dawn broke and buttered rum smeared the sky. Morning light soon dripped through the blinds of their bedroom window, and they wrestled and tugged at blankets, hoping to find a small, lost corner of night. Finally, they rose and dressed.

Quince loaded the SUV with towels, a blanket and drinks, while Sara groggily climbed into the passenger's seat, folded her petite frame in a fetal position, and closed her eyes. As she slept, Quince drove away from the city, into the eastern plateau, and high into mountains, before arriving at the lake. He drove for miles, slowly tracing the crooks and bends of the lakeshore before steering the SUV into a gravel lot. The truck rolled to a stop under a sycamore. Quince turned the key, and the engine whiffed before quieting.

Shade blanketed the truck as he watched the lake from his seat. His green eyes surveyed the harbor, nestled amid the mountains. Bulbs sprouted from summer forests, and a beard of lush grass covered the shore. Soft, teal currents dripped from the harbor, into the channel. As dawn faded, green firmly held the morning.

Quince sighed, smiling, satisfied he had chosen a perfect day. He nudged Sara's bare shoulder, and her soft, brown eyes spread; a grin lifted her cheeks. Her lips became thin and wide when she first saw the water. She grabbed a blanket, leapt from the SUV, and ran barefoot along the sandy shores. Her toes kicked moist sand into the air, and left tiny marks along the tide-grated shore. Finally, she paused, unfurled the blanket in the grass near the back of the harbor and sat. Grass was thick and soft there, sloping gently into the water.

Quince gathered towels from the truck, and followed her tiny footprints in the sand, along the shore, until he reached the unfurled blanket. He found Sara propped on her elbows, lying quietly in the grass. Dark glasses hid her eyes, but her lips were soft and peaceful as she stared into the harbor. Loose brown curls fell around her face. The sun lay on her skin, brushing color over her bare arms and legs.

It was a Saturday. The harbor was busy but serene. A small gray building stood near the water. Houseboats and long, thin vessels were anchored in slips. Fishermen fussed over their vessels. Sailboats drifted with the breeze. Later, as morning waned, a July sun dropped showers of white and gold across the lake.

Sara eventually breached the first pages of a thick paperback novel. She lay on her side, holding the open book with one hand while the other hand was tucked behind her hips. She was still except to lift a hand and turn a page, before tucking the hand away again. Her eyes were unreadable, hidden behind dark glasses, but her lips pulled and stretched when reading something that amused her. A soft breeze occasionally lifted her curls, and tugged at the pages of her book.

Quince lay on his back. His head rested in the palm of one hand while the other lay still at his side. Dark glasses and the bill of a worn cap covered his eyes and much of his face. His skin was pasty, but his chest was solid, and his arms were toned. He had the look of a lean country boy.

Sara read and Quince stared into the harbor. Once, he turned to her and grinned. The sun warmed his face. The harbor was quiet; the shores where they rested were far too distant to hear the soft groan of passing boats. He stared. His eyes seemed to lay on her, pressing against her cheeks and combing her hair with his fingers as he did last night when they made love. Finally, the weight of his stare caught her attention. She slowly lowered the book and turned. She didn't ask but her eyebrows rose above her dark glasses as if they were saying something.

Quince smiled, shrugging, "Us."

Sara nodded, "We've come so far."

"Last fall I thought I had everything I could want. My senior year. A business degree within reach. A farm I loved. Football." His lips closed, and his head tilted, knowingly, "But I was missing something. I didn't know it then but it's so clear to me now."

Sara smiled, "You came up to me as I was studying under the tree. Remember? You introduced yourself but I knew who you were." Her grin widened. "I'd watched you play every Friday night. Heard about Quince Magowan—the great football star. You were so sure of yourself. Your confidence was attractive. The records, I mean, Baxter called you Mr. Football." Quince rolled his eyes. Sara chuckled but continued, "But soon I learned there was so much more to you. Much more than football. The records. The confident, popular senior. You were sincere. Down to earth. You just did things no one else had ever done for me. If I complained, you listened. You tolerated my quirks. When I craved take-out, but didn't want to leave the apartment, you drove across town and brought it back. You took long naps with me when you weren't tired. You cared about making me happy." Sara leaned forward. Her hands slid down his arm and meshed with his fingers.

Quince grinned, "It was worth it. Every trip across town for Chinese. Every sleepless nap. The day I saw you studying under that tree was the day I stopped missing that something." He leaned forward, reaching, until Sara's chin rested in his palm, and he kissed her. As their lips parted, Quince grinned. Sara smiled and fell back onto the beach blanket. She closed her eyes, soaking up the sun and the warmth of the moment.

Hours passed. They read and slept and bathed in the sun. Finally, Quince stood and stepped into the grass with his bare feet. He pushed up the bill of his cap, and stared quietly into the harbor. Boats bounced softly in the summer tide. Some sailed between the mountains, and slid into the channel.

Sara gently closed the book, turned, and shielded her eyes from the sun. "What is it?" she asked.

Quince shrugged.

"I know that look."

Quince grinned.

Sara turned, following Quince's stare down the slope, across the sandy shore, into the harbor. Her hand lay flat above her eyes, fashioned in a weak, awkward salute. She turned back to Quince, and disapprovingly shook her head.

"I can do it," he solemnly proclaimed.

"When was the last time?" she asked as her brow rose. Skepticism had a way of lowering her voice. That morning, her words sounded admonishingly baritone.

Quince grinned, quietly weighing his answer. "I was a boy."

Sara's brow rose above her dark glasses. She gnawed on her lips as if they were candy, but Quince ignored her taunts. He stared into the harbor and answered. "I was a boy but I was well taught. You never forget."

Sara turned and watched the harbor. Finally, her chest rose and fell in a sigh, and she nodded, gathered the blanket and together they walked along the shore.

They strolled around the shack, across a deck, down steps, and along a walkway, holding hands. Sara swung her free arm with large, sweeping motions. Her sandals clacked as she walked, and wooden planks creaked over the marina waters. They strolled, watching the harbor, unaware of the day or time.

Together, they approached the first slip where an old man stood near a sailboat. A sloop. It was a gorgeous boat. Coated in cherry red, light sprung from its deep polish. The old man moved diligently around it, pulling, pushing rags gently over the wooden bow. Stooped, his old, thin face looked down, focused on the smooth surface. Bones protruded from his shoulders, and dimpled his spine while sweat glistened along his sun-beat hide.

"Excuse me," interrupted Quince, pausing aside the slip. "I need a boat for the afternoon. Do you rent?"

The old man paused. His thin face rose and turned to the couple while his body stayed contorted over the bow. Sweat dripped from his brow and glistened under the sun around his neck. "You a sailor?" he asked. His voice was wrinkled with sarcasm as he carefully inspected the young, eager man.

Quince ignored the old man's question. He was undaunted. Instead, he moved around the sloop, admiring the boat as it shined under a brilliant sun. "She is gorgeous."

The old man stared disdainfully at Quince. His wrinkled face grimaced.

Sara bit her lip, trying to restrain a smile. Her arms folded while her hands clothed her mouth. She turned, and stared at the shack as if it were something fascinating.

The old man pulled a handkerchief from his pocket and swabbed sweat from his neck. "You sail, son?" he asked.

Quince ignored him. A smile lifted his cheeks as he admired the boat. At times he stood then paused and knelt, consuming every possible view and angle of the cherry red boat. Finally, he nodded, stood and proclaimed, pointing into the slip, "I want this one."

Sara's brown eyes rolled into her brow. She gnawed at her lip, and turned toward the shack. Laughter bubbled somewhere beneath her auburn skin.

As Quince finished speaking, the old man's arm fell limp at his side. His mouth hung open as if he just witnessed something unexplainable. Then, laughter divided his lips. "She's mine. Only I man the helm."

Quince nodded. His eyes were hidden behind dark glasses and beneath the cap's bill. "I want her." He pointed into the slip.

Sara bit her lip, looking away.

The old man paused and stared at Quince. A suspicious expression wore through his tan, leathery skin and deep wrinkles, now shadowed under the summer sun. He shrugged his leathery shoulders, shook his head, turned and renewed his labor of wax and polish. Waves passed under the marina. The sloop rocked in the slip. Gentle waves smacked against the wood exterior, making the clapping sound of a sophisticated applause.

Sara giggled, snorting at the old sailor's obstinate nature.

Quince was undaunted. He slowly walked around the slip, paused near Sara, teasingly nudged her back with an elbow and proclaimed, "As a boy, I sailed with my father. We drove up here every Sunday."

The old sailor was bent over the sloop, pushing, pulling rags over the polished hull. "A boy?" he asked, chuckling.

Sara bit her lip. Laughter gurgled deep within her.

Quince's face pinched. The sailor's laughter struck his pride with the fury of a pugilistic blow. Blush colored his cheeks and he spoke. "She was red. Just like this one."

The old man kept polishing. He worked as if he were the only person around.

"Her mast was shaky. Her mainsail was frayed," Quince sighed. "But she was fast. The fastest. I tell you her bow sliced through waves like a blade." He paused. The sloop rocked in the slip. The old sailor worked. His sweat-glistened back was turned to the couple, but Quince kept talking. He gave meaning and inflection to his words as if an audience were listening and hung on every thought. It mattered not if the old man listened. Quince had faith in his words. That was enough for a Magowan to speak as he pleased. "One Sunday, my father took a brush and painted Lillian May in big white letters along her stern." Quince's head shook. His lips pinched. Air blew from his nostrils as he sighed. "She was fast."

The old man paused. His wiry arms fell. His wrinkly neck turned and his lips parted, asking, "You say, Lillian May?"

"My mother. After she died, the old man just came home one day and said he wanted to sail. So he bought a little sloop. Every Sunday, we drove from the farm to this old lake. Some folks go to church. We sailed. He saw something spiritual in it, I reckon."

Sara's smile vanished. Her features stilled as Quince spoke.

The old man stood. His thin, stiff legs, straightened as he turned, stared at Quince and asked, "Your name Magowan?"

Quince's eyes were hidden behind dark glasses, and the bill of an old cap. Slowly, his head rocked like the boat might rock in its slip.

The old sailor flinched. His head fell back as if it might peel from his thin shoulders. His lips parted and a smile rose over his long teeth. "Your old man a whisky drinking, three packs-a-day rambler named Beecher Magowan?"

A grin lifted Quince's cheeks.

"Well . . ." searched the old sailor for words, chuckling, ". . . Good Lord!" He tossed away the rag, took several steps toward Quince and offered his hand, proclaiming, "Beecher Magowan!" His words rose in reverence. "How is that old Marine?"

Quince shrugged. "Still smells of bourbon and burley."

The old sailor laughed, noting, "Beecher never knew a stranger."

Quince nodded.

"Why, I knew Beecher before Vietnam."

Quince nodded. Sara, her face still, was silent.

"Where's he been keeping? Ain't seen him in years!"

Quince shrugged. "Stays on the farm."

The old sailor shook his head, "Lonely place. Hard on a social man like Beecher Magowan." He rubbed his chin, and the scratch of his stubbly beard gave the sound of sandpaper. His eyes became lost as he looked away from Quince, and stared into the harbor. Slowly, his cheeks rose in a grin, and his eyes once again fell on Quince. "He's a talker, Beecher. Reckon he might talk the flies off a cow's hide."

Quince nodded, "And the leaves off a tree."

"Nary animal or forest is safe from Beecher Magowan's tongue," proclaimed the old sailor, erupting in laughter.

Quince laughed. Sara nodded, laughing.

Sweat glistened around the old sailor's neck. As laughter died, his lips poised and he nodded, pointing into the slip, "All right. For the son of my old friend, Beecher Magowan, enjoy. You have her for the afternoon."

Quince offered his hand, they shook, and the old sailor walked away, yelling, "Tell Beecher, Tom Shelby says hello."

Quince ignored the old sailor. He helped Sara into the boat, stooped, unfastened the line, placed a foot on the wooden walkway, and pushed, grunting as the boat skirted from its slip.

The small shack shrank as they drifted away from the marina, passing between two mountain peaks that stood guard over the harbor's entrance. Slowly, the sloop drifted below the sentry-like peaks, and into the channel. With the boat rocking lazily in the channel, Quince sighed and fell into the seat next to Sara. He slumped in the seat, and let his arms lay at his side as he watched the horizon. It was a bright day.

Sara's feet were propped over the side. A grin postured her lips. Her eyes were hidden, but they were brown and happy beneath the dark lenses. Occasionally, they squinted, ever so slightly, as she watched waves run at the boat. Once, she smiled.

The sun's reflection divided the channel with a long, lean pool of melted butter separating two green surfaces dimpled with waves. The boat rocked. Mist sprayed their faces as waves smacked against the rocking hull. The day was warm; air was growing thick. Suddenly, the sleeve of Quince's shirt flapped. He felt the cool wash of fresh air on his cheeks, and he turned to see the curls along Sara's temple jump and pull.

Quince leapt to his feet. His hands clapped, and he quickly ran to the mast and yanked the halyard. The sail quickly unfolded. Wrinkle-by-wrinkle unwrapped, running up the mast with the same urgency Quince showed as he leapt to his feet. Finally, the rope was unwound and taut. The sail stood high and erect over the sloop. Quince shook his head. He looked into the sky as the sail stood flat. He felt the burn of sun on his cheek. He sighed and his chest pounded. Air sucked through his nostrils. Quince turned to Sara before anxiously throwing his eyes into the sky. Suddenly, the sail snapped, bowing as the wind nudged its center.

The boat jerked and slid forward. Quince tugged at the halyard until the sail bulged as if it would bust. The sloop moved steady. Mist sprayed over the bow as it cut through waves. Quince sighed, then sat and threw his arm over a thin, wooden wheel. Sara watched him. Her eyes squinted, and she spoke in a soft voice asking, "When was the last time?"

Quince sighed. He watched the horizon. The sloop sliced through a dimpled surface. Wind washed his face as he answered, "A boy."

A smile lifted Sara's cheeks.

By afternoon, the breeze weakened to a whisper, and the boat settled, slowly drifting past coves and points. Sara was quiet, hiding her face in a book. Quince watched her recline comfortably in the seat with her feet perched over the edge. She was still except when a breeze blew her curls or she slowly turned a page. Peaceful and happy, her thoughts were lost in the story she held in her fingers. Late that afternoon, she stood, tossed the book into the seat, and crawled into Quince's lap, facing him. Her tan legs slid over his and her butt rested on the unguided wheel. A smile poised her lips. She lifted the cap from his head, kissed him and announced, "Autumn maybe?"

Quince's eyes were hidden beneath dark glass, but his cheeks rose as if he were hearing words long expected and hoped for. He listened.

"A simple dress to go with the season. I'll choose fall flowers for a bouquet. Mums. Yellow, I think. We'll find a small church in the country. A white fence circling the chapel. A steeple piercing the September sky. Nothing fancy. Something small and quaint. A fall wedding in a small, plain church. The kind you see on a magazine cover."

Quince's face was still as he listened. If there were any emotion in his eyes, it was hidden beneath dark glasses. The sloop rocked. Sun warmed their faces. Sara anxiously surveyed his eyes as if staring into the night. Suddenly, her face sank. "It's simple, but . . ." she paused.

"What?" he asked.

Sara shrugged, turned, and stared at the horizon.

"What?"

She shrugged, answering, "It all sounds good, but . . ."

"What?" he asked.

She shrugged. Her curls twisted in a breeze.

"Does such a place even exist?" he asked, guessing at what might be troubling her.

Sara turned and surveyed his dark glasses. She shrugged and asked, "Well?"

Quince was quiet. His face was still. Sara, he knew, expected him to shrug and say no, to say places like that only exist on a magazine cover; a photographer's creation. Made-up places. Instead, he was quiet. Dark glasses hid his eyes. His face was solemn, blushing under the sun. Finally, a breeze washed their faces. Curls danced. And a grin tugged at Quince's lips.

Chapter 4
≈ The Old Church: Autumn 1999 ≈

Silver shone in the old man's hair, and in the bark of the maple he stood beneath. Elders, old men with crisp, white hair, set tables and metal chairs around the tree. Their wives were plump old ladies who were busy arranging flowers and greeting guests as they arrived. They carried pots of garden beans and dishes of casserole from a basement kitchen, and set them on a white tablecloth. Stained aprons covered their flowery dresses. The old men and old women happily moved around the old churchyard. Family and friends mingled among the food and hanging ferns. They hugged and cried. Some laughed. Over their shoulders, a steeple pierced the blue September sky.

The chapel was small and plain and hidden in a valley of clover. It was quaint, picturesque, just what the bride wanted. The exterior was covered in thin rows of white clapboard, and the windows were clear; rich colors were forbidden by their faith. There was no giant crucifix or fancy signs quoting Bible verses, just a modest steeple crowned with a small wooden cross. A white, three-rail fence circled the yard. A bell hung from the slim white tower with a black-shingled roof that stood alone, away from the graves. A large maple fanned the steeple and shadowed the stones in the old church cemetery. Markers, dusted with mold, tilted in the moist soil. Nearby, a covered bridge rested on yellow stones that sank into a creek.

The sturdy chapel was built long ago by Quince's grandfather, Isaiah Magowan, with help from men in the community. The building was a mere forty feet wide and not more than fifty long. For decades, Isaiah worshipped in the sanctuary every Sunday. He married there and was eulogized there as a caring and devout man who had shared his love and wisdom with his family and the community. Quince's parents also married in the chapel, and there his mother was eulogized when Quince was an infant.

The Appalachian Mountains were not far from the tiny chapel. Standing on the ridge, you could see their hazy outline cut against the eastern sky. Below the ridge was the small chapel, and on that day, a wedding.

As the elders set tables, Quince stood alone near the bell tower, just inside the fence. He greeted members of the congregation as they passed, and he made small talk with family of the bride-to-be. Women hugged the groom. A dozen plump women, wearing greasy aprons, squeezed him until breath pushed from his lungs. Quince felt mashed, turned, and grease-soaked like casseroles on the table a few feet away. They were good, caring people. They had cooked and baked for two days. The food they prepared that day would have fed Napoleon's starving army.

An old man, thin and tall, wearing a blue-gray suit, emerged from the crowd, and approached Quince. The man's bony finger pointed at the old chapel. "Helped your grandfather build it," echoed his deep voice over the laughter and mutter of conversation.

Quince offered his hand, and said with a smile across his face, "Reverend Shaygrove."

Reverend Shaygrove's bony fingers gently grasped Quince's hand. "Tom Quincy Magowan." The aged pastor smiled, and wrinkles poured from his eyes. "He was a big man, too," continued the reverend, staring into Quince's eyes. "Kind. Understanding. You favor him."

Quince paused, smiled, and joked, "Better him than my rough old father."

A smile breached Reverend Shaygrove's wrinkled face. He nodded and laughed, "By miles, son, by miles. Say," he said, stiffly turning around. "Where is he, anyway?"

"Bringing grandmother," answered Quince.

"Well," the reverend dropped his head, "we all move a little slower these days."

Quince nodded.

"But," he paused, staring around at the crowd. "It's not unlike your father to make an entrance. Steal the show."

Quince chuckled, knowingly, "No sir, not at all unlike him."

The laughter trailed off, and Reverend Shaygrove's expression grew serious. "It's a tradition for the groom to pray with the elders before the ceremony." He raised his arm as if to coax Quince into the chapel. "Shall we?"

Quince nodded and walked away from the bell tower, toward the chapel, with Reverend Shaygrove. Elders followed them. Quince, Reverend Shaygrove, and a half-dozen men climbed the steps to the chapel. The railing along the stone steps was laced with yellow and white ribbons. Awaiting them at the top were double doors thrown open so the clean September air might usher out the musty smell.

The elders and Reverend Shaygrove walked down the aisles. Boards popped and moaned beneath their feet as they approached the altar. Quince, however, stood in the doorway. He paused to carefully survey the small sanctuary. His green eyes slowly crossed over the pews, clean and tidy, down the aisle where a single candle flickered on a small table near the pulpit. He sighed as moisture gathered in his eyes. Years had passed since Quince had seen this sanctuary. It was hard for him to see the inside of this church, see the place once again, after all those years. The place his grandfather, whom he had admired and loved, and his mother, whom he never knew, were eulogized.

The elders and Reverend Shaygrove paused at the altar, turned and stared down the aisle at the young man who had awkwardly paused in the doorway. Quince drew a deep breath, sucking air through his nostrils until his chest had swollen. He nodded, walked to the altar, and joined hands with them. With their heads bowed, an elder's voice cracked with age as he began to pray.

As the elder prayed, Quince lifted his head enough to peek around the circle. One by one, he surveyed the group, whispering each man's name as his eyes passed over them. They were all old, born of his grandfather's generation. Their hair was thin and white and he could feel the Great Depression in their callused hands. As a boy, he rode with his grandfather on Saturday afternoon trips from the farm to Garvey's general store. Isaiah Magowan always bought his grandson a soda before they walked to the store's front porch and joined these same men. Quince quietly sat in a dusty old rocking chair, drinking his soda and listening to stories about places with funny names like Cassino and places with scary names like Bougainville. As the elder prayed, Quince squinted and thought of those Saturdays long passed into time.

When the old man fell silent, Quince shook the hand of each man, before he slipped back outside, passing large potted ferns that hung from eaves and shepherd hooks along the steps. The colors of fall were around. September hung ribbons of burning auburn along the mountain crest. Clouds stayed away, and the sun was full and soft.

He stopped to chat with several college buddies who'd arrived while he was in the church. Baxter was there, laughing and taunting his nervous friend. He brought with him much of the old team. The offensive line was there; three-hundred-pound giants stuffed into suit jackets and choked by neckties. Gibson was there. Even Coach Simpson was there, standing beneath the maple, pulling his thick jowls into a smile as Quince approached. His hand slowly rose to congratulate his former player and record-breaking receiver. They shook hands and Quince thanked him for coming.

Absent from the team, however, was a man no one expected to show, Trimble Addison. He wasn't missed.

Quince briefly chatted with his old teammates before making his way into the cemetery. He wanted to be alone, reflect on this day, and wrestle with his nerves. He sat on a limestone bench, resting his feet in the moist grass near the first row of graves. The sun was high. A breeze combed through the clover ridges. The crowd muttered and laughed. It was a quiet, peaceful day, but Quince did not absorb the tranquility.

He was nervous. Even the confident Quince Magowan couldn't escape wedding-day jitters. His gut was tied in knots like the twin-bow ribbons hung from the railing. Drips of sweat began to trickle down the crevice of his back. His dark suit, gathering the gentle sun, didn't help. His pulse began to race. His mouth was dry. He tried to swallow but his spit choked him like sand. Succumbing to jitters, he read grave markings to occupy his thoughts. Decades, or maybe a century, of mold left the words barely legible.

"In a better place," read one inscription.

Quince lifted his head, turned, and looked around. The jitters worsened. He turned and kept reading the engravings. Another stone read, "Gone to his reward." Quince sighed. His nerves worsened, and he began to wonder if those in the graves at his feet, long dead, were better off than he was at that moment.

Finally, he looked away from the graves, and he could see the crowd had gathered around something. They were quiet; their muddled voices silent. Soon, the familiar crow of a lone voice came from within the crowd. The voice caught the autumn breeze, and echoed along the clover ridges. Shortly, the lone voice began to laugh, and in a singular, choreographed event, the crowd erupted.

Finally, the crowd broke up, and a man, unimpressive in girth and stature, emerged.

Quince sat alone in the cemetery, and watched the man walk toward him. He noticed the man's wide smile, his tan bald head, and thin white beard. As he drew closer, Quince saw the man's smile, full of bright false teeth, and the wrinkles along his forehead. Quince closely watched the man walk toward him as he had thousands of times before. He had never seen the man walk away. The man was Beecher Magowan.

Beecher passed under the maple shade, along tables filled with casseroles, pots of vegetables, and vanilla cakes. He emerged from the shade, and approached the cemetery. Beecher tugged at his pants, and sat beside his son on a stone bench near the chapel where he had married his son's mother on a September day more than two decades before. "The Big Day!" he announced, in a voice raspy with years of whisky and cigarettes.

Quince leaned forward slightly until his elbows rested on his knees. His head bowed, and he nodded, but said nothing.

"Nervous?" asked Beecher, chuckling under his words. A large, open smile cut across his whiskered face, neatly trimmed and gray.

Quince shrugged, "A little."

"Little. Hell!" said Beecher, laughing heartily. His grin was wide as the valley. His false teeth shone. "So much so that you'd rather be over here, alone with the dead?"

Quince chuckled. Beecher's humor was not lost on his son, even with his nerves. "I needed a good listener," he admitted.

Beecher laughed. His head rocked back, and his large, white teeth glistened in the sun. Laughter echoed along the ridge.

Quince continued, "Where else can a groom find a good listener when he has nerves on his wedding day, Reverend Shaygrove?"

Beecher's lips pursed, and he shook his head, "Too old-fashioned."

"A priest?" joked Quince.

"Don't know any."

"Who then?"

Beecher shrugged, answering, "Your old man!"

"My old man?"

"Yep," Beecher chuckled.

Quince turned and glanced at his father, asking, "And what words of wisdom does my old man have?"

Beecher laughed again, before answering, "Let it go."

"Let what go?"

"It," Beecher answered.

"What the hell is it?" asked Quince, jokingly sarcastic.

"It."

"That's your wisdom?" asked Quince. "Let it go?"

Beecher shrugged, "It. Your nerves. Look," he paused, wrapping an arm over Quince's shoulder, nodding toward the tiny chapel, "I stood there once, right there at the top of those very steps. Nervous. Felt like you're feeling right now. And then your mother walked through that gate. She wore a white cotton gown. Nothing fancy." Beecher shook his head. "She was a sight. Truly beautiful. A gift. She kept walking toward me, past the bell tower. Hell, I thought the bell would ring on its own on account of her passing by." His head dropped, shaking as he remembered. "As she climbed those steps, holding back a smile, it came home to me that that beautiful woman wanted me. She would be mine, and the nerves just flew away."

Quince listened. His eyes narrowed. His lips pursed, and he nodded. It was the first time he ever heard Beecher talk about his parents' wedding day.

Just then, across the churchyard, beyond the maple, an elder approached the bell tower, and tugged on a rope, setting the cast iron bell into motion.

A sharp clang echoed through the valley, over the graves, along the ridges, and maybe even to the Appalachians, their hazy outline cut into the eastern sky.

The bride approached the church.

Beecher looked at his son, smiling, "You have a good woman. She loves you. Your old man loves you. Let the nerves go. Let them go."

Quince grinned. His lips pursed and he nodded. Beecher patted his son on the shoulder, stood, and straightened his tie.

Quince stood.

Beecher straightened his son's tie.

Quince grinned, his cheeks lifted with a smile, pushing them back into the temple of his gel-slicked hair. Beecher smiled. The bell struck. The crowd turned toward the covered bridge. Their muddled conversation died away. As the two men turned and walked away from the cemetery, the elder Magowan looked at Quince and joked, "You poor bastard!" He blew up laughing.

Tom Quincy, the son, and Beecher, the father, walked away from the old cemetery, passed under the maple, beside tables filled with pots, and through the gate of the three-rail fence.

The crowd smiled and offered congratulations as they passed. Quince hugged Grandma Magowan as he passed her standing under the maple with other old women.

Father and son then climbed the stairs, turned in the doorway, and faced the country road and the covered bridge.

An elder tugged at a rope. The bell struck again, and an echo fled through the valley. The crowd fell silent.

Beyond a curve in the road, a sharp rhythm of horse's hooves clacked against asphalt.

The bell struck once more, and the elder walked away from the small tower.

Hooves clacked. Sara's carriage slowly descended the hill.

Father and son stood alone on the steps. As the carriage approached, Quince's nerves reemerged. His chest pounded and took race against the horses' hooves. Eight hooves trotted. The clacks grew louder, but slowed. Two chestnut appaloosas emerged behind the tangled limbs of streamside sycamores. Their long manes lifted in the fall breeze, washing over the reins that stretched from their bits to the soft grip of a white bearded man in a dark suit and fedora.

The driver tugged at the reins, and the horses winced, turning between yellow stone walls onto a narrow road that approached the bridge. Quince's chest pounded. His breath took race against the rhythm of the clacking hooves. He surveyed the road, but struggled to see beyond the thick-leafed sycamores.

The carriage slowed, coming down the road, swaying with the horses' gait. The rhythm of eight hooves struck the wooden floor of the old bridge. Sara sat on cushions in the carriage. Her skin was tan, matching the appaloosa's coat. The breeze bounced under her brown curls.

Quince saw her smile, a smile too wide to fit between the narrow walls of that old bridge, enclosed with wooden planks.

The bell was silent in the tower.

Guests were silent, smiling.

The silhouette of a carriage, the driver and his fedora, and Sara, petite on the large cushion, formed through the small opening on the far side of the bridge. The bridge was solid, dating back to the nineteenth century. Sturdy beams crisscrossed in the interior, and wide boards covered the side. On rainy days, water slid off a steep tin roof into the stream below. On that day, a September sun slipped between cracks in the wide boards along the walls. As the carriage crossed the bridge, it was repeatedly transformed from a shadow to illumination. Like an old camera reel, Sara's smile flashed from the bridge at Quince, as the carriage passed through light that squeezed between the boards.

The clack of eight hooves rang out.

The crowd was silent.

Quince and Beecher quietly watched from the steps. Everyone smiled.

The bell was still now.

Quince was silent, but his nerves took race against the rhythm of hooves smacking the boards on the bridge. He fidgeted, and rocked slightly, from his toes to his heels.

The carriage soon emerged from the shadows of the covered bridge, and into the sun. The sun gave color to Sara's face, her white dress, and the curls of her brown hair.

Her smile was wide, and her teeth white—whiter than Beecher's false ones. Her curls bounced in the breeze.

The carriage approached the chapel, and the crowd silently waited. A grin was frozen on Quince's face, his hands locked together behind him.

The horses turned broadside, and the carriage followed them, stopping at the gate. Sara's father, hands folded at this waist, approached the carriage. He unfolded his hands, and offered one to Sara. She accepted, stepping from the carriage, and through the gate. Guests lined the narrow path; their faces were happy and whispering. Sara's niece handed her a bouquet of mums.

Quince watched and admired his bride-to-be. She moved slowly, gracefully smiling and nodding to family. As she passed through the gate and alongside the bell tower, Quince waited for the bell to ring, to strike on its own simply because she had passed by.

Sara smiled, gestured to guests, and ascended the stairs. The train of her dress was short, modest, but long enough to waterfall up the steps as she passed the hanging ferns and twisted ribbons.

Quince grinned.

Beecher smiled, bowed slightly, and stepped aside.

Sara smiled.

Her father stopped, kissed his daughter on the forehead, and stepped aside.

With guests looking on, Quince offered his hand to her. Sara, holding the bouquet of yellow mums, grasped Quince's hand, and they walked through the double doors, down the aisle, to the altar, and paused near a single burning candle.

Guests slowly followed them, filling pews. Boards creaked and moaned under their steps. An elder gently closed the doors after the last guest entered, and the light grew dim in the old church.

Tom Quincy Magowan was calmer now. His breathing slowed. His pulse, tempered, no longer taking race against the horses' hooves.

Inside the chapel, guests sat in their cozy pews. Quince and Sara stood together near the altar while Reverend Shaygrove stood between them. Sara wore a white voile, tea-length dress. Her hair was down. Soft curls rested on her shoulders. Quince wore a dark suit. His dark hair was gel-slicked along his temple. Near the baptismal pool was a large painting of Jesus in the Garden of Gethsemane.

Reverend Shaygrove surveyed the crowd before he asked the guests to join him in prayer. His head bowed; his eloquent voice echoed through the pews. After a short prayer, he raised this thin, wrinkly face, and motioned to the choir. A small group of ladies, sitting in pews behind the altar, opened their hymnals and sang along with the piano. A candle flickered as a breeze snuck through the open windows and tugged at the flame, whispering as it struggled to stay lit.

Quince and Sara stood together, each staring into the other's eyes. Sara, holding a bouquet of mums, grinned as the petals waved with a breeze as if planted in a field.

Soon, the choir finished singing, and took its seat near the baptismal. The piano was quiet again. Reverend Shaygrove opened his Bible, read a verse, and spoke briefly about the spiritual meaning of marriage, the union's sanctity, until death do we part.

Sara listened.

Quince listened and grinned.

The pastor turned to the guests, and asked if there was anyone present who could profess a reason why Quince and Sara should not marry.

Guests sat quietly through a moment of awkward silence. The breeze sifted among them, through the pews.

Quince and Sara looked over the crowd. Sara's parents sat with her family and friends on one side of the sanctuary.

Beecher winked at this son. Grandma Magowan smiled. Quince's teammates looked on. Coach Simpson sat quietly. Baxter's eyes watered up, and Coach slowly shook his head when he saw it.

"Very well," continued the pastor. "Please repeat after me," he said to Quince. "I, Tom Quincy Magowan, take you, Sara Elizabeth Foster, to be my wife," continuing until his voice trailed off.

Quince repeated the words.

Reverend Shaygrove turned to Sara, "Sara, please repeat after me. I, Sara Elizabeth Foster, take you, Tom Quincy Magowan . . ."

"Having professed this commitment of love before the congregation, and Almighty God, I now pronounce you husband and wife. You may kiss your bride."

The couple smiled. Quince lifted his hands, cupped his bride's cheeks, and they kissed.

Guests sighed.

The couple kept kissing, and Reverend Shaygrove shifted uncomfortably.

They kissed, and the old pastor with Puritan values cleared his throat.

Finally, they finished, held hands, and turned to the guests. Everyone—guests, family, and friends—rose from their pews and applauded. As the applause continued,

Tom Quincy and Sara Magowan slowly walked down the aisle, away from the single candle. The couple smiled, gestured to family, accepted congratulations, and then passed through the double doors, down the steps, alongside hanging ferns and twin bowed ribbons. They giggled and laughed as they held hands, walked across the yard, and paused near the tables. Behind them, guests poured from the tiny chapel, down the steps, across the yard, and offered congratulations to the newly wedded couple.

Eventually, Quince, Sara, her friends and family, Beecher, Grandma Magowan, the football team, and the elders sat on metal chairs and dined under the maple. But for a few high clouds, the sky was clear. The shade of the old tree grew as the afternoon aged. It was pleasant.

Beecher talked and laughed incessantly as everyone dined. Dessert was sliced watermelon and ice cream donated by Garvey's general store. The women's auxiliary delivered a never-ending commissary, and the guests dined until they could consume no more of the garden's bounty and Beecher's jokes.

Beecher sat next to his son, who, along with Sara, sat at the end of the table. Pitchers of tea and lemonade lined the table. As the guests finished their meal, Beecher nudged Quince with an elbow. He opened his jacket, and grinned, nodding to his son. Quince peered inside Beecher's jacket at a small, silver cap protruding from a hidden pocket. He looked up to find Beecher grinning. Quince shook his head, uninterested.

Beecher shrugged, set a glass of lemonade between his legs, cautiously removed the flask, hidden under the tablecloth, and spiked his wedding drink. He returned the flask, unnoticed by the guests or elders.

Quince and Sara were laughing and enjoying conversation when suddenly the elder Magowan tapped his glass with a spoon and stood.

"Folks," Beecher interrupted, tapping the glass.

The conversation trailed off.

"Folks," bellowed his raspy voice, tapping the glass even louder.

The guests fell silent, turned and stared at Beecher who held the glass over the table.

"A toast to the bride and groom," he said, urging guests to raise their glasses with him.

In unison, elders shifted in their seats at the thought of a toast by Beecher Magowan.

The air turned from a sunny, autumn afternoon to the chill of awkwardness. "It is a wonderful day. Beautiful weather," he proclaimed, lifting his arms high, "Wonderful people." Elders smiled, pleasantly surprised. "All joined here on this beautiful day to witness the wedding of this beautiful couple, to witness the beginning of their lives together. A day God has given us to enjoy a union He has sanctified." Surprised, the elders and Reverend Shaygrove nodded in agreement. A few amens broke the guests' silence. "Quince," Beecher smiled, turning to his son, "I am glad you could join us."

Guests chuckled, knowing the groom's pre-wedding jitters, and visit to the cemetery.

"For a while I thought we might have a wedding in the graveyard," Beecher blew-up laughing. Guests laughed. Elders shifted in their seats. "But, thankfully you got through it. We all get through it . . . happens to all of us men on our wedding day," Beecher nodded, looking around as if to garner support. "Heck. Happened to me five times," the elder Magowan chuckled.

Sara, embarrassed, buried her face into her hands, smiling. Quince just shook his head. The elders shifted in unison, some cleared their throats. Reverend Shaygrove's brow rose into his forehead. A lady from the auxiliary, carrying a fresh pot of beans, froze, letting a slight gasp escape, an apron blowing in the breeze was the only movement about her frame, soft and plump in a flowery dress.

"But, thankfully you got through it," continued Beecher, undaunted by the myriad of reactions.

Guests chuckled. Quince and Sara laughed, taking it well.

"I knew you would. Once you saw your beautiful bride walking through that gate," pointing toward the chapel, "up those stairs, I knew you'd be all right. Quince, I'm glad you got through it. That you came out of that old cemetery, and took your bride." He raised the glass high, "To the happy couple." Beecher held the spiked wedding drink, and the guests joined him. They tapped each other's glasses, and drank lemonade and sweet tea except for Beecher.

As they finished, the sun did not tarry, falling quickly into the mountains. The maple's shadow and clover ridges, chewed away the yellow glow. The pots and platters were empty, the pitchers of lemonade and sweet tea, dry. Beecher, toting a flask, half-full, hidden inside his suit jacket, stood, walked around the table, leaned over Reverend Shaygrove's shoulder, and whispered something to the pastor.

Reverend Shaygrove stood, and the two men left the table while Quince anxiously watched them. Sara chatted with guests, as the two men walked across the churchyard, and paused near the bell-tower, where they briefly spoke.

Beecher was smiling as he walked through the gate, crossed the parking lot, climbed into his pickup, and drove to the covered bridge. He stopped, jumped out and walked toward the table, "Folks," shouted the elder Magowan as he approached the guests. "The time has come for the dance. It's a tradition," he happily proclaimed.

Guests, elders, Quince and Sara, and the football team stood, left the table, and made their way across the churchyard, through the gate, down a hill, and stopped near the covered bridge and Beecher's large, red pickup.

Beecher stood in the opening of the old bridge as the crowd gathered. "We have a very special treat, a fine moment in the ceremony," he proclaimed. "It's time for the newlyweds to dance. Right here," he turned, gesturing to the inside of the wooden structure. "Right here, a long time ago, after my first wedding," the elders shifted, "I danced with Lillian May, Quince's mother. Then, family, guests, gathered here, like you're doing, and Lilly and I danced. We danced to a wonderful old song." He paused for a moment, and turned to the couple, "Quince. Sara. I want you to share that moment, here, on your wedding day." With that, Beecher walked through the crowd, climbed into the pickup, turned on the radio, jumped out, slapped his hands together, and let out a whoop.

A slow melody began to pour out from the pickup, among the guests, through the dusty, wooden trusses of that old bridge, the stream below, and the yellow stones, baking in the September sun.

"Ladies and Gentlemen," announced the elder Magowan, "Mr. and Mrs. Tom Quincy Magowan."

As the music played, the couple turned to each other, joined hands, and began to dance, swaying to the slow melody of the Iceman's voice as it poured from the radio.

Chapter 5
≈ The Honeymoon ≈

Quince and Sara rose early and drove east over the mountains, across the Shenandoah, to the sandy Carolina coast. When the ocean appeared just beyond the pines, they turned and drove north along a narrow road running between trees and a white beach. Eventually, the SUV slowed, turned at a light, and crossed a bridge that arched high above the inland waterway. Sara's stomach sank as the truck climbed high above the mossy water, descended from the clouds, and landed on a narrow island. They drove for miles along the narrow road. After a while, the truck slowed, turned, and snaked along a street that was hidden between dunes, and ended at the ocean, just feet from the wave's crest.

When the SUV rolled to a stop, the couple opened their doors, stood, and stretched their sore legs. They surveyed the beach and smiled at each other. An evening tide scaled the beaches' soft grade. An ocean breeze tugged at sea oats along the dunes. Moss hanging from live oaks moved in the same twitchy motions as Sara's curls moved along her temple. Wind whispered and waves fell in the break. It was September.

They checked into a small cottage along the beach and unpacked their things. The cottage was partially hidden by a dune. Grass leaned in the summer breeze. An oak tree, with moss hanging from a limb, offered shade to a small garden alongside the cottage. Daylilies, yellow and purple, fed on sandy soil and the salty evening air. Wooden steps rose from the sand, to a small deck near the back. In the corner of the deck, a wrought iron table stood between two lawn chairs with flowery cushions.

Inside the cottage, sofas and a recliner filled a small den. Pictures of the ocean and vessels at war with angry waves covered the walls. The kitchen was in the back, near the garden. A soft bed, wide as it was long, filled a room near the den. Blue curtains hung over each window. Day and night, ceiling fans lazily turned over their heads.

Each morning, they slept until light peeked around the curtains. Then, they rose, drank coffee around the small table on the deck, and watched morning waves fall into the beach as if they were weary sailors who had escaped a sinking vessel and fell to their knees in exhaustion. They watched gulls glide along the breaks. And, miles down the beach, they watched thin silhouettes drop fishing lines from a pier.

Later, they walked along the beach, passing tiny cottages along the way before stopping to eat brunch on the patio of a diner. Sara ate and as she finished, she fell back into her chair, and watched the water through her dark glasses. Her skin bronzed in the coastal sun as she quietly sat, watching waves approach. Afterwards, they strolled along empty streets, occasionally dropping into shops filled with touristy trinkets or perused antique shops to waste time.

Each afternoon, they swam on the beach near the cottage. The tide was usually high, and waves were tall and sharp. Each time waves pushed Sara's tiny frame to the shore, but Quince plowed through them as if he were running past Antigua Sherman on his way to the end zone. Standing in the tide, salt water bubbling on his pasty biceps, he could almost hear Sherman taunt, *Not on my watch*, hear cheers from the bleachers, and see Coach with his fist pumped in the cool autumn air. Later, when they tired, they lay on towels near the water, and soaked in the sun until Quince's skin blushed.

At night, they dined on blue crab and scallops at a seafood dive near the pier. They drank. Quince began with bourbon, and finished with beer. Sara sipped lime margaritas or vodka and juice. Later, they held hands and strolled up the beach, carrying their sandals, and washing their feet in the dark waves. Back at the cottage, they staggered up the wooden stairs, across the deck, and fell into bed. Sara would close the blue curtains, turn off the lights, and they spent the evening like newlyweds.

They wanted to stay longer. Stay until the soft September air chilled the mornings, and the pier emptied of thin silhouettes. But just a week later, responsibilities of their new life together sobered their dreams and desires, and they packed, loaded the SUV, and drove down the island, over the arching bridge, and west toward the mountains. Quince drove every mile home. Sara entertained him throughout the long drive, making up stories about people they passed in cars on the highway or songs from the words on a billboard. Near Winston-Salem, they turned north, clipped a corner of Virginia and scaled the Blue Ridge Mountains. They turned west at Charleston and descended into the Kentucky Bluegrass. Home.

Chapter 6
≈ February 2000 ≈

Veins swelled with adrenaline. His heart accelerated with the velocity of a champion sprinter. His lips, once poised to dispel a light snore, tensed. Something hummed in the dark. "Shit!" Quince cursed. His eyes opened. He shifted unconsciously under a thick comforter until his face emerged, and his eyes squinted at a clock on the dresser. One hour past midnight. Hum. His head shook, and water dripped from his tired eyes. They burned a little as they focused on a cell phone lying on a nearby nightstand.

He sighed, and tried to ignore it, but the humming continued. It was relentless. The room was dark except for light from a street lamp that peeked around bedroom curtains, and a glow that emanated from the phone, and blinked like a firefly in the dark room. Hum. Light flickered.

Quince sighed, kicked the comforter from his legs, and sat forward. His feet dropped to the floor. Hum. Light flickered. He grabbed the phone, and with squinted eyes, he stared at the illuminated name. He anxiously flipped open the phone, and shouted, "Dad, is that you?" No one answered. "Dad?" he shouted. No answer. "Dad?" A mixture of muffled voices filtered through the phone and across the dark room.

Sara moaned and shuffled under the comforter.

Quince's voice grew more anxious, "Dad? Are you all right?"

Noise. Muffled voices answered.

Sara pushed the cover from her face and rose. She was scared. Her small features opened up.

"Dad?"

"Is it Beecher?" she asked.

"Dad?"

"Is everything all right? Is he OK?"

Muffled voices filtered through the phone and across the room. Sara heard them.

Quince listened. Silence. He pushed the phone against his ear, and tilted his head. Silence. Then, a slurred voice answered, saying, "It's your old man."

Music filtered from the phone. Sara watched Quince in the soft light of the open phone. His face was pinched. His head was tilted, straining to listen. He looked terribly worried.

"Is it Beecher?"

"Dad? Are you all right?" Music poured through the phone. "Where are you?"

Music, noise filled the pause on the other end. "Hole in the Wall," answered his slurred words.

"Where?"

"Hole in Wall," answered the gruff voice. "You know. On 6th and . . . 6th and . . . Hey?" The gruff voice turned away from the phone and shouted to the crowd, "Where the hell are we?"

"Hole in the Wall," chorused a few voices. Beecher turned and laughter slurred through the phone. "Smart-ass son of a bitch," he cursed.

Quince was silent.

"You know . . . Hole in the Wall?" asked Beecher. His voice slurred, washing over his words like creek-water washes over a slate bed.

"Yes, Dad. I know the place," answered Quince, frustrated and frowning.

"You're kidding?" asked Sara before falling onto her back, and pulling a comforter over her face. Concern melted away, replaced by frustration.

"You know . . . Sally . . . ?"

"Yes, Dad. I know Sally."

"It's the middle of the night for Christ sake!" continued Sara. Her words rose from under the covers.

"You know . . . the bartender?" Beecher persisted.

"Yes, Dad," answered Quince. "I remember Sally."

"Oh Jeez!" Sara exclaimed.

Quince became frustrated. "Dad, do you need something? Are you OK?" he asked.

Beecher's intoxicated lips struggled to find the proper form, slurring, "I want you to come down."

Quince's eyes bulged. "I'm not coming down there tonight!"

Sara moaned from beneath the quilts, letting go a sarcastic laugh.

"I want you to come down and have a drink with your old man," Beecher insisted.

Again, Quince squinted at the clock before he exclaimed, "It's 1:00 a.m. I'm not coming down there!"

"Well," Beecher said with chagrin before pausing as his drunk mind slowly searched for words. "You're acting married."

Quince's face opened up, briefly. "I am married," he exclaimed.

Beecher's voice was insistent, "I want you to come down here."

Sara, still buried under the covers, chimed, "You might as well go. He'll keep calling!"

Quince turned from the phone, and spoke to a lump beneath the comforter, "Easy for you to say. You can sleep."

"He's your dad," she chided.

Quince rolled his eyes. "Yes," He retorted, covering the phone with the palm of his hand, "and he's also drunk. Besides, I am supposed to be at work in a few hours."

Sara laughed sarcastically, replying, "Early classes never stopped you from staying out all night in college. What happened?"

Quince chuckled, "Got married."

A chuckle rose from the mound of covers. "He's right," she noted. "You are acting married."

Quince rolled his eyes. His brow rose, and he answered, "I reckon."

Sara laughed.

The voice in the phone continued. "I want you to come down and have a drink."

Quince paused. Air whistled through his nostrils, and he nodded, "All right. All right, I'll come down there." Music poured through the phone.

"It's about time," said Beecher. His gravelly voice echoed across the dark room.

"I'll come down, but I'm only having one drink."

Silence followed. Then, Beecher answered, "I'm at the Hole in the Wall."

Quince nodded, and closed the phone. A light on the phone paused before falling dark. It did not hum. Light did not flicker. He shook his head, and rubbed his eyes in small circles. Water dripped from them.

Sara, still buried under the comforter, let go a sarcastic chuckle. Covers bounced as her bosom rose up and down.

"Jeez," said Quince.

"What is it?" she asked.

Quince turned, and spoke to the lump, "It's only Monday."

Sara chuckled. Covers bounced.

Quince slowly dressed. He quietly shut the front door as he left, walked through the chilly night air to the SUV, started the truck, backed into the street, and drove into the city. He maneuvered through empty streets. After a while, the SUV slowed, and stopped on a street across from the bar. Quince quietly surveyed the establishment. It was late. The door was shut, but he could see a crowd through a front window. Other businesses on the street were dark. Several cars lined the curb near the bar. Frost obscured their windows.

Quince sucked air through his nostrils, opened the door, stepped out, and slammed the door behind him. He crossed the empty street, and nodded as he passed a few men mingling outside. They nodded. He pushed open a heavy, wooden door and paused. Inside, warm, smoky air washed his face. Men shot billiards in the corner. A dim light hung just above the table. They paused, observed Quince, and continued.

Quince looked around, and grinned, slightly, after seeing his father seated at the bar. Beecher wore jeans, and a leather jacket. Soft light reflected against his bald head. His short legs hung from the stool. He sat near the end, and gripped a tall beer, freshly poured, with both hands. Standing across the bar was a middle-aged woman. Her hair was yellow, and her skin had cracked from years of heavy smoke and drink. She was not unattractive, though, even for those flaws. The thought appeared to Quince that one day, decades ago, she might have been pretty. She smiled and listened as Beecher spoke. He talked and she smiled.

Quince walked across the dimly lit room, through the smoke, and slid a stool away from the bar. "Lies," he warned as he sat near his father. "Not a word of truth."

"Honey," answered Sally the bartender, "this old gal has heard it all before. I've known this old rambler for a lot a years, and I know you've got to separate the wheat from the chaff."

Beecher chuckled, smiling at the bartender.

"You mean truth from the bullshit," chimed Quince.

"Yep," she agreed. "And he piles it on."

Beecher laughed.

Sally smiled, and offered a hand, "You must be Quince?"

Quince shook her hand, and Sally nodded, grinning, "Beecher? You never told me you had such a handsome son?"

Quince smiled, nudged his father with an elbow and nodded.

Sally's head shook. Her rough voice noted, as she watched Quince, "You got your momma's height and looks."

"Now wait a second," Beecher said, pulling a cigarette from his wet lips.

"Thank God!" Quince chimed.

"Well," Beecher stated, pausing as he chugged beer, "the Lord never give me much to work with, but I sure made the best of what I had!"

"Honey," admitted Sally, "No one could argue against that. Pound for pound, no man can match you, Beecher. It's just that there ain't many pounds there!"

Beecher let go a wet, slurring laugh.

Sally smiled, poured a glass of beer, and slid it across the bar. She winked at the young man, turned and walked away.

Quince gathered the beer in his hands and drank. It was cool. His tongue tingled. The taste was a little bitter, but good. He set the glass on the bar, wiped foam from his upper lip, and asked, "Now. What is so important that I need to get out of bed in the middle of the night, and come all the way down here?"

Beecher chugged beer. Smoke trailed from a cigarette that lay in an ashtray between them. His palms turned up as he pled, "Can't you just have a drink with your old man? I ain't got no hidden motives."

Quince's hands flew back as if he were surrendering, "Just saying."

"Say what?"

Quince chuckled, "Just saying."

Beecher chugged beer. "How's Sara?" he asked as he set the glass down.

"Sleeping, like most folks," Quince retorted.

"Tom Quincy."

Quince drank. "She's fine. Doing well."

"Good. That's good," Beecher agreed, drinking. Smoke trailed from the cigarette.

Quince drank, placed the glass on the bar, and turned the stool around so that he could watch the crowd gathered behind them. Across the room, men played a game of billiards. A few women mingled around the room, toting beers as if they were trophies. Most of the men were middle-aged—some older. Women, the few there, were well past their prime. For every woman, three or four would-be suitors were crowded around, vying for her attention. They seem to enjoy themselves, laughing, chugging beer between cigarettes. A cloud of smoke filled the bar. Quince, his back turned to the bar, spoke, "Well, I see you are still keeping with fine establishments."

Beecher twisted around, "You bet." He chuckled. "These are good, hardworking people." He twisted around, facing the bar, "I'd rather be here than anywhere else." Quince chuckled, knowingly nodded his head, and twisted around to face the bar.

"So," Beecher continued, "how's the job?"

Quince paused, "It's a job."

"And the house? You're all moved in? I mean, it's all decorated?"

Quince frowned, "Well, most of it. We have a few rooms yet to fill. But it's getting there."

"You know what I mean . . ." Beecher interrupted.

The son paused, sipping beer, "It's coming along."

"Coming along?" Beecher retorted.

Quince shrugged his wiry shoulders, "Money's tight."

Beecher chugged the beer until it was empty. He grabbed the cigarette, took a drag, and pushed himself from the bar. "Come on," he begged.

"Where we going?" asked Quince.

"You wanted to know why I asked you down here."

"Thought it was to have a drink?"

"Well," he waved Quince forward. "Come on."

Quince followed Beecher through the bar, toward the back. As they passed through the crowd, each person greeted Beecher.

"Sally lets me park back here sometimes," he bragged, pushing open a thick, wooden door. Outside, frost caught Quince's breath. Cool air tickled his throat. A street lamp lit a small lot, surrounded by a privacy fence. Beecher's red pickup sat in the corner. As they approached the truck, Quince noticed a large, rectangular object protruding from the truck's bed. It was covered with a tarp.

"Parking gets mighty hard to find around here," Beecher noted as they stopped at the tailgate. Beecher hung the cigarette between his lips, grabbed the tailgate, and pulled himself onto the bumper. He let go a grunt as his short legs stretched to reach the metal bumper. Then, he threw his legs over the tailgate, and stood upright.

Quince's face pinched. Frost pulled at his breath as he asked, "What is that?"

Beecher chuckled, squinting as smoke lifted over his eyes. "A few rooms to fill yet? Well," he paused, reached down, and lifted the tarp over the object. "Thought you could use this," he said, proudly.

For a moment, Quince forgot about the cold air as he surveyed the object. It was oak. Polished legs twisted up out of the bed. Ornate decoration covered each side. Light from a nearby street lamp washed over the wood. Dozens of thin, oak spindles held the railing. It was big and decorative, approaching grandeur.

"Well," interrupted Beecher, "are you going to stand there all night with your chin on the ground, looking stupid? What do you think?"

Quince's face was open. His eyes were wide as he asked, "But . . . why . . . ?"

"Why?" Beecher cursed. "Why not? I'm your old man, ain't I?"

"But . . . you don't need to do this."

"It was nothing," Beecher shrugged.

"But . . ."

"Because I'm that little girl's papaw."

Quince paused. His persistence wavered. It was never easy to argue with Beecher Magowan. "We could get this. It was the last thing to finish the nursery. We were going this weekend . . ." he stammered.

"Look," Beecher explained, waving at his son, "I thought it would be a nice gesture. It was just something I needed to do."

Quince was silent as he approached the truck. He rubbed the soft polish along the railing.

Beecher's bearded face was proud. Smoke drifted from a cigarette that hung between his lips. "Whatcha think? Nice, huh?" he asked, squinting as smoke lifted over his eyes.

Quince swallowed, and nodded his head. "It's perfect. Sara will be thrilled."

Beecher smiled, and crawled over the tailgate. He grunted as his short legs stretched to reach the ground. "You follow me over," he said.

Quince nodded, continuing, "We'll unload it in the garage so not to wake Sara."

"The place is closing anyway," chimed Beecher, pointing at the old brick bar. He opened the truck door, and climbed into the seat.

Quince walked down the alley, crossed the street, and started the SUV. He looked across the street, into the window of the bar. Men still played billiards. Laughter spilled out onto the sidewalk. As he waited, Beecher drove along the alley, slowly rolled into the street, and passed him. Quince followed as Beecher's red pickup rolled to a stop at the light, and Quince stopped behind it. Cool air pulled at the pickup's exhaust. Beecher's skinny, tattooed arm pointed at the street sign, "6th and Haywood!" He chuckled, squinting as smoke poured out of the truck's cab.

Chapter 7
≈ Lillian ≈

A little girl was born three months later. She was small, weighing barely six pounds, with blue eyes and a crown of white peach fuzz. She was named Lilly after Quince's mother, and three days later, they brought her home. Decorations livened the aging ranch home. Balloons hung from the mailbox. A wreath hung from the front door. A sign that read, *Welcome home, baby Lillian*, stood in the front yard under the trees. Inside, the nursery was pink and green. A thick blanket, covered in a butterfly pattern, was tucked into the oak railings of Beecher's crib. The closet held baby clothes and stacks of diapers.

Sara's parents drove down from Cincinnati, and stayed with them for the first week. They helped the new mother with her baby, cleaned house, and sat with Lillian while Sara slept. Beecher visited Lillian each day. Every afternoon, he drove an hour from the farm, through the hills, down interstate, before he reached the city. He was proud of his son and his granddaughter. Months earlier, when Quince first told Beecher their intent to name the baby after his mother, he noticed a hint of sadness on the old man's face. Beecher readily agreed to it, but Quince noticed something different about the normally ebullient personality—something sad. His blue eyes became a little dull, his face, normally full of character, still. More than anything, Quince noticed that he grew quiet. Beecher Magowan was never quiet.

The Magowans settled into their new lives and their new role as parents. Quince was promoted to supervisor at a small factory across town. The extra pay helped, but it was still barely enough to cover the new expenses. Sara took a leave of absence from teaching, choosing instead to stay home with Lilly. She vowed to return someday, but she hated the thought of being away from her daughter every day while she worked. Even though money was tight, Quince agreed. Sending Lilly to daycare was simply not an option for them.

The next two years quickly passed. Lilly grew as fast as months flipped on the calendar. From sleeping to crawling, walking gingerly, then faster, Lilly grew. Her blonde hair stayed blonde, but the peach fuzz grew long and curly. Winter's snow replaced a summer wind. In the fall they went to the orchards, and fretted over Halloween costumes for Lilly. Life for the Magowans was simple, and quiet.

Chapter 8
≈ The Mountain Lake: Summer 2002 ≈

Two years passed before they took Lilly to the lake. They parked in a small, paved lot, and walked along a path littered with roots and sandstone. Sara held Lilly's hand. Quince carried a cooler and a red pack, stuffed with towels and sunscreen. Slowly, they walked along the cove, passing under a giant poplar, and near an old bench, painted with mold, sunk in the forest floor. They passed a point with a great flat rock, jutting out into the water. Lilly occasionally stopped to throw rocks into the waves, and watch geese swim in the cove. They followed the path as it hugged the crooked shoreline, and dropped the Magowans into a bed of sand. The beach was spotted by a few dozen beach towels and sunscreen-slathered families.

The Magowans kicked off their shoes, and walked barefoot across the beach. Warm sand tickled their feet until they found an open spot near the water, and spread a thin blanket. Every so often, waves threatened the blanket, coming toward the beach in a swell, rolling, and breaking as thin white crests tumbled over. Water slid up the sand, growing thin, and sliding back into the lake.

Amused, Lilly and Sara stood and walked into the wet sand, letting waves chase them up the slope. Quince wore a cap and sunglasses. Propped on his elbows, he watched them run from the cool waves as they slid up the beach. Later, they swam. Lilly was buoyed by her little floaties. The cool lake water flattened her blonde curls. When they tired of swimming, they lay on a blanket, ate sandwiches, and when the sandwiches were gone, they lay back, and soaked in the early summer sun. Later, they built sand castles, and let waves wash their feet. Quince was pale from the long winter. Sara, her skin always brown, even in the first sun of summer, was partially covered in a black bikini. Lilly was only two years old, with tight blonde curls falling over her ears and neck. Her eyes were blue.

Hours passed and the afternoon sun moved across the lake and hung over a distant cove. The Magowans folded the blanket and towels, and journeyed back along the pebbled path. Lilly held Sara's hand. Quince carried the cooler.

On the way home, they stopped at a small country store. Lilly craved ice cream so they each left the store with vanilla cones that dripped in their laps as they drove. The road was narrow and dark. The forest was heavy. Thick tree stumps were like walls, their leaves a canopy, a ceiling, holding in voices of the forest. Fireflies gathered in the fields. Quince turned the radio off, and cries from crickets and cicadas filled their ears. The air smelled of hay from the surrounding fields.

Sara's bare feet were perched on the dashboard. Her face was soft and brown, relaxed, as she stared into the hazy fields. Lilly's blonde curls floated in the wind. Vanilla ice cream dripped from her cheeks. Quince drove. His wiry, sun-blushed arm pulled the car through curves along the narrow mountain road.

Chapter 9
≈ Christmas 2002 ≈

Dimples dented her cheeks, and her blue eyes swelled as a sharp, yellow flash lit the room. She fidgeted, slightly. Then, she froze. She sat in her mother's lap, still. Sara sat on the hearth with a wide, unflinching grin. Quince knelt beside them, smiling, still. It was as if the yellow flash were a wave of glue that drenched their skin, and molded their faces.

Across the room, Grandma Magowan laughed, and leaned into a cane as she rested in a chair.

"How is it?" asked Sara.

Beecher examined the photograph, squinting under his bifocal lenses. His brow rose, "Damn," he cursed, "she moved."

"Beecher," scorned Grandma. "Don't curse around your granddaughter."

"Sorry, Ma," he repented, gazing at the digital picture.

Quince pulled Lilly into his shoulder, smiling.

Sara stared at the camera, begging, "Sit still."

"Smile for old grandpa," begged Beecher's whisky voice as he focused the camera.

Lilly fidgeted.

"Smile for old Beecher," he begged.

Sara smiled. Quince smiled, and tucked Lilly into his shoulder, holding her still.

Finally, Lilly paused, grinned, and her blonde curls fell into Sara's face.

A flash lit the room followed by a pause. Beecher squinted at the camera as Lilly's eyes fell, and snuck across the room to the corner, where a stack of gifts were wrapped and placed under a tree.

"How is it?" asked Sara, anxious.

A long pause filled the den as Beecher squinted at the camera. False teeth protruded under his thin beard, and wrinkles poured from his eyes as they narrowed. "All right I reckon."

Lilly fidgeted in Sara's lap, until Sara let her go. She dropped to the floor, ran across the room and fell to her knees next to the stack of gifts. Sara's cheeks ached as the smile disappeared from her face. Quince grunted under his breath as his knee throbbed from pressing against the maple floor.

A slow fire burned behind them. Logs popped. Embers fizzed like soda. Christmas cards stood open across the mantel. A long strand of garland lay behind the cards. One large stocking, embroidered with the face of a reindeer, and Lilly's name in thin, red letters, hung above the fire. The tree stood near the window as if it were looking out over the hills. A large, red bow crowned the freshly cut cedar. Laces lay neatly against the needles. Gold bulbs hung from limbs. The tree was wrapped with rows of tiny white lights, flickering as they pleased.

The fire burned slow, but sparked as Beecher tossed logs into the flames. Embers erupted against the stones. Logs popped. Embers fizzed. The television was muted, but flashes of light erupted from the tiny screen as scenes rolled through a Christmas program. The room was dim, lit only by the fire, tiny flickering lights, and Grandma Magowan's television. The fire warmed the room, and the smell of salty ham, and pumpkin pie filled the air.

Soon, Grandma leaned into the cane, and pushed, grunting as she leaned forward. "Ma," said Beecher, "let me help you." He feigned toward his mother, but the old woman waved her hand as if she were swatting away mosquitoes, and Beecher paused. Grunting, she finally stood. Hunched over, leaning against the cane, she scooted her feet across the smooth, maple floor, and exclaimed through a winded breath, "It's ready. You all come and eat." She slowly moved toward the kitchen.

Beecher turned, took a stick of chestnut oak from a wood rack, leaned forward, and tossed the log into the fire. Flames burst, crackling as the bark burned. Light from the fire glowed on his bald head. He jabbed the flames with a poker, and sparks erupted from the small stack of logs. Beecher quietly watched flames build as air swept over the grate, stretching high into the chimney. They became pointed, sharpened by the brisk, winter air like a blacksmith sharpens a blade. Flames moaned as they grew.

The Magowan family moved into the kitchen, and gathered around the table. It was an old table. Generations had scarred the oak finish with nicks and dents, but it was sturdy and large enough to seat a dozen Magowans. Quince sat on the end, near the kitchen. Sara sat to his right. Lilly squeezed into a high chair between them. Grandma sank into a chair opposite Sara. Next to her was Sally the bartender, Beecher's girlfriend. Beecher sat on the end, facing Quince. They talked, and Lilly pounded the table of her high chair, giggling. Grandma laughed at her great-granddaughter in that tired, old voice. "Well," she eventually proclaimed, "I reckon we should pray." The old woman lowered her face, and the others followed. The room fell quiet except for the crackling fire. Grandma lifted her voice and prayed. Lilly giggled, slamming her fist to the table. Embarrassed, Sara tried to hush the little girl, but she just giggled. "Amen," Grandma pronounced as she finished the short prayer.

"Amen," echoed others, lifting their heads.

"Well now," proclaimed Beecher. "This is a fine Christmas." He looked around, blue eyes glittering like lights blinking on the tree. His face was shiny and his bald head seemed to glow. "I have my momma who we owe for this fine meal. My girl," turning to Sally, who smiled, embarrassed. Her bronze skin cracked with wrinkles. "My son and his lovely wife. And, most of all, I have my granddaughter." Everyone turned to Lilly as she beat the table with her hands, jabbering. "Whom I believe will be a talker like her grandpa." They laughed.

"All right," Beecher continued, "it's time to carve the turkey." He stood, and pushed the chair from the table. The old, worn chair squeaked as it slid across maple boards. He grabbed a knife and a fork, and began shouting, "Come here, bird! Come here!" Sara laughed. Sally laughed. Quince just shook his head.

Beecher carved the turkey, and they filled their plates, ate and talked, and laughed at Lilly and Beecher. Beecher would occasionally stand, push away the chair, walk into the den and throw a log on the fire. The logs popped and cracked as the bark burned. He poked the logs, and sparks erupted from the fireplace as he returned to the kitchen and sat at the table.

The evening passed; the once plump turkey was a mere skeleton, and the pumpkin pie, crumbs. Lilly's face was covered and stained with pie. Everyone was full, and their stomachs felt heavy. Beecher leaned back, rubbed his pooched belly, and proclaimed, "Momma, that was some kind of good." Approvals echoed around the table. Grandma Magowan blushed, slightly. "Well," she continued, "it's good to have my family here."

"Well," Beecher continued, rubbing his belly, "I'm going to the den." He stood, pushed the chair from the table, and moved into the den.

Sally stood, turning to Grandma Magowan, "Momma, we'll get the dishes. You sit down. Rest yourself."

Grandma leaned into the cane, and pushed away from the table, moaning as she stood. "No. No. I'll help." Gathering a dirty plate with her free hand, she shuffled into the kitchen.

"Oh," said Sara, wiping pie from Lilly's face, "I'll help." She lifted Lilly from the chair, and set her on the floor, asking, "Honey, can you take her?"

In the den, Beecher stabbed logs with a poker. His bald head glowed, and his face was flush from warmth. Flames rose. Embers fizzed as he turned, and warmed his backside. "Nothing like a good fire," he proclaimed. Flames popped and cracked. Outside, a light cut through the darkness, wrapping around metal porch beams. Thick, white flakes floated from the night sky, through the light. A blanket of snow gathered on the porch's edge.

Lilly ran toward the tree and fell on her knees near the stack of presents. Plates rattled and the women chattered in the kitchen. But the den was quiet and warm. Lights on the tree sparkled. Flames threw light across the maple boards. Quince sat in the recliner, and watched the muted television. Scenes flashed across the room, and caught Quince's attention. Beecher stood with his backside to the flames, quietly watching television. Scenes showed fire and smoke, mountains, and snow. Flames lifted from a charred truck on a narrow, mountain road. In the quiet den, flames spilled out across maple boards. On television, snowflakes that poured from the mountain sky, fell onto the truck and were eaten by flames. They grabbed Quince as he anxiously watched scenes circulate through the screen, and flash across the room. Those thoughts, those places, had consumed him for months, overwhelming thoughts of home and work–they were like an insurrection to the things he had known, lived, and believed in. Quince watched the television, and his face pinched; his eyes swelled. Air sucked through his nostrils. A reporter stood on the mountain road, surrounded by grizzled men with long, gnarled beards. They hoisted guns into the air and chanted at the camera. The reporter shoved a microphone to one man's lips, and he spoke. Beecher stood quietly near the fire. Quince snatched the remote and mashed the volume. "The Soviets came," proclaimed the man in broken English, "and we fought them and killed them. Now," he shouted, "the Americans come, and we will fight them, and kill them." Men around him cheered. Some fired their weapons into the air, chanting, cheering. Their angry shouts spilled out of the television and into the den. Air sucked through Quince's nostrils. His heart raced. His face blushed.

Beecher's face sank. His head shook. "Quince, turn that off. I ain't watching that shit!"

Quince's face pinched. "This ain't shit. It's all real."

Beecher's eyes rolled. "It's shit to me!"

"We're in it!"

Beecher pointed at the television, scowling. A thick vein bulged from his bald head. It seemed his face would explode. "You heard what he said. They whipped the Soviets. Hell, they've whipped everyone who ever went there."

"What are you saying?" Anger showed in Quince's face.

"Saying they've whipped everyone else."

"Now we're in it. We're there. You're saying?"

"Saying they'll whip us," he proclaimed, his face was bright red.

"You hear what you're saying?"

"I know what I'm talking about," shouted Beecher.

"They ain't going to whip us," bragged Quince, scoffing at his father's predictions.

Beecher's face was flush, glowing, "I'm saying we'll be there for years, and it won't change a darn thing in the end."

Quince's face wrinkled, "Listen to you!"

"I am old, but I can hear my own words. We ain't got no business over there."

Quince sat there. His eyes grew wide, and his chin dropped. His face was bright and open. "Do you hear what you're saying?"

"I hear it."

"We've driven most of them out of the country already. All but a few," pronounced Quince.

Beecher's head shook violently, "They'll come back. Drag it out. Stay in those mountains."

Quince looked at Beecher in disbelief, "I can't believe you're saying this!"

Beecher's head shook.

"Not us."

"They're indigenous people. Guerrillas," his head shook, face glowing, shiny.

"They won't win," proclaimed Quince.

Beecher sighed. His distended belly rose and fell, and his whisky voice confessed, "That's what we thought in '66."

Quince leapt to his feet, stomping across the room. The empty recliner swayed forward and backward, nearly tipping over. He jerked open the thick, wooden door and slammed it behind him. Across the room, Lilly sat quietly in the floor, on a warm rug near the tree, playing with wrapping paper. Beecher turned and stabbed the fire. Sparks, embers exploded from the logs, bouncing across the stone hearth. Resting his hand on the mantel, Beecher lay his head against his forearm, staring into the fire. His complexion was flush, glowing from the flame.

Chapter 10
≈ On the Banks of the New River: Late Winter 2004 ≈

A cool, moist breeze crept away from a black tide, and mingled among a crowd gathered along the river. The evening had quickly faded into a black, soupy texture of shadows and soft light that blinked as tree limbs were blown by the wind and waved over a street lamp, taunting the meek light with bare, craggy arms. Nearby, a wide pool of choppy, brackish water elbowed the sandy soil.

Quince and Sara quietly sat amid a group of Marines and their families. An awkward silence filled the cool space between them. Sara watched him, and her soft, brown face wrinkled into a tormented, clay-like mask. Finally, she softly admitted, "It's been a long year." Quince nodded. His cheeks blushed from the cool, night air. He swabbed his dry lips with his tongue, and nodded some more. Once, his brow rose and fell.

Sara watched him. Her brown eyes carefully surveyed the nervous way he tapped his thigh, and stared into the dark pool of water. "Guess this year will be long, too?" she sighed.

Quince tapped his thigh and nodded. Silence filled the space between them until he finally spoke. He turned to Sara. His face was tormented, "Look, I realize this past year was hard on you and Lilly. I do." His shoulders rose and his head shook, "I had to do this. It was the right thing. I couldn't just watch these wars from home. From the safety of my own living room. Enjoying my peaceful little life while others my age are doing the fighting."

"What about your family? Don't we matter?"

"Of course," Quince answered in a defensive tone.

"Your father?" she continued. "He's alone now with Grandma gone."

"He'll be fine. He has Sally."

"He'll miss his mother."

Quince nodded. While Quince was away at training, Grandma Magowan's health continued to deteriorate and she passed, in a peaceful sleep, the previous winter. Beecher now lived alone in the old house.

"Well what about us?" Sara pled, moisture gathering in her eyes. "How many times over the last year have we said goodbye?"

Quince did not answer.

"Three times!" she cried, jabbing fingers into the air. "We said goodbye three times and we were apart hundreds of days!" She held a single finger in the air. "The morning you left for Basic Training. Gone for three months. And we didn't see you until we drove to South Carolina, and sat in bleachers, and watched you graduate." A second finger flew into the air. "Weeks later, we said goodbye again when you were assigned to a rifle company and left for infantry training." A third finger went up. "We cried for days when you boarded a plane and flew to California, and spent a month in Twenty-Nine Palms. Now, we're doing it again. Except this time we don't know if you're coming back." The thought of his leaving again, for seven months, left her as numb as the cold, moist air blowing across the New River. She shrugged, pitifully.

Quince shrank with every word she spoke, and every tear that spilled from her brown eyes. Her words were a giant mallet, manufactured with the tensile strength of guilt, hammering away at his pride and the efficacy of his decision to leave his family and join the service.

It was a tough decision. For months he agonized over it. His conscience was a pendulum during those months, swaying back and forth from the life he built and loved to the service he felt compelled to give. Ultimately, the pendulum swung in favor of patriotism and he joined the Marines. With a degree, he was eligible for OCS. He could become an officer. Instead, he chose the enlisted ranks. He wanted to be in the infantry—to lead Marines and avoid the politics of being an officer, even a junior officer. He wanted to serve as an NCO. Because of his education and maturity, he was quickly promoted to corporal.

That evening, tears slid down Sara's cheek as she spoke, "Lilly will sleep awhile. At least until we reach Raleigh." A breeze mingled among them, tossing her brown curls.

Quince nodded. His cheeks tingled as a cool wind crossed them. He sat on a MOLLE pack, bulging with gear and clothing, turned, and quietly watched Lilly fidget as she sat on a green sea bag that lay nearby. The little girl was bundled in a thick sweater, but the breeze tugged at her hair. She held Mickey, her favorite doll, tightly against her chest, and her face sank as if she were shielding the doll from the night's wind.

"We'll be in Charleston by two and Mom's by dinner," Sara predicted.

Quince was quiet. The bill of his cap covered his brow, and a shadow gathered around his eyes. He leaned against his knees, and watched Lilly.

Sara shrugged, turned, and stared out into the deep, black river. Her round shoulders bounced as emotion overcame her. She sniffled. Her shoulders rose and fell. Tears dropped to the sandy soil and washed down the riverbank into the water.

Quince shook his head as if he had just read the truth. He knew Sara needed him to open up, talk about the time away, where he might go, his duties, what he will eat, when he will sleep, what he will do, and what he will miss. But he couldn't talk about it. He tried but he couldn't. That simply wasn't Quince Magowan. On the surface, he was kind, friendly, a devoted husband, caring father, and loyal son. On the inside, he was as rough and hard as the rocky, cedar-scrubbed land he was raised on. He wasn't to blame. If you were raised in the hills, on a farm along the eastern plateau, it was your heritage. Deep inside, he may have felt strong emotions, but he didn't know how to show them.

Lilly fidgeted on the sea bag, shielding Mickey from the wind. Sara faced the river. Her shoulders rose and fell. Tears dropped. Finally, Quince swabbed his dry lips with a moist tongue and spoke, "Germany."

Sara turned. Her brown eyes blinked as the wind touched them, and she asked, "Honey?"

"We'll be hours at the APOE at Cherry Point. Waiting. Processing. Waiting. Sleeping. Finally, we'll board a C-17, sit next to a Humvee or a 7-ton truck for six or eight hours before landing in Germany around the time you leave for home tomorrow morning."

Sara nodded. Her eyes blinked. Torment molded her clay-like mask as she watched him. "Oh," she nodded.

"At Germany, we will disembark and sit around a stuffy room for hours while the plane is refueled. Then," he shrugged, "we'll board the plane and fly to Afghanistan. Land in Bagram around the time you drive into Cincinnati."

A soft breeze escaped from the tide, and mingled around them. Sara blinked. Her curls bounced around. She turned, saying nothing, and stared into the small crowd. Around them, MOLLE packs and sea bags were staged in the sandy grass between the pavement and the water. A thin winter moon and a street lamp were the only stationary lights.

Squad leaders scurried around, taking role, making last minute gear checks; their moonbeams (flashlights) cut the darkness.

Lilly soon complained of the cold, so Quince dug through his pack, pulled out a poncho liner and wrapped the camouflage blanket around his daughter. She fidgeted some, bundled under the poncho liner, and asked for candy. Quince smiled, opened his pack, took out an MRE, opened the plastic, beige wrapper, removed the gum and handed it to her. Lilly, her face grinning, struggled briefly to remove the cellophane wrapper, before it opened. She popped the gum in her mouth and began chewing. Her blue eyes widened as the flavors struck her tongue.

Soon, a Staff Non Commissioned Officer (Staff NCO) shouted, "1st Squad. Load up!"

Quince nodded, chewed on his lip, and stood. Others in the crowd stood. Sara wiped her cheeks with a sleeve and rose to her feet. She gingerly approached Quince and laid her head against his chest. His blouse felt like ice against her moist cheek, and she lifted her face and begged, "Be careful. Promise me?"

Quince nodded, "I'll call first chance."

He turned and knelt next to Lilly who sat on the sea bag, holding Mickey, "Sweetheart, listen to Daddy. I need you to be a big girl. Mind your mother. Do as she says."

Lilly grinned and shook her head in large motions. She voraciously chewed the gum and held her doll.

Quince grinned, leaned forward, and wrapped his arms around the little girl.

Lilly slid off the sea bag, and threw her arms around his wiry neck. As her arms spread, Mickey, the doll, fell onto the pavement. Quince kissed her forehead, gathered the doll in his callused hand, gave it to Lilly and promised as he stood, "Daddy will see you soon." Lilly pulled Mickey into her chest, nodded, and chewed the hardening gum. Then, her face fell as she hid from the wind.

Quince turned and faced Sara. Her soft features were crinkled, but she managed a smile. A soft, frigid breeze tugged at her curls. They stood quietly and stared at each other.

"1st Squad, Load up!" barked the Staff NCO.

Quince nodded and blinked knowingly. He swabbed his dry lips with a moist tongue, stooped, kissed Sara, grabbed the MOLLE pack, threw it over one shoulder, picked up his sea bag, and turned to leave.

As he walked away, Sara spoke, pointing at the poncho liner enshrouding Lilly, "You'll need this."

Quince paused, turned, and shook his head. “Let her keep it,” he begged, watching Lilly. “I’ll find another.”

Corporal Tom Quincy Magowan loaded his gear and boarded the chartered bus for the short ride to Cherry Point. Quince found a window seat and quietly watched Sara and Lilly as the bus drove away. Lilly held Mickey beneath the poncho liner, shielding the doll from a frigid wind. Sara waved. Her round shoulders rose and fell. Behind them, dark, brackish waves pecked the sandy soil on the banks of the river.

Chapter 11
≈ Nineteen hours and three cold MREs later ≈

The door screeched, crying with agonizing shrills as it fell, slow and steady, before slamming into the cold pavement. The shrill quieted, and a loud drone of jet engines hummed in their idled pace. A dim light filled the cabin. "Get off! Get your shit! Fucking move!" A Staff NCO shouted over the noise. One-by-one, Marines stood, formed a line, jogged down the metal slope, and disappeared into a dark abyss that was thrown over the valley.

Quince stood, snatched the small patrol pack he had carried onto the plane, and quietly waited his turn. Noise. Humid, fuel-scented air, rushed up the ramp and filled the cabin. Engines hummed. His chest rose and fell. Air sucked through his nostrils. He squinted and stooped forward, peering through the darkness. He desperately wanted to see something. Desert. Sand. Mountains. Anything. How would he know this was Afghanistan when all he could see was darkness and smell fuel? Was it Afghanistan? It didn't feel like it to him. Quince stood on the ramp and peered into the night, scouring the dark curtain that lay ahead for a sign of the desert; a dim silhouette of a distant mountain. Anything. His eyes narrowed. Nothing. Just darkness.

Finally, the slope was empty. It was his turn. Standing in the belly of the C-17, he squinted, scoured the dark land that awaited him but saw nothing. He nodded, sighed, and his chest rose. Then, he took a step, and then another, and then he ran down the slope, and a blast of warm, fuel-smelling exhaust slapped his face as his boots touched the pavement. Night shrouded the valley, and left Quince blind, but he ran. His chest rose and fell. Fists pumped. His boots struck the pavement with a thud. He ran hard into the wall of darkness. Far behind him, he heard the Staff NCO shouting at Marines who were still on the plane, "Go! Get the hell out! Everyone in the valley can see this light!"

Engines hummed. Quince ran. His pulse thundered in his ears.

The valley was pitch dark, blinding Quince to anything that lay ahead but he ran hard. His pulse thundered. Cold air swept across his face. Far behind him, jet engines droned in their idled pace. Soon, he heard foot steps up ahead, and the cold, ghostly silhouette of another Marine emerged from the darkness. Quince ran, following the Marine until he suddenly paused near a group of silhouettes that had gathered in a circle.

Quince quickly joined the group. His chest rose and fell. Frosty air pricked his throat as he drew deep breaths. Nearby, inside the circle, a captain with the advance party stood alone, with his arms crossed, but said nothing. Other Marines gathered around him until a Staff NCO finally shouted, "We're up!"

The captain nodded, and waved, "Follow me." Turning, he walked into the darkness. The small group followed him to a cold, metal building just off the airstrip. Once inside, they sat on wooden benches and listened as the captain stood before a map, and gave a crude briefing about the base, enemy threat, locals, and their customs. Then, he escorted them to a small, plywood hut—a B hut.

That night, Corporal Magowan, and the Marines of 1st Squad, stretched across cots and waited for the sun to rise. It had been a long journey and exhaustion quickly lulled the other Marines to sleep. The small hut soon filled with snores, and from somewhere across the base, in the darkness, came the roar of jet engines. But, unlike the others, Quince lay awake, unable to sleep. Time slowly passed. Minutes became hours as he lay across the cot, on his back, stared at the splintered rafters, thinking of Sara and Lilly. Eventually, the room grew quiet. Snores died away. Echoes of jet engines, ringing in his ears, faded. The hut was silent as Quince lay there, unable to sleep or, even momentarily, rest his thoughts of home. Once, he nodded. They're probably home now, he predicted. Cincinnati, maybe. Or at least along the Ohio River. Somewhere close.

Quince felt homesick. Lying in the dark, in a strange country, his thoughts began to wander. For the first time in his young life, this steady, measured, confident personality suffered from self-doubt. His thoughts carelessly drifted into regions of denial, and embraced ideologies that were antithetical to the patriotic convictions that led him there, all as mysterious as the sandy mountains that now stood outside the small, plywood hut where he rested. It wasn't long before his wandering mind pursued a self-torturing game of comparison. City by city. Stop by stop. He began to replay all the major points both he and his family arrived at, simultaneously, along their journeys apart. Cherry Point and Lejeune. Germany and Raleigh. Cincinnati and Bagram. Home and deployment. It was like a time and distance question on the SAT. If a chartered bus drives 50 miles an hour away from Camp Lejeune, and your wife and daughter drive 65 miles an hour away from Camp Lejeune in the opposite direction, how many miles will separate you in 1 ½ hours? Or, if a Marine is deployed for seven months and his gorgeous, smoking-hot wife is left at home, lonely, how many months before some arrogant, apathetic, penis-driven male, who has not served his country, tries to screw her? It was torturous and pathetic to think this way, and when it was over, and the roar of a jet engine racing down the airstrip distracted his thoughts, he felt ashamed for having succumbed to doubt so soon in the deployment. Maybe after months of separation, he conceded. But now? The first night? His head shook. He lay alone, staring at the rafters, face pinched and he sighed, "Two hours, Quince? Two hours of seven months and you are already homesick. You pussy!" he cursed, turned on his side and closed his eyes.

Quince slept until light crept through cracks between the boards. He blinked before his eyes opened wide with surprise. Lying there, still, he stared at the splintered rafters. Outside, men walked by the hut, offering only muddled chatter. Footsteps crunched stones scattered along the ground. Then, suddenly, a voice echoed around the hut. Long, indefinable words swept into Quince's ears, sounding as if they were from a speaker. Quince immediately thought of the old speaker that hung on a corner pole at the football field back on campus, but then his thoughts bounced back to reality.

He crawled out of the bivy sack, slid boots over his feet, laced them, and moped across the B hut, throwing open the flimsy, wooden door. He stood in the door, and cool morning air rushed by him. It was a bright morning. The sky was clear. Squinting, he looked around and saw rows of B huts, each identical to the one he slept in the previous evening, lined across the base. To his right, a deep flat valley lay beyond the airstrip. On his left, a minaret from a mosque rose above the distant wall, on the opposite side. A Muslim prayer echoed from the minaret. Far away, snow lay on mountain peaks that surrounded the valley. He sighed, nodding. It was true. Last night, darkness may have disguised the valley and left him questioning where they had landed–but not now; the rock-strewn ground, sand, tall mountains, minaret, a prayer from a foreign voice confirmed what he knew inside, beyond the ridiculous doubt. He was in Afghanistan.

Bagram Airfield was in the middle of a dusty, barren valley, surrounded by snow-capped mountains and fields of land mines. The ancient city of Bagram was nestled in a valley in the Parwan Province, north of Kabul. Cyrus and Alexander once conquered the city. Now, its shanties stood just across giant walls, crowned with concertina wire. In just a few short years since the American invasion in the wake of 9/11, Bagram Airfield was transformed from an abandoned Soviet airbase, littered with the hulls of Russian fighter jets and surrounded by fields of mines, into a thriving military city for the Americans and their allies. Thousands of soldiers, sailors, airmen, and Marines lived there. Day and night, aircraft raced down the airstrip, and lifted over the mountain peaks on combat missions.

Each morning, over the next week, Quince and the rest of 1st Squad rose, walked across base, and lifted weights in a gym under a tent. Afterwards, they ran on a gravel road that circled the airstrip, and three times a day, they feasted on meals prepared by government paid contractors. In the morning, they consumed plates of omelets, bursting with tomatoes, peppers, ham, and mushrooms; they drank coffee or juice and ate fruit. That Friday, they gathered in the crowded cafeteria and devoured steak and lobster. In just one week, Quince gained six pounds. It was Bagram.

The next week, 1st Squad boarded a Chinook and flew across the mountains to the Kunar Province on the Northeastern border. The Chinook flew fast and low, skimming mountain peaks, and dropping into valleys to avoid fire from the Taliban. Passengers swayed and their stomachs flipped as the aircraft quickly rose and fell. One Marine vomited, spewing what seemed like two weeks' worth of loaded omelets and Friday evening surf and turf across the cabin.

They flew east, and the valleys transformed from barren and beige to green, fertile lands, split by white-capped rivers. In the last valley, just below the towering, snow-covered peaks of the Pakistan border, they slid down the eastern slopes onto a dusty, rocky field. Nearby, a small, square compound, encircled with concertina wire, lay in the mountain's shadow. Each corner was capped by a tower, and guarded by Marines.

The Chinook slowly descended into the valley. Quince peered through the open hatch and saw two Marines waiting at a Humvee near the helipad. Dust swirled as the helicopter lowered and slammed into the asphalt-hard sand. Off ran 1st Squad 2nd Platoon, MOLLE packs and sea bags in hand.

They quickly formed-up, just off the small landing zone, and moved toward the base. Passing the Humvee, they saw a man lying on the stretcher; his digital camouflage trousers cut along the right leg, splattered with blood, and heavily bandaged. Two Marines hovered over his leg to shield the wound from the flying dust. Each man in 1st Squad saw the Marine's wound, and just kept walking down the path, through the gate, and into the compound.

Chapter12
≈ Candy & Concertina: September 2004 ≈

Fultz cocked his arm, and a thin, narrow bicep gathered beneath his skivvy shirt. He slung a fist through the warm, dusky air, and a piece of candy sailed over the rocks and sand, then fell. All along, his hazel eyes followed the candy closely as it rose and fell, landing in the dust just shy of the concertina wire. Fultz shook his head with disgust. Breath escaped through his nostrils as he stooped, dug through a cellophane bag, retrieved another candy and cocked his arm. His eyes darted around, determinedly measuring the distance to the wire. They were narrow, focused.

He nodded, confidently. He could get it there. He had the strength to throw the candy across the concertina. He was skinny and young but stout for his size. Deceivingly strong. He just did not look it. He had grown strong in OCS and stronger in Infantry Officer Course but his thin frame just would not hold muscle. Now, he was stubbornly determined. With an arm elevated, fresh sweat soaking the pits of his shirt was exposed. Rings of dried, salty sweat looped around the shirt along his thin back. His face pinched and his smooth complexion folded like a handkerchief. He slung a fist through the air, and the peppermint rose over the rock-strewn ground, and climbed into the valley's skyline. His thin face opened as he watched the candy. His eyes became swollen. Dried lips fell apart. Then, the candy began to fall. It had risen like a high-fly rises over the infield, then fell in a gentle slope toward the wall, seductively gathering hope from the Marine who had thrown it. Finally, the sugary projectile landed just across the wire. A cloud of dust erupted around it just before a small, dirty hand swept the candy from the ground. Others slid on their knees around the area of impact. Clouds of dust blew up. Bickering and taunting filled the quiet, dusky valley.

Satisfied with his throw, Fultz nodded. A grin spread over his thin face, but quickly fell as his eyes hung on the valley above them. "Up-armored Humvees are grounded. Staying home for the QRF," he solemnly noted, mentioning the quick reaction force.

A sigh lifted his bony chest. His youthful eyes became sad and he whispered, "Hi-luxs." Without pause, his bony fingers dug through the bag and emerged with a peppermint. He cocked an arm, and threw the candy.

Corporal Magowan quietly stood behind him. Next to Quince, Sergeant Patrick sat on a stack of sandbags, smoking a cigarette. The sun had fallen behind a mountain. The valley became gray and shadows leapt from boulders and along the riverbank. The air was still and smoke drifted aimlessly over the roof of the concrete bunker. They watched and listened to the lieutenant.

Nearby, children had gathered across the wire, along the edge of a poppy field that burst with red blooms. Each evening, as dusk settled in the valley, children waited until the Marines gathered on the roof of the old concrete building. And they ran from their shanties and mud-bricked homes, through poppy fields, stopped at the twisting wire, lined with razor-sharp blades, and begged for candy. It was a nightly tradition. They gathered and begged for candy and when the Marines slung peppermint or lemon drops or jawbreakers over the concertina, they watched and moved and positioned like an outfielder catching a fly ball.

As they waited, smiles lifted their dirt-smudged cheeks. Their clothes were soiled and ragged. Their feet were bare and callous at a tender age. Their lives were as rough and hard as the Hindu Kush Mountains surrounding the valley. They were boisterous, brave, and unafraid of the Americans. Often, they taunted and begged. All of them but one, that is, a quiet little girl with blue eyes and tangled hair that hung below her shoulders. Her face was thin and dirty. Each night, she appeared with the other children but she never approached the wire, always staying well behind the concertina, shyly standing near the poppies. Quince gave her a nickname. He called her Farrah. While the other children begged and jeered the Marines who stood on the roof, Farrah remained quiet. So it was that evening as the determinedly stubborn lieutenant tossed candy over the wire. And, Fultz was determined.

His face was pinched. His skin folded. It was like the boy who picks a spot on a tree and throws rocks until he strikes that very spot. Fultz could stand on the roof and throw candy until the bag was empty. The candy, gone. That evening, he cocked his arm, surveyed the distance to the wire, and slung a fist. Candy shot from the roof, across the sand and rocks and dust erupted as it fell just beyond the concertina. Children dove to the ground, struggled, and fought. A boy soon jumped to his feet, and displayed the candy like it was a trophy. He ran from the group, struggled with the wrapper before shoving the peppermint into his mouth.

The lieutenant nodded. He pursed his lips and, turning to Quince and Patrick, bragged, "See that shit? Like a 60mm, my arm!"

"Shit," derided Sergeant Patrick, pulling the cigarette from his dry lips. "Looked like Bryant's pull-ups. Weak. Very weak, sir." Patrick's face dropped. His head shook as if he were embarrassed for Fultz.

"Bryant?" asked the puzzled lieutenant.

"Fat-body from 1st Platoon."

"Oh," answered Fultz, "that turd?"

"A doughnut in skivvies," Patrick shot back.

Sergeant Patrick was a muscular, freckled Marine. He was a tenured sergeant, salty and sharp in training but a nightmare off-duty. A true liberty risk. Good in the field but not in the barracks. Twice he was passed over for promotion to staff sergeant. Once, he spent the night in a Jacksonville jail after a brawl in a local bar. And the previous fall, shortly after returning from Iraq, his truck clipped a telephone pole between a Jacksonville strip club and the front gate of Lejeune. He was passed over for promotion after each incident, and being passed over twice means the end. It was truly a shame. All the sacrifice, honor, everything he had given, for what? Gone. Lost to cheap domestic beer and a rode-hard class-C stripper.

So the deployment to Afghanistan was Patrick's last with the Marines. It was the end of his second tour. He would return to Lejeune in the fall, turn in his gear and go home. But, despite the unfairness, and the quickly approaching end of it all, he never stopped teaching, mentoring, taking care of his squad. That evening, a cigarette hung in his dry lips as he stood, and scratched through the bag with his meaty, Irish fingers. He cocked his arm, jerked, and the candy shot out into the gray sky of Northeastern Afghanistan, rose over the rocks and splashed into the dust well beyond the wire.

All along, children watched the falling candy. They positioned. Moved. Hands rose. They backed up well behind the wire. As the candy fell among them, they collapsed to their knees and struggled. Dust rose and the victor, a boy, ran from the others.

Patrick turned to the lieutenant. His lips were twisted in a proud, arrogant smile, and he bragged, "Like an 81mm, my arm." He shook his head. His face fell and, referring to the shorter throw by the lieutenant, he admonished, "Weak sir." He turned, strutted by the lieutenant, dropped onto the stack of sandbags and grinned. The cigarette hung from his dry lips as if it were glued there.

"Asshole," cursed Fultz.

"Bryant," Patrick retorted.

Fultz grinned. "We'll roll at 0730," he said, shifting the conversation from his weak throw and the taunts of juvenile language and comparisons to a shit-bag Marine.

"Hi-luxs?" asked Patrick.

"QRF has the two up-armors. Captain said they need them here. Something will happen sooner or later." The lieutenant stared into the mountain peaks that cut a jagged line along the eastern horizon.

"Yes sir," chimed Patrick, "but hi-luxs?"

Lieutenant Fultz nodded, helpless, "Mac, what do you think?"

Quince sighed, towering over Patrick. "Hi-luxs." His head shook. "A flea's ass has more protection." He paused, "But I understand the CO's decision."

They each nodded.

Smoke drifted around Patrick's face. Silence filled the gaps between them. There was nothing else to say about it. They would drive the hi-luxs and leave the armored Humvees for the QRF. Finally, Fultz's young face pinched. "Bryant?" he asked.

Sergeant Patrick pulled the cigarette from his lips and wielded the burley like a weapon, jabbing the air and griping. "Bryant," he adamantly stated. "How does a pussy like Bryant stay in while a DUI shit-cans a good Marine? Locked and cocked. Fire and forget weapon, like me? Fucked up!"

Lieutenant Fultz smiled, "What was her name? Diamond?"

They chuckled. Their silhouettes hardened like the Afghan soil in the dusky skyline.

"Destiny," Quince corrected.

Patrick grinned broadly, "I have a weakness for brunettes."

Fultz exploded with laughter, cracking, "With crabs and a smoker's voice?"

"Sergeant VD," taunted Quince.

Fultz nodded, chiming, "VD and DUI. Permanent marks on a Marine."

Quince chuckled, "One on his record. The other on his penis."

Patrick grinned. Smoke gathered around his face and his brow rose in embarrassed acknowledgment.

"Mac," begged the lieutenant, "you're up."

Quince nodded and smiled, playfully nudging the sergeant as he stepped forward. "Open up the highway," he demanded.

"Sergeant VD to you, Corporal."

"Mr. Destiny crabs," answered Fultz.

Quince shook his head, noting, "It was destiny he get the crabs from that club."

"Bad fitrep. Freaking double-signer," retorted the lieutenant.

Quince dug through the bag with his long, wiry fingers. He stood on the edge of that old, concrete building, staring out across the field. His eyes darted back and forth. He sized up the length, measured the distance and torque he should use. The children, their dirty faces eager for another chance, watched as the Marine carefully measured the distance to the wire, from the wire to the children, and from the children to Farrah.

"Let it go, Mac," said Fultz.

"Fire that weapon, Corporal," taunted Patrick.

Quince reared back, and his biceps pulled at the skivvy shirt. He let go a deep grunt as his arm jerked forward, and the candy shot high above them.

The children watched. Their dirty faces anxiously rose to the sky. Their eyes carefully followed the candy as it flew high above the concertina. They moved and swayed with its trajectory. Singularly, they stepped away from the concertina, near the poppies. Little Farrah, her eyes focused on the poppies, stepped forward, just slightly. She watched as the candy fell from the gray sky. Her deep blue eyes were swollen. The candy began to fall toward her. The crowd of children stepped back. They moved. Positioned. Farrah stepped forward. Finally, the candy spat into the dust between them. Farrah dropped to her knees and grabbed the candy, but the Afghan boys lunged into the dirt, falling on the peppermint, wrestling, kicking up dust before one emerged with the prize, smiling. He jumped to his feet and ran off through the poppies.

Farrah sat there, on her knees, her dirty face sank into her chest.

"Shit!" laughed Sgt. Patrick. "Damn 81mm, that arm!"

"81mm shit!" chimed Fultz. "155!"

Quince stood there, watching Farrah, not at all proud.

"Remind me never to body spar with that backwoods knuckle dragger," taunted Patrick, smoke clouding his freckled face.

Quince's face pinched. He turned, snatched a piece of peppermint, climbed over the ledge and hung from the roof before dropping to the ground.

"Where the hell is he going?" asked Fultz.

Patrick pulled the cigarette from his lips, and pointed to the little girl who stood near the poppies.

Quince walked across the barren plot that lay outside the bunker. His stride was long, determined. Children, dirt smudged on their faces, gathered along the concertina, smiling as the Marine approached.

"You have candy?" asked one boy.

"You give," demanded another. Hands poured out of the crowd, across the wire.

"Back!" Quince bellowed, "Back! Not for you."

"You give," a boy demanded. More hands poured out.

"Not for you," Quince affirmed as he reached the concertina. "For her," pointing to the girl who had risen from her knees, standing far back, near the poppies.

"Her?" the boy asked, turning to Farrah, then back at Quince with a questioning, but devious grin. "Her no candy."

"It's for her."

"Her no want . . ."

"Bullshit!" Quince barked. "Back!" shooing the others back from the wire.

The children moved back, only slightly.

Quince could see they were belligerent. He knew they would jump Farrah as soon as he gave her the candy. So he stood across the concertina, looked directly at Farrah, and waved.

Farrah, standing near the poppies, took a few tentative steps toward the wire. She was eager. Her expression was open, wide.

Quince waved.

She moved, tentatively.

Quince waved. She moved.

She moved closer, slow and cautious, and the crowd closed in around her.

Farrah jumped back, startled.

"Back!" Quince barked, pointing at the others. His face pinched. Wrinkles folded along his forehead and blush colored his cheeks. He waved and Farrah again moved forward. Then, he reached across the wire, opened his hand, and displayed the peppermint.

A small grin opened across Farrah's face, but quickly disappeared as she glanced at the other children. As long as the other children were nearby, she would not come closer. She knew they would take it from her. She knew they would knock her down, grab the candy and run before Quince could stop them.

Quince watched her. He surveyed her worried expression, how she feared the other children, and her growing trust in him.

He stepped back, away from the wire, pointed at the candy, and the dirt below his feet. He grinned. Farrah turned and glanced at the other children, their eager faces staring back. But she stepped forward, and the others looked on, staring at the little girl. Quince leaned over the wire, gathered Farrah, lifted her over the concertina, and gently set her on the barren ground.

He opened his fist, and the girl took the candy. A timid smile lifted her cheeks. She struggled with the cellophane for a moment then stuffed the peppermint candy into her mouth. Her chapped lips opened in a grin.

"Mac," shouted Lieutenant Fultz, half-heartedly admonishing the corporal for bringing the Afghan girl inside the wire. "You shouldn't be doing that."

"Let him be," said Sergeant Patrick. "Let him be . . ."

Corporal Magowan stood near the concertina wire, and watched Farrah, a filthy Afghan girl, chew a piece of peppermint. It was late evening. Long shadows grew out of the mountains. Soon, a voice sailed over the ripening poppies. The children, standing outside the concertina, ran off through the fields, chasing the voice, each to a mud-brick home nestled between the river and a mountain slope. Farrah watched them. Her nervous eyes darted up the valley, over the poppies. It was late. The valley was becoming gray, blurry. She quickly crunched the candy, looked at Quince and back up the valley. Quince patiently stood by. His arms were crossed. His lips, closed. He shook his head, smiled, and lifted the girl across the concertina, gently setting her on the opposite side. Farrah grinned and ran off through the poppies, chasing the other children.

Quince walked back to the bunker. He jumped, grabbed the ledge, and pulled himself up, onto the roof.

Fultz stood with his hands buried in his pockets. He was smoking. Patrick was sitting on sandbags, digging dirt from his fingernails with a pocketknife. A cloud of smoke hung around them.

The lieutenant pulled a half-empty pack of cigarettes from his pocket, and held it in his open palm. "Smoke, Big Mac?"

Quince shook his head, swatting his hand at them.

Patrick chided, laughing, "Not Mac. He don't smoke. He's a Puritan that way."

"Holster it, VD," Quince replied.

"So, tomorrow," Fultz continued, pushing the cigarette pack deep in his pocket, "quick patrol through town. Remind the locals we are still here. Then double back downstream. Check on the bridge."

"A morning drive," Quince followed.

"In a hi-lux?" asked Patrick, frustrated.

Fultz nodded.

Patrick, disgusted, shook his head. "We run a patrol every day, but that's it. One patrol. It's wide open—that road. They slip over the border after dark. Steal shit.

Harass locals who work with us. Riding around this valley in hi-luxs. They're going a fuck us up one day!"

Fultz nodded again, "We're on borrowed time without armor."

"What do we have to do to get armor?" continued Patrick.

Fultz paused and stared at the frustrated sergeant. He turned and stared up the valley. Drawing from the cigarette, he answered, "Go to Iraq."

Quince nodded. Patrick blew smoke through his nostrils, nodding.

Night soon seeped into the valley. They stood on the roof of that old building, staring up the river, toward the village. A few street lamps ignited in the distance, twinkling in the village. The moon soon threw reflections across the sand, and the silver concertina wire, snaking around the outpost.

Patrick and Fultz soon grew tired and left. They descended the ladder, and crossed the sandy outpost, back to their tents.

Quince was tired, but not ready for sleep. He sat on a stack of hard, unforgiving sandbags, watched the distant lights, and listened to the eerie sounds of the valley. He sat there until his ass went numb, and then he stood, descended the wooden ladder, and within a few steps, walked through a screen door just like the door on Grandma Magowan's front porch.

The door slammed behind him, and he stood in the doorway and looked around the sparse, narrow, dimly lit room. A few cots lined the wall. Bivy sacks covered them. A box of MREs sat in the corner. The deuce gear he stripped from his shoulders earlier that evening hung on a nail that had been hammered into plywood on the inner wall. His flak jacket, weighted with thick, protective, plates, SAPI plates, and a half-full camelback, hung on a T-shaped cross of 4x4 wooden beams. His Kevlar helmet rested on top of the cross. An M16A2 rifle leaned in the corner. A CD player sat on a shelf by the window. Distant chatter of Marines passing by outside, and the faint sound of music filled the silence.

Quince moved a few feet across the floor, and rolled onto a small, thin cot. This was his bed. His rack. The place he would sleep for seven months. Lying on his side, he reached under the cot, dug around in his sea bag, and took out an envelope. It was open. Days ago, he returned from patrol to find the envelope laying on his cot. He had anxiously torn open the envelope, peeling the lip with his finger and tearing a jagged edge along the top. Now, he parted the jagged edges with his fingers, withdrew the letter, unfolded it, and a small photograph fell from the creases. From the plywood floor, two familiar faces smiled back. Quince lay there. He was still. For a moment, he was frozen, staring at the faces in the photograph. The room was quiet. The music was barely audible.

Finally, he leaned over and grabbed the picture. A smile lifted his cheeks as he looked closer at the faces in the photograph. It was taken in March. A breeze pulled and tugged at their hair. Lilly wore gloves that were decorated with a cartoon. Her ears were covered with pink muffs. Sara's eyes were wide, and brown. Hair blew across her face, partially covering her cheeks that were round with a smile. They looked happy.

Quince just lay there, in his cot, staring at the photograph, studying their faces. Eventually, he held up the letter, and read it again. The words were familiar. It told of the same story he had read two days ago just after it arrived with re-supply, again after PT yesterday morning, and before and after patrol yesterday afternoon. It read the same as last evening before he went to sleep, this morning before reveille, and a dozen times since when he needed to see his wife, his daughter, and home.

He stared at the photograph and read the letter again, trading one for the other until his arm slowly fell, gently resting on his chest; his fingers gripping the worn paper. It was late. The valley was dark. Soft music played in the corner. Quince lay there. He was tired but unable to sleep. To pass time he stared at the ceiling and thought about his wife. It had become a nightly ritual to help him fight insomnia and soon, a twisted, guilty grin bent his lips as his eyes followed the cracks and chips of the concrete ceiling. It was those lines, those spidery cracks in the ceiling directly above his cot that spun their web around Quince's imagination.

Each evening, he lie on a cot, filled with anger, boredom, frustration and the web of cracks and lines twisted and turned into something good. Something he missed terribly after months, something that clouded his thoughts during every down moment as the deployment dragged along—intimacy. He was a good Marine—dedicated to his mission and committed to protecting the men around him, and so, during duty, training, listening to briefs about future missions or outside the wire, on patrol, he was focused. But after the patrol or while lounging on the roof or lying on his cot at night, he longed for Sara.

That night his imagination drew her up there, on the ceiling in the maze of cracks. He started over the window, and followed the long strips, each intersecting and sweeping around before dissecting again. The roof was shattered and splintered with cracks where her hair would have fallen over the pillow, and where her breasts gathered under her folded arms.

Her eyes he saw first, one hidden under the ridge of the pillow, the other pushed up under her cheek as she smiled back at him. It was as if she had slipped out of his sea bag, climbed the wall, and made her bed on the ceiling. Sara was there, nude as the night they were married, nude as the night they conceived Lilly, just damn, bare-all naked. Quince wasn't sure when it started or how he came to see her on the ceiling each evening, when others slept, but he did. Somehow, she was sculptured in the cracks by heat and expansion and age and Quince's loneliness; an oil painting, cracking under the weight of time but still a masterpiece to him. To him, her flaws were perfect. Lying there, that night, he wanted to pull her down, and dive into her body.

After his mind walked through a night with Sara, Quince slept. Music played. The room was dark. The valley was black and quiet. Early that night, he woke. His back ached. He twisted and shifted, grimacing. The cot was small and uncomfortable, especially for a man of his height. A few minutes was all it took for the nylon to pull under his weight, stressing the square aluminum beams and letting all the pressure fall in the valley of nylon—cutting a swath of pain in Quince's lower back. He lay there and his shoulders cramped from the pinch of the bars—his weight on the nylon pulling them narrower. He squirmed and shuffled, cursing under this breath.

It was frayed, that cot, torn and stained. It was past its prime, a relic of Marine Corps history. Quince was convinced that it began military service in Vietnam with tours in Beirut and Panama, Iraq, Somalia, Liberia, Kosovo, Iraq again, and now Afghanistan. He complained about it to Sergeant Patrick shortly after they arrived.

Upon hearing this, the dry-humored Patrick touted that the cot was the most decorated asset in active duty service, and suggested they hold a decoration ceremony for it, "We'll have a squad formation," he said. "I'll read the citation . . . you pin'm on."

Quince laughed, "We could use it for 203 practice. We'll pretend it's the cowardly bastard that killed Stanton!"

Patrick produced a wide, Irish grin, "240 Gulf for me."

Quince nodded.

Lying there, Quince grinned at the thought, squirming and shuffling on the uncomfortable cot. He tried to sleep, aggravated but tired. It had been this way for more than two months, the boredom of night. His mind had run through a night of screwing his wife. Now, he again tried, but was too tired to rekindle the horniness he experienced earlier. That evening, he lay there on the old, torn cot and wondered about things. He wondered how this camp came to be built. Who chose this place? Why here? Why this valley? Who built it? Who poured the concrete for Quince's home way up in the Hindu-Kush Mountains?

Just after 2nd Platoon arrived at Camp Stanton, a rumor swept through the camp that this small, square outpost, once home to the Soviets, had been overrun by the Mujahideen. It was a fierce battle, according to the scuttlebutt. The Afghan fighters first captured the OPs, and their heavy machine-guns, and then turned the Soviet guns on the camp, killing and wounding many.

And when the command eventually surrendered, their throats were slit, and the corpses strung up by the neck inside the room where Quince now slept.

The engineer who constructed this building would have been an officer, Quince thought, likely among those hanging from the walls in death, killed in the same room he built; his blood staining the walls he made. Quince thought about that engineer. He envisioned him as a young man, obviously educated, maybe with a young family at home. Maybe he had a pretty wife like Sara waiting for him, a beautiful daughter like his Lilly. Whatever the facts, he was long dead now. His children grown, his wife remarried, aging, his enemies aging too. Many of his enemies were still fighting in the same mountains, some with Quince and Patrick and Fultz, and some against them. That's just the way it was with that war.

He thought about the young Soviet engineer, and the building he constructed high in the mountains of the Kunar Province, near the Pakistan border. Quince knew those cracks in the ceiling came years later, after the engineer was tortured, his blood dripping down the walls. Lying there, bored, Quince's imagination took over. He wondered if those cracks were simply streams of the engineer's blood, his soul eating into the concrete, eating away at himself. Maybe the engineer's creative soul was looking to bargain with Quince, drawing Sara up there if Quince would someday kill the men that killed him. His soul completing the unfinished work, a ghost kneeling on the ceiling, chipping, chiseling away at the concrete poured by his mortal hands.

Quince thought about the dead engineer, the enemy, the building and the cracks. Eventually, he dozed off, but awoke, drifting all around sleep. Ever so slightly, he slipped into a delirium, and then it happened. His thoughts drifted back several months to a patrol.

Chapter 13
≈ The Marianas: April 2004 ≈

Like a thick, rubber cork, his boot heel twisted, boring in the sand, smashing the cigarette and extinguishing the smoldering embers. When the boot pulled away, a tinge of smoke drifted from the sand, rising from the torn burley as if it were the last breath of a dying man.

By now, the squad had gathered around him. Some leisurely kicked stones across the barren ground. Some watched him. Others stared off into a valley filled with the haze of quiet dusk. Sergeant Patrick stood among them. His eyes squinted and moved slowly over the squad, eyeing the men and judging their demeanor. A rifle was slung over his shoulder and his arms were crossed. Smoke drifted around his feet. He watched the other men but remained silent.

It was late. The sky was gray as the day's end drew near. High above them, a steep, boulder-strewn peak pierced the dull sky. Its height was menacing. It just loomed over the valley. Any man who stood at the mountain's base and looked up at the peak felt small. Tall enough to clip summer storms, at times the peak seemed to touch the clouds. Snow often dusted the peak on late April mornings. It was giant and grand, intimidating. For an unknown reason, someone called the mountain Tarawa, and the name stuck. Once, a lance corporal asked how such a mountain, one littered with boulders, sliced with gullies and crowned by a sharp peak could be named after a small, mostly flat, atoll. Sergeant Patrick laughed and in his deep, scratchy voice, reminded the Marine that . . . *Tarawa only appeared a small island. It was,* grinned Patrick's leathery face, *a mountain; its slopes rising through a turbulent ocean until the peak rose above the Pacific's crest.*

Atop Tarawa's peak laid walls of sandbags, encircling a small, square structure. Inside, a Marine squad held a dominating view and position over the ravine behind Camp Stanton and the valley along the river. The view of the surrounding valleys from Tarawa's peak was nearly panoramic, obstructed only by a few boulders that lay on the back slope of the mountain. It was a logical position for Camp Stanton's OP, observation post, but, because of the obstructed view in the ravine behind Tarawa, daily patrols were needed.

That afternoon, Sergeant Patrick held a fist above his shoulder, and 1st Squad paused outside the gates. Corporal Magowan, standing a few feet away, turned to the squad, following in trace, and pulled his hands apart. Watching his signal, the squad quickly disbursed, and dropped to a knee, facing outward, toward the mountain base.

Patrick pointed to a skinny Marine standing a few feet away and barked, "Tell Tarawa we're stepping off," pausing, he grimaced, "and the CP."

The skinny Marine, the squad RTO, Radio/Telephone Operator, stood slightly hunched, his thin frame bent under the weight of his deuce gear, flak jacket, SAPI plate, weapon, and, worst of all, the PRC-119, a heavy, burdensome radio. The antiquated radio, the scourge of every RTO, was noticeable by causing a hunch in the Marine's pack, a slight stoop in his posture, and a 3-foot antenna, a whip, jutting over the Marine's Kevlar. A black handset was tucked under the Marine's helmet, and fastened into his chinstrap.

As Patrick spoke, the RTO lazily lifted his hand, and squeezed the receiver, "Shawnee 6, this is Shawnee 2, over."

A fuzzy sound, squelch, bled from the handset as he released the button.

"This is 6. Send it 2."

"Request permission to cross the LOD."

"Standby, 2." Squelch interrupted the silence.

Moments passed. Night closed around them. Patrick became impatient. His eyes lifted into the graying Kunar sky and his hands rose and fell in despair. He turned to Quince, and spoke through exasperated breath, "Who's in the CP?"

Quince grinned, "Morehouse."

Patrick's mouth fell open, "Morehouse?"

Quince nodded.

Marines snickered.

"Light-duty Morehouse?" continued Patrick.

Quince nodded.

"Who's the OIC?" asked the sergeant.

"Gunny," Quince responded.

Patrick nodded.

They waited. Night drew closer. Squelch bled from the handset. Patrick glared at the receiver as if he were staring down Morehouse, chiding, "Come on broke-dick. Just tell Gunny we're going."

Quince's grinned broadened.

Finally, a voice dribbled through the receiver, "2, this is 6."

Squelch.

"Send it, 6."

"Permission granted. Keep in contact. Report all RPs."

"Roger, 6. 2 out."

The sky grayed. First squad, 2nd platoon, was disbursed near the base of Tarawa, kneeling.

"Tarawa, this is 2," continued the RTO.

Squelch.

"Send it 2," interrupted a deep voice.

"2 is stepping off on Marianas."

"Roger. I copy. 2 on the Marianas."

The RTO released the handset. Quince turned, motioned the men forward, and in unison, the squad rose and moved away from Camp Stanton and into the valley. The day was ending. Shadows grew from the guard posts of Stanton and slid down the slopes of OP Tarawa.

First squad snaked along the rocky valley, deep below Tarawa and another steep mountain that stood adjacent. Quince took the lead. He moved slow, carefully scanning the ridges and rocky slopes. The M16A2 he held over his chest pointed slightly down, to the left. His index finger nervously rested on the trigger guard. A dozen feet behind him walked the rest of 1st fire team, slightly disbursed. Sergeant Patrick, the RTO, and 3rd fire team, followed. Doc Sims trailed close by. Second fire team brought up the rear. Two Marines flanked out, away from the squad, on either side of the valley. They patrolled.

The squad cautiously moved up the valley. Occasionally, rocks ground under someone's footsteps, and Patrick was quick to flash a furious expression at the perpetrator. Nearby, night crept from the ravine, draining color and definition from each Marine, leaving only blurry silhouettes. Night vision goggles (NVGs) were affixed to the front of each Marine's Kevlar. A thin green band was wrapped around each Kevlar, and two squares were sewn into the band in the back. Those squares, or "cat eyes," glowed in the dark, telling the Marines in the rear the location of their colleagues up ahead.

As 1st Squad began a slow right turn around the base of Tarawa, shadows sprouted around the valley. Sergeant Patrick turned, pointed to the RTO, and whispered, "Passing RP Saipan."

The RTO paused, pressed the handset and whispered, "6, this is 2, over," releasing the handset.

The patrolled continued. The Marines kept moving.

"Send it, 2," answered the CP.

The RTO squeezed the handset, whispering, "Passing RP Saipan."

"Roger, 2. Copy. Passing Saipan."

"Tarawa, this is 2. Do you copy?" continued the RTO.

"Roger, 2," came a deep voice through the handset. "We have visibility."

"Roger, 2 out," releasing the handset a final time, the RTO nervously scanned the slopes.

Quince slowly moved along the valley on the back slope of Tarawa, a steep, rock-strewn mountain in eastern Afghanistan. The valley funneled him into a narrow, dusty path, leading him and the Marines of 1st Squad up the slope, around cliffs and boulders. His eyes were focused. His teeth clenched tight. Deep breaths pulled through his nostrils each time he approached a thick boulder, his view blocked of everything that lay beyond. He walked along the path, careful not to kick a stone or drag his boot in the sand. He moved and scanned the ridges as the sun sank into the distant mountains, and the boulders and ridges grew shadows. The patrol was 30 minutes old, moving methodically, and on pace with its point man.

Suddenly, Quince stopped and pulled a fist over his shoulder. The Marines of 1st Squad paused and faced outward. He turned, pointed to the outer flank and motioned him forward. The Marine on the left flank had fallen back as the patrol made the broad turn around the base of Tarawa.

The Marine nodded, and moved out, across the narrow valley, adjacent 3rd fire team and Sergeant Patrick. With the flanking Marine now in place, Quince motioned the squad forward and slowly they moved down the path, toward the sharp cliffs on Tarawa's back slope.

The sky soon turned dark gray. A few stars hung over the valley. Everything was still but for a dozen figures moving methodically toward a stack of large, sandstone boulders and a sharp cliff they called RP Tinian.

Sergeant Patrick gazed across the valley, scanning, reviewing the patrol's posture and disbursement. His eyes constantly moved, jumping around the valley. He scanned ridges, followed the skyline and intently watched his point man slowly descend into the valley behind a sharp cliff that was cut deep into the back slope of OP Tarawa. Patrick watched as darkness filled the valley, and Corporal Magowan's digital camouflage became a moving shadow. The sergeant's freckled, sun-leathered face pinched. His head shook as he waved a hand at the squad and flanks. With two fingers, he pointed at his face, and pulled the NVGs over his left eye. He twisted the goggles, and the dark valley flooded in a fluorescent green tide. The Marines of 1st Squad mimicked the sergeant, each pulling NVGs over their left eye. Then, Sergeant Patrick climbed the knoll before descending deep into the valley toward Tinian. Nearby, a voice interrupted the bleeding squelch, "2, this is Tarawa, over."

The RTO lifted the handset as it hung from his chinstrap, and pressed the receiver, "Send it, Tarawa."

"Roger 2, we just lost vis."

"Roger Tarawa, approaching RP Tinian. We'll confirm when we reach the RP, over."

"Roger, Tarawa out."

Corporal Magowan, descending the path behind the cliff, approached the boulders. Some massive ones were scattered around the valley. Some rested in piles. Sometime, during the ages of this ancient land, they broke free from the mountain, tumbling down the slopes, before coming to a final rest in the valley floor. They were large enough to block Quince's view of the valley, leaving only a narrow opening. On the left was a steep drop, too steep for the flanks to descend. On the right, a cliff cut the slope. It was so narrow the flanks would be forced to pull in, onto the path, until the squad cleared the boulders of Tinian. A choke point, it was the most dangerous spot of the patrol.

Quince, approaching Tinian, peered around the boulders. Using the NVGs, the giant stones were transformed from large, dominating shadows, to fluorescent, green pillars. Quince's face was solemn, still as the sandstone boulders drew close. His teeth were clenched. The valley was very quiet, even the clatter of boots striking rocks was gone, silent. He could not hear 1st Squad behind him. It was as if he were alone, a single-man patrol. He could not turn around, or take his eyes off the boulder, and fear began to grip his thoughts. *Were they still there?*

He panicked. Deep breaths pulled through his nostrils. His mind raced. His thoughts swirled, wondering if they were still behind him. Or had Patrick left? The patrol, abandoned. It was ridiculous to even think it but he did. He couldn't help himself. Unable to hear them or turn around and risk taking his eyes off the boulders, fear swept in delusions like a summer tide. His thoughts swirled.

It was his job that evening to be the point man, and identify any dangers before the main body was threatened. If he turned and took his eyes off Tinian, and something happened, men could die and Quince would never let that happen. He tried to focus, scanning the boulders, and the ground between the steep cliffs and RP Tinian. His chest pounded. His teeth clenched. His nostrils filled with cool, black air, and his thoughts raced, but his eyes were fixed on the giant, green objects covering the path. He tried to focus, concentrate on what lay ahead.

Behind him, a silhouetted 2nd fire team slowly, purposely moved over the knoll, scanning the flanks, and the path behind them. Sergeant Patrick waved his hands up and down. Having gained their attention, he used a free hand and his weapon, and pushed them together as if squeezing something imaginary. The right flank, and then the left, moved toward the path, just in front of 3rd fire team.

The valley was dark. Quince patrolled along the path. Each step carried him closer to the boulders. His thoughts raced back to stories of patrols being ambushed at this spot on Tinian. Most of them were hit and runs, quick hits by Taliban fighters who fired a few shots, harassed the patrols and disappeared into the valley. And then they stopped and patrols continued for weeks or months without incident.

Each day, patrols sank from their disbursed formation and squeezed through RP Tinian, expecting an ambush, but there was nothing. No ambush, only the dark valley, a cliff, boulders, and an anxious, later grateful, patrol. Then, last fall, before the snows came, a patrol was hit. Details of that patrol played over and over in Quince's mind as he walked along the path that night.

≈ ≈ ≈

It was early morning, hours before dawn. The patrol scaled a knoll along the path, and descended into the valley, toward the boulders, just like the patrol Quince now led. Fog sank into the mountain, and the eyes of OP Tarawa, already obstructed by the sharp cliffs at Tinian, were blinded to the valley. NVGs were useless in the fog so the squad leader limited disbursement; his flanks already close because of the cliffs. He brought his point man back.

Marine after Marine filed through the narrow path of Tinian. The valley was nearly black, quiet but for the clap of boots striking rocks. A thick fog hung over their heads, just below the peak of Tarawa. One by one, they slipped between boulders and the cliff wall. The point and flanks walked the path. The squad leader and the rest of his Marines passed between the rocks on the cliff. They each emerged from Tinian, and knelt, waiting for the others to join them.

High above them, fog blinded the OP's ability to monitor the patrol. The Marines stood, and continued patrolling through the darkness. Their boots blindly struck rocks along the path. The sounds were minor. Normally, they would have gone unnoticed but that night, in a dark, quiet valley, those sounds carried up and down the long slope like strikes of lightning.

One by one, Marines walked along the narrow path away from Tinian. Suddenly, a loud crack, followed by a whistling sound cut the air. Another followed. The cedars above the path came alive. Sharp flashes of light burst from behind thick tree trunks.

"Enemy right," screamed the squad leader. "Take cover along the path."

A few muzzles flashed from along the path. "Cease fire," yelled the leader. "Cease fire! They're between the OP and the path. We'll hit Tarawa!"

Bursts of light ignited the trees above the path. Cracks, whistles split the night air. Occasional tracer rounds lit the dark valley, running down the slope and crashing into the valley floor.

The RTO's handset came alive. "Marianas, this is Tarawa. What's your pos?"

"Fifty meters north of Tinian on the Marianas."

"Break! Break!" shouted a third voice through the handset, "What's the sit, Marianas? This is 6."

"Pinned down 50 meters north of Tinian. Enemy . . . squad size . . . between Marianas and Tarawa."

"Tarawa, do you have vis?"

"Negative, 6."

"Marianas, can you engage?"

"Negative, 6. Tarawa's in my line of fire."

A pause followed, squelch poured through the handset. "Marianas, pull back to Tinian. Tarawa, engage when Marianas clears Tinian. Get an FO down below the fog, someone with eyes on. Need eyes on for the 81s."

"Roger, 6."

"Marianas, do you copy?"

Silence, "Marianas? Marianas? Do you copy?"

Silence. Squelch.

"Marianas?" questioned the CP. "Fuck!" shouted 6.

Silence.

"6, Marianas. We got two down. Repeat two WIA. Taking heavy fire from above the path. Pulling back to Tinian. Request medevac."

≈ ≈ ≈

Quince knew the story well. He studied the after action reports, and, many nights, he and Patrick sat on the roof of the bunker, as the sun fell, and discussed how they would do it better. Do it right.

That evening, he kept moving. Within feet of the narrow pass between boulders and the cliff, he suddenly stopped, threw a clenched fist over his shoulder, and dropped to a knee. From where he knelt, giant boulders were just a few feet away. Beyond the narrow opening, lay only a few, black feet of nothing. Quince held the fist over his shoulder, and Patrick's fist soon went flying over his own shoulder. The sergeant motioned and the squad fell to a knee and faced outward. He moved along the path, and the RTO followed, until they reached the point man.

"Whatcha think, Big Mac?" Patrick asked, kneeling next to his point.

The RTO followed, kneeling next to Patrick.

"Think it's a hell of a spot for an ambush."

"Tailor made," answered Patrick.

"Fucking black . . ."

"Black as an MRE shit," noted the sergeant.

Quince nodded, pointing. "I'll move there, 30 out, and give the signal when it's clear."

Patrick nodded. "Get low!"

Quince stood and cautiously moved through the rocks.

Patrick turned and motioned for the squad to move up to his position. Near the opening, and slightly disbursed, the squad took a knee, providing as much protection to their point that the small opening would permit.

Quince moved between the boulders. His chest was pounding now, pounding through his sweat-soaked skivvy shirt, pounding through his blouse, flak, SAPI plate, deuce gear, pounding hard. His teeth clenched. Breath pulled through his nostrils. It wasn't that loud, but to Quince, internally, the sucking, pushing sounds were deafening. His lungs filled with dry valley air, before emptying, escaping, almost as if it were running away from him, running away, down the path, away from the portal of Tinian.

Quince surveyed the slope below the path. A few boulders dotted the valley. There was no sign of movement. Just sand, rocks, and darkness. He scanned the slope of the mountain across the valley. Nothing. He moved slowly, carefully placing his feet between the rocks. He was crouched, stooping. He held the M16 butt stock tight against his shoulder. The muzzle was lifted higher now. Crouching, stooping, he moved along the path away from Tinian. He scanned the slope above the path and found the grade steep. The ground was smooth. The slope was not littered with boulders but a grove of giant, thick-trunked cedars stood below the crest.

He took a knee, and surveyed the cedar grove with his NVGs. Thick trunks glowed in fluorescent green. Above them, high along the slope, hidden in the darkness, the night sky, and the brushy cedar needles, was OP Tarawa.

"Mariana, this is Tarawa, over."

"Send it, Tarawa," answered the RTO, squeezing the handset as it dangled from his chinstrap.

"Have eyes on your lead, over."

The RTO looked at Sergeant Patrick who nodded, listening to the handset as he knelt nearby.

Quince, kneeling along the path, surveyed the cedar grove with his NVGs, and saw no movement among the giant trees. Again, he scanned the valley below the steep slope, the boulders, and saw nothing move. The far slope, rising from another mountain across the valley, and saw nothing. He scanned the narrow, winding path ahead. Nothing. He was alone. He reached over his shoulder, and pulled his hand forward, through the cool night air.

Sergeant Patrick nodded, although Quince did not see him, and motioned down the path. The Marines who had been the flanks, ever vigilant for their patrol leader, stood and moved along the path, through the narrow pass and away from Tinian. Patrolling, scanning the cedar grove, the steep slope, they moved toward Quince.

Sergeant Patrick watched with eagerness. A RTO, and the rest of 1st Squad, all safe behind the boulder of Tinian, watched.

"Marianas, Tarawa, over," came a deep voice through the handset.

"Send it."

"Have eyes on your lead."

"Roger," whispered the RTO.

The flanks moved, reaching their point and kneeling in the sand. They were silent.

Quince pointed to one Marine, and then to the path. With two fingers, he pointed to his eyes, and then down the slope. He turned to the second flank, motioned toward the cedar grove, and formed the numbers 2 and 0 with his fingers.

The Marines nodded and slowly patrolled from their position along the path. The first flank disappeared over the hill, out of view from Sergeant Patrick and the Marines at Tinian. They were out of OP Tarawa's view. Only Corporal Magowan, patrolling along the narrow path, could see them. The second flank patrolled cautiously away from the path, toward the cedar grove.

"Marianas, have eyes on your lead and right flank, over."

"Roger, Tarawa," answered the RTO, watching the lead and right flank, through his NVGs. Kneeling next to him, Sergeant Patrick nervously followed his Marines on point.

Quince patrolled, scanning the rocks, slopes, and the cedar grove above the path. Nothing. He walked a few feet more before kneeling to watch the flanks. The right flank had reached the cedar grove, and begun patrolling a route even with the path. Quince watched them patrol through the trees and the site of the infamous ambush, disappearing behind thick trunks, reappearing, and disappearing again. Trees were thick fluorescent masts inside his NVGs.

He turned and looked down the steep slope.

The left flank clumsily descended the sharp grade with its loose, tumbling stones. Quince watched. He scanned the slope and boulders below the flank. Things were still. He stood, and turned, once more, to briefly scan the cedar grove. Suddenly, a sharp flash flooded his NVGs, immediately followed by a cracking sound. Whistling sounds followed again before he fell to a knee. He turned to his left. His NVGs filled with blinding light.

The quiet valley roared. The whistle of passing bullets tingled in Quince's ears. Kneeling along the path, he saw the flashes, those white explosions behind several large boulders. Quince dropped to the prone position, lifted the M16 barrel, divided the sights and squeezed the trigger. His rifle cracked. The barrel lifted slightly, and a small cloud of dust erupted along the path. The empty casing jingled as it bounced over the rocks. He kept firing, chasing explosions around the boulder. Dividing his sights. Squeezing the trigger.

He looked down the slope, and saw a Marine, the left flank, lying on his side, still. Quince stood. Stooped, and began sliding down the steep slope. The ground gave way as his tall frame pushed into the loose sand. Sharp, whistling sounds pierced his hearing and tickled his ears. Rocks around him made sharp, cracking sounds.

Sergeant Patrick was screaming. He moved the Marines forward, away from Tinian, and positioned them along the path.

“Marianas,” screamed the handset hanging from the RTO’s chinstrap. “Sitrep. Where should I position fires?”

“Break! Break! Marianas, this is 6. Sitrep, over.”

Patrick grabbed the handset, “Taking fire from below the slope, west of Tinian. One down. Have Marines in the line of fire, over.”

A sharp flash swooped down the hill, passing Sergeant Patrick who was moving furiously up and down the path. Several more whistled by, “Tarawa,” screamed the sergeant into the handset, clinched in his fist. “Check your fire! Hold fire! Marines in your line of fire.”

“Roger, Marianas,” answered the deep voice. “Holding fires. Holding fires.”

“What the fuck!” Patrick screamed. He knelt over the SAW gunner who was firing carelessly. “Put your fires there,” he screamed, barely audible among the explosions. “Right there,” pointing at a large boulder, and the origin of several explosions.

“There!” screamed Patrick. “There! The boulder,” pointing.

An anxious voice yelled through the handset. “Marianas, do you request fires?”

Patrick snatched the handset from the RTO, both kneeling behind the saw-gunner. “Negative. Negative. Have friendlies in the impact area. Standby.” Intently, he watched his point slide down the steep slope toward the wounded left flank who lie motionless on his side. He watched as dust popped around Quince’s feet; tiny explosions of dust, rock, pebbles. He slid feet first on his bottom, as if he were sliding into home base, stopping next to the Marine.

“Jenkins? Jenkins?” screamed Quince, trying to rouse the wounded Marine. “Jenkins? Can you hear me?” he screamed, leaning over the Marine.

Jenkins turned, slowly clawing at the slope, the stones, and loose sand as if he were trying to swim up the hill, up the slope below Tinian.

Quince pulled the Marine onto his back, and he flinched. His back arched. His eyes bulged. A purple stain soaked his left abdomen, near the bottom of his flak jacket. A small, trickle of blood fell from the corner of his mouth, streaming down his cheek.

Jenkins leaned forward, slightly, and spoke as blood gathered between his teeth, “Corporal Mac . . .” he struggled to speak. “Couldn’t . . .”

Their ears tingled from the whistling sounds. Dust spat.

“Couldn’t see.”

“Jenkins?”

Jenkins just stared, silent now. Trying to point, explain, apologize for not seeing the ambush. He lay there, silent, occasionally blinking. His bulged eyes stared into a sky that streaked with tracers.

"Jenkins?" Quince screamed leaning over the Marine.

"Jenkins. Fuck!" Dust spat. Quince's ears tingled. He glanced up the steep slope, where a constant flash and explosions flooded from the narrow path. Sergeant Patrick paced the lines.

Quince rose to his knees, slung the rifle across his back, and pulled the wounded Marine over his shoulder. He started up the slope, digging his feet into the loose sand. Digging. Pushing. Climbing. Then sliding back down. He climbed five feet and lost three, and so it went. Explosions from the path became sporadic. Flashes from the boulders, furious earlier, died away, rarely answering tracers that flew down the steep slope.

Quince, climbing, sliding, digging into the loose sand, drew ever closer to the path. A shadowy figure, then two, leaned over the lip of the path, down the slope, toward Quince. One figure stood above Quince. The narrow path exploded. Flames blew out over the slope, as if the rocks and sand were on fire. Quince's ears tingled. His feet dug into the sand, pushing, driving. The Marines, two of them, leaned over the path, their arms outstretched. Quince, pushing, dug his feet into the sand, but went nowhere. He pulled Jenkins from his shoulder, pushing him forward, into the grasp of the outstretched hands of those two Marines, leaning from the lip of the path. Jenkins's feet and ass struck the sand with a thud; his back arched and he screamed a loud shrill that cut through the thunderous explosions.

The two Marines, grasping Jenkins's deuce gear, pulled the wounded Marine over the lip of the path. Far below, Quince could hear the occasional explosion echo from the canyon. The sound rushed up the steep slope, through the cedar grove, and over Tarawa.

Stones around his feet popped. Quince's feet dug into loose sand, but he slipped and slid further down the slope. He slid a few feet, pulled himself up on his elbows, looked up, and saw the path exploding, on fire. He turned, looking over his shoulder. Below, the canyon roared. Sand spat around him. He turned, staring back up the slope, and a hand was stuck in his face. Behind it was the familiar grin of Sergeant Patrick, saying, "Let's get the hell out of here!"

Quince lifted his hand, grasped Sergeant Patrick's, and bounced to his feet. A few Marines leaned over the path, their arms outstretched, and pulled Quince and

Sergeant Patrick up the slope, over the lip of the path. Quince fell to the ground, lying prone across the path. He lifted the barrel of the M16, and chased the explosions that emanated from the boulders below, squeezing the trigger with each explosion. Sergeant Patrick ran to the RTO, and kneeled on the path. He snatched the handset, "6, this is Marianas," he screamed.

"Send it."

"My AO is clear. Request fires on previously established target Alpha. Hotel. Tinian. I say again, fire-for-effect on Alpha. Hotel. Tinian."

"Roger, Marianas," answered an anxious voice. "Fire-for-effect on Alpha. Hotel. Tinian. Standby."

Patrick stood and briefly walked the lines. "Fire mission is coming." He knelt again, and lifted the handset to his ear, but heard nothing, only squelch between explosions. Suddenly, from behind Tarawa, he heard several booms of thunder. Echoes bounced around the canyons.

"Rounds out," a voice broke through the squelch.

Patrick stood, running down the line. "Get down. Get your fucking heads down!" Then something split the sky over Tarawa, falling through the canyon, down the slope. The boulders below them exploded. Flames flew out of the giant rock, and pieces of stone splintered from the mass. Another hit immediately after the first. Then four more hit near the boulders. The giant stones seemed to burn.

Quince stood, walked down the path, and knelt next to Jenkins. The wounded Marine's eyes were large. His chest bounced up and down.

≈≈≈

Later that night, Corporal Magowan limped across the dusty, dark compound, exhausted. Camp Stanton echoed with voices, sifting through thick, GP tents. Dogs barked upstream, near town. Otherwise, there was only black and silence in the valley. Quince stopped in the middle of the compound at several PVC pipes planted horizontally into the sand. They were piss-tubes. With the M16A2 slung over his shoulder, he unbuttoned his trousers and pissed into the PVC pipe. As he relieved himself, light flew across the compound, and a sleepy Marine in skivvies and desert boots stumbled from a GP tent, and stopped at another PVC pipe.

Quince ignored him. He finished pissing, buttoned his trousers, and limped through loose sand to the concrete bunker. He opened the screen door, and walked across the floor. Sand scratched below his feet as he approached the cot, slipped the weapon from his shoulder and leaned it in the corner. He dropped the Kevlar on a wooden rack, slid the LBV and flak jacket from his shoulders, unbuttoned his blouse and dropped it to the floor. Then, he fell backwards into the cot and lay there. He was still. Minutes slipped by. His chest pounded. It thumped so loud it seemed as if thunder boomed behind his ribs. The pop and spit of passing rounds rang in his ears. He lay there and thought of Jenkins's horrified face. He could not escape it. The Marine's bulging, rolling eyes sprung from every shadow of that old concrete structure. The labored breathing. Dark blood that trickled from the corner of his mouth, stretched into the cracks of the concrete roof.

Quince lay on his back, and stared at the ceiling. Soft music played in the corner. Voices mumbled outside. His ears rang and whistled. His eyes were focused on the ceiling and Jenkins's horrified face slowly scratched into the cracks of the cement. His bulged eyes. Mouth agape. Blood trickling from the corner of his lips. Above Quince, along the crumbling cement, blood appeared to gather along cracks where small chunks had fallen from the ceiling. Blood pooled and dripped from the ceiling.

Quince closed his eyes, trying to think of something else, but he could not shake the whistling sound and Jenkins's face so he opened his eyes, and the blood appeared to pool near Jenkins's mouth, dripping from the roof. A stalactite of blood sank from the roof, ever lower, until it snapped from the ceiling, falling straight for Quince's face. He cowered and thrashed, desperately trying to avoid the gob of blood ominously sinking from the ceiling. He shut his eyes and Jenkins disappeared. He opened them, and there was Jenkins bleeding from the corner of this mouth. Again, Quince's hands, dusty, callused, veiled his eyes. Jenkins was gone. But in the darkness, he wondered if Jenkins was still there. Had his blood dried? Was his mouth still agape, a horrified stare across his young face?

As he lifted his callused hands, he expected to see himself drenched in the Marine's blood. He sat up and frantically searched his arms and torso and legs. He found blood across his wrist, stained along his forearm, and more on his skivvy shirt—blood from the wound to Jenkins's abdomen as he threw the wounded Marine over his shoulder.

Quince leaned forward, threw his feet to the floor and unlaced his boots. He pulled his sock feet from the boots, and rested them on the floor. The cool concrete soothed his sweaty feet. He sat there a moment, on the side of his cot, and looked around. Drops of sweat slipped down his cheeks and dropped from his chin, splattering on the floor. Soft music played from a CD player on a corner shelf. Other Marines slept in cots along the wall. Occasionally, silence broke when Marines shifted in their bivy sacks.

He stood, unbuttoned his trousers, and slid them off. He slid his bare feet into sandals, grabbed a towel that hung from a nail, and left the concrete building. Loose sand sifted between his toes as he limped through the compound. He passed a row of outhouses, and the stench of rotting shit hung in stagnate night air.

He walked into a building that sat uphill from his hooch. There was no door and the room was dark. He pulled a string and a single, exposed bulb threw light over the room. Quince limped across the room to a sink, hung the towel on a nearby hook, and positioned his face between the dirt and smudge of a small mirror. He lifted his hands and stroked the face in the mirror. The image of dried blood along his wrist and forearm, sickened him. He twisted his shoulder, all along staring at the mirror, and saw a large splatter of blood that had dried on his back.

He took a breath, sucking cool, moist air through his nostrils before letting it escape through his mouth. He pulled the shirt over his head, tossed it in the trash, slid the skivvy shorts down his legs, and limped into the shower.

Shadows filled the empty room as he stood below a dripping faucet. He just stood there. He did not use soap or scrub his skin. He stood, under the water, in the cold, dark room, letting icy water stream through his hair, down his neck, and over his shoulders. Soon, the clear, cool streams of water that ran between his feet, twirling through the drain, drew a rusted color. When the color faded again, and the water was clear, he shut the valve, dried his body, slid his legs through the skivvies, threw the towel over his shoulder, and walked back across the compound, to the concrete hooch. He walked through the dark building, and sand ground between his feet as he crossed the concrete floor. He hung the towel on a nail, slid off the sandals, and fell into the cot. The ceiling was bare, except for cracks pouring from the wall. Jenkins was gone, for now, away at Bagram Airfield, maybe alive.

Chapter 14
≈ The Next Morning ≈

A soft, gray light broke the morning shadows. Voices muttered through a window. Footsteps crossed the roof and the bustle and activity was enough to nudge Quince from a deep sleep. He blinked and scowled as light burned his eyes. Minutes slipped by before he rose, threw his feet over the cot, and rubbed his eyes and chin.

He looked around and reality finally hit him. The patrol was months ago but it still visited him at night. He wanted to leave them—chain them to the boulders on Tinian and walk away—but they kept chasing him. And, each night, they caught him. Shaking sleep, he slid into yesterday's trousers and socks. The socks were crusty with dried sweat, crunching as he slid his feet into them. His temple throbbed. He was tired.

Outside, voices muttered.

Thuds pounded the roof.

He slipped on boots, laced them, and left the hooch, pausing just outside the door.

Stanton was busy. A steady stream of Marines flowed to and from the chow hall. Some mingled outside tents. He saw the back of a Marine sitting on the concrete roof of his hooch, alone. He nodded, knowingly grinned, and climbed the old, wooden ladder. As he stepped onto the roof, the Marine sat quietly, unflinching as Quince's heavy footsteps approached.

Without speaking, Quince sat on a crate, staring at the man.

Sergeant Patrick handed him a steaming cup of coffee, asking, "Get some sleep?"

Quince took the Styrofoam cup, shaking his head.

Patrick nodded, staring at Quince. "Maybe you should talk to someone? Get some help."

Quince shrugged, looked up, and surveyed the mountains. To the west, OP Tarawa hung over the compound like a cloud in a blue sky. From the camp, he could barely make out the short wall of sandbags, and the rock and concertina as they redefined the mountain peak into a small, manmade square. Quince sighed, "Keep seeing Jenkins's face. He doesn't say anything. Just stares back at me with that help me, I'm gonna die look."

Patrick nodded, sipping coffee, "Forget Jenkins. He's gonna live. Going home soon."

Quince nodded.

"Besides," Patrick continued, "we did all we could. You," he paused, "did all you could!" Patrick leaned forward, "If it weren't for you, what you did up there, he'd be in Arlington instead of Landstuhl."

Quince's face was expressionless. He sat quietly and stared into his coffee.

"How's your daughter?" asked Patrick, hoping to refocus his corporal.

Quince's eyebrows rose and fell. "Turned four a few months ago. Had a party at the zoo. You believe that shit? A birthday party at the zoo? I never had a party like that growing up. You know? Hell. Where was your fourth birthday? What did your old man do?"

Patrick smirked, lighting a cigarette. Smoke blew through his nostrils as he smirked, answering, "Probably kicked my ass."

Quince chuckled. "My old man was drunk." Quince paused, staring down at the sand and concertina. "But at least he was there."

There was a pause. Patrick dragged from the burley. Smoke filtered through his nostrils. "What about your old lady?" asked the sergeant, grinning. "She still smoking hot?" he taunted.

Quince chuckled, "Screw you, VD."

Patrick's head twisted as he dragged from the cigarette, "Smoking hot."

"Destiny." Quince chimed.

"Ah . . . Destiny," retorted Patrick. Smoke rising from his cigarette, he stared up the valley, across the blooming poppy fields, at a small village that hung on the banks of the Kunar River.

Quince was quiet. He watched the mountains, closely surveying them as if they would move, just slide down the valley. Moments passed. The two men were silent, alone with their thoughts.

"Looks peaceful and all, don't it?" asked Patrick, dragging from the cigarette.

"I reckon," answered Quince, reluctantly.

"I mean . . . the mountains . . . river with rapids. Shit. It's a beautiful river. You know? I mean . . . the fields. It's the kind of thing you'd see at a tourist destination. See on those pamphlets. You know? When you had to piss as a kid and you bugged your old man until he stopped at those public restrooms on interstate. Remember those pamphlets?"

Quince nodded. It was strange, listening to Patrick. Those were not his words. They did not sound like him. Patrick always talked trash about the valley.

"I miss that shit. Traveling . . . being a kid. Even if my old man was a prick, I miss it."

Quince watched Patrick. Behind them, vehicles circled the compound, stacking up in a row near the concrete hooch. A plume of dust rose, lifting over the GP tents.

Patrick lifted the cup of coffee, "Here's to our old men."

Quince smiled, joining him in the toast.

"Well. It's time," Quince interrupted, standing. "Hang in there, boss," he said as he descended the ladder.

Quince entered the hooch, slid the flak and LBV over his shoulders, grabbed his Kevlar, M16A2, and joined the briefing. Several Marines mingled around four white hi-lux trucks. Quince circled the trucks, and stood with his back to the GP tents and mess hall, facing the concrete hooch. From there, he could see Patrick, still sitting alone on the roof, smoking. Smoke rose over his shoulder, but he was still, staring at the valley—the peaceful scene of a small village, nestled between two mountain ranges, on the banks of a fast moving river.

Quince watched him. Marines mingled.

Soon, Patrick tossed the cigarette to the roof, stomped it with his boot, stood, and descended the ladder. He disappeared into a tent, and reappeared a few moments later with his gear and weapon.

"Anderson," he barked, "your weapon looks like shit."

A Marine turned, grinning, "It's clean, Sergeant."

"Clean as your ass?" retorted Patrick.

The Marines chuckled.

Patrick walked among the squad, feeling the Marine's canteens and CamelBaks, assuring they had enough water for the patrol. He appeared to frisk every Marine in the squad.

Fultz appeared from a GP tent, behind Quince, and joined the squad. "All right," he shouted, "listen up!" He quickly unfolded a map across the hood of a hi-lux, and set his Kevlar nearby.

"Bring it in," Patrick shouted.

The squad gathered in close. Fultz stood over the map, leaning against the hi-lux's grill. Quince stood to his right. Patrick, to this left. The two remaining fire team leaders, and the squad, stood shoulder-to-shoulder behind them.

"Listen up!" he shouted again, briefly turning to the squad.

They were silent.

"Gather in. Close it up!" They pushed together.

"It's a long patrol. We are covering some territory today. To the village and back to the bridge. As you can see, we go in hi-luxs." Marines groaned. "Up-armors are grounded for the QRF." More groans. "I want good dispersion. Especially in the village and here," pointing at the mountains below the camp near the bridge. "The road narrows here. The mountains are steep and covered with foliage."

"Good place for an ambush," chimed Patrick.

Quince nodded.

"The patrol will enter the village, and turn right, on this street, hugging the river. We'll pass the hydroelectric station, and make our way to this point, shy of the square. There, 1st and 2nd fire teams will disembark, patrol the square, before circling back to the hi-luxs."

"A demonstration?" asked Quince.

Fultz nodded, "To remind the locals we're still here." He paused, "3rd fire team stays back to guard the vehicles."

There was a pause.

"Listen up 1st and 2nd," turning to the Marines behind him. "The square will be crowded this time of the morning. Lots of villagers in the market. Keep your eyes open."

Patrick turned to the Marines, "Yeah . . . don't fuck it up Anderson."

Marines chuckled.

"Yeah, Anderson," chimed one Marine.

"Shit-bag," yelled another.

Anderson laughed. Marines chuckled.

"Listen up," Fultz shouted, as the laughter died off. "From there, the patrol exits the village, makes its way back down the river road, through the poppy fields, passing Stanton, traveling four miles south to the bridge."

There was another pause.

"Enemy sit, sir?" asked Quince.

"Enemy sit's unchanged. Intel has small elements of enemy forces slipping across the border at night," he paused, turning to the Marines. "There's only one road in the valley. One road from Stanton to the village and from Stanton to the bridge." He paused again, "IEDs are a threat."

Another pause, as the Marines silently watched Lieutenant Fultz.

"Any questions?" he asked.

Patrick's face tightened. His head sank and began to shake. "Damn hi-lux's!" he complained.

Groans echoed from a few Marines.

"We're stepping off at . . ." Fultz glanced his watch, "0735, ten mikes." Lieutenant Fultz folded the map, tucked it in his flak jacket, and walked down the hill, through the camp, into the command post; a concrete building sunk into the hard dirt and circled by concertina and stacks of sandbags.

"All right," commanded Patrick, "weapons check."

"Weapons check," echoed Quince and the other fire team leaders.

The Marines stacked into formation. NCOs methodically examined each Marine's magazines, opening their ammo pouches, assuring they had fully loaded their magazines.

Sergeant Patrick and two Marines from 1st fire team loaded into the first hi-lux. They were lead. Patrick sat on the passenger side, while one Marine sat behind the wheel, and the 3rd in the back. Quince drove the second hi-lux. Lieutenant Fultz would ride in the passenger seat, and the last Marine from 1st fire team rode in the back. Second and 3rd fire teams manned the last two vehicles.

Lieutenant Fultz soon emerged from the command post, climbing the smooth slope of Camp Stanton, before jumping into the idling hi-lux. He turned to Quince with a wry grin, "You ready for this shit, Magowan?"

Quince did not smile. He shifted the hi-lux into gear. "I reckon," he barked.

Overhead, a handset dangled from a hook on the roof of the pickup. Fultz snatched it from the hook, mashed a button on the receiver, shouting, "6, this is Archie."

"Send it, Archie," replied a voice through the receiver.

"Request permission to depart?"

A pause, "Standby."

Squelch bled through the handset.

"Permission granted, Archie. Notify 6 at each checkpoint."

"Roger 6, Archie out," Fultz re-hung the handset, and motioned to Patrick who was turned around in the cab ahead, so that he could see the trucks behind him.

The first hi-lux clicked into gear, and sped down the slope, passing the command post. Dust rolled from its tires and poured over the camp. The other pickups followed it, each slipping through the concertina, passing Marines who guarded the entrance.

One by one, the hi-luxs turned left, and sped up the narrow, dusty road. As they turned, the Kunar River poured over rocks, racing down the valley in front of them. Tiny ripples were white with foam and the glare of the rising sun. Across the valley, a bed of green poppy fields stretched from the river up the steep mountain slopes. Pakistan loomed over the valley.

Dust lifted from each truck as they sped up the road, approaching the village.

Quince shifted gears, squinting as dust erupted from the tires of Sergeant Patrick's hi-lux. Squinting, he watched the road, and Sergeant Patrick's pickup speed alongside the river. Occasionally, clouds of dust broke and he could see the Marine kneeling in the bed of the hi-lux, staring out over the poppies. He could see the silhouette of Sergeant Patrick's head bounce as the pickup struck deep holes. Lieutenant Fultz anxiously surveyed the road and fields, but neither man spoke. Periodically, Fultz turned, and peered through the rolling dust behind them until he saw the trailing pickups.

Soon, they passed a local villager, who slowly walked along the narrow road. Dust poured over him as they sped by. Another local, a woman pulling a cart with a child, limped toward the village. Soon the fields thinned, sporadically replaced by shanties.

Sergeant Patrick's hi-lux slowed, and turned sharply right, on a road leading to the river. He briefly dropped out of sight as the road sank into a slough near the riverbank. Clouds of dust poured out of the slough.

Quince geared down and the hi-lux slowed. He pulled on the steering wheel, and it cut hard right, dropping into the slough. Lieutenant Fultz turned, surveying the trailing trucks. On their left, a row of wooden shanties hid the village. To their right, white-foamed waves rippled down the Kunar River. A mother scrubbed clothes in the ripples. Water ran through the bottom of her dress as she knelt in the river, scrubbing the dust and dirt from the garments. Nearby, children ran and splashed in the shallow waters of an eddy. As he drove, Quince could hear the roar of the rapids, water pouring over rocks and boulders as it ran down the valley.

The convoy sped up the river road. Dust flew from their tires, lifting over the river, over a woman scrubbing clothes in the rapids. Lieutenant Fultz scanned the river and the shanty windows. Quince focused on the road, and the white hi-lux in front of them. Occasionally, breaks formed in the clouds of dust and Quince could see Sergeant Patrick's silhouette, his head scanning the river, the road in front of them, and the shanties.

Patrick's pickup slowed, briefly, and his Kevlar turned right, toward the river. Dust broke as his hi-lux slowed. Quince shifted gears. The vehicle slowed, and a large, concrete building appeared through the dust. Its walls appeared thick, gray with water-soaked concrete and two tiny windows high above the rapids. It appeared to sit in the river, as if someone decided to drop a building in the fast moving rapids of the Kunar. Water struck the building, twisting and turning, grudgingly pushing around the awkward concrete structure as if passing a slow pedestrian on a busy sidewalk.

Outside, a local man stood on a bridge that led from the steep bank to the door, high above the water. A short, dark beard covered his chin and cheeks. A drab jacket shielded his arms from the harsh sun and the stiff valley winds. An AK-47 hung from his shoulder. He looked thin, tired, and bored. His face lifted as the convoy passed. His rough-hewn cheeks, wrinkled from years of sun and wind, were expressionless. Without emotion, he watched the vehicles pass. Dust poured over him.

Lieutenant Fultz snatched the receiver from the hook, "6, this is Archie, over."

Squelch screamed from the handset, "This is 6. Send it, Archie." Squelch.

Quince watched through a break in the clouds of dust. Sergeant Patrick's head turned as his hi-lux sped by the building. He seemed to be in a stare down with the local standing on the bridge.

"Roger," answered Lieutenant Fultz, mashing a button on the receiver as he spoke, "Archie passing Edith."

Fultz released the button. Squelch.

"Roger. Copy. Archie passing Edith."

Fultz mashed the button, "Archie out."

"6 out." Came a voice through the receiver as the lieutenant hung the handset on the hook. "Reckon that old boy can stop the Taliban if they decide to blow up that hydroelectric plant?" asked Quince, sarcastically.

Lieutenant Fultz chuckled, briefly. "Hell no," shaking his head.

Through a break in the clouds of dust, Quince saw Patrick's head turn away from the river, toward the row of shanties.

His hi-lux slowed, and turned sharply left.

Quince geared down. The hi-lux rumbled as it slowed.

Patrick's pickup darted up a narrow alley, disappearing.

Quince's hi-lux slowed. He geared down, mashed the gas, and pushed the truck into the alley. The sudden, steep ascent jostled the Marine riding in the back. Quince watched him stumble through the rear-view mirror as the hi-lux pulled up the hill.

Fultz's head twisted and turned as he watched Patrick's truck speed up the alley, and the trailing hi-lux's slow along the river road, before turning at the plant.

Quince chased Patrick up the alley. Dust clouds, once thick and rolling, thinned, only occasionally hiding trash piled along the alley and the deep potholes. Children ran alongside the pickups. Dogs chased and barked. Up ahead, he could see pedestrians cross an opening along Main Street, toward the market.

Patrick's pickup slowed as it approached Main. The driver geared down, mashing the brake. Suddenly, it shot left. Pedestrians scattered to get out of its path.

Quince geared down and pulled hard on the wheel. The weight swayed to the right, and Quince, the lieutenant, and the Marine in the back swayed with it. He struggled with the wheel, twisting left, then right, before the pickup straightened on Main Street.

Ahead, crowds thickened. Throngs of locals mingled among the shopkeepers in the square.

Sergeant Patrick's hi-lux was speeding toward the market.

Lieutenant Fultz twisted and turned, constantly in motion. Quince was steady. Suddenly, Quince saw Patrick's arm fly up, and point. His hi-lux slowed, before swerving left. The Marine in the back of the pickup swayed right. Quince geared down, tires scratched the hard dirt as he pulled on the steering wheel. The pickup swerved. Everyone swayed. Then they slowed again, dropping behind the sergeant's pickup as it screeched to a stop in a small, paved lot.

The Marines of 3rd fire team sprinted to meet Sergeant Patrick as he exited the hi-lux.

"One man at the entrance. One facing the garden in the back," he ordered, pointing to a stand of trees and bushes lining the back of the lot. "The other two . . . stay with the trucks."

They listened intently. Their eyes were hidden behind sunglasses, M16A2s were pulled into their abdomen. They nodded.

"You got flares?" questioned the sergeant.

The fire team leader produced a long, round cylinder.

"Roger. Pop that fucker if trouble comes."

"Questions?"

Nobody spoke.

"Roger," Sergeant Patrick pulled his wrist free of his blouse sleeve, "we'll return in 30 mikes."

They nodded and grunted before fanning out across the lot.

The remaining two fire teams were already dispersed, lined up in formation facing

Main Street.

"6, this is Archie, over," said Lieutenant Fultz, mashing the button on the receiver. Nearby, the RTO adjusted a pack that lay across his back. A single antenna jutted out of the pack, along with a black cord and a receiver on the end.

"Roger 6. Send it."

"Archie's at Kelsey's."

Squelch filtered through the receiver, "Roger. I copy, Archie's at the Kelsey's."

"Archie out," finished the lieutenant, handing the receiver back to the RTO.

The RTO hung the receiver on his chinstrap, next to his ear, just under the lip of his Kevlar, and pulled the M16A2 into his abdomen.

Fultz twisted and turned, examining the squad's posture, before looking to Sergeant Patrick, "We ready?"

The sergeant nodded, lifted his arm, and pushed his hand forward. Two Marines in front, near the street, stepped forward, beginning the patrol. Quince followed, just a few feet behind them. A few more Marines, 2nd fire team, separated Quince from the lieutenant, Sergeant Patrick, and the RTO. First fire team was dispersed near the back, providing rear security to the patrol.

Locals moved toward the village square in a steady stream.

One-by-one, Marines stepped onto the dirty, trash-covered streets, turned left, and walked slowly toward the square. Old men, standing in the shade of shops and homes, stared as the Marines passed. Quince watched them as he walked, locking eyes with them, before scanning the streets. There was a time, early in the deployment, when he refused to look them in the eye, match their stare. Maybe he was intimidated, or maybe he was worried about intimidating them. Maybe he was just unsure if it was culturally correct to stare back. He remembered thinking, *what the hell does a man from Kentucky know about eastern Afghan culture?* And that thought was naturally followed by *what the hell is a man from Kentucky doing in eastern Afghanistan?* But that was months ago, patrols ago. Months later, dozens of patrols later, hundreds, maybe thousands of eyes staring from cold, dirty faces later, he locks eyes with them and moves on, doing his job, scanning the village. He just came to understand it, not from a book, or a pamphlet, or an intelligence brief. He just came to know it, after all those months, all those patrols.

The patrol slowly moved down the street, and into the market. They were dispersed. The square was crowded, filled with small, flimsy stands whose shelves were filled with goods—meat hanging from hooks, or drying fruits or bowls of grains.

Around them, children ran through the streets. Most locals stopped, briefly pausing from their business, to stare at the patrol as it passed. A group of children soon gathered around the patrol as it moved through the square. Their young, dirty faces followed the Marines. As their confidence grew, they begged for candy.

The squad patrolled through the square. Locals, shopping the market, mingled among the dispersed Marines. Children followed them. Old men sat in the shade of nearby shops.

A large fountain sat in the middle of the square. Once painted green, the color had faded, sides had chipped. It was dry, trash and drying leaves began to fill the basin. Locals used the flat lip of the basin as a seat, and many were gathered at the dry fountain as the Marines patrolled by.

Quince surveyed the Marines. He watched children run between the dispersed Marines. He scanned sidewalks, and locked eyes with old men as they stared at the passing patrol. He scanned the streets, and watched shoppers haggle over meat and grain. He watched the crowd gathered along the dry fountain, children jumping in and out of the trash-covered basin, and men sitting along the wide edge. As he walked, he saw a small group of men gathered near the fountain. They stared, laughing as the Marines passed. Quince stared, his eyes hidden behind dark glasses. One man stepped away, quickly leaving the crowd. Before the small group could close, Quince noticed a sharp flash, a reflection pushing from something within the circle. He stared. The locals laughed. His followed the reflection, followed the way it molded over the smooth, silver barrel, then slowly rolled down through the wooden stock like lava running down a mountain.

Quince turned, locked eyes with Sergeant Patrick, and pointed toward the group of men. Patrick nodded, and signaled to the others. Their eyes locked on the suspicious group of men. The patrol dispersed, slightly, as the squad leader signaled.

Local men laughed, staring at the patrol. Another man joined them, young, just like the others, a rifle slung over his shoulder. He pushed his way into the group. Quince closely watched them, turning to Patrick and Fultz who were also watching. A third man appeared, and joined the group. Quince whistled under his breath and the Marines on point turned to face him. He motioned to the group, and the Marines nodded.

A fourth man arrived, holding a rifle in his hand. The group, still laughing, grew serious. They listened as the fourth man spoke, their faces somber. One man pulled a cigarette from his lips, tossed it to the ground, stomped it with his boot, and walked away. The others began to disperse. One man stood, lifted the rifle into his abdomen, and walked into the crowd, haggling with merchants.

Quince turned to Patrick. The sergeant motioned for more dispersion, but did not stop the patrol. They kept moving through the crowded square.

As they walked, Quince's nerves took flight. His chest began pounding, and echoing in his ears. Echoes filtered among the native voices, haggling with street vendors. Quince, patrolling, scanned the crowded market. He turned to the Marines on point before scanning the square, shop to shop. He twisted, and noticed Sergeant Patrick scanning the crowd around the dry fountain. Lieutenant Fultz was yelling something into the handset, holding it to his face, as the RTO trailed along beside him. A black, coiled cord unraveled from a slit in the RTO's patrol pack to the lieutenant's ear. Squelch bled through the handset as he released the button.

The whole patrol was tense, their Kevlars sweeping back and forth, from the market, across the dry fountain, through the square, to the shops on the other side. Back and forth they swept, scanning the crowds, locking eyes with old men gathered in the shade, watching for the four men with rifles slung over their shoulders.

The four men disappeared. They were gone, for now. *Maybe they were hiding?* Quince mused but he wasn't convinced, shaking his head. *Did you see the way they laughed? They'll return. Come back. Maybe they'll bring others?* Deep breaths pulled through Quince's nostrils. His chest pounded. Echoes rang in his ears. Claustrophobia began to shrink the village square. All around them, locals mingled around the market, between the dispersed Marines. Children followed the patrol, yelling, begging for anything the Marines would give them.

Suddenly, one of the men from the dry fountain re-emerged from the crowd; a rifle slung over his shoulder. Quince's grip on the weapon tightened. He pulled the barrel slightly higher, leaving his index finger straight, resting on the trigger. He watched the man weave through the crowd. Quince turned, hoping to see that Sergeant Patrick had noticed the local.

Patrick's face was fixed on the man as he approached. Fultz barked something into the handset, before handing it to the RTO. He turned, and motioned to the Marines of 1st fire team. They stopped on the lieutenant's signal. Two of them faced back up the street while the remaining Marines focused on the armed man.

Quince motioned to the Marines on point. They stopped and faced down the street. A second man appeared from within the crowd. Quince's grip tightened on the M16. The barrel of his rifle lifted, slightly. He watched as a third man, rifle pulled into his abdomen, walked toward them from behind the market. His chest pounded. Echoes filled his ears. Each man, separated in the market, wove through the crowds, toward one focal point. Lieutenant Fultz and Sergeant Patrick paused, their eyes darting back and forth from the locals to the Marines, assuring their men were aware, prepared. Back and forth their eyes darted.

The men walked closer before one emerged from the crowd, moving slowly, almost cautiously, toward the patrol. Quince watched him. His eyes glared beneath his brow over his dirty, unshaven face. Now the patrol was stopped. Marines tensed up. Locals, shopping the market, seemed to notice. Many paused, watching the patrol as the man approached. Some began to back away, filtering around the dry fountain and behind flimsy stands with hanging meat.

Quince's head twisted and turned, as his eyes surveyed the crowd that, by now began to move, parting as the armed men approached the patrol. Fultz and Patrick moved forward, taking a cautious step or two toward the approaching men. Patrick lifted his hand, shouting, "Stop!" The man uttered something in the Pashto. Patrick shouted back, as he and Fultz slightly raised the barrels of their weapons. Others closed in. Crowds backed away. Quince, nervously scanning the patrol, the square, the crowds, walked toward the men. Soon, the lieutenant began shouting. The men shouted something back, walking closer. Sergeant Patrick's weapon rose. Other Marines instinctively lifted their weapons. The crowd gasped, murmuring things. Quince walked closer, quickly approaching the men.

"Stop!"

The man shouted something.

"Get back!"

The man shouted and turned to the other locals, now gathered near him. A smirk lifted his cheeks. His hands rose as if he were complaining about the patrol.

Finally, another man stepped forward, away from their small group.

"Get back!" shouted the lieutenant.

The man said something, shook his head, pursed his lips and said, "Poh-leece chief," pointing through the market, toward the row of shops. He pointed again, "Poh-leece chief."

Quince stopped, watching as Lieutenant Fultz's lips mimicked the armed man's words. "Police chief?"

The man shook his head in dramatic motions as he pointed to the small row of buildings tucked behind the market. "Poh-leece chief."

"The police chief wants to see us?" Fultz pointed at the man. "You work for the police chief?"

"Poh-leece chief," repeated the man.

Sergeant Patrick began to chuckle. He turned to Quince, chuckling. His Kevlar shook as he asked, "Believe that shit? They work for the freaking police chief."

Quince nodded. His face softened, and a terse grin bent his lips. "They don't look like Barney Fife."

"Shit no," shrugged Patrick. "Figures. This ain't Mayberry." He approached the man, and lifted his arm in the direction of the market, suggesting the local lead them to the chief.

Lieutenant Fultz turned and motioned to the squad, before walking through the market. He yelled something into the handset. The RTO was close-by. The squad slowly turned and patrolled through the market, passing stands of hanging meat and the dry fountain whose basin was filled with trash.

Locals paused, staring as the Marines walked among them. Children gave chase, harassing the patrol. Old men, resting in the shade of shops, stared.

They passed through the market, under the shade of several trees, and down a wide, dirt street. Two of the armed men led them, speaking Pashto as they walked.

Patrick and Fultz talked as the patrol moved along the street. Quince and the Marines quietly followed, scanning the streets and windows, open in the fall warmth. They approached a large, gray building near the end of the street. Nearby, a small open lot sat empty except for a bench that sank into the sand. One of the local men turned, and motioned at Lieutenant Fultz, pushing his hand toward the office. "He wants us to wait here." Fultz nodded at the armed man, who smiled and ran off around the building, through the open lot and entered through a side door.

"All right," shouted Sergeant Patrick, turning to the patrol, "spread out. Get your eyes on the street." The Marines quickly dispersed, facing all directions.

Quince positioned 1st fire team south of the gray building, across the empty lot. Through a break in the shops, far down the street, he could see the fast moving waters of the Kunar River. Locals filtered down the street, shopping. The hum of water racing down the valley echoed in the distance, but there was little noise from the street itself.

The local soon emerged through the front door, pointing to Lieutenant Fultz and Sergeant Patrick. He held the door open and waved at them. Patrick turned and motioned to Quince, letting go a sharp whistle. Quince nodded, pulled the weapon into his gut and jogged across the lot.

The three Marines entered the Police Headquarters. The building was dark and musty. The floors and walls were concrete and washed in blue. Quince walked alongside Patrick. As they followed Fultz and the deputy, his arm brushed against the wall and the cool, smooth surface soothed his sweat-soaked skin. They passed an open room, with a few chairs and a table, walked down a short hallway, and into another room. The deputy stepped out of the way, and a large man appeared around the corner, stopping the Marines as they entered the office. Tall and broad, this man was so thick he nearly blocked the door that led into the office. The deputy paused and the man pulled his meaty hands into his chest and slightly bowed.

The Marines mimicked his gesture.

The large man pointed to an old couch setting along the wall, near his desk, and the lieutenant smiled, nodded, and said, "Thank you." The Marines sat, resting their M16s against the couch.

The police chief turned to the deputy, and spoke something in Pashto that sent the man scurrying down the hall. He turned to the Marines, and smiled briefly before sitting at his desk. He was a big man. Deep wrinkles poured from his eyes, down his meaty cheeks, and into his beard. Thick, gray hair fell over his mouth, covering his chin, neck and much of his chest. His eyes were steel blue. A gray jacket covered his thick frame. A turban, plain and black, covered his crown. His arms lay across the desk. Hands folded together; his fingers meshed like giant tentacles as he stared at the Marines.

Lieutenant Fultz, Sergeant Patrick, and Corporal Magowan sat there, uncomfortably staring back at the large man, the police chief for the village. The Chief stared back, unflinching. Fultz coughed and cleared his throat. Quince's head slightly nodded at the man. A smile rose across Patrick's face. His brow rose, lips parted and his eyes swelled, acknowledging the uncomfortable nature of the moment.

Soon, footsteps smacked up the hallway, and a young, thin man, entered the office. He was winded. As he entered the room, Fultz appeared to sigh. His chest sank with relief. Quince bent his lips and whispered under his breath so that only Patrick could hear him, saying, "Thank God."

Patrick whispered back, "I could hug that little guy."

The police chief turned, said something and the young man answered. The chief faced the Marines and spoke, pointing to the young man, "Eeen-gul-esh."

The Marines smiled, relieved.

The young man sank into a small, wooden chair in the corner as the police chief spoke. Each time he fell silent, the young interpreter turned to the Marines and spoke, "He is offering food."

Fultz nodded, "Tell him, thank you."

The interpreter turned to the police chief and spoke.

Chief, sitting motionless across the desk, smiled. His beard lifted and wrinkles cut into his cheeks. As his beard sank, he spoke again.

The young interpreter's mouth mimicked the old man's words. His lips pulled and pushed words the old man spoke as if lifting them from the air.

Chief fell silent, and his hands were clasped across the desk.

The interpreter twisted in the wooden chair, facing the Marines, "He says his guards told him you were in the village."

The interpreter fell silent, but Chief quickly filled the silence with this deep, scratchy voice.

He spoke. The young man translated.

"He says that you have much to discuss. He says the Taliban hide in the mountains above the valley in the day. At night, they come down from the mountains and harass the people. He says his men are few and frightened of the Taliban." The interpreter paused, and poised his lips, "Taliban killed two of his men last month as they patrolled the valley."

Lieutenant Fultz sat forward, resting his elbows on his knees. "Tell him we are sorry."

The interpreter translated the Marine's words.

Chief showed no emotion. He just stared at the Marines.

"Were they killed by a bomb? Please ask him." continued the lieutenant.

The interpreter spoke.

Chief nodded, but was silent.

"They died from a bomb. The Taliban buried it in the road at night."

The lieutenant nodded. "Tell him we have found three bombs just this month. Tell him we also patrol the roads."

The interpreter turned to the large man and spoke.

"Tell him we lost a man from these bombs. Killed on the road above the village, just before it climbs the mountains."

The interpreter spoke.

The old man's face softened slightly, and he nodded.

The room became silent. Chief, the interpreter, and the Marines stared at one another, waiting for the other to speak.

Sergeant Patrick's eyes broke free. He began scanning the room, pausing on a rifle propped in the corner. "Ask him if that is his weapon," pointing to the weapon.

The interpreter spoke.

Chief grinned. His cheeks rose, and wrinkles cut deep into his leathery skin. The beard slid up his chest like a thick, gray serpent. He stood, slowly walked to the corner and lifted the rifle to his chest. His blue eyes admired the weapon as if it were a trophy, speaking as he proudly surveyed the wood stock, lacerated with deep scratches.

The interpreter turned to the Marines. "He asks how old you are."

"Twenty-five," answered Patrick.

Chief chuckled, and spoke.

"He says the Soviets came here when you were born. Says he killed many Soviets with this weapon. Says he fought in these mountains."

Sergeant Patrick smiled and nodded.

Chief held out the rifle, offering it to Patrick. The sergeant stood, walked to the large man, and lifted the weapon from his thick hands. He admired the weapon as a trophy, much like the police chief had. Shortly, he handed the weapon back to Chief, grabbed his M16, and offered it to him. Chief leaned the weapon in the corner, took the weapon from the sergeant's hands, and inspected the polished, metal barrel and plastic. He chuckled and bellowed something in Pashto.

The interpreter turned to the Marines, smiling, "He says it feels like a toy."

They laughed.

Then, a boy entered the room carrying a platter. He clumsily set the platter on a small table in the corner, near the window, and lifted a bowl of nuts and offered it to each Marine. Each Marine gathered a handful of nuts and ate. They nodded to offer thanks. Chief devoured a handful of nuts, letting them drop from his meaty hand into his beard. The boy then poured four cups of tea, handed them to each man, and offered a bowl of shriveled tangerines to each. Each man peeled the tangerine and chewed the rubbery core. The Marines hid their disdainful expressions—they knew fruit was a delicacy in eastern Afghanistan. It took days, sometimes weeks, to deliver fruits to the remote village. They ate fruit and appeared to enjoy it.

Chief grinned and drank tea. The Marines followed. The bitter taste stung their tongues, but they ate and drank and said nothing.

Quince turned to the interpreter and spoke, "Ask him about the compound. Our base. Ask him if he fought the Soviets at our base. Tell him we have heard of a battle there."

The interpreter spoke.

The police chief offered a gentle, almost reflective smile. He began pulling at his beard, thoughtfully stroking the long, wavy hair. Slowly, he spoke. His deep, scratchy voice lifting as memories poured through the years, cascading through this aging warrior's life like the fast moving river that ran down the valley.

"We gathered deep in the mountains," translated the boy, "and crept through the valleys. Darkness covered our movement. They had men on a peak overlooking the valley," continued the interpreter. The police chief lifted his heavy arm, pushing a finger toward the ceiling. "They had a large gun pointed at the mountains to the west."

Chief paused, allowing memories to flow, and spoke again.

"We divided in the valley behind the mountains above their camp. Some climbed the mountain across the small valley. They hid behind boulders and in ditches and shot at the enemy. They shot back and we climbed their mountain on the south slope, behind them." Chief lifted his heavy arm. "They were shooting at the mountain to the north and did not notice us behind them." He paused and grew solemn. His heavy cheeks sank into his beard. "We killed them and turned their gun on the camp below. Others joined us in the mountains, shooting the camp. Finally, they gave up and we entered their camp." He fell silent again, standing, shuffling his feet across the sand-sprinkled floor. He briefly lifted the weapon propped in the corner and examined the wood and metal, before resting it against the wall. He turned to the Marines. "We were told to shoot them for what they did to us, to our village." The interpreter's eyes swelled as the police chief spoke. He no longer mimicked the large man's words, no longer pulled details from the man's lips. He was quiet, allowing words to filter across the room. Chief turned and faced the Marines. "We strung their officers to the ceiling in an old concrete shelter."

The Marines were silent. Quince nodded, slightly, but no man spoke. The interpreter was motionless. He appeared chiseled into the wooden chair.

Chief shuffled his feet across the floor, sitting at his desk. He lifted his thick arms, set them on the desk, folded his hands and spoke again. "The Taliban learned from this. Men who fought with us have shown the Taliban how to fight, how to defeat large armies. They know they cannot stand man-to-man. They will use darkness to sneak out of the mountains and bury bombs in the roads you travel." Chief fell silent. His cheeks sank into the thick beard. He stood, shuffled around the desk, to the Marines, and lifted his hand, speaking one final time. "Thank you." The interpreter fell silent.

"Thank you," retorted each Marine, shaking the large man's hands as they left.

The squad patrolled away from the gray building, down the street, crossing through the market, and passing locals as they haggled with vendors over the price of meat. They patrolled under the shady trees, passing the dry fountain filled with trash, and the children running in the dirty streets. Old men sat in the shade of the shops and stared as the patrol passed. The Marines of 1st squad loaded the hi-luxs, and drove through the village streets, turned right at the river, passing the hydroelectric plant. One lonely guard watched the pickups speed along the dusty road.

Dust flowed from Patrick's hi-lux, throwing a cloud over the poppy fields. Lieutenant Fultz grabbed the handset, squeezed the button and shouted, "6, this is Archie, over." Squelch filled the cabin as he released the handset.

"Send it Archie. This is 6," responded a dull voice.

Fultz squeezed the handset, "Roger 6, Archie's leaving the pub. Well was dry."

"Roger. I copy. Archie leaving the pub."

"Archie approaching home en route to Hauser."

"Roger. I copy. Archie en route to Hauser."

"Archie out," Fultz released the handset and squelch filled the cabin.

"Roger Archie. 6 out," answered a dull voice.

Quince focused on the vehicle ahead of them. Clouds of dust spun from the tires. Poppies, knee high, thin and weighted with a heavy red bulb, bent as the trucks sprayed sand-layered gusts.

The patrol sped between two fields before passing Camp Stanton. A Marine in the tower along the wall lifted his hand as they passed. A guard followed the hi-luxs with shaded eyes. Then, dust poured over him and he disappeared in the clouds.

Below camp, mountains reached the clouds before dropping into a small, empty field. The road crossed the field, hugging the river as it ran down the valley.

Quince and the lieutenant were quiet. Fultz occasionally turned to view the trailing hi-luxs or yelled over the rumbling tires into the handset. Otherwise, the men were silent. Quince watched dust wash the windshield, as the lead hi-lux slowly turned left, following the road along a bend in the river. On the right, the mountain's steep slope slid into the road.

"6, this is Archie, over," Fultz yelled at the handset.

Squelch poured from the handset, "Roger, this is 6. Send it Archie."

"Archie passing the Loading Dock," Lieutenant's head twisted, watching as the hi-luxs sped by an abandoned structure, built on the riverbank.

"Roger, I copy, Archie passing the Loading Dock."

Patrick's hi-lux slowed after passing the abandoned building, weaving through several sharp curves. Dust clouds settled as the truck slowed. Quince's hi-lux caught up with Sergeant Patrick in the first curve, before falling behind as the sergeant's truck pulled out of the curve. Other hi-luxs followed the same pattern. Their view of the valley was narrowed by the terrain. Cedars grew thick along the boulder-strewn slope. The river shoved the narrow road against the slope. Trees lined every bend in the fast moving river. The patrol was flanked by mountains and river. There was nowhere else to go. No field. No poppies. Only mountains and water.

Quince closed on Patrick's hi-lux in a sharp curve before falling behind as the sergeant's truck sped away, moving quickly along the base of the mountain. The mountain pushed the road out into the valley. On the far side of the river, deep green poppy fields emerged, once hidden by the cedars. As the patrol slowly turned right along the base of the mountain, beyond the poppy fields, Quince saw a dull light up ahead. It lay flat, nearly even with the narrow road, but it was smooth and reflected the rising sun.

Fultz grabbed the handset, and mashed the receiver, "6, this is Archie."

Squelch. "Roger, Archie. Send it," answered a dull voice.

"Archie has eyes on Hauser. I say again, Archie has eyes on Hauser. ETA in five mikes."

Squelch. "Roger. Copy. ETA at Hauser in five mikes."

Fultz hung the handset on the hook.

Dust clouds, tumbling from Patrick's tires, washed over Quince's windshield, but thinned as the sergeant's hi-lux turned back into the mountain, beginning several sharp curves. Quince followed. The bridge was lost from their view, hidden by the cedars and several sharp curves that lay ahead of them. Poppy fields on the far side of the Kunar were hidden by trees along the riverbank. The road grew narrow and dark in the shade of the cedars. Patrick's hi-lux slowed, and Quince pulled up to his bumper, before the sergeant's hi-lux sped ahead. Fultz twisted in the cabin, watching the trailing pickups maneuver through the curve. As dust clouds thinned, and he closed on Patrick's truck, Quince watched the sergeant's silhouette.

Patrick's hi-lux moved right along the mountain slope, before slowing in a sharp curve. The hi-lux turned sharply left as Quince pulled up to his bumper. The sergeant sped up the narrow road as Quince fought the steering wheel through the sharp curve.

Quince geared up as he drove out of the curve. Fultz turned, monitoring the trailing hi-luxs. Quince watched Patrick's silhouette; he saw Patrick's arm point to something up ahead, and suddenly, he saw the sergeant's hi-lux lift off the dusty road. A sharp, thunderous clap ran along the narrow road, between the mountains and the river. The hood of Patrick's hi-lux flew off the pickup, landing in the ditch along the slope. The cab seemed to shrink, filling with dust and smoke. Smoke poured from the exposed engine. The passenger side lifted off the dusty road before slamming down. Smoke poured from the engine as the truck slowly rolled to a stop in the ditch, resting against the mountain slope.

"What the hell?" Quince screamed, mashing the brakes, sending the hi-lux sliding along the dusty road. "IED!" yelled Fultz, opening the door before the truck slid to a stop. Fultz flew out of the hi-lux, directing the Marine in the back to engage anything that moved on the mountain slope. "Get to Pat," he shouted to Quince. He pumped his fist in the air, urging the stunned Marines in the trailing hi-luxs to move up. He sprinted along the road, deploying the other Marines against the ambush he was sure would follow. Dust from the sliding hi-luxs rolled along the road.

"Pat!" Quince screamed, running along the dusty road, toward the damaged hi-lux. He held the M16 with one hand, and sprinted, his eyes focused on the smoldering truck. He scaled the slope, running behind and then beside the hi-lux. The passenger door was jammed against the rocky slope. Quince fell to his knees, peering through the smoke as it filtered through a crack in the passenger window. Only a few inches of the window rose above the slope. He tried to fan the smoke, but it poured from the cab. "Pat?" he screamed again, but there was no answer.

Quince jumped to his feet, descended the slope in front of the pickup, and peered through the driver's side window. Smoke swirled in the cab. The smack and pop of blistering metal and rubber and plastic were the only sounds emanating from inside the hi-lux. Quince pulled the door handle, but it was stuck, jammed, bent and twisted from the explosion. Again he peered through the window. "Pat? Burton?" he screamed. Peering, his eyes stared through a cloud of smoke. A hand, bloodied with black, charred fingers, slapped the window. "Burton?" he yelled for the driver, yanking at the stuck door. Quince pulled and the hi-lux rocked. He pulled harder, and the truck swayed back and forth in the ditch. "Fuck!" he screamed. "Burton, get back. Get the fuck back!" The charred hand slipped off the window.

Quince reared back, pulled the M16 over his shoulder, and slammed the butt stock into the window. Glass cracked. Cracks webbed along the window. Again he slammed the butt of the weapon into the window and glass shattered, crumbling to the road and inside the cab. Smoke poured from the cab, rolling through the window. He used the weapon to clear the shards, dropped the M16, and reached through the window, into the cloud of smoke. Blindly he searched through the smoke until he felt the coarse texture of a flak jacket, pouches of an LBV. Murmuring, deep, incoherent moans carried through the smoke. Quince pulled and the Marine fell forward. The blackened, charred fingers grasped Quince's blouse sleeve. Smoke rolled over Quince's face, and he began to cough and choke. He pulled on Private Burton's flak jacket and the Marine's torso emerged from the smoke. His face was colored with smoke and blood and twisted with agony. Smoke had tinted his desert camouflage. Slowly, clumsily, he pulled Private Burton from the smoke-filled cab.

Burton's boots hit the ground with a thud before cutting small ditches through the dust as Quince dragged him away from the hi-lux, and lay him in the road near the second pickup. His face was black. His trousers were shredded and smoldering and blood-splattered. "Sergeant P," he murmured. He pointed to the smoking hi-lux, "Patrick."

Quince pushed his hand down. "I know. We'll get him." Turning, twisting, he scanned the patrol, the Marines dispersed along the dusty road, "Corpsman!" he screamed. "Corpsman! Get up here!"

Doc Mays bolted up the road, a green medical bag thrown over his shoulder. He slid to his knees next to Burton, and began stripping away the Marine's LBV and flak.

Quince got to his feet and ran toward the smoking hi-lux. Fultz was already there, leaning through the broken window, frantically feeling through the smoke for Sergeant Patrick. "Pat!" he screamed. His legs torqued, tensing before sliding in the dust. He rose to his toes, and his legs tensed, and his feet kicked at the slippery dust, sliding. "Damn!" he shouted. He sank onto his heels, and his torso emerged from the smoke filled cab. "Can't fucking reach him." He doubled over, bent at the waist, coughing.

Determined, Quince pushed his tall, wiry frame through the broken window, reaching through the cab until his fingers felt the coarse texture of Patrick's flak jacket. "Pat!" he screamed, coughing. "Pat, we'll get ya outta there!" He grasped the flak under the sergeant's armpit, and pulled. Patrick, lying against the passenger door, slid through the cab, moving enough for Quince to grasp the other side of his flak jacket, pulling. Coughing, choking, Quince felt something cool and sticky drip across his left hand. Quince's legs tensed and twisted as he pulled the sergeant from the smoldering cab. Patrick's weight shifted, and his torso fell into Quince's arms. His head, limp, dropped into Quince's chest. Quince grunted, cursing, choking on smoke, as he pulled Patrick through the cab. Finally, Patrick's head poked through the blinding smoke. Fultz grabbed his arms and pulled. Patrick's torso and legs emerged.

They pulled Patrick away from the burning hi-lux, and lay him in the shade of a large cedar, along the riverbank. His face was black. The explosion had shredded his right sleeve. Blood poured from nubs that once were his fingers. His trousers were shredded below the knees. The sole was sliced from the right boot, and what remained of his leg hung from a small sliver of meat and skin at the knee. Bone protruded from his thigh. He did not speak. His face drew together.

"Corpsman!" shouted Fultz. "Doc, get over here now!"

"Pat!" Quince nervously shook the sergeant. Patrick's body lay limp in the dust. His toes pointed right and left, one foot pointing to the mountain, the other, nearly separated from his leg, pointing at the fast-moving river. Quince and Lieutenant Fultz fumbled with Patrick's LBV, unclipping the plastic buckle, pulling his gear apart. Quince unsnapped the Velcro and pushed open his flak. The odor of smoke and sweat lifted from the sergeant's body, filling Quince's nostrils. He looked over and screamed, "Doc!"

Doc Mays dropped to his knees next to Patrick. His hands moved along the sergeant's leg. Blood poured from the mangled stump, creating a small stream that ran through the dust, toward the river. His head tilted side to side, "Fuck!" Mays shouted. He slid the medical bag from his shoulders, sifted through the bag, removed a tourniquet, lifted Patrick's leg, and fastened it above the knee.

Fultz leapt to his feet, running down the dusty road, passing Burton lying on the ground, surrounded by two kneeling Marines. One Marine looked up, "Sergeant gonna be all right, sir?"

Fultz kept running. He fell through the open door of his hi-lux, grabbed the handset, yelling, "6, this is Archie. IED exploded approximately . . ." twisting, looking down the road to the abandoned building along the banks of the Kunar River, ". . . 300 meters south of RP Loading Dock. Two WIA. One vehicle down," releasing the handset.

Squelch bled through the receiver, before a scratchy voice answered, "Roger Archie, copy . . ."

Fultz squeezed the receiver, his voice cracking, "Request immediate helivac. Approximately 300 meters south of Loading Dock. Seventy-five meters north of

Archie. Popping red smoke to mark the LZ." He screamed, releasing the handset.

A nervous voice ripped through the squelch, "Copy Archie, this is 6 actual. Helivac requested. ETA 25 mikes."

The lieutenant's head twisted. "Fuck!" he screamed, slamming the receiver against the seat. "Copy, 6. ETA 25 mikes."

Squelch filled the cabin, before the voice broke in, "Archie, this is 6 actual. Identify the WIA."

Fultz mashed the receiver, "Alpha Bravo, PFC type." He paused and drew a deep breath, "and 5 Juliet Papa," releasing the handset.

Squelch filled the cabin as the CP processed the names, "Roger Archie. Copy Alpha Bravo and Juliet Papa."

Fultz tossed away the receiver, and sprinted up the road, "Get ready to move," he shouted, passing Burton and the other Marines, pointing to the poppy field across the river. "Helivac in 25 mikes."

Doc Mays pulled a stethoscope from his ears, grabbed a syringe from his bag, and slightly mashed the plunger. A thin stream of liquid burst from the needle. He pushed the needle into the sergeant's thigh but Patrick was motionless.

Quince leaned over Patrick's head, holding his shoulders, shouting encouraging words that the sergeant did not hear.

"How is he, Doc?" asked Fultz through winded breathes.

Mays shook his head, continuing to work on the wounded Marine, "His heart-rate is slow, faint from the loss of blood. He's unconscious."

"When will he wake?"

"I don't know."

"We have to move him."

"To Stanton?"

Fultz shook his head, pointing to the red bloomed poppies in the field across the river, "Helivac in 23 mikes," searching his watch

"3rd fire team," he yelled, turning toward the trailing hi-luxs, "sweep the road. 50 up and back."

Four Marines stood, pulled M16s into their abdomen, and slowly patrolled down the road, passing Patrick's smoldering hi-lux. Their eyes scanned the ditches, and the cedar stumps lining the mountain slope.

Doc Mays worked feverishly on the wounded sergeant. Occasionally, he darted back to check on PFC Burton, administered morphine and checked his vitals, before returning to Patrick. Minutes passed. Quince watched, feeling helpless. He was too numb to help Fultz organize the squad but he knew it was OK. It wasn't indecisiveness. He belonged with Patrick.

Minutes moved like hours for Quince. He watched as his sergeant lay in the dirt road. He felt helpless. His hands, useless. "It's OK, Pat," he encouraged. "Doc's gonna take care of you. Bird's on its way. You'll be OK," he continued, his words cracking. Words Patrick could not hear. He was motionless. His eyes were closed. His smile was hidden behind chapped, pursed lips. Freckled cheeks were smudged with smoke.

Fultz sprinted along the road. Two Marines lifted Burton. One lifted his torso while the other held his legs, carrying him off the dusty road, and down a steep bank to the water.

"3rd provides security to the trucks. 1st carries the wounded. 2nd goes with them for security," yelled the lieutenant, moving swiftly alongside the hi-luxs.

A few Marines of 3rd fire team scattered, dispersed near the abandoned trucks. Kneeling alongside the white pickups, their eyes focused on the mountain slope that loomed over the narrow road.

"Can he go?" worried Quince, Fultz kneeling next to him.

Doc Mays just shook his head, "Lost a lot of blood. But he has to."

Quince began to lift Patrick's shoulders. "I'll help," chimed the lieutenant, grabbing the sergeant's legs. Another Marine joined them.

"Got to tie-up that leg," said Doc, "and keep it from flopping around." Mays began searching through his bag, searching, sifting. Minutes passed.

From over the mountains, a low rumbling sound tapped the blue Kunar sky.

"Shit," cursed the lieutenant, "chopper is in-bound."

Doc Mays searched, sifted through his bag. "Damn!" he cursed. "Nothing."

"We got to go!" shouted the lieutenant.

Quince lifted his blouse just below his flak, unfastened his belt, and yanked it through the loops. He tossed it to Doc Mays.

Doc took the belt, pulled Patrick's foot and calf through the dust, doubled it over his thigh, and tied them together.

"Let's go," shouted Fultz as Doc finished, disgustingly shaking his head.

The soft thunder grew louder. Minutes passed. Thump. Thump.

They lifted Patrick. Quince held his torso. The lieutenant grabbed the sergeant's mangled legs, and turned as they descended the riverbank. "Fuck!" he shouted, staring out over the poppy field across the river. "The smoke!"

In the chaos, the worry over the wounded and the safety of the squad, Fultz had forgotten to mark the LZ for the helivac.

"I got him," Quince nodded.

"You sure?"

Quince nodded.

They lay Patrick on the rocks along the fast-moving water. Fultz leapt into the current. Water pulled and tugged at his legs, pushing him down the river. He pushed through the swift current. Water splashed. The current swelled over his waist, and he drove his legs until he emerged on the opposite bank.

Two Marines carried Burton up the opposite bank. Wet boots and soaked trousers, slowed their movement.

Thump. Thump. The helos moved along a western valley.

Fultz scaled the opposite bank, passing the two Marines carrying Burton, and darted through the poppy field. He tore through poppies. His legs, heavy, weighted from the water in his boots and soaked trousers, lifted, pushed, drove. Bulbs, heavy red blooms, exploded as he ripped through the field.

Quince knelt in front of Patrick who lay unconscious in a bed of rocks near the river. He grabbed the sergeant's hands behind him, pulled them over his shoulders, around his neck, and stood. Patrick fell over the corporal's back. He carefully stepped into the current, sinking to his knees, and then his thighs. Pushing, pulling, driving, his legs moved through the fast waters. Doc Mays struggled through the strong current, moving alongside Quince, carrying the awkward medical bag. The current swept over Quince's thighs, pulling him down stream.

Thump. Thump came the deep drone of the approaching helicopter as it cleared the western mountain peak.

Fultz ran through the poppies. Moist, red blooms burst as he tore through the field. As he reached the middle, far away from the tree-lined river, he pulled a canister from his LBV, held the trigger, pulled the pin, and tossed the canister into the poppies. The canister fizzed, and the lid let go a sharp snap, spewing red smoke through the poppies. Slowly, smoke climbed over the field.

Thump. Thump. Suddenly, a helo burst over the mountain peak, flew down the valley, circling for a clear approach to the field.

Quince drove his legs through the rapid current. Patrick lay limp over Quince's back and shoulders. Blood trickled from the corner of his mouth down Quince's neck. His amputated stump leaked through the bandages Doc Mays had applied on the road.

Drops of blood, dark purple, fell into the current, stirred away in the white foam.

Doc Mays fell exhausted on the rocks on the opposite bank. Propped up by his hands, his head hung and he spit and gagged.

Quince pushed, pulled, grunted, and shouted as his legs pushed through the water. His legs burned but lifted him out of the current, across the rocks, and up the steep bank. "Come on, Doc!" he shouted.

Doc Mays pushed his hands against the rocks, grunting as he lifted the bag over his shoulder. He walked slowly, clumsily up the slope.

Red smoke floated above the poppies. The air was still for now.

The helo slowly descended below the mountains, circling over the bridge, just a mile or so down the road, turning, and dropping into the valley. Thump. Thump. Thick propellers sliced the air.

Fultz and the Marines of 1st and 2nd fire teams stood in the open poppy field.

Quince tore through poppies. "Someone fucking help 'm!" shouted the lieutenant. Two Marines ran through the poppies, and reached for Patrick, but Quince kept running. His legs, burning from the river crossing, had calmed. His muscles loosened. His pace quickened.

Thump. Thump. The CH-47 descended, slowly dropping from the blue sky, through the valley, just feet over the field.

"Back up!" waved the lieutenant. "Clear the LZ."

The 47 descended over the field. Red smoke, once floating over the poppies, dissipated. Green stalks bent and swayed as thick propellers mashed them with wind. Red bulbs bounced around, fraying, peeled by the gusts.

The Marine's trousers flapped until they nearly dried as the helo slowly descended. A deafening thunder pushed down on the field.

Quince staged Patrick next to Burton, 50 meters from the LZ and fell to his knees, exhausted. Doc Mays dropped to his knees next to Patrick, and began checking the sergeant's bandages.

Patrick's face was still except for his short, sandy hair, blowing in the wind. A stream of drying blood exited the corner of his mouth, over the side of his chin. His pale, freckled features were smudged with smoke and dirt.

Quince was numb. His face was twisted as he looked down on Patrick. His sergeant. His mentor. His friend.

Nearby, the 47 sank to the ground. Propellers pushed hard against the field as the giant helo touched down. It rocked and the back hatch fell to the ground. Three medics darted off. Two of them carried a stretcher. A third carried a bag over his shoulder. They ran through the poppies, to the wounded. Doc Mays leapt to his feet. "What do we got?" asked the free-handed medic.

Fultz pointed across the river, "IED. We were in hi-luxs."

The medic shook his head.

Doc Mays shook his head, "Two wounded. Blast amputated his leg. He was unconscious when we get to him. Gave him morphine. Pulse is weak. Messed up," shaking his head.

He pointed to the PFC, "Burton there's got some minor lacerations in his legs. That's all I saw. The blast rattled him."

The medic dropped to his knees and crudely examined Patrick, feeling his legs, examining his pupils. "He's in shock. Need to get 'm the fuck outta here!"

Two medics lifted Patrick onto the stretcher, and carried him to the helo. Propellers pushed hard against the field. Cool air poured over Patrick's still, filthy face, wrestling with his sandy hair. Wind yanked Quince's trouser legs, and the sleeves of his blouse. His face was contorted. He stared at his sergeant, lying across the stretcher.

Medics quickly carried Patrick through the poppies, under the propellers pushing hard against the field. Poppy stalks bent and swayed, mashed against the sandy Kunar dirt. The first medic stepped backwards onto the hatch, walking backwards, grunting as he bore the sergeant's weight as the second medic stepped up on the hatch. They gently sat Patrick down near the wall. A fourth medic appeared, and together, they began cutting away the sergeant's clothes. An IV was quickly inserted. Burton was helped onto the helo, and placed on a stretcher in the opposite wall. A single medic attended him.

Quince stood and watched, feeling helpless. Medics scrambled around, opening and blocking his view of the wounded sergeant. It was noisy. The powerful engine roared. Medics yelled things to each other, but Quince did not hear them. "You go with him," Fultz said, grabbing Doc Mays by his shoulders. "Tell them what happened. Watch the sergeant. Radio in as soon as you know something."

Doc Mays nodded, tossed his medical bag to the floor, and ran to the medics.

"We got to go!" shouted the lieutenant to Quince, resting his hand on the corporal's back. "You can't go with him."

Quince lifted his head, slightly nodding. He walked slowly around the medics, to Patrick's stretcher. He looked down on Patrick's solemn face.

"Corporal," shouted a medic, "you need to go. Gotta get him to Bagram."

Quince didn't acknowledge the medic. He just turned, and walked through the helo, jumping off the hatch, and slowly walking through the poppies, stopping as he cleared the propellers. Fultz walked beside him.

The hatch lifted. Propellers accelerated. The giant helicopter rocked and swayed as the tail lifted out of the field. The nose dragged before lifting over the poppies. Wind mashed stalks into the dirt. It tugged on Quince's trousers, and he squinted as the strong current pushed tears from the corner of his eyes, streaming across his temples, through the dirt and smoke caked on his face. Squinting, he watched the 47 list forward, sailing up the valley, slowly rising, lift over the skyline, turn left, flying over the river, over Camp Stanton, over OP Tarawa, into the western mountains, toward Bagram Airfield.

Quince and Fultz quietly stood in the field of poppies, watching the 47 fly away. Quince's chest rose and sank as he breathed. For a moment, his thoughts just went blank, dark. Then, he thought of home. He thought of a boy in Kentucky, going to church with his grandfather. He remembered his grandfather and the elders praying over a sick parishioner; his tanned, leathery hand, lying on the man who had knelt near the altar. Quince remembered the old man's wrinkled lips parting, and his voice saying, "God, please go with him. Pass over him with your healing hand." Standing in the poppies, watching the 47 leave the valley, Quince prayed these words. It had been a long time since he had prayed. He had nearly forgotten how. What to say. How to talk to God. But, standing on the banks of the Kunar River, the words came back and he prayed as the 47 shrank, darkened to a silhouette, and passed over the western peaks.

Chapter 15
≈ The Roof of the Bunker: That Evening ≈

Upriver a dog barked in the village. Quince sat alone on the roof of the old hooch, staring at the distant lights. For hours he watched night slowly transform the valley, seeing shadows grow from the mountains and stretch over the fields.

Quince had climbed the ladder at dusk, and nestled into a stack of sandbags that he and Patrick had shaped like a recliner. The bags were hard. Some were filled with pebbles and stuffed with coarse sand, but they loved it anyway. It was a chair. It had a back and armrests, and he and Patrick always raced to the roof to see who could get to the chair first.

That evening he wanted to be alone, and the roof was a good place to get away. He liked it there. So did Patrick. The valley lay below, and things hidden in the dusty paths were exposed at this height. Sometimes, they would sit for hours and watch the valley. Watch cooks smoke behind the mess hall, taking a break from their ovens. They saw Marines playing basketball with locals on a dirt court, laughing at their poor play. Watched men work the fields. They saw things from up there. The roof gave them something the valley floor hid. Perspective. Understanding about who they were and what they were doing.

"It's funny about this place," Sergeant Patrick always said. "You got to climb high to keep grounded." If Quince closed his eyes, he could see Patrick say those words. See him shaking his head, dragging from a cigarette or a cheap cigar. He could see his eyes squint as smoke rose over them. But that evening things were different. Quince was afraid. Scared to close his eyes. When his eyes shut, instead, he saw Patrick's blackened face, smudged with smoke. Eyes that stared into a pure blue sky, never hidden with a blink, never mashed together in a grin, or pulled apart in surprise. Just motionless. Glass. Like marbles. The chisel of emotion did not scratch or chip them. They were wide and dull. Bland as the landscape around them.

As Quince sat alone, footsteps slid across the concrete roof, scratching as they stopped. Quince turned just as Fultz offered him coffee in a Styrofoam cup. Quince acknowledged the lieutenant with a slight nod of his chin, and took the cup and sipped coffee. Steam poured from the lip as he gazed up the river at the village lights.

Fultz stood nearby, quietly looking into the valley. Occasionally, he pursed his lips and blew steam away from his cup before sipping the coffee.

"Railroad tracks," Quince said in a flat, dead tone. "A little dirt lane crossed a railroad on the ridge above his home." As he spoke, Quince looked away from the village lights, and turned to the lieutenant. "Said he always knew home was near when the car bounced across those tracks." His eyes turned and fell across the dark fields near the concertina. "His momma's home."

Fultz nodded. His eyes went blank, before pushing out over the field.

Quince's flat tone turned accusatory, "Old man was gone. Pat hadn't seen him in years. Doubt they could even find him. But his momma was always there." Quince pointed toward the valley, jabbing his bony finger into the dry Kunar air. "She's there now. Just rising for the day. Sitting on the porch, maybe, watching a morning sun climb over the ridge." Quince nodded. His lips mashed together, bending, "Those railroad tracks," he nodded. "CACO's probably crossing those tracks about now. She's sitting there thinking it's just another day and that car's gonna come bouncing over those tracks and change her life forever."

Fultz nodded. His eyes dropped from the valley. Coffee steam brushed over his tired face.

"You know," Quince laughed, "he always joked that he was gonna get his momma together with my old man." Quince shook his head, dropping his eyes to the concrete roof. His chest bounced as laughter escaped. "I told him no. Not his mother. Not my father. Don't mistake me. Beecher Magowan is a damn ball of fun. A party. Energy like you ain't never seen but he has a dark side. Has his demons. He's easy to love but difficult to know. That's him. That's my father. Old Beecher." His head shook.

There was a pause as the two men stared out into the dark valley. Fultz pushed his eyes toward the corporal, "I thought you should escort his body home."

Quince shook his head from side to side. His chin rose. Lips bent. "He would want me here. With the squad."

Fultz sipped coffee. He sighed, sucking air through his nostrils and reflectively nodding as he conceded, "You're right. You're taking 1st squad. Pat would want that."

Quince's face grew and shrank with emotion. Anger, regret, sadness, guilt, each emotion fashioned his features in different ways. His lips mashed together. His brow furrowed. His eyes shrank with angry thoughts. Guilt and regret pulled his brow high, widening his eyes. His face grew long with sadness, and he dug through a pocket, and pulled out a half-smoked pack of cigarettes. He gave the pack a sharp snap and a filter jolted free. He stooped, dropped his lips around the filter, pulled out a burley, and dropped the pack before burying his hand into his pocket and emerging with an orange lighter. He set the coffee at his feet, cuffed his hand and twisted the lighter, sending a small, weak flame swaying over the cigarette's tip. His cheeks sank. His eyes swelled, slightly, as he sucked the filter. As tobacco embers glowed, he dropped the lighter to the floor and took a drag. His hand trembled when he pinched the cigarette, pulling it from his dry lips.

Fultz watched him with curious, disappointed eyes. "A burley?"

Quince shrugged, looking into the valley.

"You hate smoking? Vowed never to start. Said you spent so much time harvesting tobacco in a humid, August field, that your lungs were already full of the stuff."

Quince ignored the lieutenant, dragging from the burley as smoke washed over his face.

"When did you start?" asked Fultz.

Quince's trembling hand pinched the cigarette, pulling it from his lips. Smoke gushed from his nostrils as he answered, "They help."

Fultz sighed, nodding as he turned away from the field, "Get some sleep," he begged. "Chaplain's coming out with re-supply tomorrow. Wants to talk with the squad." He paused and turned to the wiry Marine, sitting on a stack of sandbags, hunched over, smoking quietly. "Maybe you should talk with him. You know. Just you and Chaps."

Quince's face was dull. He seemed determined to smoke and ignore anything the lieutenant said. "And Burton?" he asked.

Fultz shrugged, "Bad concussion. Light burns."

Quince dragged from the burley. "Intel on the IED?" he asked.

Lieutenant shook his head, rested his hand on the corporal's shoulder, and walked away, climbing down the wooden ladder, crossing the compound, and disappearing into his hooch.

The burley hung from the corner of Quince's lips. He sat in a chair of sandbags and smoked and watched the valley. Upriver village lights twinkled beyond dark fields. The valley was quiet, asleep. Eventually, the burley shrank. Embers faded and Quince's eyes squinted, batting in uneven rhythms. He pinched the butt of his burley, dropped it on the roof and twisted the toe of his boot across it until a black smudge stained the concrete. He stood, turned his back on the valley, descended the ladder, and disappeared into the hooch.

Inside, he moped across the floor, dropped onto the cot and sat in silence, arms resting on his knees. Occasionally, he rubbed his cheeks or stroked his short-cropped hair. He could barely make out the forms of Marines sleeping in their bivy sacks. The room was quiet and peaceful. Light trickled from a small lamp on a table in the corner.

He unlaced his boots, pulled them from his feet, and tossed them to the floor. He dropped his shoulders into the nylon, and pulled his sweat-soaked feet into the cot. Salt from dried sweat had stained his shirt. His face was dirty. Blood had dried and cracked around his neck. Beard stubbles had sprouted under his chin, and in the ditches of his neck. He was tired. He smelled of smoke and burnt fumes and sweat but he was too exhausted to shower or change clothes. He just lay there, listening to music, his thoughts singed with burley smoke and adrenaline.

As minutes passed, his eyes curiously surveyed the room. It was late. Soft light pulled shadows from cracks along the wall, and his eyes followed them through twists and loops from a corner, across the ceiling, weaving line over line. Outside, muffled voices briefly interrupted a calm night. Music played. Quince's eyes were open, alive with movement, combing the ceiling. Soon, he noticed the shadows were growing. It was as if the music was a nutrient, fertilizing the shadows, growing them from tiny, jagged cuts to faces of people he had seen or known or places he had experienced. The distant rumble of a Humvee filtered through the walls. Outside, muffled voices passed. His eyes narrowed. The room grew dark.

Suddenly, someone pushed Quince's shoulder, causing his torso to rock, slightly, under a gortex sleeping bag. He pulled his hands from the bag, lifted the beanie cap out of his eyes and over his forehead. Squinting, he looked up, into the gray sky of Camp Lejeune. He fell asleep in the Kunar and awoke in a swampy forest where they had trained before deploying. He was confused. Disoriented.

"Get up, Big Mac," he urged, freckles popping across his face as Quince's eyes adjusted to the light. "Battalion commander is on his way. CO wants a company formation."

"What? Formation?"

"Yep."

"What the hell for?" begged Quince, sliding out of the sack.

"For the hell of it." A proud countenance enshrouded Patrick's face. Freckles danced across his leathery skin. “Looks like we got our combat tour.”

“What?” begged Quince, sliding on his boots.

Patrick nodded. Sharp creases cut along his cheeks as he grinned. Freckles popped up along his brow, over his pointy nose. “Heard it from a clerk in headquarters. We’re going to Afghanistan.”

“When?”

“Next spring.”

Quince staggered to his feet, but nearly stumbled as he heard the news. “Get the fuck out?” he shouted.

Sergeant nodded.

“Afghanistan?”

“Yep.”

“What about Iraq?”

“Reckon the battalion commander’s gonna tell us in person.”

“Reckon he wants us to kiss his ass for giving us a combat tour?” asked Quince, sliding the blouse over his shoulders.

“Kiss his ass and polish his silver oak leafs,” laughed the sergeant.

Quince buttoned his blouse and laughed. A grin lifted Sergeant Patrick’s pale face. Creases cut into his proud cheeks. His hazel eyes were full. Then, suddenly, light filled the room, washing out Patrick’s face. Quince lazily shifted in the bivy, opened his eyes, lifted his wrist and took the time: 0200. Sweat tickled down his temple, washing away the dirt, filth in its path. Music played. The soft light washed darkness from the room.

It was a dream. Memories. Nothing more.

His eyes darted around again, chasing cracks along the ceiling. Twisting, turning, they moved in and out, back and forth with the cracks. Quince’s eyes narrowed, following cracks along the ceiling. From the wall, just above the window, he followed a jagged crack across the ceiling. It bowed in the center, looping back around. Inside the crack were several small slivers. Tiny dots, cracks that were just forming, splattered the ceiling. A thick one in the center appeared to rise and fall, lifting toward the door, falling back below the window. Quince watched as it opened, and closed. It lifted and the dots became light brown. Two more creases opened, turning hazel. A crease lifted near the door. The eyes were full. Freckles popped. Suddenly, it split, opening as if it were trying to speak, to tell Quince something. Sweat beaded over Quince’s temple. Then, the crease closed. Freckles dulled and faded. The hazel openings closed, gone.

Music played. A soft light lay across the ceiling.

Quince gasped, swallowing spit to moisten his dry throat. The spit tasted like smoke but he swallowed it and sighed. As his breath settled, he rose, and threw his feet to the floor. He shoved them into his boots, left them unlaced, and walked outside, through the dusty darkness before stopping at the piss-tubes. Unbuttoning his trouser, he relieved himself, buttoned them and walked to the mess hall. It was dark and quiet. Abandoned. He poured lukewarm coffee into a Styrofoam cup, pulled up a chair, and sat alone in the dark.

Chapter 16
≈ Three Days Later ≈

Corporal Magowan moved steadily, purposefully across the dusty compound. He passed GP tents, fluttering in a morning breeze, passed the piss-tubes, reeking of stagnate urine. An M16A2 was slung over his right shoulder. His gear rattled as he moved. "All right," he shouted, "listen up." The Marines of 1st squad hushed.

Quince unfolded a map and laid it across the hood of a hi-lux. "Bring it in," he yelled, "and tighten up." The Marines squeezed around the white pickup.

"RP Burley is here," he pointed to the abandon buildings just below Camp Stanton. "RP Bourbon, here," pointing to the bridge. A few men chuckled. "Our objective is Thoroughbred. The village three clicks below RP Bourbon. Now, it's hardly a village. A few shacks. Poppy farmers. That's it. Battalion wants to make contact. Let them know we can help. Food. Medical," his head lifted from the map and he turned, facing the Marines. "This'll be a long one. We'll be gone until dusk. And," he paused. His eyes narrowed, "I don't have to tell ya that it'll be dangerous. Be ready," he finished.

"Any questions?" he asked, facing them.

"Corporal, I have a question," Anderson lifted his hand.

"Anderson," he acknowledged.

"Why us? I mean, uh, we just got hit. Just lost our squad leader. We're short, only a couple weeks left? Why us? Why all the way down there?"

Quince blinked, pausing, gathering his thoughts. He took a deep breath, and his eyes leveled on Anderson. "I didn't ask for this. I didn't want this job, but it's mine. It's my job today just like it was Sergeant Patrick's job before. After we're gone home, it'll be someone else's job. Then another's after him. It don't matter if we just got here or if we're short-time Sallys like you, Anderson. It's just what we have do."

Anderson blinked and nodded. "Yes, Corporal," he answered, dropping his head.

Corporal Magowan looked into each Marine's face. He stared each man in the eye before moving on to the next Marine; stared into the eyes of each PFC, private, each lance corporal, the two other corporals, and Doc Mays. "Our call sign will be Man O' War. We leave in 5 mikes," he said, checking his watch. He folded the map, tucked it away inside his flak jacket, and moved steadily across the compound, disappearing into the CP.

Three hi-luxs soon parked near the concrete building, Quince's hooch. The corporal exited the CP, walked through a gap in the concertina wire, and crossed the compound. He moved steady, and with purpose. He opened the passenger door of the first hi-lux, glanced at the trucks behind him, sat, and slammed the door. He pulled the receiver from the hook, mashed the button and spoke, "6, this is Man O' War, over."

Squelch flooded the cabin. "This is 6. Send it, Man O' War."

"Roger, Man O' War requests permission to depart."

Squelch bled from the receiver, "Roger, permission granted. Report all RP's."

"Man O' War out," he barked, releasing the button before hanging the receiver on the hook. "Let's go Johnson," he said, turning to the PFC behind the wheel.

"Roger that, Corporal," answered Johnson, mashing the clutch, pushing the stick shift into gear, and pressing the gas. Dust rolled from their tires, clouding over the compound. Moving along the concertina, a Marine lifted his hand, waving them through the gate. Corporal Magowan's hi-lux turned right after passing by. Johnson accelerated. Dust flew. Tires moaned. On their left, the Kunar glistened in the morning sun.

Quince twisted, turning to watch the trailing hi-luxs. Clouds of blowing dust rose between the convoy, occasionally obstructing his view. The second truck, he saw, slowed, turned right, shifted gears and closed on Quince's hi-lux. The last truck, Anderson's, slowed, almost stopping, after passing through the gate. Corporal Magowan watched; his eyes narrowed. The truck sat idle. Dust rolled. Then, as the dust cloud thinned, Anderson's pickup turned right, shifted gears, and sped down the dusty road, catching the second pickup. Quince turned, facing the road. His head shifted, scanning the road, fields, the Kunar River.

Chapter 17
≈ Leaving Camp Stanton ≈

Corporal Magowan dug through a trouser pocket. Cellophane wrapping rattled in his hands as he pulled a pack of cigarettes from his trousers and shook it. The filter of a burley popped through the opening, and he stooped, pulled it free with his lips, shoved the pack deep into his trousers, twisted a cheap lighter, and cupped his hands around the flame. A soft breeze batted the fire, but the burley tip soon began to glow. His cheeks sank as he puffed, pulling smoke through the filter, across his tongue. The burley glowed brighter. Squinting as smoke poured over his eyes, he stared across the fields. Farmers labored in their crops. Some moved through the poppies at a lazy pace. Others bent and pulled weeds from their harvest. The river moved fast. Water rushed over rocks. The valley was busy.

Quince pulled the cigarette from his lips, pinching it between his thumb and index finger. His chest lifted, swelling as he sucked smoke into his lungs. A thin stream of smoke seeped from his nostrils, over his dry, cracked lips. He watched the valley and thought of home. He was tired—fed up with dust, patrols, bare, boulder-strewn mountains, poppies, and concertina. He was tired of OPs and RPs, of bad food and flies, piss-tubes, and pungent, shit filled outhouses. He was sick of the Kunar valley. He was ready to go home. See his family.

He looked over OP Tarawa. A low, droning thud echoed over the peak. Camp Stanton bustled. Marines trickled through the walls, carrying sea bags and MOLLE packs from their shoulders. As he watched, they stopped behind the wall, dropped their gear and sat on sea bags.

Below him, concertina snaked around the perimeter. Thick rocks were scattered across the sand. Poppies grew along the edge of the concertina, but the children were gone. Above him, an echo rumbled through the mountains. Marines filed through the gate, lining the LZ. Quince pulled the cigarette from his dry lips, dropped it to the concrete, and mashed it with the toe of his boot. He turned, walked across the roof, and descended the ladder.

He gathered a MOLLE pack, and slung it over his head, the loops just catching his shoulders. Suddenly, he tossed the pack to the ground, opened a pouch, and pulled out a small, cellophane bag. Walking purposefully up the sloping camp, he paused at the outhouses and slung open a thin, wooden door. The smell of rotting shit rolled over him as he climbed a stone step into the outhouse, held the bag in his hand, and emptied it into the toilet, pouring dozens of peppermint candies into a pool of shit. He dropped the empty bag, and slammed the door as he walked away. Again, Quince pulled the MOLLE pack over his shoulder, lifted a sea bag in one hand, M16A2 in the other, and walked across Camp Stanton, passing GP tents, piss-tubes and the mess hall. The corporal's face was stubble-and dirt smudged as he left camp, tossing the sea bag into the dust beside the LZ.

Marines bustled. Some lay against their packs, faces turned to the sky as if they were sunning on the beach. Thump. Thump. The sky echoed. A long, dark, sliver cut through the blue sky over OP Tarawa. Another one followed, trailing after the first bird. Marines lifted their faces to the sky. A few men cheered as the helicopters cleared the peak.

"First chalk!" screamed gunny.

"Bout fucking time," swore a Marine.

"Shit!" replied another, "Better part of a year on the frigging-ass border," shaking his head as he cursed.

The first helicopter circled over the river, turned, and floated over Camp Stanton, softly falling into the LZ. The back wheels touched first, followed by the nose. The 47 rocked and swayed. Dust and rock flew across the LZ. The back hatch fell, and a crewmember stepped out, jumping to the ground.

"First chalk, let's go!" gunny screamed, waving his arm. Marines ran across the LZ, dragging their sea bags. They filed in, one by one, scaling the hatch, into the CH-47.

The crewmember stepped into the hatch, and the door slowly lifted from the sand. The helicopter rocked. Propellers cut through the dry air. Sand and tiny rocks sprayed the Marines left on the LZ. Propellers pushed hard against the dirt, and the back of the helicopter lifted from the ground. The front of the helicopter dragged then lifted as the 47 sailed over the poppies, turned into the valley, and rose over the river.

The second 47 descended over Camp Stanton, falling softly into the LZ. "Second chalk!" screamed a staff sergeant. Marines filed into line just below the LZ. Corporal Magowan stood in the back. He was the last man. The 47 rocked and swayed as propellers beat the hard ground. The hatch fell open, and a crewmember leapt to the ground.

"Let's go!" begged the staff sergeant, pushing his arm through the gale of dust and pebbles. Marines filed across the LZ, hunched, carrying their MOLLE packs and sea bags while weapons hung loose in their hands.

Corporal Magowan stood beneath the propellers, waiting his turn to board. The wind pushed against him, driving him away, as if it were pulling him back to the camp, back to the Kunar, back to the place he wanted to leave. Heat from the exhaust washed his face as each Marine boarded the 47, positioned their packs, their gear, and sat.

He was the last Marine to board. Turning, he saw the fast-moving waters of the Kunar reflected in the morning sun. He scaled the sloping hatch, and the gales died, replaced by a deafening drone. He tossed the sea bag to the floor, slid the MOLLE from his shoulders, dropping it on the sea bag, sat, and pulled a belt around his waist.

The hatch slowly lifted as the propellers twirled ever faster. The 47 rocked, swaying as the back lifted from the LZ. Lifting, it pulled the nose of the helo over the poppies, turned, and floated down the valley. Joining the first 47, still circling the valley, the two helicopters passed over Camp Stanton, rising over the western mountains.

Quince stared over the hatch, down to the valley. He could see how the valley was stitched with colors and contrasts. Light brown sand lining barren slopes, dropped into the fertile valley, green and red with poppies. A thin sliver of blue streaked down the center. The Kunar River shrank as they lifted over the peaks. Camp Stanton, a Bastille of concrete, high walls, laced with concertina, appeared small, vulnerable from the sky. From the last seat, Quince's eyes fell from the 47, down the slope of OP Tarawa, across the poppies, over the wall, landing on the roof of the concrete building. The sun pasted a silver glare over the concrete. It was bare. For the first time since they had arrived, it was abandoned, forgotten.

Quince sat quietly. His face was long. His brow lifted. A deep breath pulled through his nostrils. The two helos sailed over OP Tarawa, and the peak blinded him from the valley. The Kunar Valley was now gone. A memory. He was ready to go home. Ready to be Quince again.

Chapter 18
≈ The Long Flight Home ≈

"Uncover!" yelled the first sergeant. Standing near the door, his face was pruned like a dyspeptic old steward. First Sergeant always shouted. Scowling. Skin folded up his leathery neck, "I said uncover!" he shouted again. Marines removed their hats, gripped them tight in their fists, and exited the cabin. Quickly, they were ushered down the stairs, across a cold, windy runway, and herded into a room.

Large, carpeted, the walls on three sides of the room were bare, eggshell white, separated from an identical room by thick, mesh-filled glass. Quince counted each Marine in his squad as they entered the room. Nodding to the company gunnery sergeant, he walked to a corner and sat alone, on the floor, watching the others. Soon, he leaned back, shoulders propped against the wall, and closed his eyes. Marines, company strength with clean, crisp camouflage utilities, mingled in the opposite room. Some gathered in small circles, somberly talking amongst themselves. Officers stood in the corner, arms folded. Some nervously paced around rows of chairs.

Marines in both rooms wore the same, desert digital camouflage utilities but their demeanors contrasted. Marines from Quince's battalion slept in awkward positions, some lay in the floor, shedding blouses, covering their eyes to shield the light. Others talked, standing in the corner, against the wall. Occasionally, some would smile or laugh, but they were mainly quiet. They appeared tired, worn as the camouflage utilities they donned. "Hey," shouted a lance corporal. His voice was drowned, flattened through the mesh-filled glass. "Hey," he shouted, pecking on the glass with his knuckles.

A group of Marines had gathered near the window, their utilities were faded, wrinkled, worn-looking. One lance corporal turned, and lifted his brow, "Yeah?"

"Where you been?" he asked.

"Afghanistan," answered the Marine in worn utilities. "Kunar mostly. Border."

The Marine on the opposite side pursed his lips, nodding, "Hear it ain't bad over there. Hear it's slow."

The Marine in worn utilities chuckled, "It's slow in Bagram. It gets faster the farther east you go." Marines gathered nearby, laughed. He lifted his brow.

"We ain't got shit to fight with," shouted a Marine with worn utilities, "Done sent it all to Iraq!"

"And you?" followed the lance corporal.

A frown formed over the Marine's face. His young features twisted, "Ramadi."

"Damn," cursed the Marine in worn utilities. His expression was empathetic, "Good luck!"

The Marine nodded, dropped his head, and walked off, pacing around the room.

The Marine in worn utilities turned to his buddies, shaking his head.

"Poor bastard!" said one Marine. His voice laced with condescension, pity, and understanding.

"Been there, done that," another claimed.

One Marine lifted his face, "Yeah. Ain't never doing it again!" he proclaimed, arms folded.

Time passed. They slept, and talked, waiting.

Lieutenant Fultz stood among a group of lieutenants near the doorway. Occasionally, he turned and glanced around the room, watching Marines of his platoon. He noticed Quince sitting alone in the corner. He'd been waiting for him to wake, and he noticed the corporal stir, lift his head, and open his eyes. Fultz broke from the other lieutenants, approached Quince, and dropped to the floor.

"Mind if I sit?" he asked, scooting down the wall.

Quince shrugged, answering in a dead-tone, "Nope."

"Remember coming through here?"

Quince nodded.

"Hard to believe it's been seven months," continued the lieutenant. "We were anxious. Hell, I felt like those guys look," pointing to the Marines in the opposite room.

Quince lifted his brow, nodding, "Feels different now."

"Yeah," answered the lieutenant, staring into the crowd, "Wife's waiting on me at the CP. Said she'd keep checking with the XO's wife for arrival times." Fultz turned to the corporal, "How about yours?"

The corporal shook his head, "Too far. Told them to stay home. I'd be there soon enough," his wiry shoulders rose and fell. "Just be a few days anyway."

Lieutenant nodded, "Your old man?"

Quince's face pinched, his bottom lip rose, "Nope," his head shook as he stared into the crowd. "Ain't heard from him since we left."

Fultz nodded. His eyes were focused on the corporal, "Well," he continued, "I'm sure it was hard on him. His only son."

Quince shook his head. His bottom lip drifted higher. His brow sank over his eyes as if the two were trying to touch the other. "I ain't buying it. He should have written. He ain't much of a writer but he should have tried. Wrote something, you know."

"I'm sure he tried," continued the lieutenant.

"Don't matter."

Fultz nodded, knowingly. His lips bent and he spoke. "He knew what to expect before we did. Knew before we left Cherry Point. Knew as soon as you told him you were going. He's been there. Saw it before. Saw it in Vietnam."

Quince shook his head, "I don't know. Maybe."

"He knew."

"I reckon," the corporal shrugged his wiry shoulders.

Fultz nodded, "He knew to worry."

"Maybe. Doesn't change the fact he should have written."

"He was worried."

"All the more reason he should of wrote."

"Knew there would be nights like the patrol around Tarawa, the Marianas. Knew there would be Stantons," Fultz paused, his lips wiggled as if searching for the right posture. "Knew there'd be days like the one we had near the river, Archie. Knew we would see the Burtons suffer. Knew we would lose the Patricks."

Quince was quiet. Soon, water gathered in his eyes, and his head slung around. His face pinched. His hands fell against the floor, and he pushed, grunting as he stood. Waving his hand at the lieutenant as if he were dismissing the officer, he strutted away, into the company.

A second hour passed. Boredom filled the room. Finally, First Sergeant strutted into the room, poised his leathery face and shouted, "Staff sergeants, load up!"

Marines groggily stumbled to their feet. Those who had slept pulled blouses over the shoulders, buttoning them as they walked.

"Uncover!" shouted the first sergeant.

The company filed back across the cold, windy, runway, and boarded a plane. Now, their plane was a civilian airline, chartered for the last leg of their flight home. They boarded the plane and soon the airy cabin grew warm from the body heat of a couple hundred Marines. Some Marines lay back, donned sunglasses, and fell asleep. Others talked, laughed. Some cheered as the jet lifted off. "Fuck yeah!" someone yelled.

"Don't this bird fly any faster!" yelled Anderson, raising a few laughs. "Ma'am," Anderson begged a passing stewardess, "can you tell the pilot to drop the hammer. PFC Anderson needs to get home ASAP." Marines chuckled across the cabin.

"Anderson!" screamed a staff sergeant who sat behind the PFC.

Anderson, laughing at his own humor, twisted in his seat. His face flattened, a little, when he saw the staff sergeant, "Yes, Staff Sergeant?"

"Shut your cock holster," yelled Staff Sergeant. "Go to sleep. You waited seven months. You can wait another seven hours."

Anderson turned straight in his seat, giggling like a child. The Marine next to him stuck an elbow in Anderson's ribs.

"CONUS!" someone screamed near the front.

"Shut up!" yelled the first sergeant.

Quince sat near the window. He watched the plane lift off the runway, and he saw Ramstein and Landstuhl shrink. He thought of all of the wounded who had landed there—their agony.

As a child, Beecher took Quince to the old Perryville battlefield. As they walked the rolling hills and later, streets of the small town, they came across an old brick home the Union Army used as a hospital. Beecher stood near the home and told his son about the amputations, young men who walked onto that battlefield as whole men, and left without arms and legs. Beecher spoke about the agony they felt as surgeons sliced a ring over the wounded man's leg, peeled back the skin, then took his saw, and pushed through the wounded man's flesh and muscle, pushing, jerking harder as he ground through bone. "Lots of men," noted Beecher, pointing his finger like a preacher at the boy, "suffered right here. I regard this old house as some kind of holy site." Quince remembered standing quietly. He remembered how he felt, standing there as a boy near that old house. He had the same feeling now. That sour, burning feeling in his belly as he flew over Landstuhl. The thought of Patrick's lifeless body landing here just a few weeks earlier crowded his head. He quietly closed his eyes. Cool air from a small fan washed over his face as his thoughts carried him back to the Kunar River Valley.

The valley was dry. Dust was everywhere. Cool air poured through an open window of a hi-lux, and he could taste dust, a bitter, powdery film over his tongue, that scratchy feeling as he blinked. The roar of tires clawed along the hard, dusty road. A roar similar to the plane's engines, pulling the company through the German sky. Up ahead, several rows, he saw the crown of a Marine's head, twisting, turning, scanning. Up ahead, a few car lengths, he saw Sergeant Patrick's Kevlar scan the road, mountain slope, the poppy fields, and the river, white, moving fast down the valley.

Quince shook his head as if he were trying to shed thoughts stuck in his brain, shake them out through his ears, his eyes. He refused to let himself think about the explosion. Visualize it. Live it again. See his sergeant lying there in pieces. His smoke-covered features, still. He wondered if a hundred years later some father would point a finger at his son standing in front of the hospital in Landstuhl and talk about it the way Beecher had spoken about that old house on the Perryville battlefield. He wondered if people would remember. Would care. Wondered if they would understand as his father understood.

Corporal Magowan stood, slid past several sleeping Marines in his row, walked up the aisle, and pushed open a small, thin door. The plane swayed as he unbuttoned his trousers and relieved himself. After a week in Bagram, waiting for departure, he was already accustomed to toilets instead of piss-tubes. Finished pissing, he flushed, pushed open the door, and returned to his seat. The Marine beside him watched a movie. A mouse-like voice echoed through his headset. Muffled chatter rang across the cabin. The cabin warmed as the company stirred or slept. Quince dug through a pocket, took out his wallet, unfolded it, and flipped through photographs, stopping on the picture of Sara and Lilly at a water park. It was taken last July. Sara's skin was brown and smooth, large sunglasses hung over her cheeks. Her teeth were white as bone. Her tanned arms wrapped over Lilly. Lilly's grinning face lay between them. He folded the wallet, shoved the dry, cracked leather in his pocket, laid his head back and closed his eyes. He wanted to forget Afghanistan and think of home. It was that time. Time to trade memories of the Kunar for his future in Kentucky.

"Gentlemen," echoed the pilot's deep voice, "we are approaching Marine Corps Air Station Cherry Point. We are scheduled to land at 11:30 p.m. local time. Local temperature is a balmy 31 degrees." The microphone clicked off. Some Marines woke. Their groggy faces scanned the cabin as the microphone clicked on, "So, sit back, relax, we'll begin the descent in about five minutes. On behalf of the airline, the crew, we want to personally thank you for your service." The microphone snapped.

A few cheers rang out in the cabin. Marines bustled about, shifting, gathering gear. Quince blinked as his head lifted from the seat. "Sleeping beauty," said the Marine in the seat next to him. "Mac," he chuckled, "you been asleep since Ramstein."

Quince lifted his eyebrows, pushing wrinkles across his forehead. His hand pulled over his face, rubbing his bloodshot eyes. He scanned the cabin, "Yeah. I reckon."

"Well," proclaimed the Marine, "We're in CONUS now. You can rest plenty."

Quince stared through the window at the darkness of the early morning. Occasionally, he noticed a faint light, twinkling from the Carolina bottom country. A street lamp, he thought, a little, quiet country home planted near the end of a one-lane road—a quiet place for a family to enjoy their lives, and be left alone, away from it all.

The plane descended through darkness, and anticipation grew among the Marines. Laughter sprung up across the cabin. Quince adjusted the time on his watch.

The Marine next to him kept talking, "I hear it's cold at home. Colder than Stanton. Maybe not as cold as a week on Tarawa. Now that's frigging cold! Boring as hell."

Quince ignored the Marine. He stared through the window. Below, sporadic lights, once faint, shown through the black. The plane descended, teetering as it slowed. Suddenly, the black night transformed into a tree line, and the plane skirted the treetops, descending, teetering. Then, thump, back wheels screeched, catching the cold, concrete runway. Cheers rang out across the cabin. The nose slowly sank to the concrete.

"Old lady is waiting on me back at the CP," continued the Marine. "How about yours? Wife? That little girl?"

Quince shook his head, lips pulled together, "Too far. No use driving all the way down here when I'd be home in a few days."

"Not my old lady," proclaimed the Marine. "My old lady insisted. Said she couldn't wait any longer. Hell," he went on, "wanted to come here to Cherry Point. Guess battalion didn't want family here. Told them to wait at the CP in Lejeune."

The plane slowed, then turned, moving across the runway toward a giant, beige hangar and rolled to a stop. The engines died, slowly winding down before falling silent. "Yeah!" Shouted one Marine. "CONUS! Here I come!" echoed another.

Single file, Marines emptied the cabin, greeted by the crew as they exited. The first sergeant stood on the runway, near the stairs, "Uncover!" he shouted. "Get your damn covers off!"

A cold blast of air struck Quince's face as he descended the stairs. It was quiet around the runway. He could see a little town outside the gate. Dark buildings. Abandoned streets. It was a quiet night. There were no celebrations. No parades. No crowds waiting for them. They didn't expect them anyway. Didn't want them. But the place was so quiet, so desolate that time of night, it felt like they were being hidden, sneaked back into the United States.

Quince walked toward the hangar. Suddenly, he heard cheers around the corner of the large, beige building. Scattered applause followed. A few more cheers went up. Marines shouted as they neared the hangar door, but Quince was blinded by the large building. He walked closer, near the corner of the giant hangar. Cheers grew louder. Marines filing around the hangar whooped. Applause smattered. Finally, as he rounded the corner, he saw a handful of men standing alone, behind a chain-link fence, in the darkness, applauding as the Marines passed. Some cheered, and offered thanks. One man stood in the center, holding a staff. A large American flag flipped and turned with the cold breeze. He was short man. A thin, white beard covered his face. White hair ran along the temples of his otherwise bald head. His eyes were blue and sad and proud as he watched the Marines file across the runway. Around him, gathered close, were a dozen middle-aged men dressed in worn jeans, black leather jackets or olive drab coats, laced with patches. Behind them, lined along the street, was a small fleet of motorcycles.

A street lamp touched the chrome and black paint of a bike familiar to Quince. The men stood beneath the light, clapping, cheering, offering appreciation. A frosty night air pulled at their breaths as they cheered while Marines filed into the open hangar.

Quince broke from the line, walking slowly across the concrete lot near the hangar. His face was solemn, without emotion. Sadness, anger, frustration were wiped clean by the drone of exhaustion. Waving in the cold night air, the flag threw an ever-moving shadow over the concrete. Snowflakes floated out of the darkness, softly settling on the dead grass of the fields around the runway.

“Welcome back, son,” one man shouted.

Quince nodded to the small man who bore the flag. It was Beecher. The old man’s face was very still. His cheeks were ruddy, as blood pooled near the skin. A giant of a man stepped forward. Flakes gathered in his long, black beard. “Moose,” spoke Beecher, still watching his son, “you remember my boy Quince.”

Moose grabbed the staff, stepping into Beecher’s spot, “Well done. You’ve done your duty,” proclaimed the giant man. A thick, dark beard tasseled in the wind, and his giant knuckles bled white as he fisted the staff of the flag.

“Thank you, sir,” replied Quince, stopping near the fence. “Dad?” Pausing, he shrugged and searched for words in the cold silence. “Why? Why here? Tonight?” He grasped the fence near his shoulder, and leaned forward.

Beecher stepped forward. Snowflakes floated through the chain-link fence separating the two men. “We wanted to come here. Thought it the best way to thank you boys." Beecher turned, briefly, to the men around him. Aging, their faces cut with lines, hair thin, graying for most of them. "None of us are any good at saying what we're feeling. Thought just being here would say it for us."

"Dad," Quince's head shook, "you didn't have to come here. Ride all the way here in this weather. Hell," Quince looked around, "you're the only ones here. No one else came."

"That's why we came," sounded Moose's deep voice.

Beecher nodded, "Cause we know it ain't right to get off that plane and see no one."

"You done it son," smiled Beecher. Lifting his hand, he grasped Quince's fingers through the wire fence. Water pooled in the corner of his blue eyes, and his cheeks lifted, ruddy, and lined. "I'm proud of you."

Quince nodded. He swallowed spit to moisten his throat and the taste of smoke and dust was gone. He turned to the hangar, sighed and acknowledged, "Well. Reckon I better get in here." He shrugged.

Beecher smiled but said nothing, patting his son's hand instead.

Quince nodded to his father, and then to Moose and the others, saying, "Thank you."

"Thank you, son!" shouted some. "Welcome back!" shouted others.

Quince entered the hangar and followed Marines moving single file down a small hall that connected two large rooms. An administrative corporal stood next to the adjutant, holding a clipboard. The adjutant counted and Marines shouted their names, waiting for the corporal to check their names on a roster. Next, they gathered in a large, empty room on the opposite side. The cold room heated quickly as the Marines filed in. Some gathered near a large sliding door. Grunting, pulling, the door creaked, before sliding open and cool, frosty air poured through the hangar, sifting among the Marines. Quince watched as the giant beige door opened. He watched light spill onto the concrete lot. Through the darkness he saw the bikers near the fence. A black sky salted snow. The flag flipped and waved. Beecher, holding the staff, stared into the hangar.

Marines loafed around the hangar, waiting as their sea bags and MOLLE packs were unloaded from the plane and stacked in 7-ton trucks. Many slept, sprawling across the cool concrete floor, or curled in the corner. Some smoked near the entrance.

"No one leaves the hangar," shouted the first sergeant.

Quince tried to sleep. Hands tucked under his armpits, he sat on the cold concrete, back resting against the hangar wall. No matter how hard he squinted, the glow of lights flooded through his eyelids. He finally had enough. Rubbing them, he stood, and joined a group of Marines gathered near the door, smoking.

"Burley?" offered another corporal, pulling a pack from his trouser pocket.

Quince nodded and the Marine shook a pack, and the filter of a burley cigarette peaked through the opening. Quince pulled the burley from the pack, took the Marine's cheap, plastic lighter, lit the tip of his cigarette, and returned the lighter. His cheeks sank, and his eyes narrowed as he dragged. Smoke lifted over his eyes as he sucked smoke from the burley.

"Thanks," he added, gesturing with the cigarette.

Just outside the hangar, reflecting in the light that escaped the hangar, large, commercial buses idled in the cold. Exhaust from the buses danced through frosty air. Hidden by the first bus were several more identical buses, each idling like the first one.

The other Marine smoked. "So," he gestured toward the bus, "saw you talking to those men across the fence."

Quince nodded, dragging from the burley, "Yeah," slowly exhaling smoke that clouded his face. His breath misted in the cold.

The other Marine nodded, also dragging from the burley.

Each man looked toward the idling bus. The giant vehicle hid Beecher and the bikers from their view.

"Well," said the smoking Marine, "they're good-to-go." He smoked, shaking his head, "Them bikers. They didn't have to do that shit. Didn't have to come here. Could've waited with the rest of them in a warm CP at Lejeune. Those bikers are good-to-go."

Quince, dragging from the burley, pulled the cigarette from his dry lips, "Yeah," he answered, blowing smoke into the frosty air, "I reckon they're all right."

"Damn right!" continued the other Marine. "Hell," he continued, "I'll bet they don't even know any of us. Bet they just came out here."

Quince was silent, occasionally lifting the cigarette to his lips, dragging, his cheeks sinking, before pulling it away.

"Damn cold out here."

Quince nodded.

"Freaking APOE is slow as a 7-ton," cursed the smoking Marine.

Quince stared toward the bus. Guilt held his eyes in the direction of the fence for the next hour. He smoked, occasionally answering the other Marine as he spoke or asked questions. Mostly, Quince just watched for sight of Beecher.

"All right," shouted the first sergeant, "listen up." He stood near a door leading down the narrow hall. His face was leathery and well defined. He poked the air with his bony finger as he spoke. "I want 1st Platoon to load the first bus," stabbing the air toward the hangar door. "Copy?" He paused. Marines grunted as he continued. "Once we have a good count from 1st, 2nd will load the next bus, and 3rd will take the last bus with a good count from 2nd. You read me? See how this shit works?" he asked, stabbing the air. The Marines mumbled, gathering gear. Some were shaking off sleep.

Quince took a count of his squad, and flashed a thumb at the staff sergeant. The other squad leaders followed and staff sergeant waved his hand, as he and Lieutenant Fultz walked toward the idling bus. One by one, slowly, 2nd Platoon loaded. Quince settled into a window seat on the right, facing the hangar. Occasionally, he turned and peered through a window on the opposite side, looking for Beecher but his view was blocked by another bus, and he began to worry about the old man. He worried about him in the freezing night. Worried they had left. Worried he had not shown enough appreciation. Didn't show surprise. Didn't seem happy to see them. Soon, guilt seeped into his thoughts. Guilt for being angry with his father. Angry that Beecher had not written. That he disapproved of Quince's decision to join the service. His desire to serve in combat. That the old man didn't understand it. He understood. Understood it well. Beecher Magowan knew it. Lived it. Suffered it. Guilt-ridden, Quince turned, peering through the opposite window. "Hurry!" he worried, silently. "Get the fucking count and let's go!" A voice screamed in his head as he peered through a window, watching the staff sergeant count 3rd Platoon. "It's the third damn time!" Quince thought as the staff sergeant ran down the steps and motioned to the first sergeant and the officers, gathered in a circle. Finally, the circle of officers and staff NCOs broke apart. Lieutenant Fultz and the staff sergeant climbed into the bus and sat in the first row of seats, behind the driver.

"What if they left?" worried Quince to himself. "What if? Hell? I acted like I didn't give a shit. What if they kept riding right past Lejeune?" cried a silent voice. Guilt flooded his thoughts.

Outside the bus, snow flew. It was dark. Finally, the driver released the brake. He mashed the gas, and the idling bus bounced forward, swinging wide as it turned near the hangar. As it turned, Quince faced the chain-link fence. He peered through the window, waiting for the third bus to pull forward. Finally, the last bus bounced forward, and Quince saw the flag flipping in the cold night air. Beecher's face was still, his hand grasping the wooden staff. Moose and the other bikers stood silently. Some saluted as the buses passed through the gate.

Suddenly, just before Quince's bus pulled onto the empty road, the convoy stopped. Simultaneously, Beecher stepped forward, and he and Moose twirled the flag around the staff. They quickly walked away from the fence, and each man started his bike. Moose slid the flag through a ring on his seat, and then another near the exhaust.

"Those fellows want to escort you boys to Lejeune," explained the old bus driver. "Told them I don't care if they can stand the cold."

Quince listened to the driver. Standing, he peered through the front window. As he watched, Beecher, Moose, and the other bikers rolled forward, down a dark, abandoned street. Cold, frosty air pulled exhaust from the chrome pipes of their bikes. Buses bounced forward, following them.

As the convoy moved methodically along, wind tugged at a smaller flag flying over Moose's bike. It was dark, but the bus's headlights threw light over the small group of bikers. Wind blew. Flurries poured over them, but they rode on, escorting the Marines down a narrow, pine-shadowed road, through Jacksonville, and the front gate of Camp Lejeune. As the bikers slowed in a curve, Beecher's small frame leaned against the freezing wind. It tugged at his leather jacket. At the end of the main thoroughfare, the bikers circled a statue of General Lejeune, turned left, and then right, onto a small, two-lane street. The waters of the New River were still and black as the buses rolled to a stop in a small parking lot near the shore. A crowd rushed from the CP as the buses stopped. Marines quickly filed from the bus, sifting through the crowd for family members. Some kissed wives. Some hugged children and the crowd soon disappeared into the warmth of a nearby gymnasium.

Across the parking lot, bikes idled. Quince stepped down from the bus, walking with purpose across the parking lot. He approached the bikers, and stopped beside Beecher.

"How long?" asked the old man.

Quince shrugged, "Can't say. Reckon an hour. Maybe two."

A cold wind blew. Bikes rumbled as they idled.

"We'll be at the Ocean Shore Bar," Beecher paused. "You know it?"

Quince nodded, "I'll be there as soon as I can."

Beecher nodded, a smile barely lifting his frozen cheeks as he rode away. Others followed. Bikes thundered past the young Marine, away from the CP, toward Jacksonville. As they circled General Lejeune's statue, and rode along the main thoroughfare, Quince heard their chrome pipes thunder.

Quince grinned, turned and walked across the parking lot and into the gym. Inside, Marines visited with family, huddled in small groups, laughing, talking. One hour became two. Two became three. Periodically, rumors the company would soon secure trickled among them. And those hopes sank as fifteen minutes came and went.

Quince waited alone. Occasionally, he visited with families of Marines from his squad, but he otherwise sat alone on a wooden bench. As time passed, he grew impatient. His thoughts were with Sara and Lilly and Beecher. He wanted to get out of that gym, get a taxi, go to Jacksonville, to the bar, and speak with his father. He wanted to ask Beecher about his wife. His child. Pick his brain. Learn. He needed to know about home. Lilly. How much had she grown? Had her favorite foods changed?

Finally, First Sergeant strutted into the gymnasium. "Staff sergeants!" he shouted. "Form up. Company formation." Staff sergeants ushered Marines away from their families, herding them into a loose formation. First Sergeant called roll, turned, and saluted the captain who had stopped directly behind him. First Sergeant then abruptly turned walking behind the formation.

"At-ease!" shouted the captain. "Marines," he said, pacing, "It's good to be home." Some men cheered. Others grunted in affirmation. "I won't keep you long. I know your families are waiting," he said, pacing. Marines grunted in affirmation. Some chuckled. "I just want to say what a hell-of-a job you did over there. How damn proud I am of you!" Pausing, he slowly paced back and forth before the Marines. "It's been a long time," he continued. "You trained diligently through a four month work-up and a seven-month deployment. I am proud of you." Pausing, his face pinched. "Tonight, we stand in the same gymnasium where we gathered on a cold winter's night, eager to embark on this journey. Tonight," he paused, "we stand here without six of our fellow Marines. Our brothers. Five men were wounded during our deployment. They are recovering from their wounds and our thoughts are with them."

Quince listened. Thoughts of the patrol around Tarawa, the Marianas, filled his mind. He remembered the ambush at Tinian. Horror on the wounded Marine's face. His bulging eyes. How his chest bounced up and down. Standing in formation, Quince momentarily shut his eyes as the captain spoke. "During our deployment, we lost one Marine. One of the best. Sergeant Patrick. Pat lost his life from an IED on the banks of the Kunar River." Quince's lips shook. His thoughts flew back across the ocean, the mountains, sinking into the Kunar River Valley, and the day Patrick died. With his eyes closed, he saw visions of Pat's smoke-charred face. Quince felt the sergeant hanging limp across his shoulder as he forded the Kunar River. Saw poppies bend and bow as the helicopter took off.

Quince opened his eyes just as the captain paused. Holding his cover, Captain's hands fell to his side as he scanned the company. "Let's bow our heads in a moment of silence and remember these Marines and their families." His head fell, chin resting in his chest. The formation bowed their heads but Quince stared straight ahead, looking at nothing. Finally, his eyes shut, pushing water from the creases. Then, Captain's face rose. Others looked up as Captain screamed, "Company! Dismissed!"

Marines happily shouted, "Aye-Aye, sir," stepped back, about-faced, and cheered.

Through it all, Quince never moved. He did not shout. He just stood there, frozen as the company broke apart. And finally his thoughts returned. Flew back across the ocean. Back to the gymnasium. Back from the Kunar Valley.

As the formation disintegrated, Marines and their families quickly flooded out of the gymnasium. Quince waited for them to leave before going down a small lane to the CP. He opened a glass door and walked down a hallway, passing pictures and citations awarded to the unit for previous conflicts before stopping at a stack of sea bags and MOLLE packs lined along a wall. He searched through sea bags until he found one with duct tape fashioning a letter M on the bottom. He pulled the bag from the stack, unfastened the hook, and dug through the clothes. Near the bottom, just where he had packed them, he found jeans, a black hoody, and sneakers. The garments were cold, carrying winter with them as he stripped in the hall, dressed in civilian clothes, crammed his camouflage utilities in the pack, and tossed the sea bag onto the stack. Walking through the hallway, he paused before a row of pictures. "Honor," denoted a sign above the black and white photographs. Below were descriptions of the Marine's death; their heroic sacrifice. Quince paused. His lips bent and he nodded, turned, and left the CP.

Walking through a cold night, Quince passed the statue of General Lejeune, and paced down the main thoroughfare. Cars passed him as he walked in the dark. He occasionally turned and pointed a thumb at approaching traffic but no one stopped. Some blew their horn. Others sped by, pulling a gush of frosty air across Quince's face. Each time, Quince just frowned, shrugged, and kept walking. Finally, a taxi rolled alongside him, and the driver, a thin man with a black, scruffy face, rolled down the window. "Hey buddy?" he asked, a cigarette hanging from his lips. "Need a ride into town?"

Quince paused. Flurries sprinkled from the sky. Some melted on his warm cheeks as he nodded, answering, "Sure. I ain't looking forward to five miles in this weather."

Flurries sprinkled through the sky. The driver grinned. Posturing the cigarette in his yellowing teeth, he said, "Hop in."

Quince circled the taxi, opened the rear passenger door, and sat. As he shut the door, the vehicle sputtered and moved slowly along the main thoroughfare, through the front gate, before turning left toward Jacksonville. The driver attempted small talk but Quince mostly ignored him, giving short, one word answers when he had to. He was quiet, staring through the window, watching as the taxi passed a row of tall Carolina pines before bouncing across a bridge that spanned a narrow river. Boats, anchored to a small dock, rocked in the early morning tide.

Soon, small buildings and strip malls replaced the towering pines. Streetlights drove away the darkness. "Anywhere particular?" asked the driver, glancing in the rear view mirror.

"Ocean Shore Bar," Quince answered, staring through the window.

"Bar?" quipped the driver. "Son, it's 4:00 a.m. You're either a tad late or hell-of-a lot early!"

Quince sat quietly and watched small buildings and streetlights pass through the window. A few moments elapsed and he smirked, answering as an afterthought, "Not if you're on Afghanistan time."

The driver laughed as he drove. Smoke rose over his face and clouded the car. Quince stared through the window.

The taxi stopped at a light near railroad tracks. It was quiet. The town abandoned. After a brief pause, the vehicle eased through a light, crossed the tracks, and turned left onto a narrow lane. They drove by a used car lot and a pawnshop before rolling into a small, gravel lot. Near the door of a run-down, one-story shack, sat a dozen bikes. The shack was well lit. Neon lights flashed in the windows, washing the chrome bikes with intermittent splashes of greens and yellows. Flurries sprinkled over the windows.

"I'll be damned," swore the driver, surprised. "Still open this time of morning?"

"Reckon so," Quince answered, a smirk lifting his solemn face. He never doubted it. Knew Beecher and Moose would convince the bar's owner to stay open. Jacksonville was full of retired Marines and chances are the owner once served in the Second Marine Division. One Marine wouldn't deny another if asked, especially if the Marine asking was Beecher Magowan. *Hell,* Quince thought, *Marine or not, the owner would stay open for Beecher Magowan. Beecher just had that way about him.*

As the taxi idled, Quince pulled a worn wallet from his pocket, took out a twenty, and handed it to the driver. It felt odd to feel money between his fingers--to pay for something. Other than a few boxes of cheap cigars at the PX in Bagram, Quince had not purchased anything since leaving the states. For seven months, he had eaten free, driven hundreds, if not thousands of miles, flown thousands more, and never paid for anything. *Welcome home*, he thought, sarcastically.

The driver grinned as he positioned the shrinking cigarette in his teeth. He nodded, took the money, waited for Quince to shut the door and drove away.

Quince stomped up the flimsy, wooden steps leading to the bar. Loose snow painted the steps, marking his footprints. Music and muddled laughter spilled into the winter night. Quince pulled a hand from the pocket of his hoody, twisted the knob, and pushed. As he stepped through the door, music and laughter tumbled over him. A warm, smoky breeze brushed over his face. He paused and faces of a dozen drunk, red-eyed bikers immediately turned to the door. Men, gathered in circles, smoking, palming a beer, faced the door.

A few bikers broke away from a pool game, approached Quince and shook his hand. Quince reluctantly smiled and greeted the men. It felt odd to him. Strange even. It was his job to go to Afghanistan and he felt congratulations were undeserved. But that didn't stop the bikers from offering their appreciation. Moose tossed a pool stick to the table, laid his massive hands on Quince's shoulders, and awkwardly hugged the young, wiry Marine. "Good job, son! Your daddy's proud of you! I am too!" He slapped Quince on the back, and his wiry frame shook like sand.

Quince nodded, smiling some, "Appreciate you boys coming all the way up here. Know it wasn't necessary and all."

Moose's smile sank. His thick beard fell like a gnarled mop, "Reckon it was," he answered in a more serious tone. "It was important to say it in person."

"Hey! Hey!" Beecher whooped from his seat at the bar. A cigarette hung loose in the corner of his mouth. Twisting, he turned from the bar, jumped from a stool, and approached Quince. He was drunk. Small, red circles gathered at his cheeks. Tiny lines checkered his eyes. "'Bout time," he laughed.

Quince shook Moose's giant hand, nodded, and walked toward Beecher.

"Gear count. Securing a company is some slow shit," he confessed, shaking his head.

Beecher threw an arm around his son's shoulder, "First to fight, last to secure," he laughed, smoke pouring over his face. "Ain't it always that way?"

"Reckon."

Beecher pulled himself onto the stool. "Beer for my boy," he pointed to the bartender, a thin man wearing a grease-stained shirt.

The skinny bartender slid a beer under Quince's chin. Foam rose, spilling over the rim as Quince lifted the beer to his lips, tilted the glass and chugged a few ounces before setting the glass on the bar. Wiping foam from his lips, a look of satisfaction came over his features.

"Bet that tasted damn fine, huh?" Beecher patted his son's back.

Quince tilted the glass to his lips, and drank, not answering Beecher.

"How long?"

"Seven months."

"Yep," Beecher chuckled, "right fine."

Quince drank.

"Skeeter," Beecher yelled across the bar, "another one for my boy."

The skinny bartender smiled, poured another beer and set it on the bar. "They'll taste like water tonight," he proclaimed.

Quince looked up. A wry smile bent his lips as he asked Skeeter, "How did he talk you in to staying open so late?"

Skeeter threw a towel over his shoulder and pointed to Beecher, "I've known this ol' son of a bitch since Cam Lo. He ain't changed a bit. Just uglier. And shorter."

Beecher busted up laughing, "Yeah. I shrunk and Skeeter got skinnier," he retorted. "Ain't that some shit?"

"Well. Thank you, anyways," Quince interrupted, sipping beer. "Appreciate it. Needed one."

Skeeter chuckled, "Glad to do it," he proclaimed, walking away to clean tables and gather empty beer bottles that were strewn across the room.

The room was dim. Smoke hovered like a stagnant cloud. Laughter and conversation were constant, interrupted by a sharp clap as Moose's pool stick slammed into a cue ball and the cue ball slammed into a neatly stacked triangle of colorful balls, sending them flying across the table. Meanwhile, Beecher chugged beer, wiped foam from his beard, and dragged from a burley.

Quince drank beer until his taste buds were momentarily satisfied, thirsty from the long prohibition. He put the empty glass on the bar, turned to his father, and shrugged, "So much to ask. Feel like I missed it all," he confessed.

Beecher chuckled, "Reckon it does."

Quince shrugged, "How are they?" he asked. "Spoke to Sara last week. It was short. Said she was late for something. Had to go. Hell. Feels like I've missed so much," he explained, remorsefully.

Beecher exhaled. Nodding, a slight smile breached his beard, "Lilly. She's a firecracker. Just like her Grandpa." His eyes narrowed as he dragged from the burley. Smoke rose over them.

Quince grinned like a proud father.

"But. Got to admit I ain't seen them in a while," continued Beecher.

Quince's face shrank. His brow pinched together and his eyes narrowed as if shuttering from a bright light. "Lilly was supposed to spend every other weekend with you. Sara promised," he moaned, confusion mangling his words.

Beecher lifted the beer to his lips and drank. "Reckon it's been a while. Couple months. July? August maybe? Hell. I don't remember. Time passes. Anyway, I took her to the covered bridge. You know? Near Estill's Creek? It sits on those big stones?" Beecher took a drag and nodded. "Beautiful day. Took some pictures."

Skeeter poured another beer and set it on the bar. Quince nodded and drank from a tall glass. His face was furrowed and wrinkled. It was strange. Something felt wrong. Really odd. Beecher had not seen Lilly in months despite Sara's promise. Where was she? Why hadn't Sara mentioned it? It made him wonder.

Beecher noticed the worry on his son's face. He leaned over and rested his hand on Quince's shoulder, shaking the boy's wiry frame. "Oh, hell!" he cursed. "You just got home! Relax. Rest some, boy."

Quince sighed and his face opened up as he nodded in agreement. "Well," he said, resting the beer on the bar and cupping the glass between his hands. "I'll be home soon. Tomorrow, I reckon."

Beecher nodded.

"Can't wait."

"Take your time."

Quince drank.

"Get settled. Don't rush things."

"Wish I could go now. Leave. Get the hell out of here!"

Beecher set his beer on the bar and dragged from the burley. "Listen, son," he begged in a solemn voice. "You need time. They need time. It's different. Things ain't the same. You've been gone for a while now. Don't rush things."

Quince shook his head.

Beecher took a drag. His cheeks sank. His eyes narrowed as the burley tip glowed. A thin film of smoke floated like a spirit between the two men.

"Say," Quince pointed at Beecher, a grin lighting up his face, "can I bum one?"

Exhaling, a gush of smoke poured from Beecher's lips. "One what?"

"Burley," pointed Quince, grinning.

Beecher coughed, trying to find the words. "Burley?"

Quince nodded.

"When did you take up smoking?" asked Beecher, grimacing.

Quince shrugged his wiry shoulders, "Picked it up."

"Picked it up?"

"Picked it up," Quince answered.

"It's a bad habit."

"No doubt," Quince shrugged.

Beecher's blue eyes rolled. His lips bent and he sighed in capitulation. Digging through his jacket, he retrieved a half-empty pack, tapped the pack and the filter of a burley jutted out.

Quince pulled it free, put it loosely against his dry lips, and opened his palm.

Beecher's blue eyes rolled. His cheeks rose, slightly, as he smiled, and slapped a lighter into Quince's palm.

"Thanks," smiled Quince, nodding. He struck the lighter and held the burley tip over the flame. Swallowing smoke, he gave Beecher the lighter and squinted.

"There's something else. Something I need to say," Beecher continued just as he took the lighter and pushed it in his pocket.

"Yeah," answered Quince, squinting.

Beecher's lips twisted as he watched Quince smoke for the first time. He turned and lifted the beer to his lips, sucking it dry. "Skeeter," he yelled, "two more."

Skeeter filled two glasses, and left them on the bar.

"I went to town last week. Stopped by the Hole in the Wall."

"Of course," Quince retorted.

Beecher chuckled, continuing, "Stopped by the house. You know? Check on things."

Concern immediately wrinkled Quince's face. He dragged from the burley and listened.

"Looked through the front window. You know? The one on the porch?"

"Yeah," Quince answered. As Beecher spoke, Quince felt his heart run. His stomach soured.

"Saw some lights on," Beecher continued, staring into his glass. "Knocked but no one answered." Beecher paused, looking up, "You know how they were supposed to spend the summer with Sara's parents?"

"Yeah."

"Stay in Cincinnati?"

"Yeah."

"Well," Beecher's head shook. "Don't know. Maybe. But it was odd."

"How?"

"Well. The house just looked lived in."

"Lived in? That ain't right," burst Quince. "They're in Cincinnati. Sara said so."

Beecher nodded. His thin, white beard crowded together in a frown.

"Did someone break in?" Quince asked. His face was contorted. His chest ran.

Beecher's bald, shiny head shook, "Nope. I walked around the house. Checked things. Door was locked. Windows weren't broken. The neighbor. You know? The old man was mowing his back yard."

"Mr. Price."

"Yeah. Larry Price. Well, he says Sara and Lilly moved back in a month or so ago. Just came home one day. Says he don't talk to them much."

Quince's eyes narrowed. "Moved in?"

Beecher's head shook as he dragged from the burley. "Tried calling Sara but no answer. Just kept ringing. Nothing." Exhaling, smoke poured from a small gap in his beer-moistened lips.

Quince shook his head. He set the glass on the bar. The burley lay between his fingers, smoldering. "Makes no sense," he worried.

Beecher nodded. Solemnly, he rested a hand on Quince's shoulder. "Well. I'm sure it's nothing. Besides. You shouldn't trouble yourself anymore tonight. You just got here. Rest. You'll be home soon."

"Yeah," Quince agreed. Reluctantly lowering his voice, his eyes focused somewhere else, "Tomorrow I reckon."

Beecher's cheeks sank as he sucked the burley. He exhaled, slowly pouring smoke across the bar, lifted the beer to his lips and tilted the glass. Exhaling again as he swallowed, he shouted, "Drink up, son. You're home." Beecher slapped his son's wiry shoulder, climbed onto the bar, stood and shouted, "My boy's home! Let's hear it for my boy!" He shouted. His short legs bending as he shouted. A stagger formed in his step as he strutted down the bar, "Skeeter," he yelled, holding the empty glass, "another for my boy. Me too!"

Bikers cheered. Some laughed.

Beecher staggered back up the bar, "Son," he chuckled, embarrassed, "help your old man down."

Night quickly passed. Father and son and the bikers drank until dawn. As morning arrived, Quince helped Beecher down the stairs as an orange glow formed over the water. Beecher staggered across the parking lot, kicking gravel and a thin film of snow with his boots. He staggered, stopped at the bike, threw his leg over the seat and fell across the handlebars.

"No. No," refused Quince. "Where's the room?"

Beecher awkwardly pointed down a street and Quince shook his head. "Let's go," he said, pulling Beecher from the bike.

"Go?" he stammered, falling to the ground. Gravel and dusty snow rose around him.

"Let's go . . . we're walking."

"Walking?" Beecher shouted, staggering. "Beecher Magowan don't walk nowhere."

Quince held his father by the shoulders and proclaimed, "He does tonight." He led Beecher down a dim, empty street. Flurries stuck to their faces as they staggered along a sidewalk, turning left on Main Street. They swayed and staggered and laughed when the other fell, slipping on the wet pavement. A few blocks away, they checked into the hotel. Beecher slept, fully clothed, in bed. Quince wrapped himself in a sheet, sank into a recliner, closed his eyes, and finally fell asleep.

Two hours later, he woke. His eyes creased and opened. He stood and staggered across the room, and leaned over the bed, shaking his father. "Dad, let's go," he shouted. Beecher lay straddled across the undisturbed bed. The bed rocked back and forth as Quince nudged him but Beecher's small frame was motionless. He rocked like a boat on choppy waters. "Dad," Quince continued, "let's go. I'll be late!"

Beecher, lying on his stomach, rolled over. Still wearing his leather jacket, the collar fell across his face as he turned. "All right," he stammered, pushing the collar away. "All right. I'm coming." He slowly rose, rubbing his red-speckled eyes, and bearded cheeks. He looked around, disoriented, stood, and they left, retracing the route they traveled hours before. They walked along a sidewalk on Main and turned right on a narrow street that led to the bar. When they arrived, Beecher's bike was alone in the graveled lot. Beecher was sobering. He quickly straddled the seat, jumped on the kick-start and the pipes roared.

Quince sat, and lifted his boots from the gravel just as Beecher twisted the gas handle, and lifted his feet. The bike sped down a narrow street, turning right onto Main. It crossed the bridge, carrying them along the main thoroughfare. At the gate, Quince held up his ID, and an MP waved them through. As they passed from the MP's sight, Beecher accelerated down the thoroughfare, circled General Lejeune's statue, and rolled to a stop in front of the CP. Quince leapt from the bike, jogged into the CP, ran down a hall, and searched through a stack of sea bags until he found the one with a large M on the bottom. Pulling wrinkled camouflage utilities from the bag, he quickly stripped, changed, and ran into the yard behind the CP. There, Marines had already gathered.

As he walked among them, the snow had melted. A cool sun hung above the camp. The Marine company stood in brown, dying grass encircled by four two-story barracks. Quince searched through the masses, eyeing his squad across the compound. He walked with purpose, using long, deliberate strides. "Gather in. Bring it in," he said to the Marines of 1st Squad. The Marines moved closer, forming a circle around him. "I got something to say before we secure. Before we all go home. Go our separate ways." He paused, looking into each man's eyes. "It was a long time. Long work-up. Long deployment. But . . ." he paused, nodding his head as if convincing himself, "it was worth it. Hope we did some good there. Helped that village. The valley. Hope, somehow, we gave a better future to those kids who play in the fields each evening." Pausing, he looked around. "I just wanted to say I'm proud of you. You did well." Looking around, pausing, he said, "Let's all keep the memory of Sergeant Patrick with us, no matter how far we go from the Kunar River Valley."

The squad was quiet. As he finished, First Sergeant shouted, "Company! Attention!"

The masses moved like a giant puzzle, sidestepping, some moving forward, aligning themselves with the Marine ahead of them and at their side. The clapping sound of boot-heels snapping together echoed across the compound. First Sergeant completed an about-face, saluting the captain who stood frozen behind him. Captain saluted and First Sergeant stepped away. "Marines," he paused, "it's damn good to be home, uh?"

The Marines cheered. "Oorah," echoed across the compound. Captain paced around, soaking in the attention. Cold air popped from his mouth as he smiled and chuckled. "I won't keep you. Your families are waiting." Pausing, stopping, he grew solemn, "You did a damn good job out there. You earned this time with your families." Pausing, he grinned, "Stay safe. Enjoy yourselves . . ." he stopped pacing and noted, "but not too much!"

Marines chuckled.

He froze, growing solemn, "Company," he shouted, "disss-misssed."

"Aye-aye, sir," they shouted, stepping back, and completing an about-face.

The formation broke apart, filtering away. Quince moved with purpose, quickly exiting the compound. He ran into the CP, stripped, changed into the clothes he wore last night, stuffed the utilities into the sea bag, threw the bag over his shoulders, and walked down the hallway. Suddenly, he stopped near a wall lined with photographs, the same place he paused last night. But now, there was something different. A new face hung among the old, faded photographs. It was familiar. Freckles sprinkled across his nose and cheeks. A wide grin. Thick neck. Leathery skin and hazel eyes. Someone hung a photograph of Sergeant Patrick last night. Standing there, Quince's face contorted. His eyes watered. He gently laid his fingers on the glass, said a prayer, turned, and left the CP.

Beecher's bike rumbled as Quince jogged down the sidewalk, away from the CP. Now, it was time for Quince to leave. This was it. He felt done. He threw his leg over the seat, and the bike sped away, down the narrow street, passing the circle. Gathered around General Lejeune's statue were a dozen bikes, rumbling in the cold morning air. Frost pulled at their exhaust as Beecher circled the statue again and again, taking a victory lap for Quince's return. As Beecher turned down the main thoroughfare, bikers laughed and cheered before following him.

For a final time, Quince turned and looked at the dark statue. The general's face glowed in a cold sun. It was as if he were looking directly at Quince, telling him something or maybe congratulating him for his service. Quince's cheeks blushed in the frosty air. Blood pooled in his face. He felt an odd blend of satisfaction and guilt—a wanting to stay and go, each equal in their influence on him. As the statue shrank, he turned and looked west. It was time to go home.

Chapter 19
≈ Home ≈

Quince slid the sea bag from his sore shoulders, tossing it to the pavement. He stood and paused, staring at the modest brick home tucked away in a corner of an aging subdivision. It was a quiet evening. Winter had come early. Two giant oaks stood bare near the street. Across the yard, his SUV sat in the grass, near a one-car garage. Leaves had fallen, littering the windshield or scattered across the yard, drifting against steps or trapped against the wall by strong gales.

Quince paused. Silent, he stared at the house. He did not move or blink or breathe. His steps were frozen, weighted by seven months of dreams and memories of this place. Emotion bound him to the cold pavement with stronger bonds than the gravitational laws that allowed him to move free. He stood before the small ranch home in awe, the same awkward way a virgin traveler stands in the shadow of the Eiffel Tower. Mouth closed. Eyes wide and glassy, moist with wonder.

Behind him, the bike rumbled and fell silent. Beecher kicked open the stand and stood, stretching his stiff legs. “Reckon they’re home?” he asked, walking in circles, stretching.

Quince shrugged. “Don’t know,” he answered, frowning. He finally sighed and stretched his back, straightening the kinks of a ten-hour ride. The day had been long.

They had ridden far and the miles gave him time to think. He thought about what Beecher said at the bar. And, as tires hummed in his ears and he rode through the Carolina flats, up the West Virginia mountains, and down into the Bluegrass, he worried. He thought about the long deployment. Weeks that passed without receiving a letter. Weeks Sara did not write. He thought about how Sara’s letters flowed early in deployment; letters mourning his absence, filled with the promises of a good life when he returned. Letters, written in Sara’s smooth penmanship, talking of good days with Lilly and nights she cried for her daddy. How the letters flowed, flowed like the sweet waters of the Kunar River. Thought about how things were better when the letters came. Days seemed shorter. How he cherished them. Kept them in the SAPI pouch of his flak, and read them again at night, in the concrete hooch, as others slept. Thought about how they came fewer as weeks passed. Thought about how they dried up at the end.

Quince was frozen again.

"Going in?" asked Beecher.

Quince shrugged.

"Go on," he said, waving a hand.

Quince was silent, expressionless. A strange feeling overcame him. It was his home. He and Sara bought the house. He signed the papers. His name was on the deed. He lived there before deployment. A summer ago, he had trimmed the grass, and planted a magnolia on the corner and daylilies below their bedroom window. It was his home but somehow it felt wrong to simply open the door and walk in. He felt like an intruder. Too many days had gone by. Months of absence had smudged his identity. Sure. He was still Quince. Still the owner of this home. Still Sara's spouse and Lilly's father—but months were gone and he simply was unable to walk through the door and renew his old life. Take up where the old Quince left off. His feet were frozen to the pavement. Cast in the frozen ore of the Kunar River Valley.

Suddenly, the front door flew open and a thin girl with blonde curls bounced down the steps. "Daddy!" she screamed. Her arms raised high above her shoulders. A young lady, smiling, followed close behind.

Quince's features opened. His eyes swelled. Cheeks lifted.

"Lilly?" he asked. Trepidation splintered his voice as the young girl, who was too tall to be his daughter, ran toward him. As she ran, he stooped slightly and his arms breached, not wide. The young girl ran into his arms, screaming, "Daddy!" Quince pulled the girl into his arms, kissed her cheek, and began to weep. His eyes watered. Tears dripped down his ruddy cheeks.

Lilly's head lay across his shoulder as Sara jogged down the driveway, smiling. Her large brown eyes were wide, and her teeth were white as the flurrying snow. She leaned into Quince as he stooped, still holding Lilly, and wrapped her arms around both of them. "Missed you," she cried, spilling large tears from the corner of her eyes. She cupped Quince's face, pulled him lower, and kissed him. Tears trailed down her cheeks, soaking his lips. For the first time in months, Quince tasted lipstick and perfume and Sara's salty tears. For the first time in months, he felt something soft.

"Missed you," he added, smiling as their lips broke apart.

Sara stroked his face, gently rubbing his cheeks with the top of her fingers, stroking his features as if he were some statue, some likeness of her husband—a bust of Tom Quincy Magowan.

Lilly was quiet, contently holding her father, wrapping her arms around his neck and laying her head on his shoulder. Quince did not smile or laugh. He was overcome with joy, relief, but the shock of being home overwhelmed him.

"Dad," Sara greeted, throwing her arms around Beecher.

Beecher smiled and hugged Sara, who said, "Thanks for everything. Thanks for bringing him home."

Beecher nodded and grinned, flashing his false teeth.

Sara turned to Quince and admitted in a weak voice, "Sorry."

Quince's looked puzzled. "About what?" he asked.

Sara shrugged, "That we weren't there when you landed." A light frost caught her words.

Quince shook his head, "Don't be. It was too far. Too cold."

"We wanted to be . . ." she pled.

"It's OK."

"Would've been hard on her."

"You did the right thing," he insisted.

Sara smiled, reluctantly. "Come on," she begged, wrapping her arm around Quince's waist, nudging him up the driveway, "let's go in."

Beecher turned, threw a leg over the seat, and straightened the bike, lifting the kickstand.

"Dad, you ain't coming in?"

Beecher's head twisted, "Reckon not."

"Come in," said Quince.

"Yeah. You can't leave now," continued Sara. "You rode far. Stay with us tonight."

Beecher shook his head, answering in a scratchy voice, "Best get home."

Beecher leaned forward, and stroked Lilly's curls, "Pappaw's leaving."

Lilly dropped her arms around Beecher's neck. Blonde curls fell around his face, and his bald head.

"Tomorrow morning?" Beecher asked Quince. "Early?"

Quince paused, nodding. His lips folded, before parting as he answered in a flat, confident tone, "Not too early."

Beecher nodded.

His cheeks rose as his lips breached in a guilty grin. "Might sleep in," he said.

Beecher laughed. His chest bounced as he answered before starting the bike, "You earned it kid." The bike rumbled. Beecher smiled at Lilly, winked, and rode away.

Quince stood in the driveway, watching his father ride away. Watching as the bike roared down the street, slowed, turned, and disappeared.

"Come on," begged Sara, "let's go in."

Quince, Lilly in his arms and Sara at his side, walked up the driveway, climbed the steps, and crossed the threshold. Tom Quince Magowan was finally home. His war, he thought, was over.

Chapter 20
≈ The Next Morning ≈

He sat shoulder slumped over a cup of coffee. Squinting, his eyes were tightly focused on a vision—a place he held in his mind. A place hidden to those around him but one he conjured up with ease. Places like this one just materialized. They opened wide, dripping both bright and drab colors and emanating foul smells, quaint and the most violent sounds to Quince and only Quince while those near him were held hostage by the walls around them and the ceiling above their heads. These places just came to him. Pulling him into other worlds. Different dimensions. They squeezed him hard for minutes and sometimes hours before the grip reluctantly slipped. That morning, his squinting eyes blinked as steam rose from the black pool, wringing tiny beads of sweat from his brow and massaging skin pulled drum-tight over his cheeks.

He was alone in the kitchen. The lights were off but the room was dimly lit by a morning sky. Drops of rain tapped boards on a deck just outside a sliding glass door. Spongy clouds slipped east. Rain fell as he sighed and slurped the coffee. His face was calm and bland. He blew and slurped until a horn echoed in the driveway. He stood, pulled a hoody over his head, grabbed the cup, and went out the front door and into the rain. There, Beecher's giant red truck idled in the driveway. The old man's bald head glowed through a cold rain. He was hunched over as if trying to get warm.

"Damn it's early," Beecher sighed, blowing, slurping coffee from a silver mug as Quince opened the door and scooted into the seat.

"You too?" Quince chuckled.

"Damn warm front blew in overnight. Snow changed to rain," he cursed.

"Reckon."

Beecher turned, pulled the gearshift, and the truck slid down the driveway, onto the abandoned street. Beecher lifted the cup to his lips, hidden under his neatly clipped beard, blew, slurped and asked, "Think about what I told you? What to say?"

Quince nodded as if he anticipated the question. His cheeks rose, grinning as if the exercise was unnecessary.

"Aches, pains," he mocked, blowing, slurping. Outside, rain tapped the hood. Wipers swung wildly back-and-forth.

"Dreams," prodded the old man, ignoring the street as he gazed at Quince.

Quince shook his head with disgust. "I ain't telling them. Not about the dreams."

"What?"

"No!"

"We done talked about it. You and I."

"Hell no!"

Beecher's face pinched. Drew up. His bony finger bent, pointing at Quince. "We talked about this."

Quince rolled his eyes. He shrugged, "I'm not mentioning the dreams."

"We agreed."

Quince shook his head.

"What is it? What's wrong?"

Quince shrugged.

"What?"

"I ain't talking about it! It's done."

Beecher shook his head, sighed, and slurped coffee.

Quince sat quietly. He turned and watched rain though the window.

Beecher sighed again as he set the mug between his short legs. "We agreed you'd talk about the dreams. About what happened over there. You need to tell them. Let them know now," he insisted.

Quince turned. His face was flush. His lips, bent. "You want me to tell them how the drill instructor yelled at us?"

"No."

"Tell them I was scared?"

"Stop the bullshit."

"Tell them I hated loud noises."

"That's enough!" shouted Beecher.

Quince's features mashed together.

Beecher's bald head was red, afire with blood. Outside, rain tapped the hood. Wipers swung as an awkward silence faded. Beecher sighed, nodding. He sat straight and nodded. "Listen, son," he said in a calm, serious tone. "Don't underestimate the dreams. They're strange. They have ways of sticking around. Taking over until one day you just look up and your world is gone. Your life a wreck. Strange ways."

Quince was quiet. His lips were clenched and air whistled through his nostrils.

"Tell them now. While they're new."

Quince gently shook his head. Outside, rain fell as the truck wove through dreary streets, down a ramp and onto a busy thoroughfare. A few miles passed in silence as the truck turned and squeezed through a tall, black, wrought-iron gate. The gate guarded an iron fence sectioned by brick columns and crowned with stone. Beecher steered through a narrow asphalt street, and wove around giant poplars and white oaks. He slowed, turned right, and pulled into a parking space.

Quince set his coffee in a holder, opened the door, and stepped down from the truck. He turned and froze. His face opened. Eyes swelled as he looked upon the giant building for the first time. Brick, the hospital was outlined with gray stone corners. Several stories rose above ancient trees. Two sweeping stairways, made of stone, circled either side of the front door. Large blue cedars grew near the base of both stairways. Drab and motionless, they stood as if sentries guarding entry to the building.

Drops of rain tapped Quince's shoulder, smacked the crown of his head and soaked his hair. Rain trickled down his temple, dripping from his brow as he stared at the massive structure. An eerie feeling overcame him. Something surreal. Growing up, he had listened as Beecher and his grandfather talked about this old building. About long journeys from the farm to this hospital. He heard them speak of treatments and veterans who needed help. Sick. Old. Dying veterans, afflicted by common ailments and ailments uncommon to those who did not serve. Quince listened and their words formed images in his youthful mind; images of old, worn men. Men forgotten by their country except during a rare parade or sparsely attended ceremony. Those were simply well intentioned placebos, he thought. That's all. Nothing more. Ceremonies offered on occasion while these men suffered daily, long after the fireworks were extinguished and the flags taken down from light poles.

"Come on," said Beecher. "Let's get out of this rain." Hunching, he jogged across a parking lot, along a sidewalk and up a stairway. His stiff legs barely bent as he moved. On a wide stone landing, Beecher turned, opened a glass door, and held it for Quince.

Quince was frozen. Rain splashed his hair. Cold drops slid down his neck. Sighing, he walked up the stairs, water splashing at his feet as he climbed the steps. An old man, hunched, leaning against a cane, also climbed the steps. His wife, gray and bent, held his arm, lifting the man over each step. He was soaked. Raindrops pelted his fedora, and the back of his stooped neck, soaking into a maze of wrinkles. The old woman's hair became matted as the drops grew thick, falling quickly, stinging her soft, thin skin. The old couple slowly ascended the steps one stone at a time. Beecher, holding the door, saw them, let the door shut, jogged across the rain-soaked platform and down the stairs. He took the old man's free arm, and lifted him over each stone. "Here," he begged, "let me help."

"Six legs are better than four," quipped the old man.

Jogging up the steps, Quince stopped aside the old woman. "Ma'am," he said, "I'll help." The old woman looked up at Quince. Thin, gray hair fell flat over her forehead. Her ashen, wrinkled face, opened in a broad smile, and she stepped away. "Thank you," she said in a broken voice.

Raindrops fell on the pavement as Quince grabbed his free arm, and together he and Beecher lifted the old man over each step and onto the landing. Beecher let go of the old man, walked purposefully across the landing, and opened the door. Quince ran back to help the old woman up a few remaining steps while the old man limped over the threshold. Pausing, he turned, leaned on a cane, and waited for his wife. Quince ushered the old woman across the platform and inside while Beecher held open the door. Inside, the elderly couple thanked them before disappearing through a lobby and into the elevator.

Digging through his black leather jacket, Beecher produced a handkerchief, and handed it to his son. Quince stared at the white cloth, flashing a curious expression. "Seriously?" he asked.

"Go ahead," Beecher waved the cloth, offering it to Quince. "I ain't used it. It's clean."

Quince nodded. Gratitude pulled a grin over his face as he took the cloth and wiped water from his forehead and the back of his neck. He handed the handkerchief back to Beecher who dried himself, shoved the cloth in his jacket, and approached a reception desk. "Excuse me? Excuse me, sir?" asked Beecher, speaking to the man behind the desk. He was reading a newspaper.

The old man slowly dropped the newspaper. His face was gaunt, long, drooping from decades of gravity, sectioned with layered wrinkles. He wore a blue cap, adorned with gold-stitched words that read, "Iwo Jima." He did not speak but his eyes focused. His bottom lip was moist, quivering.

Beecher's blue eyes became swollen. "Semper Fi," he replied.

The old Marine offered a soft smile. His quivering lips formed, and a weak, broken voice whispered, "Semper Fi, son."

Beecher turned to Quince. "My boy here just left the Corps." Beecher laid his arm over Quince's shoulder. "It's his first time here. He needs to register."

The old Marine slowly lifted a hand, pointing a bent finger down the hallway. "Take the elevator to the second-floor lobby. Check in with the nurse at the desk." His finger slowly dropped as a weak voice faded.

Beecher smiled. "Just got back from the desert," bragged the father.

"Oh?" whispered the Marine. "Hear it's bad. Hot too. Good thing getting Saddam."

Quince's face sank. His features became still. He considered correcting the old man, but thought better of it. Instead, he shrugged, agreeing, "Yes it was."

Beecher nodded to the old veteran as they left, and disappeared into an elevator that carried them to the second-floor lobby. He looked at Quince, even as they faced the elevator door, rising between floors. "Tell them everything. Aches. Pains. Dreams. Don't matter. Say it. Get it recorded."

Quince sighed. His face rose to the elevator's ceiling as he watched two blurred reflections in the shiny metal. At first, he didn't recognize the young man staring down at him. After more than seven months in desert digital camouflage, it felt strange to be in civilian clothes. After months of carrying a weapon everywhere he went, his hands felt empty. With training and deployment, he lived with the same people, seeing them and only them each day. A family of two hundred. It was odd, intimidating even, to see so many strangers. Now, as the elevator slowly rose to the second floor, he grew nervous. His pulse raced. His chest bounced and the thought of telling a stranger about his fears made him feel like vomiting. As the elevator stopped, and the doors parted, he trudged forward.

Together, he and Beecher approached a nurse standing behind a desk.

She stared at them over thick, brown-framed glasses. "Can I help you?" she asked in a serious, flat voice.

"My boy needs to check in. He just got out," Beecher bragged.

The nurse's face was expressionless as she looked at Beecher. She assembled a small stack of forms, attached them to a clipboard, and offered them to Quince. "Here. Fill these out," she said, pointing with an ink pen to a row of seats near the desk.

Quince forced a smile, and took the clipboard.

Beecher examined his watch, "Gotta run. My appointment's on the third floor. You good here?"

Quince nodded, answering sarcastically, "Yeah. Fine. Just freaking fine."

"Meet you here when I'm done," Beecher announced, walking quickly away.

Quince stood near the desk. He looked around, scanning the busy lobby. All around him, seated in the rows of chairs, pacing halls, waiting for the elevator, were ailing veterans. Some were old; his grandfather's generation. Their thin, white hair and frail bodies stooped as they stood. Most were younger, but aging. Beecher's generation. Some were gray, others were graying. Some thin. Some fat. Some wore jackets adorned with military emblems. Others just wore plain clothing.

It was odd. The peculiarity of it sank in slowly. Standing in that busy lobby, watching ailing veterans, Quince noticed something. One simply needed to look around and see that they were all aging. All of them. Every veteran. Each one gray or graying. Not one of those patients was younger than fifty. It was strange. Peculiar. He felt uncomfortable. Like he somehow didn't belong, and questions began to flood his thoughts. These were veterans of 20th-Century wars. How does a veteran of a war still being fought fit in with these men? How does a veteran of Afghanistan fit in among these men? How does a young man, healthy, no physical wounds, fit in with these veterans, suffering from wounds of Korea and Vietnam, and the ailments of an aging body? His head shook, as if someone was asking these questions of him, and he was supposed to answer them. But he couldn't. The answers weren't there. Suddenly, guilt came over Quince. He felt ashamed for just being there.

Veterans stepped around Quince as he stood in the aisle. "Sir. Sir," complained the nurse, "please take a seat and finish the paperwork." Quince's face went flat, slightly embarrassed, as if awakened from sleep. He clumsily scanned the lobby for an empty chair, even as several men, sitting comfortably in the front row, watched him with curious faces. Quince just ignored them. He finally spotted an empty seat near the back, made his way through the crowd, sat, and began studiously completing the forms. The first form asked standard questions: name, address, height, weight. He finished that page and quickly reviewed the information. Only then did he realize he had written the APO address for Camp Stanton instead of his home address. *Are you kidding me!* A voice cursed in his head. *Dumb ass! You ain't there anymore!* His head shook as he stooped over the clipboard, writing with one hand and massaging his forehead and rubbing his eyes with the other. Finally, he sighed and reasoned that it was a simple mistake. Hell. It was home for seven months. He simply thought of it as his home since he wrote that address on so many letters to Sara.

He quickly drew a single line through the address, paused, and tried to recall his home address. Finally, he nodded and wrote down the address of the plain ranch home.

Turning the page, he quickly scanned a list of allergies. He made a check in the box that read none and flipped the page. Ailments were listed on the next page, and he checked none again. The next page asked about combat experience. Quince checked yes.

Exposure to small arms fire: Yes.

Exposure to a sudden blast: Yes.

Exposure to repeated loud sounds: Yes.

Physical wounds resulting from combat: No.

Trouble Hearing: No.

Trouble Sleeping: Quince rolled his eyes, and sighed, lifting his head. *Oh hell*, he silently cursed. He knew if he checked yes, the doctors would pry—ask him questions he didn't want to answer. Prescribe things that won't help. But sitting there, he could hear Beecher's raspy, whisky voice, chastising him to check yes. *Go on. Mark it down. Tell them.*

Quince sighed and checked yes. He stood, walked to the desk, handed the clipboard to the nurse, and returned to his seat. Nurses, wearing light blue scrubs, darted around ailing patients. A loud drone of chattering voices filled the lobby, occasionally interrupted by a voice shouting a patient's name. Nearby, veterans searched the lobby, watching as an old man stood, and followed a nurse down the hall. And as they disappeared, others went about their waiting, fidgeting, watching, listening, or browsing through an old magazine. Some dozed. Most just sat, bored.

Occasionally, Quince looked around the lobby, but mostly he just stared at the floor. After a while, he felt the burn of someone's stare. He felt the weight of someone's eyes focused on him. Minutes slowly ticked away and the burn began to irritate him, even as his eyes focused on the dirty tiles beneath his feet. Then, a deep, scratchy voice, asked, "Waiting on your father?"

Quince looked into the man's eyes, partially shadowed by the bill of a cap. A thick, graying mustache hung from his lip. The collar of a plaid shirt rose out of his jacket, hiding a turkey neck.

"Nope," Quince answered, shaking his head.

"Saw that man with you. Figured he's your old man."

Quince nodded.

"So you're waiting on him?"

"Nope," Quince answered, a stern texture in his voice. "Waiting to see the doc."

The man's eyes swelled, growing full and round as an awkward moment passed. "Doctor?" he asked.

Quince nodded.

"You a veteran?" asked the old man.

Quince held his stare, nodding.

The man's eyebrows lifted under the bill, pushing the cap even higher. His bottom lip buckled under an un-trimmed mustache.

Quince nodded.

The man turned, staring straight ahead. He seemed mystified as thoughts tumbled across his tongue, "We don't see many your age." His head twisted, as he said, "Reckon they'll get younger seeing how we got ourselves involved in two wars. But we ain't seen them yet. At least not here."

Quince sat silent. His face was still, motionless. His hands were buried in the pockets of his hoody.

"Reckon the VA needs young men like you."

Quince said nothing.

"You young fellas are here to replace us old men."

Quince shook his head, "I ain't here to replace anyone."

"Ah," growled the man, "just look around." The old man lifted his arm, waving a bent finger across the lobby. "Anyone can see. Just look around."

"I'm just here to register. That's all. I won't be back. Not here," explained Quince.

The old man ignored him, continuing, "Just look around. What's missing?"

Quince was silent. He didn't bother to answer or lift his face to scan the room as the old man asked. "Young men," proclaimed the stranger. "We're all old here. Every darn one of us." The aging man shifted in his lobby chair, sitting up, leaning into Quince. "Look, the VA's treated me right here, in this very hospital, since I got back from Vietnam in '68. Nearly forty years," he exclaimed as eyebrows pushed his cap higher. Then, he turned, pointing at an old man sitting in the front row. "Now you take Harry." The old man's bald, sun-freckled head, leaned back, stiffly attempting to turn upon hearing his name. "Harry served in Korea. Uh, what year was you in Korea?"

"Huh?" grumbled the old man, attempting to twist his stiff neck.

"I say what year were you in Korea?" shouted the man, leaning forward.

"Oh . . . Fifty two," answered the old man.

The man leaned back into his lobby chair. "That old man," he said, pointing to a frail person whose gown hung loose from his thin frame as he rode in a wheelchair across the lobby. Pushed by a nurse, he sat with an elbow nestled on the armrest. His chin sat neatly in the palm of his wrinkled hand. "That old man was on Guadalcanal."

The stranger's bent finger waved around before pointing to the tile floor. "He's been treated here for 60 years. Right here, in this old hospital."

Quince broke his stare with the stranger, and his eyes wandered around the crowded lobby. All around, old veterans filled the lobby chairs or moped away from the elevator, down the hall. A deep drone echoed from the tile floors, a melody of chatter, coughing, footsteps. The lobby looked tired and ill.

"I'm sick," proclaimed the man. "I'm here all the time." His head shook. His bottom lip buckled under his mustache. "I ain't never seen a man young as you here. Not from these wars. You're a first."

Quince sat silent.

"Makes sense."

"I reckon," answered Quince.

"Boys over there are losing arms and legs. Sure . . ." he professed, crossing his own arms, and resting his chin against his chest. "Those things happened in Vietnam. Korea. But," nodding his head, "it's different now. These wars are different." He sat up, twisted in his seat, and leaned into Quince. "Saw a boy on TV just the other night." The man shook his head vociferously. "He was burnt head-to-toe," his head shook, "ears . . . eyebrows . . . even his nose . . . gone." The old man grew quiet. He crossed his arms, and his face fell still.

Quince tucked his hands into the pockets of his hoody. Flashes of the Kunar River jumped around in his head. Smoke from Sergeant Patrick's hi-lux tingled in his nose.

The stranger pointed a bent finger across the lobby, "It changes things. Yep. Things will change someday soon. No longer will it be a VA of old men suffering with old men ailments." His head shook. "Young men and new wars will bring different sicknesses. It changes how they treat veterans. What they treat veterans for. Thousands more, maybe millions, will need help. More buildings are needed. New equipment. Doctors. It's new medicine." His bent finger waved around the lobby, "In all these years I been coming here, things ain't changed. Same old building. Few new coats of paint," his head shook, "but that's all. Paint, not concrete. Just Band-Aids."

Quince held a stare with the stranger. Deep wrinkles spilled from the corner of the old man's eyes. His cheeks were tan and sallow, split open as if sliced by a knife, cut with wrinkles. His eyes were full and watery and sad. They were asking something of Quince—pulling something out of the young veteran.

Suddenly, a woman's voice shouted, "Magowan," and the muttering crowd fell silent. Quince broke the stare, looking around, finding a nurse scanning the lobby from behind her thick-framed glasses.

Oddly, Quince did not answer. He quickly turned to face the aging man who yet stared at the young veteran. “Magowan!” echoed her voice but Quince held his stare with the stranger. The nurse held a clipboard to her eyes, focused, and dropped it again, letting it smack against her thick, round thighs. “Tom Quincy Magowan,” she shouted in a slightly agitated voice.

Quince finally nodded, stood, wove through the crowd and approached the nurse.

“Magowan?” she asked.

Quince nodded.

She sighed and wrote something in the clipboard. “Follow me,” she begged, moving determinedly through the hall before ducking into a small office.

“Have a seat,” she said, pointing to a metal chair near the wall.

Quince nodded, sat but said nothing. His face hung low. His eyes were stuck to the tile floor.

The nurse sighed as she sat at a desk with a computer, pounding a keyboard, giving Quince time to survey the room. It was nothing special. A patient’s chair sat in the middle. Around it, another metal chair was tucked away in the corner. A plain, white sink stood on the far side of the room. A radiator heater, twisted pipes smeared with layer upon layer of white paint, stood near the desk. The room was clean but old.

“All right,” said the nurse, “let’s get your blood pressure.” She stood, took a sphygmomanometer from the desk and approached Quince. “Roll up your sleeve,” she ordered.

Quince reached over his back and pulled the hoody over his shoulders. His head slid through the shirt. Wearing only a white undershirt, he offered the nurse his arm.

The nurse wrapped the cuff around his arm and pumped. “Hmmm,” she grunted. “Little high.”

Quince rolled his eyes.

The nurse removed the cuff, turned and began pounding the keyboard. “Do you smoke?” she asked.

“Just started,” retorted Quince, staring at a far wall.

“How long?”

“September 3rd.”

The nurse’s face twisted. One eye shut as she turned away from the screen, and faced him, “You remember the day?”

Quince paused, speaking in a low, solemn voice, “Was an important day.”

"Must be," retorted the nurse.

Quince sighed, nodding.

"How many packs a day?" she asked in a flat tone.

"Two."

"Drink?"

"Yes."

"How many alcoholic drinks do you consume in a week?"

Quince paused, thinking about the answer. "Depends."

"On what?"

"The month."

Her face twisted, "Month?"

"Yes."

"How does your alcohol consumption change within a month?"

"Doesn't. Not within the month. It's just changed a lot this year."

"How so?"

"Well," he paused, mentally reviewing a calendar, "last spring, before watching a game or something. I didn't drink during deployment. Weren't allowed. They would NJP our ass."

The nurse's face was flat, still as she listened.

"Only been back a few days. Since then . . . I've drank."

"How much?" she asked.

"Every day."

"How much each day?"

Quince threw a hand into the air, "I don't know . . . six or eight a day. Maybe more."

The nurse straightened her body, and began pounding the keyboard.

"Guess I'm trying to catch up on all the drinking I missed when I was in the Kunar." A thin smile lifted his cheeks.

"We have alcohol cessation classes. Are you interested?"

"No," he quickly answered.

"Your chart says you experienced a loud explosion?"

"That's right," Quince's face pinched.

"How close were you to the blast?"

His shoulders lifted then sank. "Fifty feet, maybe. Not really sure. I was behind the truck that got hit. We were driving fast . . ."

The nurse pounded a keyboard. "Do you have serious or frequent headaches?"

"No."

"Ringing in your ears?"

"No."

The nurse sighed. "After deployment, have you had trouble sleeping?"

Quince paused. Whispers of Beecher's voice bounced around in his head. *Tell them everything. Get it on record.*

Quince sighed, shrugged and answered, "Never slept well anyway."

The keyboard fell silent. "How many hours each night do you sleep?"

"After deployment?" he asked.

The nurse nodded.

Quince paused, shrugging, "I don't know. Four or five. Sometimes more. Sometimes less."

The keyboard clapped as the nurse typed. "Have you experienced bad dreams or nightmares about events that occurred during your deployment?"

Quince paused, expelling a sigh in frustration. His head twisted. His lips bent and a nod threw his head forward.

"Do these dreams occur every night?"

Quince nodded.

"Do these dreams involve the same incident?"

Quince nodded. Water gathered in the corner of his eyes.

"Have you experienced increased anger or frustration toward family or friends?"

Quince shook his head.

"OK." The nurse stopped typing. The keyboard fell silent again and she stood, walking toward the door. "Sit tight. The doctor will be here in a minute," she ordered, closing the door as she left.

Suddenly, Quince was alone. The room was quiet, empty. Five minutes passed. And another five. Quince looked at his watch. Twenty minutes became thirty. He waited. Silence settled into the room. Quince was patient. Waiting was something he was accustomed to. Waiting and boredom were a big part of his last year.

Finally, the door swung open and a middle-aged man, wearing a white coat, walked in and sat at the desk. His face was buried in a chart hung on a clipboard. He said nothing.

Quince offered a suspicious stare. Squinting, he watched the physician and waited for the man to speak. This was his office after all. His workplace. The man was entitled to speak first. Say what he needed to say.

Moments passed before his face rose, and he stuck out his hand. "Dr. Kimble," he greeted. A brief smile lifted his cheeks.

Quince shook the doctor's hand, answering in a dead tone, "Quince Magowan."

"So, Quince," he said, flipping a page, "you just got back, huh?"

Quince nodded.

"Well," he said, turning a page. Reading. "Everything looks good. Blood pressure is slightly elevated but that's likely due to your trouble sleeping." He paused, "Do you take anything to help you sleep?"

Quince shook his head.

"Well. If it continues, take an over-the-counter medication. Call me if that does not help . . . or, I should say, call the nurse. I am leaving soon."

Quince's face pinched. Suspicious eyes poured over the physician as he leafed through his file. "Leaving?" asked the young veteran.

"Yes."

"Where to?"

"University Hospital."

Quince nodded.

"Not sure who they will assign you."

Quince's eyes fell to the tile floor.

"I see you've experienced dreams about events that occurred during deployment."

Quince nodded.

"How long have you had them?" he asked, lowering the clipboard.

As the conversation progressed, Quince began to feel a certain comfort with the doctor. His soft voice was clean of accusation or sarcasm. Cleansed from judgment. He seemed experienced, as if he knew things to ask, to question. He was about the truth and Quince appreciated the brevity of it all.

"Couple months," he answered.

"Was there a significant event that occurred this year?"

Quince nodded, his lips bunching up.

"And what was that event?"

Quince paused. Water gathered in his eyes. "Saw things. Saw guys get shot. Buddy got killed. I was right behind him when it happened."

"And that's when the dreams first occurred?"

Quince nodded, "Had a few dreams before that but they're worse now."

"Are the dreams persistent? Do they occur most nights?"

Quince nodded. Lips bunched.

"Are they mostly about your friend? The day he died?"

Quince nodded again.

"Says here you have not shown anger against your family?"

Quince paused, "Yeah. I just got back yesterday. Barely seen them."

The physician leaned forward. "You are one of the first Iraq and Afghanistan War veterans I have seen here but I have heard about this. I know veterans have reported these symptoms."

Quince sighed.

"PTSD it's called. Post-Traumatic Stress Disorder. Brought about by sudden or persistent exposure to combat—or really any traumatic event." he continued. "It's not a diagnosis but you have some of the symptoms."

Quince's face pinched. His green eyes rose and leveled with the physician. "I ain't no coward," he said in a stern, aggravated voice.

"Of course not. It's just . . ." answered the doctor.

"I can handle what I've seen," he interrupted. "Hell. It ain't as bad as what most boys are going through in Iraq right now," Quince's face was flush. He jabbed a pointed finger into the air.

The physician paused, staring over the clipboard at the young man. "It's nothing new. Veterans of your father's and grandfather's wars experienced similar symptoms. It's been a symptom with veterans from all wars. Though I think . . ." he paused, reflecting, "I think it will be different for veterans of these wars."

Quince was silent, listening. His features softened, slightly.

"Wars have changed over the last century. Their nature has changed. World War II battles were fought with a defined line. You were either on the front lines or in the rear. But Vietnam . . . well . . . battle-lines were less defined. Sure, they had base camps but you were rarely in the rear as they say. Now," he paused, "with these wars . . . there is no rear. The enemy is everywhere—mixed into the population. In front of you. Beside you. Behind you. Persistent exposure to danger."

Quince listened, nodding as the physician fell silent.

"Well, I've carried on long enough," he said. "I recommend you see a clinical psychologist. A nurse will call you in the next few days to set up an appointment." The physician offered his hand to Quince and they shook. "Good luck, son. Welcome home," he said, smiling. He slapped Quince's shoulder and left the room.

Quince slumped into the metal chair. Silence quickly filled the room. Minutes passed. Beard stubble scratched as he rubbed his face, massaging stress from his tense features. Sighing, he nodded. *Not so bad*, he thought. *Talking about it. Hell. Dad should be happy. At least he'll get off my back now!* Soon, a nurse opened the door, "Mr. Magowan. Please follow me."

Quince stood and followed the nurse down a whitewashed hall. She stopped in a doorway and pointed to a row of chairs lined against the wall of a small waiting room. A placard that read *Hearing* hung from two thin chains above the door. "Wait here—they'll call you."

Quince sat in a chair near the door and waited. Soon, he was called for a hearing test, and he passed on the second attempt. A nurse told him to go downstairs to the lab and so he went down four flights of stairs to the basement. It was a cool, dark stairwell, and his steps echoed against the dungeon-like walls. In the lab, a nurse took several vials of blood, wrapped a bandage around his pierced vein, and dismissed him. The VA, she said, would call him or send a letter with the results.

Hands tucked into the pockets of his hoody, Quince slowly scaled the stairs, and walked down a hall to the main lobby, waiting for Beecher. Quince's eyes squinted as he sat, looking around the crowded room for his father. *Odd,* he thought. *Dad should be finished by now. He should be here waiting for me. Well. Maybe he bumped into someone he knew? Hell. He knows everyone.* A soft grin parted Quince's lips as he sighed. Bored, he began sifting through a stack of old magazines spread across a small end table. He eventually settled on a four-month old hunting magazine, and began leafing through it. It was missing pages, and the remaining pages were ripped and well worn, but photographs of camouflage-suited hunters, smiling over the carcass of a fallen deer, or a fisherman holding a striped bass on a boat in the swamps of Okeechobee Lake, were enough to distract Quince from his wait.

The magazine was published in June. It was a Father's Day edition. Page after page was filled with photographs of fathers and sons happily posing over their trophies, smiling in the frost of an autumn field or under the warm sun on a summer lake. Suddenly, Quince's lips parted and his eyes became creased. Looking at that photograph, he thought of a morning from a long time ago, where, as a boy, he stood on a flat rock near the cove of a mountain lake. He thought about holding a trophy smallmouth bass he had just caught. Thought about how proud it made Beecher. He thought about how Beecher had been there for him.

Some folks saw Beecher for what he showed on the outside—saw him for a man who had married five times. They saw him for the alcohol, and the cigarette that was always between his fingers. They saw him as a many-married drunk who talked a lot. But Quince knew better. He saw him as an imperfect man who had lived and experienced hardship and tragedy, and dulled the pain with vices and talk. He saw him as a man who was there for his family, devoted to his dying mother, dedicated to a farm his father adored—a man who loved his only son and his only grandchild. A man who loved his first wife, Quince's mother, Beecher's rock, his compass. She was the only woman in the world who could have leveled Beecher Magowan, and when she died, Beecher was destined to struggle with direction in his life. Most folks didn't see that part of Beecher. They couldn't. He disguised it with jokes and laughter, clouds of cigarette smoke. He soaked it all with the burn of stiff bourbon.

"They take care of you?" asked Beecher's voice from behind the hunting magazine.

Quince dropped the magazine, tossing it to the small table. "Yeah," he nodded. "Where've you been? Thought you'd finish before me?"

"Well," Beecher answered, looking into the crowded lobby, "it takes longer sometimes. You know? It's crowded and all." Beecher scratched his white beard as he spoke. "Let's get out of here," he said, urging Quince to his feet.

Chapter 21
≈ A Week Later ≈

She smiled. Brown, flirtatious eyes admired a man sitting across the table. A candle burned on the table between them. A soft, yellow flame washed their faces. Long, thin, the flame was composed, swaying only when patrons passed by or with a gush of laughter. When she grinned, the flame warmed her stare.

Occasionally, her thin fingers gently slid under the goblet, around the stem, lifting the bowl ever higher, before tilting and resting the rim on her thinly parted lips. Even as she drank, her eyes never broke with his. She sipped chardonnay, quietly setting the glass on the white-clothed table. Her motions were soft, easy.

His elbows lay on the table. Hands folded, his fingers were webbed together. Leaning forward, he grinned. "Your fettuccine?" he asked.

"Filling," she smiled. She fell against a cushioned seat back, rubbing her belly.

"And the wine?" he asked

Leaning forward, her fingers slid under the bowl, then lifted the glass to her lips and drank. Afterwards, she asked, "Your Malbec?"

He shrugged. "The truth?"

She nodded, smiling.

"Let's just say it's not a beer." He chuckled, shrugging, "I tried."

She nodded, "You like beer."

"I like a brew," he conceded.

"But you tried for me."

He nodded, grinning.

Her eyes softened as she leaned forward. A hand gently slid across the table, covering his hand.

He smiled, stood, and circled the table, stopping over her chair. He gathered the thick, dark coat, and pulled it apart at the collar.

Sara stood, brushed her hands across a thin dress, and slid through the opened coat. They turned, and walked confidently among a room of tables, lit by burning candles. Quince nodded to a hostess, who held the door as they left.

Outside, a hazy light lit the night sky. Street lamps glowed above them as Quince held open the door for his wife. Sara smiled. "Thank you," she grinned, stepping up into the SUV. Quince circled the truck, opened the door, and drove away.

Sara fidgeted with her phone. "Mom left a message. Lilly is already asleep. They've been playing hide-n-seek all evening."

Quince nodded knowingly. "She could hide in that big house all night and not be found."

Sara nodded, "Said she was exhausted."

Quince chuckled, "Lilly or your mom?"

Sara giggled. "Both . . . I'm sure."

As the laughter faded, her hand slid across the console, resting on his thigh. "Thank you, Quince, for this evening."

He turned, saying nothing. Her head was tilted, and she stared with a guilty grin. "You know," she announced, her face rose, gazing across the street, glowing from the light of street lamps, "I think I would like another glass of wine." Her brow rose and dropped, as she stared at him. "You?"

Quince's head shook, "I think I'll pass."

She laughed, clapping her hands. "We have beer at home."

Across town, Quince parked, opened the door, and circled the truck. Sara did not wait for her husband. One heel awkwardly stretched to reach the pavement. She slid, falling, but Quince stooped, grabbing her shoulders. Sara giggled like a child.

"Another glass of wine?" Quince asked, laughing.

Sara stood, and walked along the sidewalk. Her finger rose, "Just one more."

Quince grinned, shaking his head. He pulled keys from his pocket, opened the door, and Sara, then he, stepped inside.

Sara walked through darkness, across the den. Quince followed, flipped a switch and light flooded the empty home. His wife awkwardly swayed toward the kitchen. He smiled, loosened his tie, and followed her. Bottles clanked as Sara sifted through the refrigerator. She rose, hoisting a dark, brown bottle. "Beer for the man," she announced, stooping again.

"Thanks," Quince grinned, twisting the cap, and pulling the bottle to his lips.

She soon rose, holding a long, narrow bottle, slammed the door, grabbed a glass from a rack, popped a half-seated cork, and poured the glass full of red wine. Drops splashed the counter. "Oops," she laughed. Not bothering to clean the counter, she awkwardly swayed from the kitchen, down the hall, into the bedroom.

Quince followed his wife down the hall. While Sara disappeared into the bathroom, Quince dropped on the bed, unknotting his tie. He pulled the beer to his lips, drank, and set the bottle on a nightstand. The tie hung over his neck, dangling like two lifeless arms. Tired, he fell back, throwing his arms out as if he were a child flopping in the snow. The room was dark, illuminated only from light seeping around the bathroom door. A ceiling fan slowly spun overhead. A soft breeze brushed over his face, tearing up his eyes. He blinked, and moisture blurred his vision. He blinked again, and opened them. Across the bed, a blurry vision floated near his legs. Quince rose, propped up on his elbows, and blinked. Near his legs, Sara stood in lingerie. A soft, lavender top exposed her shoulders, and the top of her breasts. Quince smiled. A candle burned on the nightstand. Sara danced under the breeze, taking her lead from the swaying candle flame. She pulled the glass to her lips, drank, and set the glass near Quince's beer. Leaning across the bed, her lips dropped across his chin, rising to his lips; curly brown locks tickled his cheeks. She pulled her lips back, smiled, and grabbed his tie. Leaning, she pulled him upright, kissing him. She slid the coat from his shoulders, jerked the tie free, and unbuttoned her husband's shirt. Quince's hand brushed along her thighs, over her waist, and lifted the lingerie above her breasts, through her brown locks. She pushed the shirt from his shoulders, and kissed his chest. He kissed her neck and small, round shoulders.

Overhead, the fan slowly turned; wooden arms twisted like a windmill in a lazy breeze. The candle burned. A flame swayed in the soft breeze, and the gush of their twisting bodies. Quince slowly fell on his back, pulling Sara on top of him. She kissed his chest, rising, along his neck. Quince paused. His hands slipped from her shoulders, falling to the mattress, lifeless as the tie that once hung from his neck. Kissing his neck, Sara paused, falling back on her knees, sweeping hair away from her eyes. "What's wrong?" she asked, her face pinched.

Quince was still, a bewildered look on his face. "I . . . I'm not sure."

A soft smile lifted her lips as she stooped over him, kissing his chest. "It's been a while. Remember? The night before you left?"

Quince was still. "Yeah," he whispered.

Kissing his chest, her lips rose along his neck.

Quince lay there. His hands lifted, embraced her shoulders, and gently pushed them.

Sara fell back on her knees, sweeping hair from her eyes. “What’s wrong?” she asked.

“I don’t know.”

“You can do this.”

His head shook, “I can’t.”

“It’s just been a while . . . that’s all,” she begged.

“I know.”

“I’m your wife.”

“I know. I just can’t.”

“I don’t believe this.” Her head tilted, and she stared into the swaying flame. Her face pinched, disgusted. “What’s wrong? This is the third time.”

Quince blushed, “I’m trying, OK?”

“I know. It’s just that . . .”

“What?” he asked in a defensive voice.

She shrugged, looking away.

“What?”

“It’s just been so long.”

Quince was quiet. In his embarrassment, words left him, and he lay there in awkward silence.

Sara slowly turned, waiting for him to say something, but he was speechless. More than anything, he wanted to tell her how he felt, but he couldn’t find the right words. His face flush with embarrassment and frustration, he was unable to describe what was happening to him.

Finally, Sara slid off the bed, grabbed the lavender top from the floor, covered her breasts, and stormed down the hall.

Quince lay still, staring at the ceiling. Overhead, the fan slowly turned.

Chapter 22
≈ The Dreams ≈

His eyes twitched and fell open as the alarm on his phone rang. Quince slipped an arm out of the comforter, and clumsily searched the table until he found the phone and pressed a button. The room was silent again. He grunted and rubbed sleep from his eyes. It was dark and quiet. His legs slipped over the side of the bed, and he sat.

Next to him, the comforter slowly shifted as Sara squirmed. She pushed the comforter from her face, staring at the shadowy back of the figure leaning against the bed. Groggily, she said, "You've got to do something."

Quince turned halfway. He was silent. Across the room, the light of dawn leaked through a soft, beige curtain.

"You tossed and turned all night. Mumbled. Held conversations."

He chuckled, asking tersely, "With who?"

"I don't know," she answered.

"What did I say?"

"I don't know . . ."

"Who was I talking to?" Quince began to enjoy this.

"I don't know."

"A woman?" he joked.

"What?" she asked with a stern face.

"Now. If I were talking to a woman."

Sara sat, leaning against a pillow along the headboard. Her face was bland. "I'm serious," she continued. "You need to treat this. Get help. You've been home for more than a month and not once have you slept through the night. Not one time!"

Quince's voice became defensive. His face pinched. "I slept last night," he protested. "All night. Never woke."

"Quince," she said, "you tossed and turned."

"I slept."

"Talked in your sleep."

"I slept all night."

"Quince!" she interrupted. "You screamed."

"What'd I say?"

"I don't know."

"What?"

"I couldn't understand it."

"What was it?"

"Something about a bridge."

"Bridge?"

Sara nodded, "A bridge and a river."

"A bridge and a river?" he said sarcastically.

"Patrick, Dammit!" she shouted. "You screamed for Sergeant Patrick!"

Quince's face fell. He was quiet. Nodding, he turned and faced the wall.

Silence filled the dark room. Finally, Sara continued, her voice softer, calm. "Quince, you have these dreams every night. Not one time have you slept through the night without them. When are they going to stop?"

Quince was quiet, listening.

"When Quince? They're having this effect on all of us. They wake Lilly," she continued, her arms flailing as she pointed down the hall toward their daughter's room. "They wake me. You're not sleeping. Something's got to change. This is hard . . . We can't keep doing this."

Quince shrugged, turning to face her. "What do you want me to do?" he asked, anger lifting his voice. "Huh? I can't make them stop. I don't want them! You think I want them? You think I like sleeping a couple hours each night only to have this dream . . . this dream that seems so real . . . only to wake to see my friend's face? His mangled leg? His pain? Dying in agony? You think I like seeing that shit every night?" he shouted, jabbing a finger into the comforter.

Sara was quiet. Her face was twisted, frightened as she sat on the corner of their bed.

Suddenly, a small voice cried across the room, "Mommy?"

Startled, they both turned, falling silent when they saw Lilly standing in the doorway, blonde curls falling over her sleepy face. "Mommy, I can't sleep," she continued, struggling to hold a thick, plastic doll as it lay over her shoulder. Quince's face became smooth. His cheeks lifted as he forced a smile, watching the little girl shift the doll from shoulder to shoulder.

Sara slid her legs out of the comforter. Pushing it away, she moped across the room. “Honey, you need to go back to bed. It’s early.” As she passed him, Sara glared at Quince. “Come on, Bugs,” she begged Lilly, nudging the girl down the hall. “You can have milk if you promise to go back to sleep.” As the door shut behind them, Quince sat alone on the bed. A small black clock, with red digital numbers, lay on the dresser. It read 5:37 a.m.

Chapter 23
≈ A Night of Honor ≈

On the sink sat a small glass jar, filled with lavender scented wax. A thin ribbon, tied in a bow, adorned the jar. The flame bent and swayed as Sara pulled the blow dryer over her long hair. The smell of lavender filled the bathroom, spilling out into the bedroom.

Quince slipped a silver-plated watch over his wrist. It was heavy. It looked bulky and expensive. His arms slid through a suit coat, and he shifted, adjusting his shoulders as he stared into Sara's full-length mirror that hung from a closet door. His hair had grown fast since he came home two months ago. The neatly cropped high-and-tight was gone, and his hair was long enough to part.

Quince didn't mind short hair. Honestly, he preferred it to long hair. He didn't care for standing in front of a mirror, combing, spraying or smudging gel. A man shouldn't do those things. Not him. He enjoyed quick showers. Getting out and just going without worrying about how his hair looked. Before, he knew how it looked. Short. Neat. But Sara insisted he let it grow out for this evening. She bought him teeth-whitener and hair gel and a special cologne she thought a man with wealth would wear. Quince didn't know why she thought he should wear it. She demanded Quince shave the short-stubbed beard he enjoyed wearing on weekends. She bought him a new navy blue suit and a watch, a bulky silver-plated piece.

Quince stood and stared into the mirror. The face staring back looked different. Maybe it was the mirror, he thought. Mirrors do that. Have that effect. They make the fat look skinny and the skinny look fat and ugly people prettier. Maybe it was the mirror. For seven months, he stared into the dirty, cracked mirror that hung from a concrete wall in the shower of Camp Stanton. Now, two months after leaving the Kunar Valley, he saw a different face in the mirror. A face that had changed. The short-cropped hair was long. Short sideburns grew below his temple. He was thinner. The muscle he added with daily workouts was shrinking. Desert camouflage was replaced by navy blue suit.

He was transforming. Changing. He no longer looked military. Sure, he still stood straight, and occasionally he caught himself standing with his hands locked behind his back at parade rest just as he stood so many times during company formation. But things were different. He had changed. He no longer looked Marine. He was a civilian.

Quince hated this primping. So he grabbed his wallet from the dresser, shoved it in a pocket, and left. Walking into the den, he flopped on the couch, grabbed the remote, and turned on the television. Down the hall, he could still hear the hissing sound of spewing hair spray. He glanced at the bulky watch, before staring down the empty hall into the bedroom. His head shook. His lips pursed.

The television was running an infomercial about a class-action lawsuit. An old, distinguished man was speaking. Wearing a dark suit, hair thick and gray, the lawyer begged viewers to call a phone number and join the suit. *Call now*, he pled. *They have done you wrong*. Quince rolled his eyes and whispered, “Rodent.”

Bored, he noticed his old watch lying on a stack of books on the end table. It was the same worn, dirty piece he wore throughout deployment. He glanced down the empty hall and flashed a sneaky, guilty grin. Quickly, he grabbed the old watch and examined the face. It was rough. The plastic face was scratched. Smudged. The Velcro wristband was frayed. But it had memories. For seven months, he watched time pass by the numbers on that old watch. Seconds of his deployment, his time in the Kunar River Valley, ticked away on that old dirty piece. Now, it was relegated to a watch he wore while working outside. Cleaning the garage. Raking leaves along the fence in the backyard. It was filthy and scratched, and Quince loved it.

Quince again glanced down the hall. Again, he looked down at the old watch, before glancing at the new, shiny watch Sara had given him. He grinned, unfastened the silver-plated watch, tucked it away behind the stack of books, and fastened the old watch around his wrist.

Minutes passed. Quince sighed, flipping channels until it landed on the news. Quince watched as a female reporter, wearing a black flak jacket and a plain blue helmet, was speaking to the camera as she walked through a dusty street. She passed a stone building, walking with a squad of soldiers. The street was sparsely crowded, littered with clothing. Over her shoulder was the hull of a burning car. Shards of glass, metal, and shredded tires were strewn across a street. Remnants of a market stood behind her. A few wooden stands smoldered as a fire weakened. The camera flashed to the market hours earlier when civilians were scattered across streets. Men scurried around, directing, pointing, carting away wounded. An old woman, burka blown off, was hoisted onto the shoulders of two men who whisked her away. Her arms fell limp over their faces. As Quince watched he dropped the remote as flames rose from a burning hull. Smoke rolled over the market. Men scurried around streets. Quince watched. The burning hull and rolling smoke reminded him of that morning on the banks of the Kunar River. Water gathered in the corner of Quince's eyes as he watched, remembering Sergeant Patrick's hi-lux explode; watching it burn.

Suddenly, an eager voice spoke, "Come on." Quince did not move. He was frozen, paralyzed as Sara approached the television and pushed a button. The screen went dark. "I won't be late tonight—not to this event," she vowed, smiling.

Her back turned, Quince wiped his eyes with the sleeve of his coat, leaving a smear over the fabric.

Sara turned and faced her husband. "How do I look?" she smiled, posing.

Quince stood, and forced a grin. "Wonderful," he answered, his voice splintering as they left.

Later, Quince drove through dimly lit suburban streets. He was quiet as Sara talked of former classmates, girlfriends, sorority sisters. Tess, she said, married Jimmy Stiles. They met in the student center their sophomore year, and were inseparable through graduation. They have a daughter, but Sara had forgotten the little girl's name. After college, they moved into a small house in a new subdivision outside town. It was a beautiful home. She had a healthy family, a good job, and youth but it wasn't enough for Tess. Last summer, she filed for divorce. She had been given all anyone could want, but Tess just wasn't ready to settle down. She's dating a man from the bank. The CFO or maybe COO, Sara had forgotten. Regardless, they would attend the reunion that night.

Sylvia was Sara's closest friend in college. They were roommates and sorority sisters. They shared every secret, helped the other study for exams and wore the other's clothes. Sylvia often spent weekends and holidays with Sara and her parents. They still talked almost every day. Sylvia, Sara contended, helped her get through Quince's absence during deployment. They talked each night and emailed most every day. They stayed on the beach last summer. In the fall, they walked corn mazes and painted pumpkins. *I never would have gotten through it without her,* Sara would say.

Quince suspected Sylvia did not care for him. He always had that feeling about her. It was just the way she acted around him. Cocky attitude. Short conversations. More than once he caught Sylvia rolling her eyes at something he said. Sylvia was a petite blonde with long, straight hair and soft features. She never married. Never stopped going to clubs after college. Never stopped serial dating. Never stopped using her looks to get what she wanted. Quince didn't trust Sylvia. Through deployment, he worried when Sara and Sylvia were together. He knew what she was capable of and he knew Sara would listen to Sylvia. Sylvia, Quince suspected, felt Sara could do better than the wiry farm boy she married. After all, what did he have going for him? A talented wide receiver, he broke records, but college was over, a memory. The best Quince could offer, Sylvia felt, was mediocrity. He had a mediocre job as a warehouse supervisor. They lived in a plain, aging, ranch home. They drove cheap cars. Their lives were plain, predictable, mediocre. But more than anything, he knew Sylvia was good friends with Trimble, the former quarterback and Sara's college beau.

Trimble's family was wealthy and well connected. The Addison name was as old as the town itself, and so was their money. Trimble graduated with a degree in political science and went to work as an aide to the Mayor. Since college, he had not aged. He hadn't lost hair or gained weight. He walked around flashing his looks and money—a small-town playboy. He acted like a high roller, and Quince laughed at him, but he knew, in a small town, most people view a man like Trimble as someone important, powerful, even if he were just a frat boy who had been given everything in life. Quince mocked him. Beecher called him a piss-ant.

That night, Main Street was alive with lights. Soft, cylinder-shaped glows fell from street lamps along the sidewalk. Shops and boutiques were still open. Marquees hung above their doors. Shoppers mingled along the sidewalk, gazing through storefront windows at sharply dressed mannequins hoisted on pedestals. It was a cool, but mild winter evening.

Quince mashed the brake pedal, and the SUV slowed at a stop sign. He was quiet as he drove. Sara stared into a mirror on the visor, touching up her makeup and lipstick. He turned at the stop sign, away from the lights of Main Street, and through several dark streets with large homes. He kept driving and eventually street lamps re-emerged in the skyline. Those lamps formed in a large, oval shape around the edges of the coliseum. The coliseum sat on a hill above campus. Several stories of brick and stone, it was painted white with one end of the oval open, like a horseshoe, so that the students could see into the coliseum from their dorms below. A street passed by the opening before it turned, following the hill down into campus. Sara turned, staring into the coliseum as they passed. Quince stared at the street ahead, ignoring the lights and the field where his record was achieved and still stood.

They turned, followed the street down the hill, into campus, passing several plain brick buildings. Quince applied the brake, and the SUV rolled to a stop beneath the portico of a large, black-glass building. Thick marble columns supported the building. Red stones were a foundation for the portico. Stopped, Quince opened the door, and stepped out. A valet handed him a tag as he walked around the SUV and opened the door for Sara. Sara dropped her feet to the ground, and slid from the seat. She was elegantly dressed. A thin, black cocktail dress hung to her thighs. Gray fur covered her round shoulders. Soft brown curls fell across her ears.

Hanging from a chain, a chandelier threw light over the stones of the portico, refracting tints of yellow and white. A necklace twinkled as Sara accepted Quince's hand, and gracefully moved across the portico. Her heels clapped as they struck the stones.

Sara was popular in college, and she reveled in the comfort of being admired by her peers. She had given that up in the years following graduation, accepting roles as the wife of a warehouse supervisor, a mother, and finally a military spouse. Now, just the idea of an evening with her college friends gave her so much joy and excitement. It was a chance to pull back the curtain separating months of loneliness she experienced while Quince was away training or on deployment from the carefree days she knew in school.

But Sara felt anxious as she walked into the event that evening. Excitement lifted her cheeks, fashioning a permanent but nervous grin. Holding Quince's hand, she led her husband through a rotating door. Glass panes twirled the couple around a tinted cylinder as they quickly stepped through an opening, allowing the panes to sweep by, disappearing back into the cylinder. It was a spacious, grand room. Marble tile, colored in earth tones, surrounded a fountain. A nude statue stood on a pedestal, holding a tilted vase. Her soft smile welcomed visitors as she poured water into the pool. Light from the moon dripped through a skylight. The room was warm. Large ferns sprouted from pots. Columns were posted like sentries in every doorway. The foyer had the feel of a museum and an atrium.

The couple paused, scanning the room for familiar faces. Guests mingled near the fountain. A couple sat on stairs across the foyer. Nearby, a lady, hips swaying in a royal blue dress, crossed the foyer, passing the fountain. She held a margarita glass with thick salt crusted around the rim as if it were a trophy. Raven hair fell across her shoulders, and her skin shared Sara's dark tone. She turned, and a smile exploded across her face. Her cheeks lifted, "Sara Foster!" she exclaimed. "Oh my God!" One arm lifted, while the other steadied the margarita as she clopped across the foyer in high heels. "Tess!" she shouted. Sara dropped Quince's hand, ran across the foyer, and embraced her friend. They hugged and stomped and giggled like children. Lime margarita splashed across marble tiles as they danced, laughing. "I'm so glad you made it!" Tess continued.

"Oh," moaned Sara. "Nothing would keep me from this night!"

Quince approached the two women. He stopped, standing quietly behind his wife. The sound of falling water echoed across the foyer. His eyes surveyed the room, fountain, and naked statue. He examined things around him. He noticed the hidden things. How the water was silver as it slipped over the brim of the vase, dyed blue as it fell across the light of a neon sign hanging above the bar, and yellow as it passed the rays of a distant lamp. How the bark of a magnolia, hidden in the corner, curled outward like pointing toes. A young lady, Quince's age, flirted through her cell phone as she passed the fountain. Her voice was drowned by the sound of crashing water, and the rumble of loud music from a distant room. He noticed how only the lilt of her giggles lifted above the music and sank as her laughter died away. Lifting, sinking, the lilt of her voice gasped for air.

He was bored. Like Sara, it was his reunion, but he felt out of place. Tom Quincy Magowan was the leading receiver in the conference. His record stood just as he stood in the foyer, or like a naked statue stood in a fountain, but he felt no kinship with those students or the school. For them, college was the glory days—days to remember and long for, and reminisce about. Not Quince. He rarely thought of those days. It was not as if he never knew them. The memories were there. They were simply hidden by time and events; buried behind the demands of today, the here and now, and the clutter of memories and feelings he brought home from Afghanistan. And he knew it. That was the hard part for Quince. It was sad. Having something and losing it is harder than never having owned it at all. He once had it, relished it, relished the record, cheers, the applause. Now, it was gone forever, and he knew it.

"And who's your handsome date?" Tess asked Sara, attempting conversation by flirting.

"Oh," Sara curtsied, "just the star receiver."

"Star receiver?"

"His record still stands," bantered Sara.

"Well, I need a hug from the star receiver," Tess proclaimed, brushing past Sara. Lifting her arms, she dropped them over Quince's shoulders. "Glad you're back safe," she said in a soft, serious tone.

Quince nodded, halfheartedly embracing the woman. His cheeks rose and quickly sank.

A tall man, older than Quince, stomped his feet as he paused near the fountain. He grinned with confidence. Holding a glass to his chest, he smiled at the group.

"Dale," bellowed Tess, noticing the man as she stepped away from Quince. She quickly approached the fountain, hips swaying, and twisted a hand around the man's arm. "You guys," she paused, "this is Dale McDonald." A proud smile lifted Tess's face. "He's the CFO of United Bank."

Sara smiled, offering a hand as she approached the man. They shook. Quince slowly moved across the foyer. His face was still. His arms lay at his side.

Water slipped over the brim of the vase, and crashed into the pool. Music rumbled from a distant room.

Dale McDonald smiled and offered a hand. Quince squeezed his hand, and stared at him with a motionless, uninviting face.

"Heard you were in Afghanistan?" asked Dale, still smiling.

Quince nodded. His lips bunched.

"Well. Glad you're home safe."

Quince nodded again. "Thanks," he answered, managing a terse smile.

"Well," interrupted Tess, "shall we go? Others are waiting."

Together, they walked around the fountain, across the foyer, toward a distant room. Tess and Sara walked ahead, their heels smacked the floor. Quince and Dale followed behind them. "So, how long were you over there?" asked Dale, lifting the glass to his lips, and drinking. He swished the drink around his teeth, swallowed and smiled. Confidence seemed to permanently fashion a smile over his face. His teeth were white, straight. His hair was sandy with gray speckled around his temple. Soft wrinkles cut down his cheeks, across the forehead.

Quince shrugged, answering, "Seven months. Most of it on the border."

Dale's eyes swelled. His head turned, as he asked, "With Pakistan?"

Quince nodded.

"Hear a lot about that area. Not as much as Iraq, though, but when they talk about Afghanistan, they talk about the border."

"Well. What province?" he continued.

Loud music rumbled. Crashing water echoed in the background.

Quince stared at the floor as he walked. "It don't matter," he said.

"It does."

"You probably ain't heard of it anyway."

"I'd like to know," Dale persisted.

Quince turned, pausing. His face pinched. His eyes narrowed. They stood below a handful of steps as music poured through a door, cascading down the tile steps where the men stood. "You know much about the border?"

Dale's shoulders shrugged.

"Kunar," answered Quince.

Dale's face sank.

Quince rolled his eyes, starting to ascend the steps.

Dale grabbed his arm. Quince paused. His face pinched. He jabbed an open hand, striking Dale's wrist, freeing his arm from the man's grasp.

Sara and Tess climbed the stairs, alone in their conversation.

"It means something," pled the banker.

"To you?" Quince asked, his voice sliced through the music in an arrogant tone.

"That's right."

Quince's lips bunched. "Tell me." His shoulders lifted, hanging above his neck. "Name a town, a village, province, anywhere on the border."

Dale was silent before softly answering, "Khost." His face was long. His smile disappeared. He looked different. Absent confidence, he appeared smaller. "I have a nephew there. Just out of high school."

Quince's wrinkled face smoothed.

"His mother, my sister, well . . . she's worried sick."

Quince listened. Dale's words pierced his armor, bleeding the arrogance from his veins. His features softened.

"Just got there few weeks back. His tour is a year."

Quince's head shook. His shoulders sank.

"What do you know about it, Khost?"

"The truth?' asked Quince, a brow lifting into his forehead.

Dale nodded.

"I'd be lying if I told you it wasn't bad. Bad as the Kunar."

Dale nodded. He laid a hand on Quince's shoulder, but Quince didn't move, didn't strike the man's arm or knock it away. "Thanks. Appreciate your honesty."

Quince nodded.

"You two, come on!" screamed Tess, waving her hands at the men.

Dale and Quince climbed the steps. They were silent now. Music thundered across the foyer. Tess and Sara smiled, dancing to the rhythm as they begged their dates to join them. "Come on!" Sara pled, waving her arms at Quince. The room was dark as they approached the door. Music, laughter, and muddled conversation tumbled around the spacious ballroom. It was very dim. Hundreds of silhouettes bounced across the dance floor.

The two couples stood at the threshold, staring at the room as if it were a murky river, and the threshold the shore. Suddenly, Tess and Sara leapt across the threshold, joining the crowd as it bounced around. They danced, bouncing across the floor, laughing. "Get out here!" screamed Sara.

Tess cupped her hands near her painted lips, taunting the men, "Stiffs!" Swaying across the room, back to the threshold, she grabbed Dale's hand and jerked him into the crowd. The room bounced like waves down a river. Sara danced her way back to the threshold, grabbed her husband's hand, and smiled, nodding, "Come on. You know this night is important to me!"

Quince's lips bunched. He hated to dance. He never learned, and he always felt awkward when he tried.

Sara nodded, motioning him toward the dance floor. Her lips were open, and her white teeth shone like candles in the dimly lit room.

Quince sighed. A reluctant smile lifted his cheeks as he nodded.

Sara pulled him away from the threshold, into the river of bouncing silhouettes.

"Wooohoooo!" bellowed Tess, as the couples danced. Tess and Sara swayed. Dale snapped his fingers, turning in small motions. Quince kept his hands at his waist, awkwardly twisting back and forth. Music thundered. The crowd bounced around the ballroom like water sailing down the Kunar River. It was dark. Dale danced. Tess and Sara danced and swayed. Quince moved in awkward, twisting motions. Suddenly, the music stopped. The speakers silenced. Screams and cheers were replaced with muddled conversation. Applause smattered.

A young lady, Quince and Sara's age, emerged from the crowd, and stepped behind a lectern. Her face was full, and she was short. Her heavy cheeks barely hung above the lectern.

"That's Tamara Watson," Tess whispered to Sara.

"That's Tamara?" asked Sara, her face contorted.

Tess's eyebrows rose into her forehead. She nodded. "Three kids . . ." she said.

"Ladies and gentlemen," Tamara spoke. Muddled conversation died. "Ladies and gentlemen please be seated. Placards with names of each guest are placed on their respective tables."

The crowd broke apart. Guests scrambled, surveying each table for the placard with their name. The room once again filled with conversation.

"We're over here," Tess noted, dragging Dale toward a table in the middle. Sara and Quince followed the couple, weaving through the crowd until they reached the table with their placards. A candle flickered inside a glass dome, circled with greenery, near the table's center. Crystal stood guard among utensils and plates, catching the soft flame. White paper, folded in a triangle, listed names of each guest in thin, black cursive.

Quince's eyes surveyed the placards as he circled the table. *Dale McDonald*, read one placard. Next to it, the placard read *Tess Handly*. "I'll be damned!" cursed Quince, smiling. *Baxter Samples* was the name printed on the next placard. *Shelley Samples* was on the placard to the left. Quince kept walking, circling the table. A flame flickered in the crystal. *Sylvia Tibato*. Quince's brow wrinkled. He kept walking, circling. A flame flickered. Suddenly, Quince paused. A deep furrow folded across his forward. His lips bunched. He examined the name splashed across the next placard. It read *Trimble Addison*.

Quince's eyes rose from the table, and searched for Sara. Sara, Dale and Tess were already seated. Tess was laughing. Tipsy, she drank her margarita. Dale laughed. Confidently, he smiled, enjoying the company of his attractive, somewhat intoxicated, date. Meanwhile, Sara sipped champagne.

Quince stooped, whispering in her ear, "Can I talk with you in private?"

Sara frowned. She reluctantly pulled her lips from the crystal, set the glass on the table, pushed her chair from the table and stood. "Be right back," she shouted through the chatter.

Tess winked, raising the margarita over her head. "Sara Magowan!" she screamed, laughing.

Sara followed Quince as he wove around tables, and through the crowd. Away from the crowd, he paused in the corner, turning to his wife.

"Trimble?" he asked in a strong voice.

"What?" she asked. Her face was dismissive.

"He's at our table?"

Sara shrugged, looking away.

"Sitting next to me?" Quince jabbed a finger at his own chest. His face was pinched, his eyes narrowed.

"I didn't know they would seat him next to you!" she shouted, her eyes flashing as she spoke.

Quince was furious. His shoulders straightened. His hands lifted, coming to rest on his hips, and he sighed. “You reserved our seats.”

“I didn’t know he would sit there.”

Quince’s eyes narrowed, and he stooped once more. “You reserved seating for the guests at our table.”

“For the table. I didn’t know they would seat him there!” she shouted. Her face twisted in anger.

“Trimble at our table?”

Sara crossed her arms, and she looked away.

“Why?” he asked.

“He was your friend,” she explained.

“Friend?” he gasped.

“OK,” she admitted, “but he was your teammate.”

“He was an asshole, and we hated each other. He was jealous of the record.”

Sara rolled her eyes.

“And he was jealous I took you,” he shouted, a deep furrow wrinkling his forehead.

“You didn’t take me,” she answered sarcastically.

His face pinched.

Sara shrugged, exasperated. “I’ll sit next to him,” she conceded. “You can have my seat.”

Quince stood straight. Hands resting on his hips, he looked across the room. Most guests were seated. The room was filled with muddled chatter. Elevator music played in the background. A steady stream of waitresses emerged from behind the kitchen. Wearing black suit-pants, white shirts and black vests, they scurried around each table with platters filled with wine bottles.

Quince sighed, shaking his head, but he wasn’t finished. He felt betrayed. Trimble, he thought? That cocky asshole!

“Well. They’re serving and we’re standing here arguing. This is embarrassing!” she proclaimed, stomping away.

Quince looked across the room. Sighing, he walked with confidence, weaving among white-clothed tables, black-vested waitresses who balanced bottles of wine and champagne on platters, to his table in the middle. A flame flickered in the crystal as he approached the table. Guests glowed as they smiled, laughing.

“Hey, hey!” shouted someone from across the table. “Ladies and gentlemen, there he is! That record breaking wide receiver!" Quince looked around as a stocky man, of medium height, smiled. The man moved quickly around the table, lifting a hand. "Good to see you, my friend!" he said, shaking Quince's hand.

Quince grinned, almost laughing. "Baxter you son of a bitch!" he cursed. "How the hell have you been?"

Sara grimaced as her husband cursed.

Baxter laughed. Shaking hands, he grabbed Quince's shoulder with his free hand, and embraced his old friend. "Apparently better than you, pal. Afghanistan, huh?"

Quince nodded. His smile faded.

"Well, you're back now and that's all that matters. It's all behind you!" he continued, smiling as he spoke. Baxter turned to the guests at their table. "Ladies and gentlemen, for those of you at this table who are not alums, this man holds a record in receiving-yards. And," he pointed for emphasis, "the record still stands today."

Quince smiled, blushing as his old friend bragged about his feats.

Baxter immediately returned to his chair, stooped, lifted a glass of champagne and toasted, "To the record!"

Quince's cheeks blushed, smiling. Looking around, he surveyed faces of the guests gathered around the table. Sara smiled with grudging pride, still angry with her husband. She sipped champagne. Tess hoisted the margarita to her painted lips, and tilted the glass. Dale smiled, nodding, drinking champagne. Shelley Samples, Baxter's wife, smiled and hoisted a glass of wine. The flame flickered, reflecting off the crystal. He watched Sara as her eyes darted uncomfortably around the table. Finally, they stopped and peered to her left. Quince traced them, following them over crystal, bubbling champagne, skirting the flickering candle and stopping on an attractive woman with long, blonde hair falling below her shoulders. The woman sat quietly and without emotion. The small features of her face were tan and painted. Her blue eyes were fixed, steadied across the flickering candle. She appeared to ignore the toast, sitting quietly as if she were at another table. Quince looked closer, watching the woman as Baxter went on about the record. It had been years but he recognized the face, blonde hair and paint. It was Sylvia.

Quince's eyes narrowed. He continued to survey guests sitting at the table. Visible just below him, beneath the beer he held, was the crown of a man's head. Like with Sylvia, Quince recognized the features. It was like carrying a picture of an old friend in a wallet, and pulling it out years later. Through the wrinkles, fading and sweat soaked material, you immediately recognize some quirky feature about that friend, a feature you'd forgotten. He had not forgotten this man's features. Thick, sandy hair. He remembered looking down on that crown in the auditorium during philosophy. And, in a huddle, those sandy locks lay behind the stranger's facemask, near his temple. Quince recognized them. Years had passed, but he knew them. It was Trimble Addison. Trimble was quiet. His eyes were hidden from Quince, but he could picture them. Like an old photograph, he could see them, creased, emanating a cocky stare across the table.

"Everyone raise a glass," commanded a moderately intoxicated Baxter, hoisting crystal over his head. Sara, Tess, and Shelley hoisted their drinks, smiling, humoring their intoxicated friend. Sylvia and Trimble sat still. Sylvia's hands were folded across her lap and her legs were crossed. Over Trimble's shoulder, Quince saw the man's hand, grasping a bourbon and ice, release the glass, and slide the hand across the table, dropping it onto his thigh beneath the white cloth.

"Everyone," stammered Baxter, "a toast to the night Quince broke the record." Across the table, glasses were hoisted even higher. Sara sat back. She let one arm fall into her lap, and she hoisted the glass, but looked down, as if staring into her plate. The soft sound of crystal tapping against crystal filled the table. Baxter tapped Quince's beer bottle, and they drank. Guests drank. Quince swished beer around in his mouth, through his teeth, and smirked as he swallowed. His eyes fell on the sandy-haired crown beneath him.

Baxter slapped Quince's shoulder, smiled, and said, "Good to have you home." He then stumbled around the table to his seat.

Guests around the table watched him. Quince felt the weight of their stare. He took a few steps and sat. Staring at Sara, he lifted the beer to his lips and drank. The candle flickered. Light danced across his forehead.

Trimble turned, and gazed at the man's profile. "Quince," he greeted, tersely.

Muscles in Quince's jaw tightened. His eyes batted, and he slowly turned and answered, "Trimble." Quince smirked, amused at Trimble's arrogance. His eyes shifted and he greeted the blonde to his right, "Sylvia."

Sylvia's lips were twisted. Her eyes were wide, and filled with the naive disgust of an immature, vain woman. "Quince," she answered, sarcastically, her arms now crossed.

Quince smirked. Lifting the bottle to his lips, he drank. Breath escaped from his nostrils as he laughed.

Guests shuffled in their seats, fidgeting uncomfortably through the silence. Torment disfigured Sara's face.

A server paused near the table, dropped a stand, kicked it open, and slowly lowered a large tray to the platform. Quickly, he set salads on the table in front of each guest.

"So, Dale," interrupted Trimble, slapping his hands together. "How are things in the world of banking?"

Dale sipped champagne, slowly lowering the crystal from his lips. Nodding confidently, he smiled, "Very good. We just acquired Morgan Regional."

"Morgan Regional?" asked Trimble.

"Small chain . . . has an office on the corner of Maple and Broadway. Satellite offices around the area."

Trimble lifted the glass to his lips, and sipped bourbon. Ice cubes rattled as he lowered the glass.

"And how are things at City Hall?" asked Dale.

Light flickered across the table. Guests sat quietly, eating salad, sipping their drinks. Sylvia and Tess ate quietly, occasionally smiling with pride as their dates talked of their prestigious careers.

"Very good," he answered, grinning.

"Busy?"

He sipped bourbon, smiling, "Running a city this size keeps you busy."

Quince ate salad. His face lowered to the plate, he turned to Sara and rolled his eyes.

Sara's face pinched when she saw his mocking gesture.

"The election?" Dale continued.

"Promising. The Mayor's almost assured re-election to a second term."

"Job security. Here's to it," Dale quipped, hoisting his glass.

Trimble grinned, hoisting his glass, tilting it to his lips, and sipping bourbon.

"So, Quince," said Trimble, turning to face him, "how are things down at the warehouse?" Trimble's cheeks lifted, and his smile was wide.

A slight gasp erupted among the women. Sara ate quietly, staring at the salad.

Quince tilted the beer to his lips and drank. He moved slowly, letting the beer burn his tongue before setting the bottle on the table. His fist clenched as he released the bottle. He wanted to punch Trimble, hit him in the face, knock his perfect white teeth through the back of his head. His face rose from the plate, and he gazed at him. "Things at the warehouse are good," he answered in a stern voice.

Trimble's arrogant smile grew wider.

His smile burned inside of Quince. His face blushed. His eyes began to swell, and he said in a clear, resolute voice, "It's honest, hard work. It pays the bills. But you wouldn't know about hard work since you were born with a silver spoon in your ass!"

A gasp erupted from the table. Sylvia's mouth fell open, and a half-chewed leaf of salad dropped into her lap. Sara's face disfigured. Dale and Tess fidgeted uncomfortably, dropping their heads. Baxter laughed. He nearly spewed champagne across the table.

Trimble's smile disappeared. His lips bunched up, and his eyes narrowed. Quince sipped beer, and gazed at Trimble. He wanted Trimble to make a move—to give him reason to hit the man. He wanted Trimble to stand, so he could punch him, drop that arrogant bastard in front of everyone.

"Ladies and gentlemen," spoke the former Tamara Watson from the lectern. "Sorry to interrupt your dinner but we have a special recognition to make. If we could get all members of the varsity football team to come up and stand right over here," she asked, pointing to the left of the lectern.

"Hey! Hey!" shouted Baxter, leaping up from the table. "Duty calls."

Quince and Trimble sat there, staring at one another. Baxter circled the table. "Come on, big Quince. That's us," he begged, his hand on Quince's shoulder.

Quince grinned, stared at Trimble, stood, and crossed the floor with Baxter at his side.

Trimble pushed his chair away from the table, staring at Sara as he stood.

Sara's lips moved silently, mimicking, "I'm sorry."

Trimble crossed the floor, and stood near the end of the line of former players.

"The 1998 Varsity Football team set three records on their way to placing division runner-up. Led by quarterback Trimble Addison," Trimble grinned, hoisting a hand, "running back Baxter Samples," Baxter grinned, teetering as he stepped forward, "and the record-breaking performance of wide-receiver Quince Magowan," Quince hoisted a hand. Trimble's lips bunched. His eyes rolled. "We would like to show our appreciation of your performance that season with these rings, each bearing the inscription of that season's accomplishments." Tamara continued, holding a gold ring over the lectern. Guests applauded. Tamara walked the line, handing each player a ring. She returned to the lectern, and leaned into the microphone, "And now we have another recognition. In his varsity season, he set a single season record for yards received, catching for 1800 yards, and scoring 16 touchdowns."

The crowd listened. The dark, hazy room blurred their faces. Dale, Tess, and Shelley quietly listened. As Quince surveyed their table, Sara and Sylvia whispered. The candle flickered. Light brushed over their faces.

"Tonight we honor Quince Magowan with a special trophy for his record-breaking performance during our varsity year. Even today, Quince's record is unbroken." The former Tamara Watson pulled a small trophy from the bowels of the lectern, and gracefully passed along the line of former players.

Former players applauded, turning toward Quince who stood emotionless near the end. Trimble Addison lowered his face as Tamara approached Quince. Baxter smiled. Wobbling slightly, he tapped Quince's shoulder with the palm of his hand. Tamara handed Quince the trophy, shook his free hand, smiled, and returned to the lectern. Leaning into the microphone, she said, "Ladies and gentlemen, that concludes our recognitions. You may return to your seats. Please enjoy your dinner."

Quince and the others returned to their seats. He set the trophy on the table, in front of him, near his empty beer bottle. A gold-plated collegian, arms outstretched, hands cupped, legs poised in a leap, was balanced on a marble-toned base. It was short, barely taller than the empty beer bottle, but shiny and beautiful. He smiled. It was difficult for him, but he let himself be proud.

A server circled the table, pouring champagne from tilted bottles. "Another beer, sir?" she asked and Quince nodded. A second waiter slid a stand from his shoulder, kicked it open, and slowly lowered a platter to the base. Quickly, he dispersed the entrée, and removed the empty salad plates.

A waiter leaned over Quince's shoulder, and gently set a beer next to his trophy. They ate. The sound of silverware tapping plates set the room to a symphonic chime. "Quince," interrupted Baxter, pointing at the trophy, "pass it over." The bottle was tilted to his lips. He drank beer, pulled the bottle from his lips, gathered the trophy with his left hand, stood, and leaned over the table. Baxter stood, leaning across the table.

Quince's sleeve slid up his arm as he stretched.

"Magowan, you didn't need a trophy, you need a watch," quipped Trimble. Sylvia burst into laughter, nearly spewing wine across the table as she saw the worn, dirt smudged, timepiece fastened to his wrist.

Sara's face was anguished. Blush leaked through her tan cheeks.

"Sara wouldn't let you leave home wearing a piece of shit watch. Not tonight," said Sylvia, laughing through her words.

"It's all about class, Quince," continued Trimble, an arrogant smile lifting his lips. "You never had it."

Quince handed Baxter the trophy. The candle flickered. Light brushed over his forehead.

"It's important to most, but obviously not you. That watch is trash," continued Trimble.

"I bought him a new watch. He was supposed to wear it tonight," announced Sara, angrily. "Why aren't you wearing . . . ?"

"It's not trash!" Quince insisted.

Trimble disagreed, a smirk lifting his cheeks. "Look at it. It's dirty, scratched. It's trash."

"It was earned!" Quince insisted, his face pinched as he stood over Trimble.

"It's filthy, Magowan. A relic like your record."

"You have a new watch. Silver-plated. Why aren't you wearing it?" nagged Sara.

"These scratches. They were earned."

Trimble chuckled. His lips were open; the flame brushed over his white teeth.

"Earned. Something you don't know shit about."

"Classy, Magowan."

Baxter pushed himself away from the table, and stood. Dale, Tess and Shelley sat quietly. Sara grew furious at her husband. Sylvia was drunk, observing the argument with amusement. Uncomfortable silence absorbed the room as guests from other tables listened.

Quince blushed as blood rushed to his head. His eyes were wide, afire. "Trimble, everything you own came from your dad's wallet."

Trimble's face pinched. Blush leaked from his cheeks. "What are you saying?"

"Saying you never stood on your own ground."

"Don't talk to me about earning it, Magowan. I'm a senior aide to the Mayor. You work at a factory."

"You always followed a path cleared by your father," Quince said, his voice lifting to a shout. The ballroom was quiet. Silence absorbed guests as they listened.

Trimble's face pinched. "And your father's path. What was it, Magowan? Half a dozen marriages. Drunk and disorderly. A farmer. Class, Magowan." Trimble's arms folded, and his chest rose and sank as he laughed.

Gasps absorbed the room. For months, Sara devoutly invested her hopes and dreams of a glamorous evening. Now, as Trimble and Quince argued, and their former classmates listened, her dreams melted, dissolving like the ice in Trimble's bourbon.

"Quince . . . sit down," begged his wife.

Quince's eyes narrowed. Light brushed over his face. He stooped, slapping Trimble's chest, grabbing a handful of the man's blazer.

Trimble's eyes swelled. "Son of a bitch!" he shouted. Sylvia nearly fell from her seat.

Guests erupted in a single, consonant gasp. Sara screamed.

Baxter quickly circled the table, wrapping his arms around Quince's chest, pulling him away from Trimble. Baxter tugged. Quince's grasp tightened. Trimble smacked Quince's hand as if he were swatting away a pesky insect on a summer evening.

"Get him off me!" shouted Trimble.

Baxter tugged.

Dale stood, and reluctantly assisted Baxter, pulling Quince's arm. They tugged. Quince's fist shrank. "My father . . ." he shouted, gasping for words.

Sara stood and stepped back, cowering away from the altercation. Her hands cuffed her mouth.

Baxter and Dale tugged. Quince's grasp loosened. "Get him away," begged Trimble, swatting Quince's arm. Blush leaked from his cheeks.

Dale tugged at Quince's arm. Baxter, arms wrapped around Quince's chest, tugged. Quince's fist opened. His hand slipped. Arms dropped to his thighs. A sigh blew across Trimble's lips.

Baxter gently tapped his cheeks. "You all right?"

Quince nodded.

Trimble straightened his blazer.

"We're leaving," stated Sara, snatching her purse from the table, and storming across the room.

Tess ran behind her.

Quince gazed at Trimble. His lips were tight. Eyes, narrow. Turning, he slowly walked away as silence absorbed the room. Guests stared as the wiry former receiver disappeared into the expansive foyer.

The candle flickered. Nearby, two beer bottles and a trophy sat on a table. Light brushed across the gold-plated collegian, arms poised for a catch.

Chapter 24
≈ Dreaming about the Kunar Valley ≈

Quince woke from a sound sleep. His body lazily shifted inside the bivy sack. He groaned. Water seeped from his blinking eyes, burned by morning light. Last night, a bright moon hung over Camp Stanton. At dusk, it jumped into the valley as a performer would leap onto stage. Slowly, it rose over the poppy fields, the small village on the river, and the clear water moving swiftly down the valley. It rose above the soft, white peaks, pulling shadows from their rocky hideaways. Quince lay there, in a small cot, inside a sleeping bag, and tried to sleep. Occasionally, the deep drone of voices echoed outside the concrete walls, and shadows darted across the ceiling as Marines passed by his window.

Soon, as he lay there, staring at the gray ceiling, a shadow peeked over the dark wall. It was still. It did not run or dart across the ceiling. It was as permanent as the night. Quince tried to sleep. Ignore it. He closed his eyes and thought of home, of Lilly and Sara. He tried to convince himself that he was asleep in his own bed at home, back in Kentucky. He focused on little things, details about home, sounds and smells. He thought about a small clock that hung above the family portrait in the hall. How it ticked away the seconds of his life, faint clicks that were insignificant, muffled during the bustle of everyday life—sounds of a busy kitchen, a children's channel playing on the television in the den, a little girl brushing her teeth before bed. The clock was so quiet during the day, but at night it found a voice, and marked every lonely second in the dark. Quince closed his eyes and prayed to hear the clicking sound of that small clock. He prayed but only silence answered.

He closed his lips and sucked air through his nostrils, hoping to smell perfume lifting from Sara's neck as they spooned, naked, in bed. Instead, the musty smell of a bivy sack, unwashed for weeks, and the bitter smells of smoke, and singed hair pulled through his nostrils. His arms opened, hoping to feel Sara's petite body. Each night, as they spooned, Quince's fingers walked down Sara's mid-section, cuffing her thin waist.

Tonight, his hands postured, but felt nothing, just the cool Kunar air.

His eyes opened, and the shadow had grown into a long, thick cylinder with a square hole along the top. Quince could see straight through the hole of the shadow. It grew as the moon fell into the valley. Soon, it was there, a cylinder at its full height. Quince shrugged off sleep. His eyes were wide as he watched the tower hang from his ceiling. He watched as a man stepped from the shadow, into the clear hole. The man's frame was clearly outlined against the ceiling. He strolled across the opening. He stopped, lifted NVGs to his face and surveyed the valley. The man dropped the NVGs from his face, and pointed across the camp. He pointed with insistence, jabbing a finger at the cool, night air. He waved and pointed again. Finally, with arms hanging at his waist, he stepped into the shadows, disappearing once again.

Quince rose and pushed the bivy sack away from his legs. Pulling boots over his feet, he grabbed his M16, and went out into the darkness. He walked directly toward a guard-tower across camp. Dust rose from his boots as he walked. Quince's feet dragged as he passed the piss-tubes and outhouses in rows near the shower. The cool night air tempered the stench of rotting feces as he passed them, turned left and walked under a tower. He stopped near a small shack. In front, a small, sandy yard was encircled by chicken wire strung along ten-foot poles. Quince, the M16 slung over his shoulder, grasped the sling of the weapon, and stared at the shadowy figures inside. They were thin. Most wore black or gray. Some sat quietly in the sand while others walked laps around the small yard. Black hoods covered their faces.

"Corporal Mac?" someone asked. Quince turned, staring into the darkness as a Marine approached from outside the chicken wire. "Corporal Mac, what are you doing out this late?"

Quince's lips pursed, and his head nodded. He shrugged, "Couldn't sleep."

The Marine nodded. His face dropped slightly. "Did we catch them, Corporal Mac? Catch the bastards that planted the IED?"

Quince shook his head. "No. Not yet." Quince turned again, staring at the shadowy figures behind the wire. As he watched them, his lips pinched and his teeth clenched. He blushed as his anger grew. He hated them, these thin, dirty men. At that moment, he wanted to kill them. All of them. Lower his M16A2, set the weapon on burst, and shoot them dead. Standing there, in the dark, his face flush with hatred, he suddenly thought of Lilly and his anger waned. His face dropped into his chest as he turned and walked away.

He walked along a sandy road, ducking as he passed through an opening in the wall that led to a small compound. Inside, a dozen vehicles were strewn around the walled compound. Tires were missing from some vehicles. Hoods were up, bent, or missing. Pieces of engine littered the sand around them, as if the vehicle were somehow human, intestines spilled out into the sand. There were Humvees, a 5-ton, even a small red car. In the corner sat a white hi-lux. The hood lay next to the pickup, warped. Tires were missing.

The compound was dark and abandoned. The captain decided to build a wall around this compound to keep these damaged vehicles out of sight. *Out of sight, out of mind*, First Sergeant would say, but it never escaped their thoughts while in the Kunar River Valley. Quince drew a deep breath. His grasp of the sling tightened as he approached the vehicle. The smell of smoke, burning plastic, hung like a cloud around the hi-lux. Both doors hung open. He stopped at the driver's side and laid his hand on the inside of the door. The window was shattered. The glass, gone. He leaned on the door, and peered through the cab. It was dark, but the moon gave enough light that he could make out the steering wheel, charred plastic seat, a gearshift.

Quince slid the M16 from his shoulder, leaned it against the hi-lux, and sat down at the driver's side. Sighing, he lifted his hands and rested them on the steering wheel. The compound was dark and quiet; no one could see him.

Quince began pulling, twisting the steering wheel as if guiding the vehicle through the narrow road winding along the river. Twisting, turning, his wiry arms flexed as he steered the hi-lux. He imagined the road, a narrow, dusty lane he had driven so many times. He imagined the long curve in the field below Camp Stanton. He imagined dust pouring over the windshield as he followed Sergeant Patrick. He twisted the steering wheel, mashed the clutch and shoved the gear forward. He could see it, the road. It was fresh in his memory. He pictured the patrol. It was fresh, only that morning, just a few hours ago. He imagined pulling onto the bumper of Sergeant Patrick's hi-lux, before falling back in the curve. He twisted the wheel, pulling out of the curve, edging ever closer to Patrick's bumper. Then, he saw fire. He saw the hi-lux lift from the road, and roll helpless into the ditch, against the mountain.

He imagined what it was like as the explosion lifted the hi-lux into the air and tore a gaping hole in the floorboard. Quince imagined the agony of fire and rock and metal and plastic tearing through his legs, imagined the loud clap bursting their eardrums. He imagined smoke and fire filling the cab as the truck rolled into the ditch and Patrick drew his last breaths. Just hours before, a man, Quince's sergeant, his mentor, his friend, was mortally wounded in this truck. Quince held the steering wheel before letting his arms fall to his thighs. He imagined death. How it came sudden, too quick to resist, to fight, to run away from. It just took him and left before anyone could stop it.

Quince's eyes grew narrow and watery. His eyelids mashed together, and tears poured out, falling across his cheeks. He leaned forward, rested his forehead against the steering wheel, and wept.

He wept then sought composure. Sitting upright, he used his bare fingers to wipe water from his eyes. From the corner of his eye, through the blurring tears, he saw something. He felt as if someone was there. He felt a stare. He was frozen. He didn't want anyone to see him like this, to see him weep. He rubbed water from his eyes, and slowly, nervously, looked into the rear-view mirror that hung loose from the windshield. His eyes slowly lifted, passing along the compound, ever higher along the windshield, onto the mirror. Inside the thin mirror were the eyes, the face of Sergeant Patrick. Quince's eyes bulged. Sergeant Patrick's face was contorted, bloody and charred, but his eyes were open, starring at Quince through the mirror. He was silent. He just stared at Quince. Tears gathered in Quince's eyes. His eyelids shut, and he rubbed them with bare fingers. Again he looked into the mirror, and there was Patrick's face. Quickly, his head twisted, staring at the seat where Patrick sat.

Quince screamed as he sat up. Sweat poured from his face. The mattress beneath him was soaked.

"Are you OK?" Sara asked in a frantic tone. Her hands lay across Quince's wet shoulders.

Quince's eyes were wide. They scanned the room, disoriented.

"Mommy, what's wrong?" asked Lilly, standing in the doorway, whimpering.

"It's all right, honey," Sara assured.

Quince's eyes danced around the dark room.

"Is Daddy scared?" she continued.

"Daddy's fine. He just had a bad dream."

"Go back to bed," begged the mother, pointing down the hall. "I'll be in later to tuck you in."

Lilly stood there. She sniffled, stared at her father, turned and left.

"Quince, are you OK?" asked Sara once Lilly was gone.

Quince's eyes focused, and he nodded.

Sara pushed the comforter from her legs. "That's it!" she exclaimed, jumping to her feet, before stomping across the room. "That's it!"

"What are you doing?" he asked, sobering.

"I'm getting you help," she exclaimed. Grabbing her cell phone from the nightstand, she began dialing.

"Who are you calling?"

"Help."

"Who?"

"The hospital."

Quince shook his head. "Forget it." He pulled his hands from the comforter, and rubbed his eyes.

"I'm getting you help," she insisted.

"Yeah," he grunted sarcastically.

"Yes," Sara answered, ignoring Quince. "My husband is a patient. I need to speak to a nurse."

Sara listened. "Oh," she mumbled.

Quince shook his head. His lips were bunched.

"His ailment?" she asked. "He suffers from nightmares. He has them every night. He wakes up screaming. He spoke with Dr. Kimble about them," she continued.

Quince pushed the comforter from his legs and rolled his eyes.

"When can he speak with a doctor?"

Quince shook his head. Sweat dried on his face as he began to dress.

"Nine a.m. tomorrow?" she nodded.

Quince shook his head.

"OK. He'll be there," she answered, hanging up.

"I'm not going," he insisted.

"They can help."

"Not this."

Sara was adamant, saying, "How do you know? Dr. Kimble said they have treatments. They can help."

Quince was not convinced. "That's just talk. That's all it is to me. Just talk." He pulled a shirt over his shoulders. His dog tags clanked as his head slid through the neck hole.

Sara shook her head. "You're just saying that because you don't want to go."

"I'm not making it up!" he yelled.

"They can help. You're going?"

"I'm not."

"Quince, look at me," she demanded, sitting on the bed next to her husband as he dressed. "You've got to. Do it for me."

Quince dressed.

"For Lilly?"

He paused.

"Try?"

He sighed. Air rushed through his nostrils. He reluctantly nodded, and left the room.

Chapter 25
≈ Back to the VA ≈

Juice dripped from his fingers. Mayonnaise, ketchup, and grease squeezed from the patty, dripping like a sponge onto a paper plate. His molars ground the patty; jaw swinging in two or three large, deliberate motions, then pausing, and a bubble sank through his throat. Teeth parted, his head tilted, and what was left of the burger dropped into his open mouth. It was not vile, the way he ate, but it was loudly rude. All around him, patrons were crowded into the small cafeteria. Some watched him, amused or disgusted. Nurses, gathered in a corner booth, giggled at him. Their blue scrubs wrinkled as they stooped over a table, laughing.

During his short service, the Marine Corps had taught Quince two basic tenets of personal conduct that he swore he would never forget: sleep when you can, regardless of where you are, and eat fast. That afternoon, sitting among a crowd of strangers in a VA cafeteria in Lexington, he inhaled a greasy, ketchup-soaked burger with just a few healthy chomps and with disregard to those who watched or the opinions they formed. Quince simply ignored them. He dried his palms with a napkin, crumbled it, dropped it into the plate, stood, and walked across the room. He flung open a glass door, and the aroma of bleach seeped through the cafeteria.

Hands buried in his pockets, Quince quietly walked through the hospital. His face was lowered, resting on the perch of the sternum. Suddenly, nurses burst from a room, shouting, maneuvering around the young veteran, but he ignored them and kept walking. An aged veteran, wearing a light-blue bed gown, jacketed with a bathrobe, prodded a metal stand with an IV. His feet scooted across the tiles. A free hand occasionally grasped the railing for balance. Quince walked by him, face down.

As he walked, faces greeted Quince, but he did not see them. He was lost in thought. This promised to be a tough day for him. He was eager to finish the meeting. Do it and leave. Sara asked that he go for Lilly and he agreed, but he was anxious, nervous. He had not the slightest desire to be courteous or acknowledge others that day. It was a mission.

During the earlier visit he made with Beecher, Quince had registered at the veterans' hospital. Walking down the stone stairs, he silently bade goodbye, believing in the purity of his conscience that he would not return until afflictions of age forced him back up those stairs. Now, only months later, his physical instruments intact, Quince returned. This visit did not set right with the young veteran. It was hard for him. He walked down the hall, frustrated.

Turning a corner, he passed rooms filled with veterans, sick and ailing. As he walked, moisture gathered in his eyes, singed from the sharp, slicing smell of bleach, or the putrid odor of urine. Televisions shouted from each room; volumes lifted by worn, wrinkled fingers, compensating for hearing they lost during a long life, and in the thunder of war, decades ago.

Down the hall, an old man sat alone in a wheelchair. He was bald with a slim, wrinkled face. Bruises speckled his scalp and forearms. As people walked by, he spoke, but dementia twisted his language. Some paused, attempting to communicate with him. Others quickly passed, hoping to avoid his shouts. Hands buried in his pockets, Quince approached the ancient veteran, and the man lifted his arms. Opening them, he began to wail, but the tongue of Alzheimer's shredded his words. Face lowered, hands buried deep in his pockets, Quince walked down the hall, around a corner.

His gait was long. The tiles were simple and beige, and worn through their exterior coating. They swept under his feet as a road passes under the feet of a child who's riding on the tailgate of a pickup. Quince mused about generations of veterans who marched across these tiles. Quince realized, walking quietly through the hall, how veterans of every 20th-century war had marched here. Not one army or one war.

He turned a corner and walked through a metal door, stomped up a flight of steps, and entered through another door. Echoes of his steps rattled through the stairwell, lost as the door slammed behind him. Standing alone, his shoulders sank, face low, like a traveler abandoned on the dock of a train station in a distant town. He sighed, and quickly gathered himself. He despised self-pity, but it grew like a cancer in him these past few months. He hated the dreams, and the festering paranoia. He promised Sara he would try counseling or speak with the chaplain. Try the VA. Sighing once more, his face lifted, and turned. On his left, a wall, whitewashed and bare, blocked the hallway. He sighed. Silence, then laughter erupted down the hall, on the right. Quince turned, stepped forward, approaching a linoleum counter. As he approached, he noticed two middle-aged women sitting at a desk behind the counter. Computer screens partially hid their faces. Turning to each other, they failed to see the young veteran or hear him over their conversation.

"Chaplain Griggs, please," said Quince, looming over the counter, looking down at a woman wearing burgundy-framed glasses.

Her expression grew serious. She turned, and faced the computer screen, never bothering to provide meaningful eye contact. "Name?" she asked, bluntly.

"Magowan," he answered.

She typed. "Last four?"

"2764," he answered.

She typed.

Quince leaned against the counter, looking around. Stacks of pamphlets littered the desk below. Pamphlets with fancy graphics boasted of veterans' benefits, job fairs for veterans, and the Montgomery GI Bill.

The woman typed.

Quince leaned across the counter, lifting a pamphlet from the desk. Pinched between his thumb and index finger, he reviewed the pamphlet's cover. A wounded soldier, leaning on crutches, smiled at a physician. Dog tags hung from the neck of the stooping soldier. An attractive woman stood near the soldier, grinning, shaking hands with the physician. A girl adoringly watched her soldier-father, standing at his cast-covered feet. It was a joyous scene. Letters, written in a sweeping font, read, *VA Medicine: Here to serve those who served us.* Quince opened the pamphlet, thumbing through its thin pages. Inside, paragraphs detailed innovative medicines developed to treat wounds from Iraq and Afghanistan, therapies for burn victims, and amazing technologies for prosthetics.

The typing paused. Looking over her glasses, the woman said in a bland tone, "The nurse will come for you. Please wait in the room."

Quince looked around.

"Around the corner," she directed, pointing with a pencil.

Quince turned, and walked away, leaving the pamphlet open on the counter.

As he walked away, laughter once again erupted, flowing over the counter and down the hall. Quince quietly walked. Entering the waiting room, he paused in the doorway. The room was empty. A row of plastic cushioned chairs lined the wall, separated by an occasional end table, littered with old magazines. His head cocked left, but the chairs were empty. To his right, a half-empty cup of coffee sat on the floor. A television was perched on a pedestal that hung from the ceiling. It played to the empty chairs and half-empty cup.

Quince moped across the room and sat. He looked around at the empty chairs and frowned. A round clock hung on a wall. Thick black hands marked passing minutes. He sighed, leaned across an empty chair, and grabbed a hunting-and-fishing magazine from the small table. He scanned the torn cover and pages, and noticed small, white letters in the top left corner that read, "Summer 2004."

Quince mindlessly thumbed through the magazine, quickly flipping pages, glancing at images. The television shouted at empty chairs, a plastic cup, half-filled with cold coffee, old magazines, and one young veteran. Suddenly, the television fell silent, pausing between programs. The rumblings of idle conversation flowed through the empty waiting room. The television program shouted once again, drowning the conversation. Thirty seconds later, it fell silent.

Quince stood, dropped the magazine on the table, and walked curiously through the hall. Turning left, he walked, ears poised, tracking the conversation. It grew louder. Down the hall and across from the empty waiting room, Quince turned, and faced the doorway of another waiting room. As he stood there, conversation poured across the threshold. Nearly every cushioned chair was taken, filled with old men, and men aging. Some were quiet. Most talked. One by one, they noticed Quince, lifting their faces from conversation, and stared at the young veteran standing paralyzed in the doorway.

Confused, Quince turned, and walked the hall. He stopped abruptly, and leaned over the counter. Lifting a hand, he pointed a thumb like a hitchhiker. "There's another waiting room."

Typing, the woman peered over her glasses.

"Why am I in the empty room? The other room is nearly full." His voice was accusing, strained. He sensed that somehow he was being cheated, or, worse, separated.

"The room on the left is reserved for patients who seek counseling for psychological illnesses. You," she paused, "are here to see Chaplain Griggs. The room on the right is reserved for patients needing general medical care."

He paused, thumb poised like a hitchhiker, leaning across the counter.

Emotions swept through his head, and there they hid. He was quiet; confusion paralyzed his tongue, far worse than words spoken by the ancient veteran, words shredded by Alzheimer's. The ancient veteran sat alone in a wheelchair, avoided like a leper by those passing by. Now, Quince somehow felt kindred to the old man. He appeared healthy; he was tall, thin and wiry, healthy. He wouldn't shrink, shrivel or bruise for decades, but he felt different from the other veterans. He had a stigma. For the first time since the dreams began, he felt different.

Quince slid off the linoleum counter, and quietly walked down the hall, into the empty waiting room, and sat. A television program shouted at empty chairs, a half-filled coffee cup, old magazines, and the young veteran, but Quince did not hear it. He sat alone. Magazines lay undisturbed on the table.

"Magowan," yelled a nurse, pausing in the hall.

Quince stood, and left the empty waiting room. The nurse waved a clipboard, and together they walked down the hall, passing the second waiting room. Idle conversation poured into the hall but grew silent as Quince and the nurse passed. He walked, face sunk, eyes focused on the tiles at his feet, but he saw them, veterans watching as he passed by the doorway. The nurse paused, and turned before a tiny, closet-sized room. "Step on the scales, please." She said, tapping the clipboard, poised to write.

Quince frowned. *What the hell does my weight have to do with dreams*, he quietly wondered? Eventually, he nodded, and walked up the scales, arms hanging at his side. The nurse tapped a clipboard. Red, digital numbers twisted on the scale. Finally, they settled on 172. Quince nodded, "It never changes," he boasted, stepping off the scale. The nurse did not respond. She noted his weight, and waved the clipboard. "Wait in here. Chaplain Griggs will be with you momentarily."

Quince stood in the threshold, peering into the room. It was small and plain, like any other examination room. A small metal chair sat aside a desk and computer. An old water coil heater rested below a window. Outside, an oak limb swayed in the breeze. An examination chair sat in a lounging position near the center. Thin, white paper ran the length of the blue-cushioned seat.

Quince sighed, fighting self-pity. He felt it coming on as one feels an illness. Nodding, his lips pinched. His eyes briefly closed as he stepped across the threshold, and sat in a metal chair. The nurse quietly closed the door behind him. Quince, again, was alone.

A small, round clock hung above the door. The hands were narrow, black. The numbers were plain, black, nothing fancy or cursive about their form. The background was eggshell white. It did not tick or sound the hours. It just turned, a razor thin hand running laps around two, slower, bulky hands. "Saddest damn clock I've ever seen," Quince said aloud, chuckling.

Quince sat alone. Time passed. Ten minutes became fifteen, and the humor he initially found in the quiet, bland clock faded as the hands turned. Outside, the hallway was quiet except for the occasional echo of a door slamming or someone's footsteps. Beyond the window, an oak limb, bent like a contorted arm and lined with coarse bark, bounced in a light breeze. Fear of re-living his dreams began to overwhelm him. Just the thought of talking about that day in the Kunar Valley, driving along the river, and watching Sergeant Patrick's hi-lux explode, terrified the young man. Suddenly, it felt as if the walls were closing in on him. Beads of sweat sprinkled his forehead.

He glanced at the clock, and the second hand appeared to race around the cylinder as if it were the arms of a third-base coach, waving home a runner. That small, boring instrument he'd just laughed at was now waving on the walls, cheering them to move closer—crush the young man who stood in their way.

As the walls drew closer, Quince had enough. He leapt from the chair, burst through the door and down the hall, passing the waiting room crowded with veterans. He passed the empty waiting room, the television shouting at empty chairs, and cold coffee. He passed the linoleum counter. "Should we schedule a follow-up?" asked the aging woman, staring through burgundy frames.

Quince ignored her and kept walking. He pushed open the metal door, stomped down a flight of stairs, and turned on a landing, glancing through a window that overlooked a paved lot. The lot was crowded, cars parked in the grass, under trees. Quince paused and approached the window. Parked beneath a catalpa tree, in the grass, was a red pickup. It was oddly familiar; big tires, a scratch cut down along the driver's side door, the tailgate always folded down. He stood there, staring through the window, at the pickup, when a small man walked purposefully across the lot, maneuvering through a maze of parked cars. Overcast, soft light reflected from his bald scalp. Pausing, he scratched around in his pocket, hung a burley cigarette in his lips, cupped his hands, and lit it. His lips puckered and face pinched as smoke twisted from the burley. The man stood far away, partially shielded by cars, but his mannerisms, the way he lit a cigarette was something Quince had seen thousands of times. It was Beecher's way of smoking.

Quince turned, bouncing down steps, and burst through the metal door, into the hall. He ran. He passed patients, doctors, nurses. He passed the ancient veteran who wailed at him with a tongue twisted with Alzheimer's. He ran fast, nearly tumbling over nurses in blue scrubs as they left the cafeteria. Bursting through a door, he leapt down the sweeping stone stairs, and ran.

Across the lot, under the catalpa, Beecher jerked the door open, leapt into the seat of his pickup, and drove away. Running, Quince's legs slowed before stopping. He stood alone in the parking lot with arms braced on his knees, winded from the run. He was confused. Why was Beecher there today? He hadn't mentioned an appointment. The farm is more than an hour away. He always told Quince when he'd be in town. Why not now?

Chapter 26
≈ Ambush ≈

Autumn's fallen leaves lay in the grass, soggy. It was early—a cold spring morning. The sky was dark and moist. Dawn was away in the east.

Quince stood on a dark porch, beneath the eave. His head tilted and cocked. Vertebrae creaked, loosening muscles in his neck. His eyes blinked, washing moisture over them, before he opened them again. He gazed south, toward the city center. A moon hung over the towers. Like a campfire among trees, glowing street lamps touched the tower walls.

North, he gazed. A giant maple, foliage stripped by winter's wind, stood near the street. Limbs waved with a crisp breeze; craggy, skeletal fingers pointed, heralding the north. Above him, along the eave, dew bubbled and fell onto his bare neck.

Suddenly, a crisp breeze pimpled the skin along his arms, nudging Quince from the porch. He leaned forward, skipped down two front steps, and lunged as if hopping over puddles. Landing softly in the grass, he ran. Icy dew soaked Quince's shoes, leaking through his socks. Quince ran and the moon slowly fell, clawing at a black sky, stretching for stars as if they were ledges of a cliff. It was easy for Quince to keep a good pace. His stride was long, rhythmic. Tall, wiry, he was made to run, and run he did that morning. Sneakers slapped the pavement as he navigated streets and alleys. Lamps hung above him. Far north, beneath the stars, a skyline rose and fell along soft ridges. A compass, they guided him north.

It was quiet. The usual pedestrians slept in their beds; cars sat idle in driveways. He ran and lamps drew white circles over the sidewalk. Stoplights turned patterns; a red glow painted an intersection, and the street blushed. He soon settled into a comfortable pace, passing empty boutiques and flower shops, turning left at the courthouse, onto a street lined with tall brick houses and antebellum mansions. He ran under the umbrella of giant oaks. He ran.

His breath was deep, controlled. Trickles of sweat cooled his skin and warm air poured from his scalp. His chest rose and fell beneath a gray sweatshirt. Moisture bubbled along his brow, muscles loosened, lungs stretched. Quince ran through a winding street of blue-collar homes. Porch lights winked as he passed. Houses were quiet. Windows were black and cold.

His stride carried him along the bypass, and a narrow road through farms and hills and streams, north. His muscles relaxed, pushing and pulling Quince over every hill and around curves. The air was thick with the smell of fresh-turned soil. Cattle grazed in the fields. Dogs barked. He was alone now, running. The trickle of rolling water echoed against a hill. Quince ran and the trickle grew loud. The road sank over a knoll, and wound along a simple, quiet valley. A rusty, barbed-wire fence paralleled one side; on the other side, broken stalks yellowed in a field.

He ran between barbed-wire and yellowing stalks, and the road softly fell into a valley, toward a line of trees, and a shadowy mountain. Ahead, the dim, gray road disappeared; the mountain simply swallowed it. It was gone, lost to a dark cloud enveloping the valley. A wall of trees stood below the mountain slope.

Nearing the trees, his stride shortened and his breath labored, and Quince's sneakers softly slapped the asphalt. Soon, he began to walk, resting his hands atop his head. Trickling water echoed across the road as he neared the trees. Asphalt slowly rose to a bridge, resting high above a stream.

Quince paused, turned, and dropped his hands onto a concrete wall overlooking the water. Dew had gathered on the ledge, and the concrete was cool, moist to his warm fingers. Below, murky water swiftly passed under the bridge. Sycamores stood on the edge of the pasture. Steep, muddy banks sloped into the water; roots, twisted and gnarled, burst through the mud like veins across flesh.

Laboring to breathe, his face sank, and sweat dripped from his brow, falling in a perfect, vertical descent, splashing into the smooth current below. Upstream, water was shallow, swiftly passing over a bed of slate and tumbling into a fallen sycamore.

Something was familiar about the river. As a boy, during the summer, he waded these waters with Beecher, casting for smallmouth and bluegill. But, it wasn't childhood memories that drew the familiarity—there was something about the sounds of trickling water, pungent smell, the cool air—it was something he had felt as an adult.

Quince pulled his hands from the wall, and slowly walked away from the bridge, stepping off the road, into the high, wet grass. At a fence, he rested one hand on a rotting, coarse post, and the other between barbs on the wire. Lifting a leg over the wire, he leapt, and pushed against the rotting post. Clearing the wire with his other leg, he landed in the soft, wet grass.

Quince wiped sweat from his brow, squatting in the grass. Below, fog clouds sailed downstream, as if fleeing from something evil. Water swept over slate rock, crashing into a fallen tree. Upriver, a farmhouse sat alone on a knoll overlooking the valley; light from a window flooded the farmer's yard. A dog yelped from the porch.

Quince squatted near the walnut, listening. As a boy, hunting deer, Beecher taught him to listen beyond the surface noise, ignore a barking dog, a gust of wind, and listen, however briefly, to the dead spots. *Just chanticleers*, he often said of noisemakers. If a dog barked, Beecher, whispering in a whisky voice, would say, *Wait for the old bitch to swallow*. When trees shook with a fall breeze, he warned, *Listen beneath the wind*. In the Kunar Valley, Quince often listened beneath the wind. Squatting near the walnut, on the banks of a stream, Quince closed his eyes and thought of the Kunar Valley.

≈≈≈

Smooth, silky was the petal he pinched from the red bloom. "Waiting," cursed Jenkins, "... fucking blows!" Quince ignored him, rubbing the petal between his index finger and thumb. The silky petal soon tore as he stroked it with his coarse fingers. All around him, poppies swayed in a soft breeze.

"Corporal Mac ... it's hell, waiting. I say we go ... get to the river."

Quince ignored the Marine, examining the petal. His coarse fingers twisted in circles over the flower until it fell in small pieces to the sandy soil. Peeling the sleeve over his wrist, he cupped a hand over the watch, pushed a button, and ignited a light. Quince turned to the RTO, squatting next to him. "Thirty mikes," he whispered. "Reckon it's time."

The RTO nodded, pressing a button on the handset hanging from his chinstrap. He pressed the button two more times, and waited until he was answered by the sound of three clicks. Turning to Quince, he nodded.

"All right," Quince leaned into Jenkins, "we'll set up on the back side of the sand bed. Low-crawl down the bank and keep your weapons out of the sand." He dropped his finger into the sandy soil, between rows of poppies, and drew a straight line. "Ramirez, Thomas, in tight," he motioned.

Two Marines scooted closer.

"River," he pointed to the line, drawing circles on one side, "Pakistan mountains," drawing another circle on the opposite side, "Camp Stanton." His face lifted, and he surveyed their eyes. "The sand bed is here. Should be coming down the river, but," he paused, "can't say for sure. Cover 180 degrees, north to south. They could be going or coming. Hell if I know. But we'll have our backs to the riverbank and Stanton. Now, you three will cover 90 to 180. We got up to 90," pointing to the RTO. "Just like we briefed today."

Jenkins nodded.

"Roger that, Corporal," whispered Ramirez.

Thomas nodded.

Quince continued, whispering, "Those fuckers been slipping across the border to bury IEDs in the road. Gone before daylight. Use the river as a path to hide from Stanton and our patrols. Tonight, if they come," he paused, "we'll be waiting."

"Oorah," grunted Ramirez.

Jenkins nodded. So did Thomas.

Quince and the RTO crawled on their knees between rows of blooming poppies. A soft wind blew. Thick, heavy blooms swayed in the wind, rocking back and forth, tapping the Marines on the shoulder as they crawled. Quince paused on the bank. A narrow strip of metal held NVGs to the front of his Kevlar; a mechanical arm acted as an elbow, allowing them to rise and fall. He lifted a hand, tugged on the NVGs, and they dropped over his left eye. His right eye squinted shut as he surveyed the river below. The water ran down the valley, running swiftly over stones and around sharp bends. For ages, a swift current sliced the sandy soil. The water was powerful. As the snow melted, and the currents swelled, the river cut deeper into the valley floor. When the water subsided, boulders had tumbled miles downstream, and sand beds littered the river.

Quince surveyed the valley, listening. Upstream, light from street lamps lay across the village streets. A dog barked. A soft breeze whistled in his ears. Squatting in the sandy soil, beneath the poppies, he listened. He listened between barks, and beneath the wind, and soon, he nodded to the RTO, fell forward, on his stomach, dropped his elbows over the lip of the bank, and slid down into the riverbed. He walked with his elbows, hoisting the M16 in his hands, and kicking his knees. He slid down the slope, and through a shallow tributary, adjacent to the main river, and onto the back slope of a steep sand bed, overlooking the water. Twisting, he faced the village. The RTO quietly crawled out of the tributary, onto the sand bed, a few feet from Quince. He slowly pushed the M16 forward, and pointed the barrel at the mountains. Jenkins,

Ramirez, and Thomas slid down the riverbank, through the tributary, onto the sand bed. Jenkins faced the mountains; Thomas and Ramirez, south, down the valley.

Quince pointed the M16 north, up the river. His chest, groin, and thighs were soaked—sand stuck to them like glue. The sand bed was narrow, and his feet lay in the tributary. A soft breeze floated down the valley, across the sand bed, and through his wet clothes. It was cold. He began to shake.

He laid the brim of his Kevlar on the weapon's rear sight post, and surveyed the river. Upstream, street lamps glittered like tiny, green constellations in the dark valley. Minutes passed. The moon sailed over the valley. Wind whistled in his ears. Across the river, below the mountains, blooming poppies swayed in a night breeze. The Marines were quiet, still, listening.

Squinting, he surveyed the riverbed. Water tumbled down the valley. Waves were dipped in a creamy light of the moon. North, the riverbank slid into a narrow bed of stones, filling the river with bowling-ball size rocks. The stony path, a dozen feet across, wound from the sand bed north, before turning left and disappearing behind a steep bend.

Slowly, Quince lifted his Kevlar off the weapon, and opened his right eye. He could see the RTO in his periphery. He lowered the Kevlar, resting the brim on the rear sight post, and surveyed the area with NVGs. Light from the moon-frosted stones along the path. Glittering waves swept down the valley. A dark shadow lay across the river at the bend. Hours passed.

He shook. His feet lay in the tributary; cold water ran between his toes. Wind whistled. His cheek rested against the cool, plastic stock. His frosty breath fogged the M16's metal barrel. His body shook, twisting in the sand with tiny convulsions. His fingers were icy. Poppies swayed and waves tumbled. Everything in the valley shook.

A dog barked in the village. Wind whistled in his ears. Water trickled. His frosty breath fogged the metal barrel. "Listen beneath the wind," whispered Beecher's whisky voice from two decades past and an ocean away. He sighed. Sucking air through his nostrils, Quince held his breath and listened. Wind whistled, and he exhaled. Wind whistled, and died. His breathing paused. Around the bend, north, the faint clap of stone striking stone seeped from the shadow. Wind whistled. He exhaled; frosty breath fogged the metal barrel. Stones lay still along the path. Waves emerged from the shadowy bend, glittering in the creamy moonlight. Squinting, he saw nothing; the stones and waves and sand beds were alone.

Water trickled. Wind whistled. Quince, lying on the slope of a sand bed, held his breath. Around the bend, in the shadows, stones clapped. He listened. Exhaling, he drew another breath. There it was, again. This time he heard it between the trickling waves. Squinting, he surveyed the river, but saw nothing. The stones and waves were alone.

Slowly, his Kevlar rose from the rear sight post, and he turned south, looking downriver. "Pssst," he whistled, and the RTO looked over. "You hear that?" Quince whispered. The RTO paused, and his Kevlar shook.

Quince's face pinched and he turned, faced north, slowly lowered his Kevlar, and squinted. Upstream, street lamps projected green, fluorescent shapes across village streets. Squinting, he surveyed the river; the stones and waves but saw nothing. Drawing a breath, his lips closed, and he listened. Water trickled. Wind died away. Stones clapped in the shadows. His feet lay in the tributary. Cold water seeped through his boots. His clothes were soaked, but he ignored the cold. His body lay across the sand bed, still. A small, black box was affixed to the barrel below the rear sight. A thin, red laser poured from the box, north, at the shadow. Quince leveled the laser a few feet above the stony path. Stones clapped, coming ever closer.

Slowly, his thumb brushed across the butt stock. It was cold, icy. He turned a small lever, and it snapped, ready to fire. He turned it again, and the weapon was on burst, ready to send three rounds each time he squeezed the trigger; three rounds into the shadow, the clapping stones. Wind whistled. Stones clapped. His lips were pressed together, but the pressure of his breath pried them open. Quince leveled the laser over the stones. His chest bounced in the sand. His finger lay across the cold, icy trigger. Stones clapped. Soon two fluorescent green forms emerged from the shadows. Voiceless, they moved slowly, cautiously along the stony path. The thin red laser shook, then leveled on the chest of the figure near the water. Slowly, Quince squeezed slack from the trigger. The laser was steady. A sharp, crisp line needled through the dark riverbed. The two figures moved cautiously, unknowingly toward the sand bed.

Patiently, Quince lay on a sand bed; his feet soaked in the tributary. Stones clapped. The figures walked along the stony path. They walked closer, and their fluorescent forms took the shape of humans. Their frames, imposing in the shadows, narrowed in the creamy moonlight. Their stride narrowed. Their faces were smooth and round. Squinting, Quince's face pinched. His finger dropped. Stones clapped. The figures stepped onto the sand bed. A soft voice spoke in Pashto. They laughed.

"Down!" Quince shouted. "Get down!" Waving his barrel at the two figures, the red laser sliced across their thin frames.

"What the fuck!" Jenkins screamed, surprised.

"Cover me," Quince shouted.

"Roger."

"Damn!" Jenkins shouted.

"They ain't our guys. They're kids," answered Quince. He stood, pulled his feet from the tributary, and approached the figures. He pushed the NVGs from his eyes, pulled a flashlight from his vest, and shined the light in the children's faces. Their dirt smudged features trembled. Their eyes were wide. Quince surveyed them, shining light across their thin frames. The children whimpered. Their hands were empty.

"Shit! Where did they come from?" Jenkins cursed, leveling his weapon at the children.

"These ain't our guys," said Thomas.

"No," Quince nodded. "Let them go."

Water tumbled down the valley. Wind whistled, and died. A dog barked in the village. Stones clapped as the children walked north, along the river, toward the village. The Marines waded the tributary, climbed the riverbank, and patrolled quietly through the swaying poppies. Red blooms tapped their thighs.

≈ ≈ ≈

Quince lay in the soft mud below the riverbank. The pungent smell of rotting leaves rose from the stream. He stood. Mud was caked to his face and soaked his clothes. Disoriented, he surveyed the stream. A car passed over the bridge. The pasture and fields were gray; orange quilted the hills and peaks. The moon slipped over the hills in the west. Quince sighed. His eyes moistened. He stooped, sat in the mud, and wept. After a while, he stood, climbed the bank, passed the walnut tree, the dewy pasture, and leapt the fence. His stride had length, and his feet clapped against the asphalt as he ran south, away from the stream.

Meanwhile, back at home, the snap of percolating coffee filled the kitchen. Sara opened the refrigerator, poured milk in a small pink cup, and handed it to Lilly. She smiled, and ran fingers through her daughter's blonde curls. A clock on the coffee pot read 8:47 a.m. She poured a cup, and leaned over the table, gazing up the street. Lilly sipped milk, sitting at a small glass table in the nook. "Where is Daddy?" she asked, milk across her upper lip.

Sara blew steam from the coffee, tilted the cup to her lips, and sipped. Pulling the cup away, she answered. "Sometimes . . ." she paused, "your daddy likes to run."

Lilly frowned. "At night, Mommy?"

Sara sipped coffee. She exhaled, stared across the yard, and confessed, "At night." She turned, smiling as Lilly pulled the cup to her lips and drank.

Suddenly, the front door opened, and footsteps echoed across the floor, approaching the kitchen. Sara turned, facing the den. Lilly turned, sipping milk. Footsteps echoed, drawing nearer. "Quince? Is that you?" she asked.

Footsteps echoed, drawing closer.

"Quince?" asked Sara. Face pinched. Her voice, frightened.

Muddy shoes stepped from the carpet, onto the linoleum floor. Sara's eyes slowly rose, along the legs, across the mud-soaked knees, up the mud and sweat soaked torso. Water dripped from his brow. His cheeks were spotted with dirt. His hair was soaked. He was still. Mud, sweat dripped across the linoleum.

Sara's face was long. Her eyes swelled. Lilly, sipping milk, gently set the cup on the table. Her eyes were scared.

Quince stood there, still. His mouth opened, stammering, but couldn't find the right words. He knew he owed them an explanation. Instead, his face sank. He turned, and moped down the hall, disappearing into the bathroom. Muddy prints marked his path across the carpet. He showered, walked naked across the room, crawled into a bed, pulled a comforter over his face, and closed his eyes. He slept and, once again, the dreams came.

Chapter 27
≈ A Mud-bricked Home ≈

Wind whistled through camp. Tents bent and swayed. Torrents of dust scratched windows. Rain pelted the concrete roof over Quince's cot. He lay still, listening as the storm sailed over the valley. Hours earlier, thunder shook the camp. He stood on the roof, lit a cigarette and watched a dark cloud move up the Kunar River. Gusts of wind and rain shook the fields, and soaked mountain slopes. Poppies drew lightning from the cloud. Thunder shook the valley.

Quince dragged from a burley, and watched the valley. Clouds passed over the bridge, along the fields where Sergeant Patrick once lay dying, and over shanties on the riverbank. Quince dragged, exhaled, dropped the cigarette, and crushed the embers with his boot. He stepped down the ladder, walked along the sandy road and into the concrete room. Lying in his cot, he stared at the roof, listening as the storm passed over Camp Stanton, and moved toward the village. Wind whistled through camp, shaking tents, scratching windows. Outside, a horn blew, echoing across camp. Voices shouted over thunder, and whistling wind.

Quince sat up, dropping his feet to the floor. He quickly pulled boots over his feet, laced them, and ran across the camp. Rain and sand pelted him, soaking the skivvy shirt as he traced the commotion. Two Humvees were parked near the entrance, just inside the concertina, on the camp's south side. It was a small, wooden shanty. Outside the door, a sign marked with fat, red letters, read BAS for Battalion Aid Station.

Men huddled near the open door of a Humvee. A man shouted in Pashto. Rain soaked his thin, black beard. A younger man listened, and shouted in English. A corpsman in a skivvy shirt leaned over the Pashtun man. Marines gathered nearby.

"What is it?" Quince shouted, pausing near a Marine who stood near the Humvee. Rain streamed over his brow, along the back of his neck.

The Marine squinted, shaking his head. "Little girl, Corporal. Wind blew over a wall. Guess the rain weakened the bricks, and the wall tumbled over on her."

"How is she?"

"Doc will fix her up, Corporal."

Quince pushed through the crowd. Her father shouted at the others. His face was panicked. Doc shouted, urging them into the shanty. Rain pelted them. The young interpreter shouted. Quince wiped his eyes, peering through the rain. In the arms of her father, lay a small, rain-soaked girl. Mud caked her cheeks. She was pale, still, but her eyes were open, staring gauntly at the heavens. Quince peered through rain, leaning closer. Suddenly, his face pinched. Her eyes were blue. Her hair was long and dark. "Farrah?" he whispered.

His eyes swelled. She was pale, still, but her eyes were open.

Doc shrugged. "Her ribs are broken. Maybe worse. Won't know until tomorrow. Helivac can't fly in this weather. Need to get her to Bagram."

Doc fell silent as they rushed Farrah into the shanty. A corpsman blocked the door, keeping the Marines outside. "Go back to your hooch," he shouted, standing in the threshold, bracing the door with each hand. The Marines slowly grumbled, moping across the muddy compound.

Quince stood in the rain. Water streamed over his brow. His skivvy top was soaked. Muddy water ran over his boots. He peered through the pelting rain, into the well-lit shanty. Doc frantically worked. Her father wailed. Quince turned, and went across the compound to his hooch. He changed into dry clothes and fell into the cot and lay there, unable to sleep, until finally, sometime that night, the room fell dark.

The next morning, light peeked through the window. Quince blinked, and sat upright in the cot. Thunder echoed across the valley. Quince's feet dropped to the floor, and he pulled boots over them, boots still soaked from last night. He laced them, and ran across the compound. He waved at the Marines in the tower as he slipped through a hole in the wall, jogging toward the rock-strewn landing zone.

A Marine was walking away from the landing zone, toward camp. "This for the little girl?" he asked the Marine.

"Yes, Corporal," he answered, still walking.

Quince jogged up the hill. Several Marines were gathered around a Humvee where Farrah lay quietly on a stretcher inside. Her father stood nearby. His face was noticeably calmer. Overhead, thunder rumbled. A CH-47 crested the mountain peaks, and circled the valley. Quince quickly approached the Humvee. He wove through the small crowd, to the vehicle's door just as Doc pronounced to the others, "Best I can tell it's just broken ribs. We'll know in Bagram. She'll need an x-ray to rule out internal damage. Regardless, she's gonna be fine."

A smile lifted Quince's face. He leaned into the Humvee, over the little girl, bundled in blankets, and gently patted her shoulder. Farrah's blue eyes watched him. She smiled, and softly spoke. As she finished, and her tiny blue lips closed, her father looked at the Quince and nodded, slightly.

"She says you are the candy man," shouted the young interpreter.

Quince smiled, patted her shoulder, nodded to the father, and walked down the hill, into camp.

Overhead, the CH-47 sank to the landing zone, and Farrah was loaded on the helicopter. Her father and Doc ran alongside the stretcher, and stepped into the helicopter just before it lifted, circled the valley and crested the mountain peaks.

A week later, a Humvee drove between the poppies, along the Kunar River. The village was a mile away when it turned onto a small dirt path, and drove between poppy fields, toward the mountain slope. Quince road in the passenger seat. Doc drove. Farrah, swaddled in bandages, a robe, and a blanket, sat with her father in the backseat. A young interpreter rode with them as they drove up a valley, through the mountain's shadow, and stopped near a slope.

Quince circled the Humvee, and surveyed the rocky ground above them. The M16A2 was pressed against his torso; the plastic stock was cold on his bare fingers. Doc and the little girl's father helped Farrah from the Humvee. She was stooped, favoring her fragile ribs, walking across the yard, toward the mud-walled compound. Quince followed them, knelt near the door, scratched through his pocket, and produced a small bag of peppermints. He laid them in Farrah's hand, and a smile lifted her soft cheeks. Her blue eyes opened, watching him, and he grinned, rose to his feet, and surveyed the slope, and the fields below them. Doc and the interpreter disappeared through mud walls.

Shadows grew over the valley. Soon, they emerged from the compound. It was getting late. Farrah's father smiled, and spoke. Quince listened. The young interpreter listened, and turned to the Marine. "He says you are very kind to his daughter."

Quince smiled.

The father spoke.

"He says his daughter speaks of you often," continued the interpreter.

Quince smiled, turned to the interpreter, and asked, "We're leaving soon. Do they need food for the winter?"

The young interpreter turned to the father, and spoke. The father listened, before speaking, waving his hands as he talked. Quince watched him. The man's thin, black beard bounced around as his chin rose and fell. His skin was wrinkled, coarse, but Quince guessed the man was no older than 35. His finger pointed as he spoke, and his hands appeared bent, scarred. He was thin. The valley had aged him.

The young interpreter turned to Quince, and spoke, "Says the summer has been dry, but they will have a good harvest."

Quince nodded.

"It is true for families across the valley," continued the interpreter, staring out across the Kunar Valley. Red blooms swayed in a breeze. Water ran briskly down the valley.

Quince nodded.

"Tell him I will return in one week to check on his daughter," said Doc, crowded near the men.

The father smiled, and shook hands with Doc. He grasped Quince's hand, and spoke.

The interpreter listened, "Says you are very generous. He is grateful for your help."

Quince smiled, turned, and walked away. They loaded the Humvee, and sped away, down the valley, through fields of poppy.

≈≈≈

Coarse, gray smoke spewed from his nostrils. Lifting the cigarette to his dry lips, his cheeks sank, embers burned, and his chest lifted. Again, he pulled the burley from his lips, paused, and exhaled. A cloud of smoke gathered around him. His eyes squinted, staring north, toward the village. It was evening. The air was dead. The valley, quiet. Quince smoked alone, standing on the roof of the concrete hooch. Nearby, his blouse lay across a stack of bulging sandbags. A thin skivvy shirt covered his chest. One arm hung lifeless against a thigh; the other mechanically lifted a burley to his lips, and jerked it away. His eyes blinked in the smoky cloud.

"Corporal Mac," shouted Doc, standing behind the walls.

Quince turned, nodding.

"We're headed up the valley to see the little girl." He threw a finger in the air, toward an idling Humvee, asking, "Go with us?"

Quince nodded, dropped the cigarette, and stomped the tobacco with the toe of his boot. Embers blackened, smudged across the concrete roof and smoke lifted from them. Sliding the blouse over his shoulders, he dropped down the wooden ladder, and walked through a screen door.

Doc waited in the road.

Quince soon emerged, wearing a flak jacket and LBV; an M16A2 hung from his hand; a green strap hung from the weapon, swaying as he walked. Together, they walked across the compound, loaded a Humvee, and slowly drove north, along the river road, through poppy fields. Dust spat from their tires, and rolled over red-bloomed plants. Doc drove. The young interpreter sat alone in the back. Quince rode in the passenger's seat, staring at the dusty lane ahead of them. He watched as Doc turned from the river road, onto the small, narrow lane running between fields. Shadows dropped over the fields, throwing a dusky texture across the small valley and the mud-walled compound.

The Humvee slowly rolled across the yard, and paused near the compound. Quince's face pinched. A thick, wooden door, leading into the compound, hung open. Trash littered the yard. A filthy dog lay quietly outside the door. Flies swarmed over it; syrupy blood pooled in a dark, purplish tint below the animal's stomach.

Quince pulled the M16 into his chest. His thumb slid under the trigger guard, flipping a lever. His index finger lay against the trigger. "You two stay with the vehicle," he ordered, waving at Doc and the interpreter. "Doc, get word to Stanton. Tell them to standby. Something's happened." Flies swarmed the blood-soaked wound, as he passed the dog's carcass. Quince squinted as stench lifted from rotting flesh. Water gathered in his eyes, but he moved forward. His head was tilted, leaning across the M16's stock. His eyes scanned the compound, following the long, black barrel of the weapon. He scanned the mud walls, sweeping the weapon left-to-right. His chest pounded. Heartbeats thundered in his ears. The weapon's muzzle passed between the mud wall, and his boots softly traced behind, crossing the wooden threshold. Pungent air sucked through his nostrils, down into his lungs. He coughed, and spat, washing the stench from his tongue.

Inside the compound, he swept the muzzle left, then right, scanning the walls. Both corners were empty. He sighed. He scanned. Trash littered the compound, outside the small, home. Footprints covered the dusty ground. Prints were carved in the soft dust like a mosaic. Quince cautiously moved toward the home, the wooden door, ajar. The M16's muzzle was pointed at the door. Quince followed it; the muzzle acted like a yoke, pulling him forward, across the compound, toward the building. His chest pounded; his ears filled with thundering heartbeats. Near the door, his left hand slipped from the muzzle, and carefully pushed the wooden door. Rusty hinges cried out, squeaking as the heavy door opened, alerting the compound to his presence. His chest pounded. He prayed the squeaking would stop, but the door slowly turned, and the hinges cried out. He scanned the room and saw that a back door was open. Dim light tattooed the dirt floor. The home was otherwise dark. Pungent air rushed across the threshold. Flies swarmed, buzzing mysteriously around him, in the shadows.

Quince pulled a small flashlight from his LBV, clicked it on, and swept light across the floor. Empty pots were scattered around. A rough wooden table stood nearby. The light swept to his right, where chairs were strewn, overturned. Portraits were torn from the wall. Light swept against the wall, across the threshold of another room.

He sighed and walked across the front room, holding the light in one hand. The weapon, pointing at the doorway, he held with the other hand. Walking, stooped over the weapon, Quince moved cautiously through the front room. The muzzle passed over the threshold. His boots followed. It was dark. In his periphery, two shadows lay prone. Light swept toward them, and his chest pounded. Hands shook, and the light trembled. Instinctively, he dropped to a knee, and his finger poised on the trigger. The light steadied. Dark, shiny hair slid over a mattress, and hung like olive-tinted ivy. The woman's face was pinched. Her body lay contorted; arms thrown over her head. The mattress was white and purplish. Quince swept light across the room, steadying on the figure lying in the floor. The man lay with his face in the floor. Quince moved closer, stepping between the man's opened legs. Stooping, Quince steadied light over the man's face. His eyes were open, staring at the dusty floor. A thin, black beard grew around his parted lips. Syrupy streams carved rivers in the dust around his neck.

Quince stood upright and turned, sweeping light across the walls, and another doorway. He stepped around the man's legs, softly placing his boots in the dusty floor. His chest pounded, ears thundered, as he approached the final room. Walking, Quince felt the toe of his boot kick something. It was soft, noiseless, but he felt the push of something against his toe. Light swept across his feet as he knelt, and reached for a small object lying in the floor. It was soft in his hand and he squished the object as he held it to the light. Soft, white fur; black eyes and nose; penciled smile. Quince recognized the stuffed bear. It had been his daughter's. Lilly sent him the bear last summer, after he wrote her about Farrah, and asked that he give the doll to the little Afghan girl. Standing, he pushed the bear into his pocket, and swept light across the room. Blankets littered the small, dark room. A small bed was overturned; a mattress spilled across the floor. Suddenly, Quince's toe kicked something again. Like before, it was soft. He knelt, and swept light across his feet. Clothing rose like a snowdrift against the wall. Quince brushed away the clothing, stopping, as a cold object touched his hand. He swept light across the pile of clothing, noticing a tiny fist emerging from the clothes. Quince sighed. His chest pounded. Louder than before, heartbeats thundered in his ears. Brushing away clothing, an arm was exposed. His heart pounded, punching the flak jacket like a fist. He lifted and tossed clothing, and swept light along the arm, to a tiny face. His heart pounded. The flashlight shook violently. Quince's brow pinched, and his mouth fell open, sucking pungent, stench-filled air down his lungs. He tried to steady the light over the tiny face, but his hands shook. The little face was dirt-smudged. Deep blue eyes looked up, in horror, helpless. A small, purplish stream had trickled from her scalp, down her temple. It was dry.

Kneeling, Quince laid the M16 across his thigh, and put the light on clothing near Farrah's face. His face lowered, dropping into his cupped hands, and he began to cry. His face soon rose. He sighed, gathering confidence, and dropped his hands into the littered clothing, sifting through them like sand. Clothing fell away as Farrah's lifeless body rose from the litter. Quince held her and wept.

"Corporal Mac?" shouted Doc from the compound. "Corporal?" he shouted again, sweeping light through the mud-bricked home.

The interpreter's high-pitched, youthful voice screamed in Pashto.

Light swept across the small, clothing littered room. "Corporal Mac?" asked Doc, approaching Quince.

Quince's shoulders bounced as he knelt over the little Afghan girl, weeping.

Doc swept light over Quince's shoulder, across the little girl's face. His head tilted, and his eyes rolled. "Fucking cowards! All cause we helped them."

"QRF's is en route," Doc proclaimed. "Captain ain't taking chances."

Quince stood, sniffling, sucking snot through his nostrils. Gently, he laid Farrah in Doc's arms, knelt, picked up the M16, went out into the open. Down below, light swept across the poppy fields. Humvees raced up the valley.

≈≈≈

Quince wept, choking himself awake. Sitting forward, his eyes bulged. Dazed, they searched for something familiar, recognizable through his blurry, wet sight. Soon, a wall clock stuttered under the tongue of the second hand. The refrigerator clicked to life. A ceiling fan whistled in the bedroom. Outside, a car slowed at a stop sign and turned south, toward the city. The moon watched over town. Bright and heavy, light peeked beneath the blinds, fogging the window with white breath. Alone in a dark, quiet room, only silence and shadows in their suburban forms, joined him.

Quince leaned forward, and tapped the remote. A dark screen began to speak. The voice was strong and creviced with inflections. A suited man soon materialized. He was handsome and groomed, a qualifying owner to the voice. Sighing, Quince fell back into the chair, grimacing. His back arched. Cold sweat had soaked through his shirt. Reluctantly, he lay back, and the cold, moist fabric stuck to his back. Quince muted the suited man's voice. Settling deep in the recliner, one leg stretched forward, and the other cocked high against the armrest. His wrist hung over the knee, and he tapped the remote, surfing through channels. The flashing screen washed the dark walls of the den. The light brought warmth to walls, beating back the night's breath. They could have been flames climbing canyon walls in some old western.

Quince sat in silence, amid the boredom of night. The clock slapped away dark, quiet seconds. Surfing channels, he stood, dropped the remote in the chair, went into the kitchen. He pulled the refrigerator door, and light soaked the floor, spilling like milk across the tiles. Bottles clanked as he pulled a beer from the refrigerator, twisted the cap, lifted the bottle to his lips and drank. Quince grabbed another beer, and slammed the door. Tossing the cap on the counter, he went back in the den and flopped into the recliner. Tapping the remote, he surfed channels and drank.

Quince pulled the bottle to his lips and drank.

"Daddy?" asked Lilly's soft, half-asleep voice. Standing in the hall, blonde curls fell across her face. Her pajamas were wrinkled. "What are you doing?" she continued, walking sleepily toward her father.

Quince pulled the beer from his lips, swallowing discretely. "Daddy couldn't sleep," he answered.

The television flashed, silently. Light washed the den.

"Can I stay up with you?" she asked, standing near the recliner.

Quince set the beer down on the table, leaned forward, and pulled Lilly into his lap. "Sure, but only for a minute. Your mother doesn't want you up this late."

"OK," she whispered, her socked feet dangling over Quince's knees. She lay in Quince's lap, quietly watching her father surf channels.

"Daddy?" she asked, watching the television.

"Yes?"

"Why is your shirt wet?" she asked.

Quince paused. "Daddy just had a bad dream."

"Oh."

Quietly, Quince pulled the beer to his lips and drank, returning the bottle to the table. Light flashed. A suited man materialized. Quickly, though, his face was swept away by scenes of burning wreckage, and frightened soldiers. Blood-splattered civilians ran across the screen.

Lilly watched. She was quiet. Quince watched as scared figures ran through streets, pleading to the camera. Light flashed. Shadows leapt from the screen and ran along the walls. The flames and choking black smoke kindled along the neck of Quince's half-empty beer bottle.

Sitting quietly, Quince's thoughts slipped back into the Kunar Valley, and the small mud-bricked home beneath the mountain slope. His eyes dimmed, closed and he slept. When his eyes opened, he saw a filthy, dark room, littered with clothes. He was back in the Kunar. Kneeling, he brushed away clothing, until the flashlight he held swept over Farrah's smooth, round cheeks. Leaning forward, he saw the girl's features, softened in the dim light. A small, round nose, her thin brows, a dimpled chin, Quince held her lifeless body.

Suddenly, her blue eyes, frozen open in horror, blinked. Her lips pursed, focusing on the young Marine stooping over her. Quince began to smile, laughing through tears. He couldn't believe she was alive. Had she just been unconscious? Hiding from the Taliban under the clothing? Was she really alive? Purplish blood streamed down her temple, dried, but she was alive! Moving. Watching Quince. "Farrah?" he asked, disbelief whispering his voice.

Her eyes focused.

"I'm here," Quince answered.

She attempted to speak. Quince leaned closer so that he might hear faint words. Her lips poised. Breath passed through her lips as they postured. Quince tilted his head. His ear hung above her lips, listening for her soft voice.

"Go away," whispered the voice.

Quince's face pinched.

His head tilted.

"Go away . . ." whispered the voice again.

Quince leaned back. His brow fell over his eyes.

"Leave," she demanded, her voice strengthening. "Leave my family."

Quince was horrified. His lips stammered, pleading, "I just wanted to help."

"Go away," answered her voice, growing mature with each word.

Quince stammered. "We tried to help you."

"You brought pain."

Quince rocked back on his heels, kneeling. "We helped you. When . . . when . . . you were hurt . . . we helped you."

"You brought pain to my family."

"We just wanted to help. Fix you."

"You killed me . . ." she said.

Quince stumbled back, falling on his ass. He began to scoot away from the girl. His eyes were bulging, horrified.

"Leave us. Leave the valley," demanded the little Afghan girl. "Leave the valley."

Quince scooted across the dusty, clothing-littered floor. Scrambling to his feet, he ran from the home, through the poppies. He ran hard. His legs pumped, boots digging in the soft, irrigated soil. Red blooms burst, exploding as he ran through poppies. He ran between fields, crossing the river road, running as hard as he could. His chest bounced, air sucked through his nostrils. Dust spat around his boots as he ran, feet pumping, digging into the soil. Running, he could hear the rushing water below the ledge. Arms pumping, his chest bounced as he ran, leaping from a sharp ledge, tumbling head first into the river, crashing through the strong, icy waters of the Kunar River.

≈≈≈

Quince wept, choking until he woke. He screamed, pushing the little girl away from him; scooting away until the recliner overturned, scrambling away until he struck the wall. Lilly began to scream, wailing as she lay on the floor, watching her father. Quince's eyes bulged. They were lost, away somewhere, in some forgotten valley.

"Lilly!" screamed Sara, rushing from the bedroom. Kneeling next to her daughter, she pled, "What's wrong? What happened?"

Lilly whimpered, pointing to her father. "Daddy threw me down."

Sara's eyes followed the little girl's finger as it pointed across the den, to the overturned recliner, emptied beer bottles, spilling across the carpet, to her husband, cowering against a far wall.

She looked back at Lilly, "Are you hurt?" Lilly shook her head, standing slowly. "OK," continued Sara, softly kissing the girl's forehead. "Go on to bed. I will be in soon to tuck you in."

Lilly stood, glanced at her father, and walked gingerly down the hall, to bed. Sara stood, and approached Quince. His eyes began to narrow, slowly lifting as she paused over him. "I have asked you to get help. Now look what you've done. You frightened her half to death, Quince." Sara paused, crossing her arms. Her face was stern, pinched as she glared at her husband. "We're leaving tomorrow. You can have the house. I don't care about it." She stood and watched him, looking down at her husband, cowering against the wall.

The channel turned. Light flashed, washing the den.

Chapter 28
≈ Leaving ≈

Quince rose early the next morning. Rain fell. The sky was gray. It was a dreary spring morning. Sara and Lilly slept as he dressed and left for work. It was inventory day. Each Friday, Quince walked the aisles, carrying a clipboard, counting pallets. It took all day, but he enjoyed the job. He worked alone, and it was a nice, mindless activity to finish the week.

During breaks, he sat at a desk, and reviewed inventory. Often, during the day, he dialed Sara's number, listening as the tone buzzed in his ear, followed by Sara's voice smoothly announcing her name, and begging the caller to leave a message. Each time, Quince listened all the way through the message. Her voice was soft, and happy and sexy and when the message ended, Quince hung up.

When break was over, he went back to inventory. At 4:00 p.m. a whistle blew, echoing throughout the warehouse, between aisles, around pallets. Quince laid the clipboard on the desk, and joined a steady stream of workers pouring from the warehouse. He walked quietly among them, waiting as the crowd exited one-by-one through a turnstile. Rain was light. Drops sporadically struck his scalp, or dripped down his neck. Friday afternoon laughter echoed throughout the crowd. Jason Norris, a fellow supervisor, turned to Quince, and asked, "So . . . what's the weekend plan?"

Quince was silent; his eyes gazed aimlessly ahead.

"Magowan," Jason Norris insisted, "did you hear me? Hey?"

Quince's eyes focused, gazing at the young man's face.

"Quince?" asked Jason Norris, nervousness shaking his voice.

But Quince stomped ahead of the line, and pushed his way through the turnstile.

Those he cut in front of heckled him, but Quince ignored them. He walked across the parking lot, started the SUV, and drove away.

It was a quiet drive home. The radio was off. Wipers occasionally squeaked across the windshield. Quince thought about last night. He knew Sara was serious. He never doubted her threat. By now, Sara had taken their daughter and left. They were gone.

The house was empty. It was over, finished. He knew it. Felt it all day. Suddenly it felt like the end. It was real.

Quince drove through quiet streets, wondering where they had gone. Where were they at that moment? What were they doing? He just wanted to forget about the last six months. Go back to Cherry Point and get off the plane from Afghanistan again. Start over. But he knew that wasn't possible. Good or bad, time had passed. What's done is done. Instead, he drove. Wipers squeaked across the windshield. Like moisture on glass, Quince wanted to simply brush away those months, but he realized the damage was done. He had inflicted wounds that would not heal.

Quince drove. He swerved through a parking lot, pulled to the curb in front of a strip mall, left the truck running, walked into a liquor store, and purchased a bottle of bourbon and a case of beer. He drove through quiet streets, pulling into the driveway of his house, sat in the truck, and stared at his home. It looked quiet. Abandoned. Lights were off in the den, but the porch light glittered in the falling rain. The evening sky was gray. It was a dreary evening. Eventually, he tired of sitting there, pulled the phone from his pocket, and dialed Sara's number again. It buzzed. He listened. Sara's soft voice spoke through a greeting. The message ended. Quince turned it off, grabbed the bourbon and beer, and went inside.

Inside the den, he flipped on the lights, and surveyed the room. The couch, recliner, end tables, were all there, but the room felt empty. Portraits were missing; walls were bare where paintings and decorations once hung.

Quince moped across the den, into the kitchen, and set the bourbon and beer on the counter. He slowly walked down the hall, surveying things as he passed. Things looked different. Empty. Bare. Cold. Large stains dotted the wall where family portraits once hung. Small things were gone. Candles. Stacks of books. Things Sara used to decorate. She had that touch. That gift. The ability to fill a house. Things you don't notice when they are there but you miss them when they are gone. Instead, he stood in the doorway of their bedroom, and stared at an empty bed. It was bare, stripped of sheets, pillows, and a comforter. Sara always kept a stack of books on the nightstand. They were gone, along with a small, ornate jewelry desk that stood in the corner, near the closet. As he stood alone, memories played through his mind. He thought of the night they conceived Lilly, and the many nights they screwed on that bed. Memories of the first night Lilly came home from the hospital, and slept between them. Images of the night before he left for Camp Lejeune on his way to Afghanistan flooded his mind.

Soon, those memories became too much, and he turned, and walked down the hall, into Lilly's room. It was nearly empty. Her closet doors were open. A few plastic hangers dangled on a closet rod. Her tiny bed was gone. Holes dented the carpet were it once stood. It was too much for him. Quince sighed, turned, and walked purposefully down the hall, opened a closet in the den, and pulled out a sea bag. He unsnapped the hook, and dug through the bag, tossing clothes across the floor. His hand dove deep into the bag, surfacing with the stuffed bear. He kicked the sea bag into the closet, slammed the door, and moped down the hall, into Lilly's room. It was so empty. It made him feel as if he had lost his daughter. As if he were no longer a father. He couldn't take the feeling. He set the bear on its haunches in the middle of the room, and nodded. At least the room wasn't empty, he thought. He turned, walked down the hall, into the kitchen, tossed beer into the refrigerator, grabbed two bottles, and walked into the den. Afterwards, he dropped into the recliner, and began to drink. As the night dragged on, bottle-by-empty-bottle lined the counter as he finished them.

Late in the evening, Quince's phone buzzed, vibrating across the end table. Quince's heart raced. Was it Sara? Did she regret leaving? Does she want to come home? He wanted to hear her soft voice. Instead, the phone read *Beecher* across the screen. Quince held it for a second, before dropping it on the end table. He simply wasn't ready to tell his father about their break-up. He needed time to think about it. Let it sink in. He needed to drink, and drink he did, killing a half case of beer that night. After finishing each beer, he drunkenly swayed to the kitchen, set the empty bottle on the counter, grabbed a full bottle from the refrigerator, set it on the end table, and swayed down to the bathroom. He unzipped, swayed over the toilet as he pissed, closed the zipper, and swayed back to the recliner. Well into the night, frustration boiled in the young veteran as he drank. Then, as the counter filled with empty bottles, alcohol finally dulled his pain. After midnight, he passed out.

Chapter 29
≈ The Sandstone Cliffs ≈

Light seeped through the den window, brushing over his eyes as he slept. Quince squirmed to avoid the light, blinked, and used his fingers to push sleep from his eyes. Dazed, he sat forward, and looked around. The house was quiet. His hair was disheveled; face, unshaven. His breath smelled of bourbon and beer. His clothes were wrinkled. He rose, stood in the doorway of their bedroom and thought of Sara, lamenting the last six months. He walked over to Sara's side of the bed, and lay on the mattress. Over the years, perfume had soaked from her skin, into the fabric. He could smell her as he lay there. He sighed, whispered something, stood, and walked down the hall into Lilly's empty room. In the center sat the stuffed bear, resting on its haunches. Quince knelt, gathered the doll, and pulled it into his chest. He began to weep, falling on his ass. When the tears dried, he gently set the doll on the floor, stood, and left the house, carrying a bottle of bourbon.

He drove around town a while, slowly navigating the quiet Saturday morning streets, thinking. His post-war life had been difficult. He knew and accepted that reality, but he felt helpless against the dreams, and firmly believed he was misunderstood. His pain was unappreciated. As he drove, his stomach rumbled, but he was not hungry. He hadn't eaten breakfast, or drank coffee, shaved, or showered. Hung over, he was exhausted from the dreams, the helplessness, and now they had taken his family.

Tired of the streets, Quince steered the SUV from town, down interstate, toward the mountains. As a young boy, Beecher took his son hunting in a forest above the eastern plateau. Quince took his first deer in those forests; a six-point buck he shot with his grandfather's 30.06. Often, while they hunted, he and Beecher would climb the sandstone cliffs. They would stand on a ledge, looking down at the valleys and trees, misty with snow. When Quince arrived in the Kunar Valley, and first climbed OP Tarawa, he got the same feeling. Below, poppy fields were green and red like

Christmas candy. Mud-bricked homes dotted the valley. The river was white and blue, and ran down the valley like the spine of something alive.

As he drove alone, hills gave way to mountains, green pastures to forests as he crossed the plateau. It was quiet. The radio was off. Trees whisked by as he drove deep into the forest. Finally, he turned down a graveled road, and followed a small stream up a valley, parking in a lot that lay beneath a mountain. He grabbed the bottle, slammed the door, and moped along the stream, further up the valley. The sound of trickling water filled the woods. Spring rains softened leaves lying on the valley floor, cushioning his feet as he walked. Occasionally, birds swept from treetops, shaking yesterday's rain from the leaves. Squirrels scampered along the valley floor before scaling a tree trunk, disappearing high above the passing stranger.

A few miles up the valley, Quince stooped over a rock, and sipped from the stream. His tongue slurped the cool, mountain water. He rose, and used his sleeve to wipe water from his chin. Walking awhile longer, he turned, and climbed a steep slope, sliding in the soft, leaf-slicked ground. His chest bounced as he crested the slope and walked across a plateau, stopping near a cliff wall. His face rose and he surveyed the steep cliff, mentally mapping out a path up the sandstone wall. Finally, he was ready. He tucked the bottle under his belt, behind him, and began climbing. His fingers dug into the sandstone. His feet stuck to the scratchy sediment as he scaled the wall, rising high above the valley. Slowly, he rose above the trees. Wind tugged at his pant-legs and his hair. Near the top, he grabbed a cedar sapling, and pulled himself over the ledge.

For some time, he walked around, enjoying the view, staring down into the misty valleys. Wind brushed across his cheeks and nudged pine trees along the peak. Orange pine needles lay in beds on the sandstone. He walked to the ledge, sat in a bed of needles, and dropped his feet over the side. He pulled the bottle from his belt, twisted the cap, and drank. Bourbon tickled his tongue as he swished it around in his mouth. He swallowed, lifted the bottle to his lips, and drank again, grimacing. Last night, he drank a dozen beers. His stomach was sour, and his throat was scratched. That morning, bourbon tasted like poison on his tongue, but he drank, and the pain softened as the bottle emptied. Eventually, he grabbed a handful of orange needles, and dropped them over the ledge, watching them fall. Slowly, they twisted, tumbling down the cliff, falling softly as if they were feathers of nature. Twisting, they slowly fell before a gust of wind swept them into the wall.

Next, Quince leaned forward, and pulled his wallet from a back pocket. He unfolded the leather, and removed a picture of Sara and Lilly sitting on the banks of a stream. In the background, an old covered bridge hung over the smooth water. Soggy yellow leaves speckled the surface. It was fall. Quince began to weep. His eyes moistened. Tears spilled from them, ran down his cheeks, dripped from his chin, and were swept across the valley by a passing breeze. He pulled the bottle to his lips and sucked down the last ounce. Then, he held the empty bottle over his feet, and let it slip through his fingers. The clear, glass cylinder passed between his feet, careening down the steep wall, through treetops, and exploded against a sandstone boulder on the valley floor.

Quince sighed, weeping, wiping tears from his cheek with a sleeve. Finally, he returned the picture, shoved the wallet in his pocket, and stood. Wind brushed across his face as he looked down the cliff wall. Drunk, his legs bent and swayed. His toes hung over the ledge. Everything was numb to him. The last year had been one horrible, long dream. The Kunar River Valley. Jenkins lying wounded on a path below OP Tarawa. Sergeant Patrick blown apart on the river road. A little Afghan girl, Farrah, who stood in a poppy field and begged for candy, killed by the Taliban. His dreams about them all. A night rarely passed when the dreams did not come. Over the months, they brought him a constant thirst for alcohol, anger, paranoia, and distance from his wife and daughter. A year ago, Quince never dreamed of standing on this ledge, atop a sandstone cliff, drunk. Now, it was the only thing he knew would help. Standing atop the cliff, a year later, he could not imagine climbing down, and going home to an empty house.

Quince stood on the ledge, swaying, mustering courage. Praying. Wind brushed over his cheeks. He swayed, drunk. He sighed, whispered amen and nodded. His foot rose from the sandstone cliff, dangling above the valley below. His eyes closed. His torso leaned forward but suddenly, the phone buzzed in his pocket. Vibrations tickled his leg. His foot once again rested on the sandstone. Swaying, he dug the phone from his pocket and read the screen. *Beecher*. He hadn't spoken to his father since seeing him leave the hospital last week. Questions about why Beecher was there troubled him and suddenly distracted Quince from his purpose. He began to think about it. Wandering away from his suicidal thoughts. It's just that way. Small things lure away a drunk man's thoughts. He thought about it. It didn't make sense for Beecher to go back so soon after his annual exam. Suddenly, the vibrations paused before buzzing twice more. A small emblem of a phone popped on the screen. Quince opened the phone, and pressed a button, and Beecher's scratchy voice erupted, "Quince . . . it's your dad. Call me when you get a chance. Need to talk about something."

Quince's face pinched as he closed the phone. He wondered. Did Beecher know about Sara leaving? His head shook. Not this soon. Was it about Beecher? Is that why he was at the hospital? Quince stood on the ledge, swaying, wondering. Questions flooded his mind. Thoughts drifted away from him, blown by the gusts of spring wind, to his family. What would his father do if he didn't come back? Quince's pain would end, but Beecher would lose a son. Lilly, a father. Sara would remarry. She was young, beautiful. She would remarry someday, and her new husband would become the only father Lilly would remember. She was five. She would barely remember Quince. Sara would remarry. Her new husband would become Lilly's father, and where would Quince be? Dead. In a cold grave. Forgotten.

The outcome of his death on the lives of his family was too much for him to accept. Thoughts of his not being there for Lilly and for Beecher, sobered him. Sara marrying a man who would become Lilly's father, bore a new breed of anger in him. Wind brushed over his face as he stood on the ledge, looking down into the valley. He nodded, drew breathe through his nostrils, and pulled the wallet from his pocket. He stared at the photograph of Lilly smiling, there on the banks of a small, lazy stream, and he began to weep again. After a while, he shoved the wallet in his pocket, sat in a bed of needles, and slid over the ledge, climbing slowly down the sandstone cliff, down below the treetops, to the leaf-slicked ground.

Chapter 30
≈ The Farm ≈

Sunday morning, Quince poured a stainless steel mug full of black coffee, walked from the kitchen, through the den, and slammed the door behind him. He backed the SUV onto the street, pushed the gear in drive, and steered northeast, away from town. Sipping coffee, he drove along the interstate, away from the horse farms and gated communities, into the hills.

An hour later, the SUV exited the interstate on a wooded ridge, turned north, and lazily rose and sank through foggy hills and valleys. Green fields lined both sides of the road. Cattle grazed in pastures. Dew dripped from spring grass. It was a good drive. He enjoyed going home, and being on the farm. It was a place to get centered. Everything about the farm offered comfort and perspective to anyone in need. Whether he was a confused teenager grappling with the loss of a girlfriend, a young man debating marriage, or a husband and father contemplating service to his country, Quince sought refuge in the pastures and woods of the Magowan farm. That morning, two months had passed since he was home.

Quince sipped coffee, and enjoyed the country. Each passing hill, each rotting fence post, swept away the pain he had felt so severely the morning before. The dreams were still there, each night, haunting him, calling him back to the Kunar Valley. His home was empty—Sara and Lilly, gone. The pain of those losses he would always feel. But this morning, Quince sought refuge in the farm. He wanted to heal.

So he drove. The SUV rose and sank through the hills, slowing as it passed through a sleepy country town. Old men moped along the sidewalks. A light flashed at the intersection. Quince turned at an old abandoned brick church, speeding through the hills, along country streams. He sipped cooling coffee, and watched the hills as he drove.

Eventually, his SUV slowed at a rusty mailbox, and followed a barbed-wire fence. Cattle gathered along the wire, near the road, as Quince drove up a graveled driveway. A large black Labrador bounced alongside the truck, between the driveway and the barbed wire. Atop a small, sloping hill, in the middle of the pasture, sat a two-story, whitewashed house. It was a small structure. Black shutters guarded windows like sentries. Red paint peeled from the front door. A large red pickup rested under a sycamore in the corner of the yard. Barbed wire sectioned a fat square from the pasture. A giant black barn sat further up the driveway, behind the house.

Quince parked aside the red pickup. “Shadow,” he yelled, sliding from the SUV. The Labrador bounced; its front paws landed against Quince’s belly. “How are you, buddy?” he asked, pausing to rub Shadow’s ears. He slammed the truck door, and walked across the yard, stomped up wooden steps, and across the porch. Quince knocked on the door, looking around as he waited. Two rocking chairs sat on either side of the door. An empty beer bottle, filled with cigarette butts, sat near one chair. Quince smiled when he saw them, shaking his head.

He knocked again and waited. Nothing. So he walked across the porch, stooped, and peered through glass and a filthy screen that covered a window. He looked into the front room. It was dark and empty. A coffee cup and a dirty plate rested on newspapers scattered on a small table. The television was off. Down the hall, he could see the dryer and a few feet of the kitchen counter. He pounded the door with a fist. Pausing, he listened for footsteps. Nothing. Again he pounded on the door.

Finally, he crossed the porch, leapt from the ledge, into the soft grass, and walked across the yard, up the slope. He gazed up the hill, and saw the barn door was open, a light hanging from rafters in the breezeway. Shadow bounced alongside as he unhooked a chain, and pushed open a metal gate that blocked the gravel road leading to the barn. He let Shadow through, closed the gate, hooked the chain on a rusty nail, and went up the hill.

The smell of manure tickled his nostrils as he neared the barn. Small piles of cow shit dotted the pasture. As he walked, sunlight broke through the clouds, warming his shoulders. Across the pasture, cows gathered in the shade of a walnut tree along the fence. Except for his faint breath, the farm was quiet.

“Dad,” he shouted, nearing the barn. Nothing. He walked closer. “Hey . . . you in there?” he shouted again. Soft, damp shadows cooled his shoulders as he walked through the open door, into the breezeway. Tiny strips of tobacco leaves were scattered across the barn floor. Brown, mangled, they freshened the damp barn with a sweet, pungent odor. Quince looked around, peeking into the dark stripping room. “Dad,” he shouted louder, then listened. Inside, a potbelly stove sat alone in the corner. A short table was empty along the wall.

"Back here," answered a familiar, scratchy voice. Quince walked through the breezeway, toward the back. Cigarette smoke filtered through a door that led into a small room.

Quince stood in the breezeway, looking through the door. "Hey," he nodded.

"There he is." Beecher greeted. Examining a tool, he didn't look up.

"Got your message," Quince continued, stepping through the door onto a wooden floor. Smoke filled the small room.

"You can't call your old man?"

Quince shrugged. "Been busy."

"I reckon," Beecher retorted. "How long has it been?"

Quince shrugged again, "I don' know. Few weeks, maybe?"

"Maybe," answered Beecher, as his stern eyes passed over his glasses toward Quince. Again, they sank to the knife he held, "How's my granddaughter?"

Quince nodded, "Growing."

Beecher chuckled, grabbed a cigarette that hung over the ledge of the table, pulled it to his lips, and took a drag. "And Sara?"

Quince shrugged, "All right, I guess." He was uncomfortable, off guard. He'd planned to tell his father about Sara and Lilly leaving, but not yet. He didn't expect the conversation to advance this quickly.

"You guess?" Beecher asked, flashing stern eyes.

Quince paused and fidgeted. "I need to tell you something."

"I'm listening."

"Sara left. Took Lilly."

"Left?" Beecher asked.

Quince nodded.

"And?"

"It was me. The drinking."

Beecher nodded.

"She just tired of it." He nodded, looking away from his father. "She couldn't take the dreams another night."

Beecher gently laid the tobacco knife on the table. "Come on," he waved, "let's take a seat." Beecher hung the cigarette in the corner of his dry lips, turned, walked into the breezeway, and sat on the wagon. His short feet hung over the wooden wagon bed. Even though the old man wore boots, Quince was a head taller than his father. Quince slid along the wagon's planks, resting his shoulders against the wooden slabs forming a wall on the rear of the wagon.

Beecher took a deep breath and spoke. “Son,” he said, “I had five wives.” The old man turned, gazing at Quince. Behind the wrinkles and thin white beard, his face twisted in embarrassed pride.

Quince nodded, knowingly.

“Between them, I shacked up with many more. Hell. Don’t know how many.” Again, a shallow smile lifted his cheeks. He sighed, “Except for your momma, they all left me or I left them before they could leave.”

Quince smiled.

Beecher stared straight ahead. Smoke trickled from the embers of his burley cigarette. Quince chuckled. “Yeah . . .” he joked. “Well, momma would’ve left your old ass had she lived.”

Beecher burst into laughter, nodding. “You bet she would have.”

Laughter trailed off. Beecher sighed. “Folks used to say, Beecher could find them but he couldn’t hold them.”

Quince was quiet, listening.

Beecher’s head shook. “Some blamed drinking. Some a temper. Others, a wandering eye.” He turned, facing Quince, smiled and turned away. “Maybe that was some of it, don’t know.” His head shook. “But the wives and girlfriends all slept next to me, and they’d all tell you those dreams were the worst of all.” His head shook. Smoke rose from his cigarette into the rafters. “I just couldn’t forget that place . . . couldn’t forget what I saw over there.”

Quince listened, quietly. Moisture gathered in his eyes.

Beecher turned to his son. His head shook. “Don’t end up a lonely old man. Get them dreams taken care of.”

“I tried.”

“Try again,” Beecher snapped in a crisp, angry voice.

“I just couldn’t talk to them.”

“Go back. Try again. Keep on until you can. Until they listen. Somebody will help.”

Quince nodded.

Beecher’s bony finger pointed at Quince. “You promise your father?”

Quince nodded.

“Promise your father you won’t give up.”

Quince nodded.

Beecher nodded. Moisture gathered in his eyes. “All right,” his head sank, and he slipped off the wagon, “let’s get a bite.” He waved at Quince.

Quince slid off the wagon, and walked with his father through the breezeway, down the gravel road. As they walked, he laid his arm over Beecher’s shoulder. “Bum a burley?” he asked, smiling.

Beecher’s head shook as he scratched around in his pocket. “Can’t get over you smoking.”

Shadow, the black Labrador, bounced along in the pasture.

Beecher handed a burley cigarette and a lighter to Quince. The younger Magowan hung the burley in the corner of his mouth, cupped his hands, and lit the cigarette. Quince’s cheeks sank as embers reddened on the burley’s tip. He handed the lighter back to Beecher, pulled the burley from his lips, exhaled, spewing smoke through his nostrils, and nodded, “So, you had something to tell me?”

Beecher’s head shook as he walked. “It was nothing,” he said.

Chapter 31
≈ Back to the VA ≈

Early the next morning, fog hung above the farm. Quince and Beecher rose early. Quince had slept in his clothes on the couch. He rose, folded a blanket, walked to the kitchen, and began frying bacon. Beecher sat in the porch chair, smoking. He watched clouds slide over the hill, and blurry images of fat, Black Angus cattle graze in the pasture. His legs were crossed and he sat in the most relaxed way, slouched. One boot was perched on the opposite knee as he methodically pulled the burley from his lips, exhaled, and re-hung the cigarette in the corner of his mouth. Finally, he dropped the butt in an empty beer bottle, opened the front door and walked through the house, toward the kitchen. That morning, the two men ate fried bacon, drank coffee, and talked about small, innocent things. After they finished, Quince washed dishes, and left for home.

Driving through the hills, Quince felt a sense of peace. The things that had gone wrong in his life were still fresh, eerie, and he struggled against the guilt of it all, but his mind was clearer while he was on the farm. He grew devoted to the idea of healing. It was an idea he'd abandoned over the past six months. Now, driving through hills, he resolved to find the old Quince somewhere in this new life. The old Quince could fix his marriage and regain his family. He found hope again.

Quince left work early the next afternoon. He drove across town, slowed on a busy street, and turned through high, brick walls, between two open, wrought iron gates. He circled the campus of buildings that surrounded the archaic structure in the center, and parked in the grass. Pulling keys from the ignition, he walked quickly across the grass. It was Monday afternoon. The sun was high and warmed his shoulders. Summer was being born.

Quince bounced up the large, sweeping steps, walked across the stone landing, and swung open the glass door. Inside, he walked determinedly through the lobby, ignoring everything around him, went up the stairs, and passed through a blue door.

His footsteps echoed quickly around the stone walls inside the stairwell. A blue door slammed behind him as he turned left, and quickly approached the linoleum counter.

"Quince Magowan to see Chaplain Griggs," he said, not waiting to be asked.

Behind the desk, the woman stared at him over her burgundy-framed glasses. "Do you have an appointment?" she asked as her fingers pounded across the keyboard.

Quince's head shook. "Nope, but I need to speak with him."

The woman paused from her typing, "Honey," she said, leaning forward. "Chaplain Griggs left."

"Left?"

"Retired," she said, leaning against the backrest of her chair.

Quince's face pinched. Blood gathered in his cheeks. "Well . . ." he stammered, "is anyone available?"

Her head shook, "Not today."

"Is there a doctor to replace him?"

"Dr. Gates will arrive next Tuesday."

Quince nodded, determined, "Tuesday it is. I'll be here."

"He won't be available for counseling sessions the first day. Is it an emergency?"

"Well . . . no," Quince paused. "Guess I can wait."

"His first available session is Monday the 23rd."

"That's three weeks," Quince responded, blood coloring his cheeks. Quince sighed, looking away from the woman, shaking his head in frustration. "All right," he said, facing the woman, "put me down for the 23rd."

"Last four?" she asked in a flat, dead tone, all along typing furiously on the keyboard. "We have you scheduled to meet with Dr. Gates on Wednesday, the 23rd, at 8:30 a.m. The VA will send you a letter detailing the appointment and call you the day before to confirm your attendance."

"Thanks," Quince answered tersely. His elbow slid from the linoleum counter as he turned and left.

He stomped down stairs, pushed open the blue doors, and wove through the crowds until he reached a busy lobby where he stopped at a vending machine. Digging through his pockets, he fed the machine coins, mashed a button, and a soda dropped into the carrier. Quince stooped to grab the soda.

"Hell. They let a Magowan in here?" bellowed a voice above him.

Quince's face pinched. He rose, and turned. It was a deep, angry voice and Quince postured, closing a fist.

"Wow!" laughed the man. "Take it easy, son."

Quince's face opened, lips lifted into his cheeks as he looked up. "Yeah," he laughed, posturing with cockiness. "Magowan, hell. They ain't worried about Magowans when Sasquatch is running around." All along, Quince gazed up at the giant, hairy man. He towered over the young veteran. A scraggly black beard hung over his pooched belly. Balding, black and gray hair dropped from his temple, down his broad shoulders. He wore a green t-shirt, covered with a black leather vest, black boots and worn jeans. His eyebrows were thick and black, and nearly ran together. Beneath them, giant, round eyes made others feel small.

The giant man laughed.

"Moose," Quince greeted, "how the hell you been?"

Moose smiled, nodding. "Getting old and tired."

Quince chuckled.

"Ain't seen you since we left Camp Lejeune for home. How you been?"

Quince shrugged. "Busy."

"Well . . . being a civilian looks like it agrees with you."

"I reckon."

Moose nodded, seeing Quince's frustrations. "It'll take a while, but you'll adapt."

Quince shrugged.

"So," Moose scanned the busy lobby, asking, "are you here with your old man?"

Quince's lips pursed. His brow furrowed. His head shook.

"Just thought you might have brought him down for treatment."

"Treatment?" Quince's face pinched.

"Yeah. Hate to hear about it. He's a good one, your father. None like him," Moose's big, hairy, scary-ass face softened. Moisture gathered in his eyes.

Quince played coy. He began to piece together life's subtle hints. Beecher's message while Quince stood on the sandstone cliff, asking his son to visit. Beecher's reluctance to tell Quince after his son first mentioned his family problems. Coy, Quince asked, "So . . . Dad don't like telling folks about it, but, except for me, you know him better than anyone. Just how much did he tell you?"

Moose's face knotted up. "Just said it was bad. Said he thought it come from the Agent Orange but who the hell knows?" Moose's giant head rolled, a smile lifted his scraggly beard. "When we were in Vietnam, he always swore he'd get shot in the ass. Damn colon cancer. He's says this to me just the other day. Says they got him. Says it took them nearly forty years, but he was right. They done got him. Right in the ass!"

Quince's face pinched. Moisture gathered in his eyes. His features fought to mask the pain, and a light smile lifted his cheeks.

Moose waved his big, meaty hands, "Oh . . . hell . . . your old man can whip this. He's the toughest old bird I ever done know. Hell . . . he may out live us all."

Quince nodded, blinking the moisture in his eyes. "You seen him lately?"

"Lately? Hell . . . I just saw him. He was just here. Said he's thirsty, and smiled. You know Beecher Magowan? It won't take his smile."

"Well . . . I gotta run," Quince said, throwing a thumb over his shoulder.

Moose nodded, "Tell the old man I'll call in a few days. We're planning a ride through the mountains."

Quince smiled, turned, and left the hospital. The sun was falling as he bounced down the sweeping, stone steps. He was numb. Life's surrealistic punches had struck another blow to the young veteran. He walked down the sidewalk, through the grass, and opened the SUV's door. He sat, closed the door, and wept. He was encouraged after speaking with Beecher on Sunday. His father was right; he needed to try, if not for himself, then for Lilly. And, as he drove through the hills, leaving the farm, he was ready, committed. He wanted to get healthy. As his feet bounced up the stone steps, he had expected a long, productive talk with Chaplain Griggs. Now Griggs was gone, and a new doctor was coming; a doctor he had not met. Another stranger. Now, sitting alone, none of that mattered to him. The thought of his father with cancer made him physically ill. His stomach knotted. Soured. His throat dried. His heart raced until he pushed open the door, leaned over the grass, and vomited. He vomited hard, heaving until his stomach was dry, and then he wiped his lips with a sleeve, sat back, opened the soda, lifted the can to his lips, and drank. Rinsing his mouth, he spat soda in the grass, started the truck and drove away from the hospital, through the streets, toward town.

A green arrow, pointing left, flashed across the dashboard as he mashed the gas, turning through traffic onto a quiet street. The SUV rolled to a stop along the curb. Quince pulled the keys from the ignition, pushed open the door, slid from the seat, slammed the door behind him, and jogged across the street.

It was early evening. The sun had fallen from the town's sky. Shadows lay across the sidewalk. A soft light hung from a window. Men were playing pool inside as Quince passed through the light, pushed open the wooden door, and quietly entered. Immediately, he felt the weight of staring faces. Although his demeanor was calm, his emotions were anything but relaxed. Confused, angry, worried, violent emotions surged through his mind. Why didn't he tell me? He's stubborn. What if he had gone to the doctor sooner? Did he wait because of my health? Was it my fault?

Quince surveyed the smoky room. A stereo sat on a window seat in the corner. Music was loud. Men playing pool leaned on their pool sticks. One stared at Quince. He was older, unshaven, and he suspiciously watched the clean-shaven young man.

He walked slowly across the room, sat on a stool, and leaned over the bar. Clouds of smoke hung over the room like fog. Golf was on the television over the bar. "Beer, honey?" asked the bartender. Quince nodded, "Sure, Sally."

Sally grinned, but her eyes were sad. She poured a beer from the tap, and gently set the glass on the bar. Quince's stone face managed a smile. He pulled the glass to his lips and drank.

Smoke rose from a cigarette lying in an ashtray on the bar, but Quince ignored it. He grabbed a saltshaker, methodically sprinkled salt across a moist napkin, and set the beer down. Quince stared into a mirror behind the bar. Beneath the mirror, bottles of bourbon and vodka were stacked along a ledge cushioned with felt. Behind him, men played pool. Some stood, leaning onto those thin, wooden sticks, waiting for their turn. Beside Quince was a small man wearing a white beard. Mechanically, the man pulled a glass to his lips, drank, set the glass on the bar, and with his other hand, hung the cigarette in his moist lips, sucked the filter, and pulled the cigarette away, flicking ashes into the ashtray. Both hands lifted and pulled. He consumed vices like a starving man consumes nourishment. The small man focused on the game, staring at the television above the bar. Quince watched him through the mirror, occasionally pulling the beer to his lips, and drinking. "Since when are you a golf fan?" he asked.

Beecher pulled the glass to his lips, drank, and set the beer down. "It's OK." He shrugged.

"You hate golf."

"It's May. Bad time for sports. It's either golf or you go fishing. Well, I can't fish here at the bar, and I sure as hell ain't watching home improvement shows. So," he drank, "it's golf until September or until the next time I can wet my line in the lake."

"I went to see Chaplain Griggs this afternoon," Quince noted, drinking.

"Yeah?"

Quince shook his head, "Gone."

"Gone?"

Quince nodded. "Retired."

Beecher's eyes rolled into his brow.

"Replaced by some shrink," continued Quince. "I have an appointment in three weeks."

"Figures," Beecher said sarcastically. "Listen, son," his words becoming serious, "you keep trying. Don't give up."

Quince nodded, pulling the beer to his lips.

"I mean it," insisted the old man.

Beecher turned, facing the game.

Quince stared through the mirror, watching his father. His mind churned. He wanted to scream at his father. Ask him why he had not told his son about the cancer. He wanted to hug him, and promise him that he would be there during his illness. His lips poised, fashioning the emotion of each thought. He pulled the glass to his lips, and drank, set the beer on the bar, stared into the mirror, and spoke, "So, did I tell you? I ran into Moose Law at the hospital." His eyes focused on the mirror.

Beecher gazed at the game. His expression was emotionless. "Is that right?" he asked in an uninterested tone.

Quince nodded. "You guys are good friends."

Beecher nodded. "Known Moose for nearly 40 years. Served with him. Good man."

"How long has it been?"

"Since?"

"You last saw him?"

Beecher shrugged, "A month or so, I reckon." Eyes gazing at the game.

"A month or so?"

"Reckon."

"Dad?"

"Yeah?" he answered, watching the game.

"He told me."

"Told you what?" asked Beecher, pulling the beer to his lips.

"Cancer."

Beecher blinked. He gently set the glass on the bar. He hung the cigarette in his lips, sucked the filter, and pulled the burley away. Beecher exhaled. His chest sank. Smoke poured from his nostrils. His blue eyes gazed at Quince.

"Why didn't you tell me?"

Beecher was calm. His demeanor was peaceful. He shrugged, slightly lifting his shoulders, and said, "You didn't need the worry."

"Why not?"

Beecher shrugged.

"You got enough of that."

"I'm your son!" Quince said. Anger lifted his voice.

Beecher nodded. "You had enough to worry about."

"Because of my health."

Beecher was quiet.

"Dreams?"

Beecher chewed on his lower lip. Beard stubbles tickled his lip as he nodded.

"I can handle it."

"I know."

Quince sighed. He pulled the beer to his lips, and drank. The television aired golf. Fans cheered. Men played pool behind them.

"What has the doctor told you?" asked the son. He stared into the mirror across the bar, and watched Beecher, searching for truth in the man's bearded expression.

Beecher frowned. "Said to enjoy life while I can."

"Dad."

"Make a will."

"Dad, stop it," Quince rebuked, his voice stern.

Beecher sighed, blowing air through his nostrils. "They run some tests this morning. Took x-rays. Had me in that damn cave-of-a thing they call an MRI for nearly an hour. I don't care to remember how many times my ass has been poked by fingers and tubes lately." He scowled...

Quince's lips pursed. "Colon?"

Beecher nodded. Again, he became distracted by the game. His eyes lifted to the television.

"When do you go back?"

"Next week."

"And the doctors will know something by then."

"I reckon."

Quince sighed, he pulled the beer to his lips, and drank. "Dad," he said in a serious tone, "I'm gonna take you."

Beecher's head shook. "You got work."

"Fuck work."

"You'll get fired."

"I got time. I can take it."

"You got enough to worry about."

"I'm OK."

"Ain't gonna trouble you."

"I can't worry about that now."

"I can do it alone."

"I'll come up Saturday. Stay the weekend. On Monday we'll go to the hospital."

Beecher sighed, staring at the game. "Dad?" Quince begged. "Dad, look at me?"

Beecher's eyes dropped from the television. Slowly, they slid down the mirror but stopped, watching his son between the bottles of bourbon and vodka. Beecher Magowan had always been alone. He didn't ask anyone for help. He was proud. That was Beecher. Beneath the pride, he knew trips from the farm to town would be difficult. He knew treatment would be hard. He was going to be sick, nauseous beyond any hangover he'd ever felt. He would feel pain above any broken bone, or shrapnel wound. For the first time, Beecher Magowan needed someone's help. He sighed, and nodded. Beecher stared at his son's reflection.

Quince nodded. He pulled the beer to his lips, swallowed the last drink, set the glass on the bar, and stood, digging through a pocket. He tossed a five on the bar, nodded to Sally, and left.

Quince methodically worked through his shifts at the warehouse. All week, distractions lured his mind away from its daily duties. Dreams woke him each night. Thoughts of Sara and Lilly never left him. Every shelf stocked, every box lifted, every inventory, they accompanied him. And, joining them was Beecher with cancer. Each worry hung like a yoke from the young veteran's neck. Days were long and slow. He was tired. At night, he slept in an empty house.

Chapter 32
≈ A Reckoning with Trimble Addison ≈

"Mayor to Discuss Controversial Zoning Plan During Council Meeting," was written in bold, black letters on a newspaper. Papers were stacked on a counter near the energy drinks. Soft music played from ceiling speakers.

A clerk pecked at the register, and said, "Your total is $15.99."

Quince pulled his wallet from his pocket, took out a twenty and slid the bill across the counter. He leaned over the stack of papers, reading. Below the headline, lighter, smaller text read, "Mayor chooses growth over culture. New codes permit development of famed Hickory Forest Horse Farm."

The clerk pecked at the register as music played. He smiled, and handed Quince change. Quince shoved the change in his pocket, and kept reading. "The Mayor has a bold plan for growth. This new industrial park will add hundreds of jobs to our city's economy, noted Trimble Addison, a senior aide to Mayor Johnson." Quince's eyes rolled up into his brow. "Prick," he whispered, nodded to the clerk, and carried the beer from the store.

He drove across town, and pulled up the driveway. It was June. The evening air was warm.

He unlocked the door, went to the kitchen, opened the refrigerator, and slid the box across an empty shelf. He tore the box, grabbed a beer, opened a thin box on the top shelf, tore a slice of pizza from a cold pie, and kicked the door shut as he went into the den, falling into the recliner.

He quickly tapped the remote, opened the beer and tossed the lid across an end table. The television came alive as Quince drank and chewed cold pizza. He tried to forget work; shed the details, tasks, and calls from a bad week at the warehouse. His watch read 4:47 p.m.

Quince devoured pizza, drank beer, and went to the kitchen for another. He made several more trips before 6:11 p.m. when someone knocked on the door. "Who the hell?" he whispered, slowly climbing to his feet. The house was always empty, he thought. A visitor had not come there since Sara and Lilly left.

He walked across the den and slowly opened the front door, not bothering to peer through the peephole. Through a dirty screen, he saw a man wearing a worried grin.

Baxter's smile broadened. "Can't an old friend stop by?"

Quince opened the screen. "Depends."

"On what?" asked Baxter, stepping through the door.

"His motives."

Baxter chuckled.

"Beer?" asked Quince.

Baxter shrugged. "Sure."

Quince nodded, and went into the kitchen. "Good," he proclaimed from the kitchen. "I need another, anyway."

Baxter looked around the den. A blanket was crumpled on the couch. Cushions were strewn across the floor. Beer tabs littered the end table. The carpet was dirty.

Quince walked into the den, and handed Baxter a beer.

"Love what you've done with the place," Baxter remarked.

Quince smirked. "Yeah. Well. It definitely misses a woman's touch."

Baxter chuckled.

Quince waved a hand, saying, "Have a seat."

Quince flopped into the recliner. Baxter pushed aside the blanket, and sat on the couch. He pulled the beer to his lips, and drank.

"So. What brings you here?" asked Quince.

"Done said. Just wanted to check on my old friend," Baxter explained.

Quince pulled the beer from his lips. "Bullshit."

"What?" asked Baxter.

"Old friends know each other. This friend knows it ain't like you to stop by here without calling first."

Baxter pulled the beer to his lips, and drank. "Well . . ." he sighed.

Quince frowned. His chest began to pound. Here it comes, he thought.

Baxter leaned forward, elbows resting on his knees. "This isn't easy."

"What is it?" Quince asked, his voice growing impatient.

Baxter sighed. His eyes danced around before settling on Quince. "Sara has been dating Trimble."

The television played. Baxter's face was long, sad.

"What?" Quince asked in a shaken, whispered voice.

"I heard it from Tess. She wanted to tell you, but didn't want to get in the middle of anything."

An embarrassed, uncomfortable expression formed on Quince's face.

Baxter kept talking. "They've been talking for a while now."

"How early?"

Baxter sighed, "Last year."

"Last year?"

Baxter nodded.

"When I was gone?"

Baxter's lips pursed. He nodded.

"Trimble?" Quince asked. His chest pounded, thundering in his ears.

Baxter nodded. "Quince. Tess said they were calling each other last year."

"What?"

"It just grew from there."

Quince's chest pounded. "When I was gone?" he asked, his voice shaken.

Baxter nodded. "I'm sorry. I didn't know until now."

Quince slowly looked around the den. His eyes were disoriented, twitching in small, circular motions. He gently set the beer on the table, stood, and paused.

Baxter's voice was careful and solemn. "Hey. Why don't we go out tonight? Nothing crazy. Just old friends. Shelley won't mind."

Quince walked across the den, and opened the front door. "I want to be alone."

"Quince," pleaded Baxter.

"Please leave."

"Listen, you shouldn't be alone."

"Thank you, Baxter," he said, struggling through the words. "You are a good friend. I needed to know."

Baxter sighed, set the bottle on the table, and slowly walked across the den. He paused in front of Quince, searched for words, but they were lost. He nodded, laid his hand on Quince's shoulder, and left.

Quince gently sank onto the recliner. His face wore a stunned look. Thoughts flooded his mind like a spring torrent. His brain throbbed against his skull as if it had swollen with the news Baxter delivered. The television played, and he sat there, leaning forward, on his knees.

To Quince, it was the death of his marriage. Marriages experience ups and downs.

We can work through them, he promised Sara before they wed. But I can't forgive two things so don't ever do or say them. Don't ever cheat, I can't forgive infidelity; and never say one bad word about where I came from or my family. I can't forgive these things—they were blasphemous to him. And to cheat with Trimble Addison was the most damning sin of all.

He sat there, alone. It was the true death of his family. Beneath the anger, he mourned his marriage. He remembered better times. Sitting there, in the recliner, his mind twisted through the curves of his life with Sara. From the time he saw her from the library steps, sitting cross-legged, studying beneath a maple, through graduation, work, marriage, Lilly's birth, boot camp, diapers, weekends away at reserve drill, potty training, and, at Camp Lejeune, when he loaded a chartered bus for Cherry Point, and then to Afghanistan. All the time together, and all the time away was now over. He sat there, stunned. The evening slowly passed.

After a while, he glanced at the watch on his wrist–6:49 p.m. He nodded to himself, stood, walked into the kitchen, opened the refrigerator door, grabbed two beers in each hand, kicked the door shut, and walked into the den. He twisted open a bottle, set the other on the table, and sank into the recliner, drinking as he fell into the chair. He drank and stared at the television, ignoring the programs as they changed. He just stared at the screen, lifted the beer to his lips, drank, and stared. When one bottle was empty, he set it down, and opened another. He drank the last bottle, glanced at his watch. It was 7:41 p.m. He set the empty bottle on the table, stood, walked across the den, opened the door, and left. The door was open, and the television, playing.

The SUV rolled to a stop in traffic, before a row of two-story buildings. Quince surveyed the buildings. On a sign above the entrance of a tall, stone structure was a sign that read, City Hall. He looked to his right, across the street; a large, brick building sat on a hill. Granite monuments stood like sentries in the yard, below two thick oaks. In the corner of the yard, a faded historic marker leaned over the sidewalk.

Traffic crept along the street. The SUV rolled forward, turned on a cobbled street across from City Hall, in front of the Courthouse, and parked among other cars. The street was crowded with cars. Lights were on inside City Hall. A few pedestrians loitered outside. Quince turned the key and the engine died. He sat alone, quietly watching the door of City Hall. A hint of sunlight shone between buildings, and on treetops. Sunlight sat atop the roof of City Hall like a crown. He glanced at his watch —7:58 p.m. Quince nodded. The council meeting would end promptly at 8:00 p.m. Mayor Johnson, and his senior aides, would exit City Hall, walk across the street, down the sidewalk, and up the steps, into the Courthouse, and the Mayor's office.

Questions filled his thoughts. How had it come to this? Should I have seen this earlier? What will happen with Lilly? And then, his thoughts took a leap into the what-if future. What if they marry? Sara Addison made him cringe with anger. Trimble as a stepfather to Lilly infuriated him. His heart raced, chest pounded, thundering in his ears. His mouth was dry so he repeatedly swallowed, gathering moisture across his tongue. He watched the foyer of City Hall, looking through two metal doors with glass windows. Inside, a wooden door led into the council chamber. Quince watched, waiting. The sun slid from the top of City Hall, off the stones, into the valley of distant mountains. He stared down the cobbled street, across Main, into the foyer.

Suddenly, the wooden door flew open; out poured a crowd of people. Lights flashed. Quince's chest pounded. He pulled the lever, pushed open the door, slammed it behind him, ran across the cobbled street, down the sidewalk and across Main. Policemen stood along Main, just north and south of City Hall, blocking traffic for the Mayor and his aides to cross. Quince ran by a policeman who stared suspiciously at the man running toward City Hall.

Quince paused near the door, standing beneath one of many ornamental pear trees on the sidewalk along Main. He watched the doors as the crowd rumbled inside the foyer. The two metal doors flew open, and people poured out. Lights flashed as a photographer from the local paper snapped pictures of the Mayor departing the controversial meeting. The Mayor was a short, portly man, with a raspy voice that Quince heard above the shouting crowd. A policeman walked alongside the Mayor, struggling to push aside the crowd so the Mayor could cross the street. Quince watched. His face pinched. Walking alongside the Mayor was a tall, neatly dressed man. It was Trimble Addison.

Quince's chest pounded, thundering in his ears. He stepped forward, jogging toward the crowd. From the corner of his eye, he felt the weight of a policeman's stare. He jogged closer. "Watch him!" shouted the policeman, pointing at the suspicious man running toward the Mayor. His words, though, were drowned by the crowd's shouts. Quince ran. He didn't care. He ignored the policeman. He ran into the crowd. Policemen on the street watched him with suspicion, unable to leave their post due to the stalled traffic.

Trimble Addison walked confidently beside the Mayor. He was speaking with a reporter, who held a microphone to his face. A separate reporter poked a microphone in the Mayor's face. Both men boasted about the Mayor's plan for development. A group of preservationists walked alongside, shouting at the Mayor. The crowd moved across the sidewalk, between the pears, and onto the street.

The policeman walking alongside the Mayor was busy wrestling an angry preservationist. The crowd shouted. The policeman blocking traffic shouted.

Quince ignored them all, and stepped toward Trimble. "You son of a bitch. You've been with Sara?" he angrily shouted.

Trimble stammered, embarrassed. "No," he insisted.

Quince stepped in front of Trimble, swatted away the reporter's microphone, and pushed a hand deep into Trimble's chest. Trimble staggered onto his heels, and his face lifted from the microphone.

"You son of a bitch!" Quince shouted.

Trimble's face pinched before opening with surprise. His eyes grew wide and frozen as if they were staring at an oncoming train he could not avoid. They showed dread, awaiting pending humiliation. "You been with her, I know," Quince continued.

"I don't know what you are talking about. Can someone get this man away from me?" he pleaded, pathetically looking around for help.

"You've been with Sara!"

"Get him away from me!"

"You've been with her!"

"I haven't!"

Unknown to Quince, the crowd had stopped, and the shouting trailed off.

"You've been seeing Sara!" Quince persisted.

Trimble shrugged, "You know . . . so what if I have? You're separated."

"You've been seeing my wife!"

The crowd gasped. Mayor Johnson flinched.

"She moved out. You're separated," Trimble said, pathetically looking at the Mayor.

Mayor Johnson watched quietly, stunned.

"You're seeing her!" Quince stepped forward.

Trimble shrugged. Mayor Johnson, the crowd, the preservationist, watched.

"You've been seeing my wife! You were seeing her when I was gone!"

"No."

"You were screwing my wife when I was gone!"

The crowd gasped.

Trimble looked around, embarrassed. "Can someone get him away from me?"

Nobody moved.

"You were!"

"You left her. Then came back, and turned into a drunk. You abandoned her."

"I had to go!" Quince shouted, reasoning.

"You abandoned your wife, and came back a drunk. You can't blame her for wanting someone stable."

"You screwed her when I was in Afghanistan!"

The crowd gasped.

Quince began to weep. His face sank.

"You left her, and now you're a drunk, just like your old man."

Quince's face rose. His chest pounded, and his teeth ground together to the point of breaking, chipping apart. His hand clinched. He stepped forward, and swung a fist at Trimble's smirking face. The crowd gasped as Quince's knuckle landed flush against the man's cheek. Trimble sank to the street, and lay prostrate across the double-yellow line. The crowd gasped. Quince stood over him. A disgusted expression contorted his face. His fist throbbed. Suddenly, a thick arm wrapped around his neck, choking him. He struggled, before being shoved to the street. They jerked his hands behind him, and cuffed his wrist.

Quince was pulled to his feet. The crowd watched, stunned. Trimble struggled to stand. Mayor Johnson's face was aghast. A policeman ushered the Mayor across the street, down the sidewalk, up steps and through the courthouse doors. From behind, a policeman shoved Quince across the street through the open door of a police car.

Blue and red lights swept across the row of buildings along Main. A siren screamed. The squad car sped away. Two blocks away, it turned up a hill, and slid to a stop along the curb of a whitewashed building. Quince stooped forward in the back seat. His arms were fastened behind him. He grimaced as the cop slung open the door, and jerked him from the back seat. "Come on!" he shouted.

Quince's face rose, surveying the building before he was shoved through the front door—it was large, two-story, white-painted brick. Above the door was a sign with "1892" written in black letters. Quince was ushered through a lobby, his arms fastened as he stood over a desk. A deputy in uniform looked at the prisoner.

Quince's hair was disheveled, and he grimaced with anger.

"What is this, Bill?" he asked, poised to begin typing.

"Assault on the Mayor's aide," answered a deputy holding Quince's arm.

Quince smirked.

"You been drinking?" interrogated the deputy.

Quince's head shook.

The deputy jerked his fastened arm. "Don't lie to me, son. I smell it."

Quince's head shook.

"How much have you drank?"

Quince was silent.

"Son, if you want this to be difficult we can accommodate you!"

Quince smirked.

"Looks like he's gonna take a Breathalyzer."

Quince grimaced.

"All right," he conceded.

"I thought so. Now," paused the deputy, "how much have you drank today?"

Quince shrugged. "Six-pack, I reckon."

A smirk lifted the deputy's cheeks. "Add public intoxication to the list of charges."

Quince grimaced.

The deputy sitting behind the desk began to type. "Your name?" he asked

"Magowan?" Quince answered.

"Full name, son."

"Tom Quincy Magowan."

A deputy scratched through Quince's back pocket, lifted his wallet, opened it, and removed the driver license. He briefly examined the license, before handing it to the other deputy. "Here," he noted, "this should help."

The deputy's fingers pounded a keyboard. "Assault and Public Intoxication," whispered the deputy to himself. He smacked the keyboard, and his face rose from the screen. "OK," he announced, "cell three."

Two deputies shoved Quince across the lobby, pausing as a thick, metal door opened. Quince stared through a tiny glass window, lined with chicken-wire, into the cell room. It was bright inside. Bars lined about a half-dozen cells. Thick concrete walls blocked each cell. The door clapped, and slid open. Deputies shoved Quince through the door, down the hall, passing the first two cells. One deputy rattled a set of keys, unlocked the bars, and pulled them open, while the other shoved Quince into the cell. The deputy slammed the door. "Turn around," he demanded. Quince went up to the bars, and slowly turned, facing the wall. The deputy unfastened the cuffs, pulled them away, and both men walked off, down the hall, closing the thick, metal doors.

The jail was quiet. Quince wasn't sure about the last three cells, but the first two cells he passed were empty. He was alone, again. Deep rings were sliced in his wrist from the handcuffs. He rubbed the sting from his wrists, and looked around. The floors and walls were whitewashed concrete. A slab of concrete hung over his head. A toilet sat next to the small, thin bunk; a sink next to the toilet, and a metal sheet hung over the sink as a blurry mirror. Thick bars hung like stalactites from the ceiling to the floor. It was bare and cold. Except for the toilet, and bars that hemmed in the bunk, the place reminded Quince of the concrete bunker at Camp Stanton.

Quince sighed as he stood, looking through the bars, at a small window, high above the floor, on the opposite wall. From where he stood, the limb of an old pear tree dangled over the window. Behind the limb was the gray sky of a June evening.

Quince's chest began to settle. The thundering he had experienced in his ears all evening, since Baxter gave him the terrible news, had subsided, passed like a spring storm. His face grew long; his eyes moistened as reality set in. The buzz from the beer began to fade. The adrenaline from the fight subsided, leaked from his veins. Sara and Trimble were going to be together, a couple. The thought of it all felt like a blow to the stomach. He was sure they would marry. It wasn't a leap in logic to believe that. They were college sweethearts. Trimble came from money. Money was important to Sara. At first, new love masked that feeling in her. But later, after they were married, and settled into their plain, small life, Quince began to see her dissatisfaction.

Now, they were together. And knowing that prick would be a father figure to Lilly turned Quince's stomach. He could hear her soft voice say, "Daddy Trimble took me here. Daddy Trimble bought me this." The reality was hard for Quince. His stomach soured. Sitting on the bunk, his eyes moistened; stomach turned. He quickly leaned into the open toilet, and vomited. The moan of each heave echoed through the empty, stone chamber.

"Well, well," smirked a deputy. "Looks like our criminal can't handle his beer."

A deputy standing beside him laughed. Quince heaved.

The deputy slid a tray of food through a small, thin opening. The metal tray hung on a hook, just inside the bars. "I doubt you'll want this–but we're told to leave it anyway," said the smartass deputy. Both men chuckled as they walked away, disappearing through the thick metal door.

Quince's face lifted. A putrid taste of partially digested beer clung to his teeth. His eyes were red, moist. He wiped his lips with a sleeve, lay back on the cot, turned to the wall, and closed his eyes.

That night, a clank echoed across the empty chamber. Quince squirmed. Light rinsed his eyes. He blinked. He twisted around on the cot, blindly rubbed his cheeks, before his eyes opened. Footsteps moved across the concrete floor. Quince rose, and threw his feet over the cot, onto the cold floor. He anxiously watched the bars. He was sober now, and reality quickly set in. His mind frantically searched through the events of last evening, interrogating memories from every step along the way. In a moment, the interrogation was finished. Memories had spoken. His estranged wife was dating a man he despised. He was in the county jail. His family was gone. His dignity, disappearing. Quince's face grew long. Footsteps echoed across the chamber.

His eyes anxiously watched the bars as a deputy walked in front of them, paused, and turned, facing into the cell, "It's all 'bout who you know. Right Magowan?"

Suddenly, footsteps echoed across the chamber. Worn leather boots stomped forward, and paused. A short, balding man, with a thin beard and a small pooch distending his plaid, button down shirt, stared into the cell. "Mayor talked Mr. Addison into dropping charges. A favor to your father. His great service to our country." The deputy scoured the young veteran who sat pathetically on the cot in the cell. "And yours." He reluctantly admitted. The deputy poked a key into the door, and turned it. It clanked, and he pulled open the bars.

Quince stood. His appearance was unimpressive. Whiskers had sprouted from his chin. His clothes were wrinkled. His legs were stiff, and ached as he stood. He was embarrassed. It was difficult for Quince to look at his father.

Beecher's face was stolid. He resembled a marble statue facing the cell. The deputy looked on. Beecher's lips poised, and he said, "Mayor done told me everything."

Quince grimaced.

"Trimble, huh?"

Quince nodded, and sighed. Breath slipped from his lungs, and his chest sank.

The deputy smirked, holding the bars open.

Beecher slowly nodded, sighed, and proclaimed, "You should of hit that prick harder."

A smile slowly lifted Quince's cheeks. His eyes moistened.

The deputy's jowls fell open. His eyes swelled.

Beecher's face grew soft, sad. His eyes glistened under a hallway light. His lips were sewn together, mashed against one another like two narrow cushions. The old man's lightly bearded chin nodded, his cheeks lifted, and his eyes narrowed. "Come on, son." He beckoned, waving an arm to Quince. "Let's get out of here."

Quince stepped forward, walking with his father down the stone hallway. Their feet echoed across the chamber.

Chapter 33
≈ Beecher's Treatment ≈

Quince rode with his father through the hills to the family farm. Exhaust from the red pickup thundered across pastures, and through hollers. It was Saturday morning. They spent the weekend farming, feeding cattle. Rusted barbed wire had snapped on the fence along a stream near the back of the farm. Quince and Beecher pulled new, silver-toned wire between the rotting, gray poles. Each evening, they sat in rocking chairs on the porch, smoked, and drank beer. On Monday, they loaded the red pickup and drove out of the hills, back to town, arriving at the hospital as the fog lifted.

As always, Beecher parked under the catalpa tree on the hospital's campus. It was crowded. Only a few parking spots were available, even during that early hour, but Beecher didn't care. It had become his favorite spot, and he would park under the tree even if the paved spaces were empty. He reminded Quince about the catalpa tree next to the creek on the farm, and how they would pull worms from the tree, bait hooks, and drop them in the old pond. "Yellow catfish loved catalpa worms," he said, walking slowly across the grass. "We caught a bucket full." Quince grinned, but said nothing.

It was hard for Quince to remember himself as a boy. He listened, trying to assign an age to the boy gathering catalpa worms with his father, but the memory had faded. A photo of Quince taken in fourth grade hung in a wooden frame over his grandmother's bed. Lately, Beecher often talked about when Quince was a boy. When Quince was unable to recall them, he simply removed the boy from the still-framed picture, and set him in the memory; his imagination breathed life into the child with the purposeful stare in the picture, a bruise on his cheek from playing football with his father.

Together, that morning, they climbed the sweeping stone stairs, and entered the hospital. They stopped in a large, crowded lobby, poured plastic cups full of steaming coffee, and walked down the hallway.

"Beecher Magowan," he proclaimed to the woman behind the counter. The woman looked up, and a smile dropped from her face. "Yes." She grabbed a clipboard, stood, and walked around the counter. "Come with me, please." The nurse led them down a hall, and stopped near a weight scale. "Please step on the scale," she begged. Beecher, holding the coffee cup, stepped forward.

"Does it matter if I hold this?" Beecher joked, displaying the steaming coffee as if it were a trophy. The nurse shrugged. "It's about 5 ounces in the cup, and 5 ounces in my gut," he chuckled. The nurse forced a grin. "171," she announced, reading red electronic letters on the scale. "That can't be right," protested Beecher. "That's four pounds lighter than last week. Even then I was three pounds lighter than normal. Hell, 178, I have always weighed 178."

The nurse forced a grin. "Please come with me." She turned, and continued down the hall. Beecher's face was puzzled. He slowly stepped from the scale, and followed the nurse. Quince walked alongside his father.

The nurse opened a wooden door, and stepped inside a room and said, "Please wait here. The doctor will be right in." Beecher and Quince entered the room. "Mr. Magowan," she said to Beecher, "please sit up here." The nurse patted a blue-cushioned chair, turned, and left the room, shutting the door behind her. Beecher rested in the chair. Quince sat on a metal chair near the doctor's table. It was a cold, quiet room. Father and son waited, but did not speak. A thin, black hand turned in a clock over the door. Minutes passed before the door opened, and a man in a white lab coat walked in; his face buried in a chart fastened to a clipboard. He looked up, and offered a hand, "Mr. Magowan."

They shook hands.

Beecher nodded, "Doc."

The physician turned, facing Quince, "And this is . . .?"

"My son."

"Quince," answered the younger Magowan.

The doctor nodded, offering a hand. "Doctor Tomasky," he answered. "They call me Dr. Tom."

"Dr. Tom."

"Quince."

The Doctor turned to Beecher again, scanned the clipboard, and sighed. "Well," he said, "your results are back." He paused, referencing the clipboard.

Quince's chest pounded. Thunder rang in his ears. His mouth dried.

"During the endoscopy, we removed four polyps from your colon. We tested those polyps, and found three to be cancerous."

Quince's chest pounded.

Beecher's face was stolid.

"Now . . . it appears from the MRI that small spots have developed on your liver and we noticed one spot on your lung. The cancer is spreading." Doctor Tom paused, sighing.

Quince's mouth dried. "Can you treat it?" He asked.

Doctor Tom's eyebrows lifted, and sank. "The cancer is aggressive."

"Doc?" Quince barked.

Doctor Tom paused. "Treat it? Yes. Slow it? Maybe." he paused again,

"Doc," Beecher interjected, "we have a saying in the hills, when bad news is coming." Beecher paused, "Give it to me with the bark off the wood."

Doctor Tom's face became solemn. He dropped the clipboard to his thigh. "We can treat it, maybe contain it, but there's no promise we can completely eradicate the cancer."

"How long?" asked Beecher, frustrated.

Doctor Tom sighed.

Quince's chest pounded.

"A year, maybe?" answered the doctor.

Beecher nodded. His lips pursed.

Those words sucked the breath from Quince's lungs. His eyes moistened.

"When do treatments begin?" Quince asked after gathering his breath.

"Immediately. Next Monday and every Monday for a while. Difficult to say how long but we need to determine if the treatment is effective—if the cancer is responding," answered the doctor.

Beecher nodded, and slipped from the blue-cushioned chair. He had heard enough. He offered a hand, and Doctor Tom shook it. "Thank you," he said.

"The nurse will call you tomorrow. She will provide the day and time and other specifics of the first treatment."

Quince stood, and shook Doctor Tom's hand, and the Magowan men left, walking down the tiled hallway, through the lobby, and down the stone stairs. As they crossed the grass, Beecher scratched through his pocket, pulled out a cigarette and hung the burley in his dry lips. He lit and sucked the burley, occasionally pulling it from his lips. It was late June. The air was warm. They drove through the hills with the windows down.

≈≈≈

Quince and Beecher worked the farm all week. At noon, each day, they drove into a small hamlet that sat on a hill a few miles east of the farm. The pickup rolled to a stop in a graveled lot, outside a small country store. Father and son would walk in, and ask the old lady behind the counter to fix them bologna sandwiches.

In the evening they rested on the porch, smoked burley cigarettes, and watched fireflies spark like flint rock across the dark pastures. One evening, sitting there, Beecher asked Quince to move to the farm. They could share the meager income. Everything was paid for. Bills were small. Besides, it would be his soon. Quince sighed, and nodded. It made sense. His old life was gone; the old Quince, dead. A death that began in the Kunar Valley, and suffered palpitations for nearly a year, was finally to the point of succumbing. He did not want to live in the house in town anymore—too many memories. He hated working at the warehouse, and wanted to quit. Quince nodded, and it was settled. They smoked cigarettes and watched fireflies.

On Monday, they drove from the hills to town. All day, Beecher lay in a chair while an IV dripped medicine through his veins or was shuttled out of the room to receive other treatments. When he could, Beecher slept and watched television. Quince sat in a chair next to the bed, and read hunting and fishing magazines.

That afternoon, he took Beecher's keys, left the hospital, and drove across town, to the small ranch home. Quince parked, walked up the steps, and peered through the screen door. The large, wooden door was still open. Inside, the television played in the den. In his anger over Trimble and Sara, Quince had left the television on over a week ago when he stormed from the house, and drove to City Hall. Quince opened the screen door, and walked around the house. It was empty, but no one had been there.

He went to the closet, pulled out his sea bag, and filled it with his clothes. Quince carried the bag into the den, dropped it, and sat in the recliner. He pulled a cell phone from his pocket, dialed the warehouse, and told them he was not coming back. He sighed, and stared at the phone for a moment. Finally, he dialed Sara's cell phone, and the tone rang until her soft, smooth voice asked the caller to leave a message.

Quince wanted to speak with her. He wanted to talk about Trimble, and tell her about Beecher. He wanted to hear Lilly's voice. Instead, he hung up when Sara's voice paused, and a beep echoed from the phone. Quince sighed, stood, walked across the den, down the hall, into Lilly's old room. In the middle of the floor sat the small stuffed bear he had given Farrah, the little Afghan girl, and brought back for Lilly. The doll had sat on the floor since the day Sara and Lilly left. Quince dropped to the floor, held the doll, and wept. After a while, he carried the doll into the den, and pushed it into the sea bag. He looked around one last time, nodded, and left.

Chapter 34
≈ Megan ≈

June faded and July quickly passed. In the heat of summer, Beecher changed. Around his temple, his thin, gray hair disappeared. His beard thinned, but he refused to shave, leaving a mangy tuft of hair around his chin. The sickness drained his strength and personality. He grew quieter. He was weak. He mostly lay on the couch or rocked in a chair on the porch. Occasionally, he walked to the barn with Shadow. Otherwise, Beecher stayed at home. He had good and bad days.

Quince worked the farm. Each morning, he rose before dawn, and left to tend the farm. He always returned, and asked Beecher if he was hungry and wanted breakfast. The smell of eggs turned Beecher's stomach so Quince fixed toast and bacon, and they ate at the large wooden table.

On the morning of the 18th, Quince stood before a calendar that hung on the wall in the kitchen. Each day, he noted Beecher's treatments, penciling a few words on the calendar. He also erased a reminder of an appointment with Dr. Gates at the VA. The eraser washed those words away. It was the 3rd time he'd missed appointments. Later that day, his cell phone rang, but Quince eventually turned it off, and deleted voicemails without listening to them. He had given up on his treatment. Beecher's health became his focus.

As weeks passed, Quince became even more anxious to see his daughter. One night, as Beecher slept, Quince walked out onto the porch, and dialed Sara's cell phone. As her voice asked the caller to leave a message, Quince sighed, waited for the beep, and told Sara about Beecher's cancer. He stood on the porch, staring into the pasture. It was nearly pitch black. The hills were thick, plump shadows. All around the farm, fireflies sparked across the dark hills.

He sighed, turned, and went to bed. The next week, Beecher's nausea worsened two days after the chemotherapy treatment. He could not eat, vomiting until he dry-heaved. Quince would hold a small trashcan as the old man sat on the couch, leaned forward and vomited. Finally, Quince had seen enough, and walked Beecher to the pickup and drove him to the hospital.

Beecher was badly dehydrated. He was admitted to the hospital, and given a room with three other ailing veterans. Nurses worked to hydrate him, and reduce the nausea. At night, Quince slept in a chair next to Beecher's bed, but sleep was difficult. The chair was uncomfortable, and the ailing veterans in the room snored and moaned. Each was old, and sick. "He's 91," said the old veteran in the bed next to Beecher's. He pointed to a man lying in a bed across the room. "But his mind is gone, crazy with the Alzheimer's. He's got pneumonia." The old man's head shook, "He won't last."

Quince listened as the old man spoke. "I turned 84 last week. Had by-pass. Funny thing," he said, pulling down the nightgown, "my chest is sore, but the real pain is in my legs." The old man pushed the sheets away from his legs, and raised the gown, revealing one long scar on the inside of his leg. "Oh well. The trials of getting old. Now," the old man pointed to the veteran lying in a bed near the window. "He's got diabetes real bad. Took his leg off two weeks ago, but it won't heal."

Quince listened, nodding, grimacing as the old man spoke.

"That your father?" he asked.

Quince nodded.

"What's wrong with him?"

"Colon cancer. He's dehydrated from the treatments," Quince explained.

The old man shook his head, "Trials of getting old."

The door opened, and a nurse walked across the room, to the veteran with Alzheimer's.

"Well," greeted the talkative old man. "Good morning."

The nurse smiled. She was petite. Baggy scrubs hung from her small frame. Blonde hair lay across her back in a ponytail, and her smile was soft and genuine. "My . . . aren't we chipper this morning!"

"Well, when you are as old as I am, it's always nice to see such a pretty gal."

The nurse chuckled, and her cheeks blushed.

The talkative old man turned to Quince, "Ain't she pretty?" he asked.

Quince nodded, partially hidden from the nurse by Beecher's bed. "Very."

The nurse looked at the young veteran, and blushed. Her face dropped, and her eyes focused on the old man's IV. Then, almost immediately, her brow furrowed, and her face rose. Her green eyes leveled on Quince. "Say. I've seen you here before."

Quince's eyes lifted from the hunting magazine. His head shook. His brow shrugged.

"Yeah. A few months ago. In the cafeteria."

Quince shrugged. "I've stopped there once or twice."

"Yeah," she continued, the revelation opening her eyes, lifting a smile into her cheeks. "That was you."

"Did we talk?" asked Quince, smiling.

The nurse shook her head.

Quince's face was happily perplexed.

"I was sitting in a corner booth with other nurses."

Quince shrugged.

"You were eating breakfast."

Quince shrugged. His brow lifted and sank.

"You were eating like a starved man."

Quince smiled. "I always eat like that."

"We snickered at you. The way you ate."

Suddenly, Quince remembered. He came to see Chaplain Griggs, and stopped at the cafeteria. He nodded. "I remember now. You snickered like a school girl."

The nurse grinned. "You ate like a starved dog."

Quince smiled, "I was."

The nurse replaced the empty IV with a full bag. The old man slept. She leaned over, patted his cheek, walked across the room, and pulled a thermometer from her pocket, poked it in the ear of the amputee, and shook her head.

Quince watched her. He positioned the magazine where he could slyly watch the pretty nurse without it being obvious. He wanted her to stay. Keep talking. Their conversation was left unfinished. He desperately thought of something to say, something to keep her there, but words were elusive. Suddenly, the door swung open, and a middle-aged nurse leaned into the room, holding the door for balance, "Megan," she said, "patients in five and twelve are calling for a nurse."

Megan, paused, looked around at the four patients in the room, and nodded. "I'll be right there."

The nurse pulled the door shut.

Megan's soft, pretty face became sad, quietly frustrated. She sighed.

Quince dropped the magazine below his chin. "Are you OK?" he asked.

Megan nodded, and her eyes moistened. "I just can't get to everyone. I'm the only nurse on this shift, and I have the whole floor."

Quince pointed to the door. "And her?"

Megan nodded. "She's managing the nurse's station."

She regained composure, and approached Beecher's bed. "Is this your father?"

Quince nodded.

"He's so sick," she proclaimed, rubbing Beecher's arm as he slept.

"Has the vomiting stopped in the last two hours?" she asked.

Quince's head shook, "It has slowed."

"Hopefully it will stop soon, and he can hold fluids."

Quince nodded.

Megan smiled at Quince, and she turned. "Mr. Ames, I will be right back."

The old man smiled, and nodded. "Sure. Sure. Take your time. I'm all right."

Megan quickly walked across the room, swung open the wooden door, and darted down the hall. Quince had not realized it, but his chest was pounding, and his mouth had dried. For the first time in months, he smiled. He had forgotten, however briefly, about the troubles in his life.

The hospital was tiring, but he stayed with Beecher two more days. One night, he slept in a chair, next to his father's bed, and awoke covered with a blanket. He had fallen asleep without one, and did not know who covered him during the night.

During the day, he read at Beecher's bedside, making occasional trips to the lounge to watch television and drink coffee. Several times a day, Megan popped into the room and tended the ailing veterans. Quince made small talk with her, but she was always too busy to chat long. On the morning of the third day, Beecher was released. The vomiting had stopped. His body began to hold fluids. He was hydrated, and ready to leave.

The Magowan men returned to the farm, only leaving the small, whitewashed house for short trips into the nearby hamlet, or to drive around the farm just before dusk. Each Monday, they drove from the hills to the hospital where Beecher continued treatments. On a Friday evening, Quince strolled onto the porch carrying a beer, and smoking a burley cigarette. He pulled the phone from his pocket, and dialed Sara's number. The rings gave way to Sara's soft voice, seeking a message. Quince sighed. His chest throbbed. The phone beeped, and words poured from his mouth. "Hey," he began awkwardly, just like he used to leave messages. He sighed, "I think we need to talk. I need to see Lilly. It's been two months. I need to see my daughter." Quince paused. His mind flooded with thoughts, emotions. "Something's happened with dad. Lilly needs to spend time with him." He paused, sighing. "Sara . . . I . . . I . . . I'm sorry about everything. I . . . I . . ." stammering, his pride was unable to release the words. "Please call me back," he asked, and hung up the phone.

It was late. Fireflies sparked across the dark pasture. Cattle gathered under trees along the fence near the barn. Their bellows echoed through the hollows. Quince pulled the beer to his lips and drank. He rinsed his teeth with the beer, swallowed, hung the cigarette in his moist lips, sucked the burley, held the smoke in his lungs, and pushed it through his nostrils. Beecher lay quietly on the couch. The television spoke through the screen door. Suddenly, Quince's phone rang. He looked down, and the name Sara was written across the illuminated screen. His chest pounded. Thunder rang in his ears. He pulled the phone to his ears, and spoke. "Hey, it's me."

A deep, crass voice spoke through the speakers. "Quince, this is Donald Foster, Sara's father," he answered, as if Quince did not know his own father-in-law. His voice was professional, all business, clean, crisp, the excess of pleasantries and kindness were cut with a tool-and-die tongue.

"Mr. Foster," Quince greeted.

"Listen, Quince, Sara can't bring herself to speak with you," he paused.

Quince's eyes moistened.

"But she realizes you need to see Lilly."

Quince nodded. A sense of success lifted his spirits.

"That would be good, Mr. Foster."

"When will you be in town?"

"Monday," answered Quince, thinking of Beecher's treatment.

"Monday," Mr. Foster whispered to someone.

Quince listened closely. He thought he heard Sara's voice speaking softly, but he was unsure.

"Meet us in the mall parking lot at 10:00 a.m."

Quince nodded. Moisture gathered in his eyes. "I'll be there."

"Oh. Quince."

"Yes Mr. Foster?"

"Your message said something about your father. Is something wrong?"

"Dad has cancer. Treatments make him terribly sick, and he's real tired."

"I'm sorry to hear that. Give him our best."

Quince nodded. "I will," he vowed, and hung up.

On Monday, Quince drove Beecher into town, parking under the catalpa tree in front of the hospital. He walked with Beecher across the grass, through the crowded parking lot, and up the stairs. They walked through the lounge, down the hall, and into the large room where Beecher took his treatment. He stayed with Beecher until the treatments began, and then left, leaping into the big, red pickup, pulling away from the hospital campus, and speeding across town.

The blinker ticked in Quince's ears as he waited to turn through traffic into the parking lot. The street was crowded with passing cars, and Quince impatiently watched for an opportunity to turn. At one point, he glanced into the lot, and saw a black sedan parked near the grocery. The windows were dark. He was unable to see inside, but he knew Lilly was in the car. His chest began to pound. It was the first time in months he felt sincere joy. Finally, Quince spotted a small opening between passing cars. He mashed the gas, and the large tires squealed as the pickup shot across the street, into the lot, and rolled to a stop near the sedan.

Quince glanced in the mirror. Until that morning, he wore a scruffy beard. Wanting to impress the Fosters, he'd shaved, and dressed in his best jeans, a buttoned, plaid shirt, and brown dress shoes. He sighed, opened the door, and slid from the tall seat all along wondering if Sara was in the car. He doubted she would come, but he couldn't help but wonder. Slowly, he walked toward the sedan, and the tinted window on the driver's side dropped. A distinguished face, crowned with white hair, watched him. "Quince," he greeted, nodding without emotion.

"Mr. Foster," answered the young veteran.

"Where's Beecher?"

"At treatment."

Mr. Foster nodded.

The passenger door opened, and a middle-aged woman rose from the seat, glanced at Quince, turned, and opened the back door.

A smile lifted Quince's cheeks. It was as natural as anything he'd ever felt.

Suddenly, a mop of curly, blonde hair leaped from the backseat, and ran around the sedan. "Daddy!" shouted the little girl.

"Lilly," Quince shouted as moisture gathered in his eyes.

Lilly threw her tiny arms around his waist.

Quince stooped, and pulled the girl off her feet. "I missed you, precious," he said.

"Missed you, Daddy."

"We'll meet you here in two hours," interjected Mr. Foster.

Quince's face rose. Smiling, he nodded.

The sedan drove away as Quince lifted Lilly into the truck's seat, jumped behind the wheel, and sped off.

"Where should we go? You pick," he asked, leaning toward the blonde girl.

Lilly shrugged, "I don't know. How about the park?" she suggested.

"The park it is."

The pickup rolled through the city park, and stopped near the tennis courts. Father and daughter strolled along the path, among thick, bushy conifers. Quince slid coins into a vending machine, grabbed a bag of chips, and they kept walking, swinging their hands as they moped along the asphalt path. At a small lake, they walked out a pier, opened the bag, and tossed chips into the water. Geese swarmed the water around the piling, diving for soggy chips. When the bag was empty, they climbed a hill, and Lilly sat in a swing.

Quince pushed her, and the little girl laughed, and swung, kicking her feet each time the swing rose. Eventually, her laughter trailed off and she became quiet. Wind tugged at her blonde locks, and gently brushed across her face. Quiet, it was as if she were thinking about something, wondering about a time not long ago when her father and mother would bring her here, and watch as she played on the jungle-gym, and applauded as she built poorly formed sandcastles. Quince pushed, watching her. Moisture gathered in his eyes, but he quickly wiped them dry. Like Lilly, he wondered what had happened to his family, how his life came to that moment. But now, standing in the mulch, he was content to savor the moment, and push his daughter on a swing.

After a while, they left, drove across town, and stopped at a small diner. Quince devoured a hamburger. Lilly ate fries, and drank a chocolate shake. He paid, and they left, drove a few miles, and pulled to a stop next the black sedan in the parking lot. Quince opened the door, and lifted Lilly from the seat, gently lowering her to the asphalt. He walked her to the sedan, opened the door, hugged her neck, and kissed her cheek. Afterwards, he circled the sedan, stooped, and waved at Mr. Foster who nodded, and offered a terse smile. Quince peered through the back window, smiled, and waved at Lilly as the sedan drove away. It was only two hours but Quince was happy. It was a good day.

Quince drove back to the hospital, parked, ran across the grass, and bounced up the stairs. His feet were light. He felt as if he were flying. A smile lifted his cheeks as he bolted through the glass door, down the hall, through a lounge crowded with veterans, down another hall, and into the treatment room. Beecher was lying in the cushioned chair, watching a daytime soap. "Never expected to see this," ribbed Quince.

Beecher chuckled, "Me neither but hell, these ain't half bad."

Quince nodded.

"Well, how'd it go?"

Quince nodded again.

"Good. Hell, it was great!"

Beecher grinned.

"She's grown," Quince's head shook.

"And the Fosters?" asked Beecher, sarcastically.

Quince's head shook, "Same, I reckon."

Beecher nodded.

"Never mentioned Sara."

"There ain't much for them to say about it. Reckon there ain't much anyone can say about it now."

Quince nodded.

"There's a time when you can change things, but then it's just done. Can't what if things the rest of your life. It is what it is."

Quince stood, and sighed. "I'm going for a cup of coffee."

Beecher grinned. "I'll be here. Enjoy your coffee."

Quince nodded. "Enjoy your soap."

Beecher raised a thumb and grinned, turning to the television.

Quince went down the hall. Reliving the afternoon with Lilly easily lifted a smile across his face. It was unconscious, but each time he paused to relive a memory at the park, or in the diner, a smile rose into his cheeks. The memory lifting and dropping them like a puppeteer.

He walked through the lobby, down the hall, into the cafeteria, poured a cup of coffee, and sat alone in a booth, facing the door where he blew and sipped coffee, and enjoyed himself.

"Not hungry today, Magowan?" asked a soft voice.

Quince's eyes slowly rose. He smiled and nodded. "Ate earlier. Guess you missed it."

"We were hoping to watch you devour a hamburger," she taunted, pointing to a few nurses who'd gathered in a corner booth.

Quince turned, nodded to the nurses before looking back at Megan. "No hamburger today, but I'll buy you a cup of coffee."

Megan grinned, nodded and slid into the booth as Quince went to the counter, poured a cup of coffee, and gently set it on the table in front of Megan. He slid into the booth across from her, sipped coffee, and smiled. Megan's lips poised as she softly blew away steam, drank and asked, "How's Mr. Magowan?"

Quince shrugged. "OK. I reckon."

"Is he here for treatment?"

Quince nodded again.

Megan sipped coffee. Her brow furrowed, and she stared at Quince with a curious expression. "You seem different today."

Quince shrugged.

"Happier, I think."

Quince paused, and nodded. "It was a good day."

Megan's lips bunched. "And what made it good?"

Quince shrugged. "Spent the afternoon with Lilly," he said, saying his daughter's name in the most obvious fashion, as if he were saying Elvis or Gandhi or Shakespeare.

"Lilly?" she asked, the question furrowing her brow.

Quince embarrassingly dropped his face. "My daughter."

Megan's face opened up. "You have a daughter?"

Quince dug through his pocket, pulled out a wallet, unfolded the leather, and held up a picture of Lilly.

"Blonde curls. She's beautiful."

"Thanks."

"I can't tell," she continued. "Does she resemble you or your wife?"

Quince shrugged. "Both."

"I haven't seen your wife. Do you have a picture?"

Quince closed the wallet. "No."

"Well. You and your wife must be proud."

"We are. But," Quince paused, sighing, "we ain't together anymore."

Megan was sipping coffee, but paused. "I'm sorry."

Quince's lips bunched as he shrugged. "Separated a few months back."

Megan nodded.

"How about you? You have kids?" asked Quince, anxious to shift attention away from his marriage.

Megan smiled, leaning back, and shaking her head side-to-side. "With this shift? No way. But maybe someday."

"Married?" he persisted.

Megan's head shook. "Same story. Married to work. This hospital."

Quince lifted the cup. “Here’s to someday,” he toasted.

Megan lifted her cup, and tapped his cup. “Someday.”

Quince grinned. Blush slightly colored Megan’s cheeks as she glanced at her watch. “Oh. I need to go. Sorry. Shift is starting.”

The smile dropped from Quince’s face as she stood, and said, “Thanks for the coffee,” before turning to walk away.

“Megan,” she turned around. “I don’t know your last name?”

She giggled, “Tucker.”

“Tucker,” Quince repeated. She paused in thought, “Magowan, I just realized, I don’t know your first name.”

His chest lifted as he laughed. “Quince.”

“Quince,” she repeated.

Quince pointed to the booth, “Lunch, here, next Monday, Megan Tucker?”

“Lunch here, Quince Magowan.” Megan turned, and left the cafeteria. Quince grinned. It was a good day for Tom Quincy Magowan.

Chapter 35
≈ The Farmer ≈

The summer sprinted through July on its way to August. Quince worked the farm as Beecher rested inside the house. Each Monday, Quince drove his father to the hospital. It was always a full day. He would sit with Beecher, read, eat lunch, or take walks with Megan, and, every other Monday, he met the Fosters at the mall and took Lilly. They would first visit Beecher in the hospital before leaving for the park or a playground. Sara never rode with her parents during the visitations. Quince had not seen her since the night before she left.

One Monday, as visitation ended, Mr. Foster told Quince that they had a buyer for the ranch house in town. A neighbor wanted to buy the house for his elderly mother. The mother lived alone in Cincinnati, but she was no longer capable of caring for herself. They wanted the mother to move closer. The neighbor offered to pay off the house, with a little extra if he and Sara agreed to leave the furniture. They both agreed; neither needed nor wanted the furniture. It was perfect for everyone.

Three weeks later, Quince drove into town, and, for the final time, stopped in the driveway of his house. He went inside, and began packing the few personal items that remained. He'd taken most of his clothes to the farm soon after moving in with his father, but he had left a stack of books, which he carried to the truck. Returning to the house, he walked through each room one last time, pausing to briefly recall memories of better times. Then, he drove to a bank in town, sat with an attorney, and signed a stack of papers. When the final paper was signed, he got back in the truck and drove through the hills, to the farm. A sense of relief filled the young man. The yoke of a mortgage payment on an empty house was lifted from his neck. He had finished another chapter. Deep beneath the sadness, he felt a sense of tempered joy.

One Saturday afternoon, Quince walked across the pastures to the farmhouse.

It was mid-August. The lower fields were thick with grass. He'd been on a tractor all morning, and well into the afternoon, cutting grass. Dust was caked across his face. Walking across the pasture, he spat a mouth full of dirt. Dust scratched his eyes, and lined his teeth. A deep tan colored his arms and neck. He wore an old cap, and a thin shirt that was soaked with August sweat. He walked into the house, and made two sandwiches. He and Beecher sat on the porch, eating sandwiches, and drinking Ale-8s, talking about the hay he would bale on Sunday. When they finished, Quince scrubbed plates, took a shower, pulled a clean shirt over his shoulders, slid on jeans and his good boots, doused cologne across his neck, and left.

He drove through the hills with the windows down. Wind blew across his face as the red pickup rose and sank along the winding road. He drove into town, maneuvered through Saturday evening traffic, and parked on Main Street. He glanced in the mirror, opened the door, and slid from the pickup, bouncing down the sidewalk as traffic slowly crawled by. Ducking into a corner restaurant, a pretty hostess smiled, and asked, "How many?"

Quince peered through the crowded restaurant, "I'm meeting someone who's already here," he answered, straining to see over the booths. That someone waved from a corner booth along the back wall. In the dim lighting of the dark restaurant, her features appeared small and soft. A grin lifted into her cheeks, and blonde hair fell across her shoulders. Her hair was straight and long; it was the first time he'd seen her without a ponytail. A black tank top hung from her shoulders, and her skin was lightly tanned. Quince waved, nodded to the hostess, and walked across the room.

She smiled as Quince slid into booth.

"Sorry," he confessed. "Saturday evening traffic."

"I didn't wait. Hope you don't mind?" she asked, tilting a glass of beer to her lips.

Quince nodded. "Thanks," he said, pointing to a glass of beer on the table.

Megan nodded, smiling.

Quince tipped the glass to his lips, and drank. "So" he asked, resting the glass on the table. "Beer?"

Megan shook her head, "Sometimes I enjoy bourbon but I prefer beer." Her shoulders shrugged. "Guess I'm not a fruity drink kind of girl."

Quince nodded.

"You look nice," Quince complimented.

"Just shorts and a tank top."

"It's nice on you."

Megan smiled.

A waitress slipped over Quince's shoulder, poised with a pencil and pad, "So, are we ready to order?"

Quince gestured to the lady, and Megan ordered. "I think I'll just have the house sirloin. Medium rare."

Quince nodded. "Perfect. Same for me."

The waitress scribbled on the pad, smiled, and walked away.

"You're impressing me."

"Why?" she asked.

Quince's lips bunched, restraining a smile.

Megan shrugged. "I'm not much for putting on a public face. I'm just plain old Megan."

"Nothing plain about being who you are," said Quince.

Megan shrugged.

"Besides, it's refreshing. I'm not used to it."

Megan pulled the glass to her lips, and drank. "Sara was different, wasn't she?"

Quince nodded, and his face dropped.

"You miss her?"

Quince shrugged. His lips bunched. "It's done now."

Megan nodded. Her face grew serious. "How's Beecher?"

Quince shrugged. "Same. Doubt he'll get better."

Quince pulled the beer to his lips, and drank.

"And you?" she asked. "Are you sleeping?"

Quince shrugged. "About the same, I reckon."

Megan listened.

"Work is hard. I'm tired at night. Sometimes that helps. But it usually doesn't matter."

"You still won't see the new doctor?" she asked.

Quince nodded. "I tried."

"I hear good things about Doctor Gates," she persisted.

"With the farm, and dad being sick, I'm too busy now."

Megan frowned, and she stared at him with questioning eyes.

"How do you know Gates can help me?"

Megan pulled the beer to her lips, and drank. "I've heard good things about him."

Quince's brow lifted. "Such as?"

"He's worked at other VA hospitals. Been in the system for much of his career."

Quince stared across the table with a disbelieving look.

"Look. He's devoted his life to caring for veterans. He's treated others with PTSD."

"Not at our hospital," insisted Quince.

Megan nodded.

Quince's brow lifted.

"There are others?"

Megan nodded.

"From Iraq and Afghanistan?"

Megan nodded. "Yes. Several now."

Quince's face was stunned, "I used to be the only one."

"Not anymore."

Silence fell between them.

"Will you see him?"

He glanced away, staring across the crowded restaurant.

"Try."

Quince shook his head.

Megan slipped her hands across the table, and over his hand lying next to the half-empty glass. "For me?"

Quince stared across the table, into her wide, green eyes. Her face was gentle but solemn, sincere.

He sighed and shrugged.

As the evening passed, they drank, and ate steak. Later, they left, walking along the sidewalks, gawking into the well-lit shops along Main Street. Once, Megan spotted a mannequin wearing a summer dress she liked. They went inside, and Quince stood and patiently waited outside the dressing room while Megan slipped into the dress, reappeared, modeled it for Quince, and asked for his advice. For the next 30 minutes, she disappeared into the dressing room only to reappear minutes later wearing a new dress. Finally, they tired, ducked into a bar, rested, and drank a beer on an open patio, enjoying the soft warmth of an August evening. They drank and watched pedestrians pass along the small, wrought iron fence separating the sidewalk and the patio. Megan pushed her stool next to Quince's, and, as the booze and the warm evening air softened her anxieties, she laid her head on Quince's shoulder.

Quince pulled the bottle to his lips, and drank. His face dropped as he turned to Megan, "Wake up. It's only 10:30."

Megan's sleepy face rose from his shoulder as she whispered, "Long shift last night."

"Still ain't hired help for you?" asked Quince.

Megan's head shook, and she rubbed her sleepy eyes, yawning.

"OK," he announced, setting down the bottle. "I'll walk you back to the car." Quince gently pushed the stool from the table, and stood.

Megan shook her head.

"What?" he asked. "You want to stay now?"

"No," her head shook. "I want you to come back with me."

Quince smiled and blush colored his cheeks.

"Will you?" she asked.

Quince nodded.

Together, they held hands, and walked through the bar, past the wrought iron fence, down sidewalks, passing expensive boutiques, and crowded bars. They stopped beside Megan's car as she turned to ask, "Follow me?"

He nodded as Megan rose to her toes, kissed him and slipped into her car. Quince followed the small foreign car through the streets, and along the bypass leading out of town. They turned into a gated apartment complex, drove to the back, passing a small square with a statue pouring water into the fountain. They walked up three flights of stairs, and Megan opened the door, turned, and smiled at Quince, pointing, "There's beer in the fridge." Then, she flipped on the lights, and disappeared down the hall into a bedroom.

Quince walked across the room, into the tiny kitchen, opened the refrigerator, took a beer, twisted the bottle cap, and tossed it on the counter. He walked around, gawking at photographs, and cheap, department store art Megan had hung in the den. Noticing a balcony, he moved across the den, opened the door, and stepped outside, onto the small wooden platform. The sound of crashing water filled the square below as Quince pulled the beer to his lips, and drank. Suddenly, soft, thin arms slid around his waist, and he felt gentle, moist lips touch his neck.

He set the bottle on a wooden rail, turned, cupped Megan's face in his callused hands, and kissed her. She was soft and smelled of freshly sprayed perfume. A white T-shirt hung to her bare thighs. They kissed, and Quince slowly pulled his lips from hers. Megan grinned, as Quince gathered her in his arms, carried her through the door, and across the den, down the hall, and into the bedroom.

Across the room, a candle burned on a dresser. A sweet scent filled the air, and a soft flame offered the only light. Quince gently laid her on the bed, and leaned over her, kissing her neck, rising across her cheek, over her lips, and back down. Megan's hand slid across his back, pulled the shirt over his shoulders, and kissed his chest. Next, Quince slid the T-shirt over Megan's round shoulders, kissed her neck, across her chest, fondled her small breasts, and kissed her nipples. Across the room, on the dresser, a small flame flickered atop a jar of wax. The air was filled with a sweet scent. Quince and Megan kissed, and pulled each other's clothes off, and screwed until the wax melted, pooling in the small jar. Outside, water crashed into the fountain below the statue's stone feet.

The next morning, Quince awoke to the smell of brewing coffee and burning grease. Megan's side of the bed was empty. The comforter was pushed back, and small indentations were creased into the pillow where her head and her butt lay. Quince pushed away the comforter, pulled the jeans over his legs, fastened them, and went into the kitchen where Megan stood over the stove with her back turned. The T-shirt barely covered her butt. Quince slid his arms around her waist, and kissed her neck. She smiled, turned, and kissed him. Later, they ate on the balcony, overlooking the fountain. They drank coffee, and soaked in the morning sun. Quince helped her wash dishes, kissed her soft lips, and promised to call her that afternoon.

The red pickup sped through the hills, toward the farm. Quince drove up the long, graveled driveway, and saw Beecher rocking in a chair on the front porch. A cloud of smoke gathered around his chair—a cigarette hung in the corner of his dry lips. Quince slid from the truck. Shadow bounced and jumped as he walked across the yard.

"Where the hell you been?" asked Beecher, rocking.

A grin lifted Quince's cheeks. "Oh . . . just out."

"Uh huh," Beecher grunted. "You spent the night at Megan's?"

Quince nodded as he climbed the porch steps. A wide grin cut his face.

"Bastard," proclaimed Beecher.

Quince flopped into a rocking chair.

"Don't get comfortable. You got to rake and bail that whole field of hay this afternoon."

"I just got here."

"Ain't my fault you been out all night," joked Beecher.

Quince grinned. "She's special, dad."

Beecher nodded. His dry lips bunched up. "I know. Many times I've talked to her about you. She seems to be a good, honest woman. She's hardworking and sincere."

Quince nodded, stood, walked across the porch, and laid his hand on Beecher's shoulder. "Can I get you anything?"

Beecher shook his head.

"All right," proclaimed Quince, "I'll be in the field."

Chapter 36
≈ The Old Churchyard ≈

The morning was warm. Humid air seared the pastures at dawn. Quince rose, fried bacon and brewed coffee. He and Beecher sat on the porch and ate.

"I told Reverend Shaygrove we'd come by today and patch the roof of the old church."

"When did you see him?" asked Quince.

"He stopped by yesterday morning," answered Beecher, rocking. "Winds from that last thunderstorm blew off some shingles. More storms are on the way so we need to get it done."

Quince nodded, carried in the dirty plates, and washed them. He walked across the pasture, and disappeared into the barn. A few minutes later, he reappeared, carrying a ladder, hammer, and a carpenter's pouch. He loaded the tools in the bed of the truck, and he and Beecher climbed into the cab. Shadow leaped into the bed, and they drove through the hills, turning, and crossing the covered bridge that spanned the small stream. The pick-up stopped in the gravel next to the whitewashed fence. An old man, wearing a straw hat with a wide brim, limped across the cemetery, toward the pick-up.

"Reverend," shouted Beecher as he slid from the seat. "It's too hot for you to be out here. You'll have a heat stroke, old man."

Reverend Shaygrove was a supremely devout, sincere, and serious man. Every word that slipped through his lips was serious and had a purpose. He commanded respect. Beecher Magowan was not disrespectful to the reverend. It was just his way. He spoke his mind. And, if he poked fun at you, it meant he liked you. Ribbing was Beecher's way of showing endearment, and Reverend Shaygrove knew it.

The reverend just shook his head. "Weeds are about to overtake the cemetery. Just pruning."

Reverend Shaygrove pulled off his glove, and offered a sweaty hand. "Quince. Haven't seen you in a while."

Quince shook hands with the old man. "Better than two years, I reckon."

"I reckon," agreed the aging pastor, "Hope to see you in church. We need young folks."

"Maybe soon," answered Quince.

Reverend Shaygrove circled the pick-up, and shook Beecher's hand.

Quince opened the tailgate, and Shadow leapt from the bed. He pulled the ladder from the bed, carried it through the gate, and around the small sanctuary, gently leaning it against the eave. Beecher handed Quince the carpenter's belt, which he fastened to his waist, and began climbing. Reverend Shaygrove stood in the grass, and gazed at the roof. "We lost some shingles on top, along the cap."

Quince gingerly stepped from the ladder onto the steep roof, and climbed the sharp slope to the top. The wind had ripped shingles from the roof, throwing them into the ancient cemetery below. "I need two," Quince shouted. Beecher nodded, and moped toward the truck.

Quince took the claw of the hammer, and pried away the exposed roofing nails. He wiped away a few small pieces, turned, and slid down the roof, stepping onto the ladder. It was terribly hot. Sweat dripped from his brow. Moist patches had already appeared on his shirt.

"Yes sir," proclaimed Reverend Shaygrove. "It is warm. I appreciate you gentlemen helping the congregation this way."

Quince grinned.

"Glad to do it," Beecher answered, packing a handful of shingles over his shoulder. He lifted one foot onto the ladder, and said, "We may not be faithful churchgoers, but we help when we…ahhhhh." Grimacing, Beecher moaned, and collapsed, falling from the ladder, into the grass.

"Dad!" shouted Quince, sliding down the ladder. Reverend Shaygrove kneeled next to Beecher, who lay on his stomach, holding his back. Shadow barked. Quince knelt next to his father. "Are you OK? What is it?"

Beecher moaned. "My back!"

"All right, we're gonna get you to the hospital," Quince promised. "Can you walk?"

Beecher moaned and struggled to pull his legs under him, before collapsing again.

"OK, I'll carry you." Quince slid his arms under Beecher, and grimaced as he lifted the small man. "What can I do?" asked Reverend Shaygrove.

"Reverend, can you take Shadow back to the farm? He'll be all right. He has food in the barn."

"Sure," promised the old man. "We'll be praying."

"Thank you, reverend," Quince said. He carried Beecher across the yard, through the gate, and laid him in the cab.

Reverend Shaygrove slid the straw hat from his head. "God bless you, Beecher," he prayed.

Beecher, who lay slumped over in the seat, opened his fingers, and barely lifted a hand, waving. "Thank you," he whispered. Then, he shouted in agony.

Quince leapt behind the wheel, and started the truck. He slammed the door, mashed the gas, and slung gravel across the churchyard. The pick-up shot through the covered bridge, turned, and sped away.

Chapter 37
≈ With the bark off the tree ≈

"You look exhausted," she noted, handing Quince a cup of coffee. His brow rose and fell. Without a word, Quince took the cup, blew steam from the coffee, and sipped.

Megan stood next to Quince, and stared at the man lying unconscious in the bed. "Tests are all finished," she said. "Dr. Tomasky should be here with the results soon."

Quince's lips were pinched. A distinct whistling sound occurred as he sucked air through his nostrils, and stared at Beecher.

Beecher was covered in a white blanket. His mouth hung open. Periodically, he snorted, and his eyelids twitched.

"The anesthesia is wearing off. He'll wake soon," Megan noted.

"Will he be in pain?" asked Quince.

Megan shook her head. "No. He has a morphine drip," she pointed to the IV tube that dropped from a bag, across the bed, and disappeared into Beecher's arm.

Beecher's head began to rotate, and his mouth slowly closed. Soon, his eyelids popped open, and he stared nervously at the ceiling.

Quince leaned forward. "Dad. I'm here," he said.

Beecher's head slowly turned. His eyes focused on Quince, but he said nothing.

"The morphine will probably keep him disoriented for a while."

Beecher's chest rose as he sucked a deep breath into his lungs. "Naw," he said, looking up at the ceiling. "I know who I am. And," he paused, "why I'm here," his chest fell as he exhaled.

They were quiet. Beecher lay still, and stared at the ceiling.

Quince sat nearby, sipped coffee, and watched his father. Megan paced around the room.

Another hour passed, when the door swung open, and Dr. Tom entered. He nervously fumbled through papers fixed to a clipboard before he spoke.

Beecher sighed. "Let's have it, doc. I told you before. The truth. Give it to me with the bark off the tree."

Dr. Tom sighed, and his eyes lifted from the clipboard. "Since your last exam, the cancer has become much more aggressive. It has spread throughout much of your lower colon. And," he paused, "into your pelvic bone." He paused.

"And?" asked Beecher in a gravelly, perturbed voice.

"X-rays show a small spot, about 1 centimeter, on your pancreas."

Moisture gathered in Quince's eyes. His mouth hung open, and he gasped. It was like someone had struck him in the stomach.

Megan began to sniffle. Tears trickled down her soft cheeks. Beecher's face was solemn, but emotionless. His jaws were thin, and clinched tight. Thin sprigs of white beard sprouted across his cheeks. Wrinkles furrowed under his eyes, and his eyelids were loose, heavy. His eyes were nearly closed, and, if there was any emotion in them, it was hidden from the loose skin, and the shield of an old, hardened man.

"So," asked Beecher, "where do we go from here?"

Dr. Tom's face was pensive. He pushed his hands behind his back. "Well. We can attack the cancer with a more aggressive treatment. That may . . ."

"You mean more chemotherapy?" interrupted the ailing man.

"Well, yes, that and radiation."

"I can't take no more!"

"But we can . . ."

"I'm done with the juice!"

"Dad!" interjected Quince, trying to reason with his father.

"A more aggressive treatment can prolong . . ."

"That's right!" shouted Beecher. "Prolong the end."

Dr. Tom's face sank.

"Ain't that right, doc? We're talking about stretching it out just a little longer, right? We ain't talking about a cure?" said Beecher, frustrated.

Dr. Tom sighed. "Yes. That's correct."

"Dad," interjected Quince, "maybe you should try."

"How long?" asked Beecher.

"You can't just give up!" Quince insisted.

"How long?" asked Beecher, angrily.

Dr. Tom's shrugged, exasperated. "Maybe three months. Maybe less if the cancer continues to attack this aggressively."

A difficult silence fell across the room. Megan stood over Beecher's bed, whimpering. Quince sat nearby—his face was long and pinched. Beecher lay there, staring at the ceiling. He was silent, but his eyes creased, then opened, as if he were staring into the sun. Suddenly, his head began to shake, and his lips pursed. "I don't want it."

Silence again followed Beecher's words. His head shook. "I don't want it. Two extra months don't mean much if I'm sick."

Dr. Tom nodded, and sighed. "I understand. But, I need to tell you that some patients initially choose to forego treatment, and later change their mind when the realization of death sets in. By then, it's too late."

Beecher nodded. "Not me. I don't want it. I want to go home."

Dr. Tom nodded. "As long as your pain is under control, I don't see why you can't go home tomorrow. Hospice will visit with you before you are released. A nurse will come to your house each week." Dr. Tom walked to the bed, and gently patted Beecher's shoulder. "I'm sorry. I wish I could have done more."

Chapter 38
≈ Cigarettes and Ale-8-One ≈

Beecher Magowan went home the next morning. Quince took care of the farm. Most days, Beecher lay on the couch in the den, watching television and sleeping. Every few hours, he would drop his legs from the couch, onto the floor, scoot his feet across the den, open the front door, and drop into the rocking chair on the porch. He would scratch through his pocket for a burley, hang the cigarette in his dry lips, light the tip, and smoke. When the cigarette had burned down to the filter, he dropped the butt into an empty beer bottle, stood, opened the door, scooted his feet across the den, and lay down. Morphine kept much of the pain away. Occasionally, on some afternoons, when the pain was bearable, Beecher walked to the barn. Mostly, though, he just lay there, the television played to an empty house and a man whose sharp wit had dulled with the delirium of morphine.

A front blew across the farm one afternoon. Rain poured from dark clouds. Lightning struck the hills. Thunder rumbled, vibrating the small farmhouse. When it was over, Quince walked the pastures, checking on the cattle, the barns and fences for damage. The air was humid but summer had begun to fade.

The next morning, Quince rose early. He drove to the country store, bought a carton of cigarettes, and a dozen Ale-8s, and brought them home.

Beecher winked at Quince as he opened an Ale-8 and a pack of cigarettes, and set them on the coffee table. He stooped over the small man lying on the couch, kissed his forehead, and left.

Later that morning, the red truck drove up the graveled driveway. Beecher sat on the porch, smoking, staring out across the pasture. The passenger door flew open, and a small, thin girl with curly blonde hair, slipped from the seat. She ran across the yard, smiling and screaming, "Papaw."

A grin lifted Beecher's thin cheeks. He struggled to stand, opened his arms, and wrapped them around the little girl as she ran across the porch. That afternoon,

Quince lifted Lilly into the red pickup, before setting the frail man beside his granddaughter. He dropped the tailgate, and Shadow leapt into the truck bed. He opened the gate, and drove to the barn, where he stopped, walked into the barn, and re-emerged with three fishing poles.

Soon, the pickup bounced through pastures and passed the corn crib, through the lower fields, forded a shallow creek, and stopped near a tall tree adorned with wide leaves and stringy tassels. Beecher sat in the cab, and watched as Quince and Lilly scoured for worms along limbs of the old tree. Lilly bounced and screamed as Quince pulled worms from the limbs, and dropped them into a Mason jar. When the jar was full, they drove along the shallow creek, and parked on the banks of a pond.

Mallard ducks squawked, and flew from a stand of cattails as the trio stopped near the water. Beecher slowly bent, and sat in the dirt on the bank. Lilly squealed as Quince baited each hook with catalpa worms. He reared back, jerked the pole, and the hook flew across the pond, splashing in the still, murky water. He coached Lilly, holding her hands, showing the little girl how to drop the pole over her shoulder before jerking it forward. Beecher, sitting in the dirt, slung his line into the water.

Quince, Beecher, and Lilly sat in the dirt on the banks of the old farm pond, and studied their fishing lines, watching for that slight tremor as a catfish nibbles on a worm. The afternoon sun warmed their faces. Canadian geese cackled in the blue sky, flying to the cornfields along the river bottom. A soft, peaceful grin lifted Beecher's emaciated cheeks. "I could go for fresh catfish tonight," he proclaimed, staring across the smooth, green water. "Been a while since we had fresh catfish."

The stringer was nearly full when the tip of Lilly's pole began to bounce. Beecher pointed, excited, "There he is! He's nibbling that old worm." Quince knelt behind Lilly, and wrapped his arms around the little girl, helping her hold the pole. Beecher watched, and shouted. "He's nibbling."

The pole shook and bounced. "Jerk it!" Beecher shouted, laughing. Quince and Lilly jerked, and the tip of the pole bent. The line zigzagged across the pond. Together, they pulled and reeled until the catfish lay flopping on the bank. Lilly danced and screamed. Beecher laughed, and clapped.

Later, they drove back to the farmhouse. Quince and Beecher filleted the fish, breaded the fillets, and fried them in a skillet. That evening, they sat on the porch, drank Ale-8s and ate fresh catfish. When they were finished, Beecher and Lilly lay on the couch watching television. Soon, both were asleep. Quince unfolded a blanket, tucked them in, and sat in the recliner, watching them. Later, he stood, walked down the hall, into his bedroom, and went to sleep.

The next morning, Beecher's eyes moistened as he handed Lilly a small locket. "That's your grandmother," he explained, pointing to the faded picture inside. "You and your daddy never knew her, but she was special."

Lilly stared at the locket, "And you, Papaw."

Beecher nodded, "I added a picture of your old papaw so you'll remember him. I want you to have it."

Lilly wrapped her arms around the frail man. A tear dropped from Beecher's eyes as the little girl walked across the yard, climbed into the truck, and waved as she and Quince drove away.

A week later, Beecher lay on the couch as Quince slept. All day, he lay there, restlessly fidgeting, whimpering, moaning. That night, as the farmhouse was dark and quiet, Beecher's moans grew louder. "Dad. What is it?" asked Quince, groggy as he stood over the frail man on the couch.

"My legs and my back. They hurt so I can't stand it," he cried.

Quince quickly dressed, packed some clothes, and carried Beecher to the truck. They drove through the night, across the hills, down the highway, and arrived at the hospital before dawn.

Chapter 39
≈ A Quiet Knoll ≈

"We've increased the treatments," explained Dr. Tom. "Morphine acts as a sedative. The stronger the dosage, the less cognizant he will become. You need to be prepared for this. His pain will become so great, the morphine required to ease that pain will likely keep him unconscious, or delirious, at best."

Quince and Megan stood in the hall, and listened. Quince sighed. Red streaks lay like a spider's web across his eyes. Dark circles hung below them. He was exhausted. Moisture gathered in Megan's eyes as she listened, and patted Quince's back.

"Just make him as comfortable as you can," begged Quince. "I don't want him to suffer. No suffering. He wanted to die with dignity. That's all he asked for."

"Sure," Dr. Tom said, nodding. He patted Quince's shoulder and walked away.

Beecher lay quiet, still under a white blanket. At night, Quince slept in a chair near the bed. Two older veterans were in the room with him. One of them, suffering from dementia, moaned all night. The other veteran cursed and complained. Though the hospital was crowded, Megan convinced the staff to place Beecher in a room by himself, and he was moved the next day.

Quince pulled two chairs together, and slept each night next to his father. During the day, Quince read, and occasionally sat in the lounge, and talked to strangers. Sometimes, he would take a book, and sit under maple trees on a knoll overlooking the hospital. It was September and the sun was warm and comfortable. The sting of summer's heat was gone. The sun washed his face, and a gentle breeze rattled the drying leaves. He was alone there. The knoll overlooked a sprawling hospital compound, but it was tucked away near the back, along a tall fence overgrown with vines. He sat there, under the trees, read, and thought about the last two years. How the winding, unpredictable path his life followed led him to this spot, under these maple trees, without a family, unable to sleep at night, a dying father lying in the hospital.

After a while, when his mind tired, Quince closed the book, walked down the slopes of the knoll, along the sidewalk, and into the hospital. It became an evening ritual for him, relaxing under a tree on a quiet knoll. He found solitude there, a place to think, understand things lost in the chaos of sickness and death.

Chapter 40
≈ Names on a Note ≈

One night, Quince came into the room after dusk, unfolded a cover, pushed the chairs together, lay down, and closed his eyes.

"Son!" shouted a muddled voice. "Quince!" screamed a gravelly voice, echoing as if it were underwater.

Quince's eyes were barely open. In his delirium, he recognized the voice of his father. He shot straight up, rising so fast that the chair holding his feet slid across the room.

"Quince!" screamed the voice.

Panic tugged at Quince's face. His eyes bulged. His chest pounded, thundering in his ears. His eyes frantically searched the room until they fell on Beecher. The old man was propped up on an elbow. His emaciated face was pinched.

The door swung open, and a nurse burst into the room. "What's wrong?" she asked, running to Beecher's bedside.

Quince's chest rose and fell. Suddenly, he felt something slide down his back. His shirt was soaked. Sweat pimpled across his forehead.

"It's all right," pronounced Beecher. "We're OK," he said again, then fell onto his back, laboring to breathe.

"Mr. Magowan. You have to rest," she scolded.

Beecher waved her away, nodding sarcastically. "Why?" he asked. "What am I saving it for?"

The nurse frowned, "Mr. Magowan."

Beecher sighed, nodding. "We're all right. Give us some time alone."

The nurse stared at Beecher, then looked at Quince, who stood, disheveled, soaked with sweat. "Your father needs to rest," she scolded, turned, and left.

"Quince," Beecher sighed, exhausted, "Listen to me, son. Sit down."

Quince nodded and slid into a chair.

Beecher lay still. A thick, white blanket covered his thin frame, falling just below his shoulders. Only his face, with a thin, white beard, and his bald head, poked from the blanket. His dull eyes stared across the room, at Quince.

"When I came home from Vietnam, I took a construction job building bridges with an outfit from Maysville. I traveled the state, working. Pay was good. I learned how to tie steel. Learned concrete. Picked up some engineering." He chuckled. "Even thought I might go to school, and become an engineer. On weekends, I came home to the farm. Some nights, well, I couldn't sleep. Kept thinking about things I'd seen overseas. I began having these dreams." Beecher's bald head shook. "They got so bad, your grandfather told me to get some help." His head shook. "But, I was embarrassed. Frustrated. I just wouldn't try. So, he told me to get out. It worried them, especially your grandmother. About that time," he paused. "I met your mother. We dated on weekends when I was home. That summer, we rented a tiny apartment. Your mother decorated it the best she could. I was happy for the first time in a long time."

His head nodded, "But those dreams never went away. Your mother finally talked me into going to the hospital. And," he paused, nodding, "I did. I had these talks with a doc at the VA. Once a month, the doc would come to the VFW in town, and we'd sit in a circle and talk about things we'd seen. Troubles we each were having." Beecher nodded, and looked away. "It helped some, but, eventually, I just quit going. Hated talking about it. That fall I lost the job. The next year, my old man had a heart attack, and needed help on the farm. And I ain't done nothing but farm since."

"I never went back to the VA to talk about the dreams. Now, here I am, all these years later. Several failed marriages and a lifetime of drinking and loneliness. Listen, it's gonna be worse with you boys. War is different. I see it on the news. See them boys get blown up. Hell, every time you go out, every street you drive down, every road, you don't know if a bomb is under your tires."

Beecher shook his head. "It's different. A lot of them boys is gonna have dreams like you got. Lot of them. Lot of them got burned up real bad. Lost arms and legs. For decades, this old hospital has treated pneumonia and cancers, diabetes, and heart disease, and the burns but the dreams and the prosthesis was just minor stuff." Beecher paused, drawing a deep breath, "Wars are more than dates. More than battles that take place between surprise attacks and treaties. They don't end when the guns are silenced, and the troops come home."

Quince sat quietly, and listened. Sweat dried along his temple.

"Now," continued Beecher. "Megan done told me about this Dr. Gates."

Quince's face sank, and twisted, sarcastically.

"Listen to me, son," Beecher scolded. "I don't know if this man can help your dreams, but you got to try."

Quince listened.

"Will you do that? Don't wind up a broken down old man who's had five wives, but who has been alone his whole damn life. Don't do it for me? I'm gone soon. Do it for yourself. Your daughter."

Moisture gathered in Quince's eyes. His face was blank. Then, his lips bunched up, and his head shook. "I can't. I done tried. This man ain't no different than the last one." Quince stood, walked across the room, swung open the wooden door, and stomped down the hall. He stopped at the nurse's station, and leaned over the counter. "Can we talk?" he asked in a stern voice.

Megan was sitting at a computer, typing. "Sure," she answered. She stared at the young veteran with confusion written across her soft features. She stood but paused as Quince began shouting.

"Why are you talking to my father about Gates?"

Megan's green eyes blinked. She shrugged. "I . . . I . . . I just mentioned him."

"My dreams ain't none of your business!" he shouted.

"I was just trying to help," she explained.

Quince's face was red, flustered. His eyes were open wide.

"Your father's worried about you."

"I trusted you. What I told you about those dreams was between us."

"Dr. Gates can help."

Quince pointed across the counter. "I don' ever want to hear you mention those dreams to anyone."

Megan's brow lifted, then sank. Her eyes narrowed. "I'm not giving up. I'm gonna keep talking to you, and Beecher, and Dr. Gates until you try."

Quince's finger pointed at the pretty blonde nurse. "I've done asked you. If you talk to him again, that's it. Means I can't trust you. Means we're finished." Quince turned, and stomped down the hall.

Megan's lips pinched. Moisture gathered in her eyes.

Chapter 41
≈ Things Changed ≈

One afternoon, Quince sat under maple trees, overlooking the hospital campus. It was warm. The air, dry. The sun washed grass bearding the knoll. Quince sat, and read a newspaper he'd taken from the lobby. As the sun dropped, he folded the paper, tucked it under his arm, and walked across the grass, along the sidewalk, and through a white metal door. He walked down an empty hall, turned a corner, pressed a button, and waited on the elevator doors to open. His face was low as he stood. Waiting, a man appeared and stood next to him. Quince did not look at the man; he didn't care to acknowledge the stranger.

Red lights ignited behind numbers as the elevator sank. Suddenly, a bell rang, and the chrome doors opened. Quince walked through the doors, stooped, and pressed the number 3, and the man followed him. He was tall, wore glasses, and a white lab coat. His brown hair was graying, and combed to one side.

"Where to?" asked Quince.

The man peered at the numbers. "The same."

Quince nodded, and stood in the corner, staring at the floor. He felt a weight from the man's stare. It was strange, but he knew the man's spectacled eyes were staring right at him.

"Are you Quince Magowan?" asked the man's deep voice.

Quince's face lifted, and he nodded.

The man's long arm stretched across the elevator, and his hand opened. "I thought so. Megan spoke to me. I'm Blaine Gates."

Quince glanced at the man's extended hand, left it empty, and looked into his eyes. "Did you follow me in here, doc?"

Dr. Gates's head shook. "No. Of course, not. I recognized your face from a picture on Megan's desk. She showed it to me as we spoke."

"I ain't got time to talk to you, doc."

Dr. Gates nodded. His brow sank over his eyes.

"My father is dying. I got to take care of him. Can't worry about myself right now."

"I understand. I'm sorry about your father. Megan told me. Listen, I would like to speak with you sometime. When you feel you can talk. When you want to talk, please stop by my office or call. Here's my card."

Quince took the doctor's card. The bell rang, and the doors flew open. Dr. Gates nodded, walked through them, and down the hall.

Quince sighed, walked down the hall, and stopped at the nurse's station, but it was empty. He pushed open the door to Beecher's room, and Megan was sitting in the chair, talking to the old man. She offered a faint smile as he stood in the doorway. Beecher turned, and looked at his son.

"I told you about talking to Dr. Gates," he shouted.

"Quince," shouted Beecher.

Megan stood. Her face was frightened, but she said nothing.

"I done warned you about it."

"Quince, that's enough," Beecher scolded.

"If I ask you, and you ignore me, that means I can't trust you." His head shook. "If I can't trust you, I don't want to be with you. I've already been through that with one woman. I ain't going through it again."

"Quince," shouted Beecher.

The young veteran turned, and slammed the door as he left.

≈ ≈ ≈

Beecher Magowan fell asleep a week later, and slept for days. His pain worsened, and more morphine was prescribed, but the medication lulled the thin, frail man into a deep sleep. Dr. Tom warned Quince that the end was near. And, he warned that Beecher might not wake again.

Megan and Quince stopped speaking to each other. Occasionally, Quince's phone would vibrate, and Megan's name would flash across the screen, but he refused to answer it. His emotions were twisted inside out, and he had not the strength to patch a relationship when his father lay dying. Megan visited Beecher in the afternoons, when she knew Quince was gone, reading in the grass on the knoll, overlooking the hospital. She tended the dying man during her shift. When she came into the room, and Quince was there, he would leave without saying a word.

One morning, Quince left the room, and walked down a busy hall into the lobby. He poured a cup of coffee, spotted an empty seat, maneuvered through the crowded room, and sat. He thumbed through an old magazine, and sipped coffee until the Styrofoam cup was empty. He'd been awake most of the night. He had pushed two chairs together, tossed a blanket over his legs, and closed his eyes, but sleep never came. He fidgeted a while, but eventually gave up. Finally, he sat up in the chair, and watched the small, frail man sleep. All night, he sat in the dark, and watched the shadowy form of a man, lying under a white blanket. The blanket slowly, softly rose and fell with every shallow breath.

That morning, Quince finished the coffee, but he wasn't ready to return to Beecher's room. He walked through the halls, up the stairs, and passed the nurse's counter. The old woman stared through her glasses as he passed. He wanted to stretch his legs, walk around, get some exercise, and avoid a hospital room that had come to feel like a prison cell. He walked down the hall, toward the sound of a television, and approached the small room where he once waited alone to see the psychologist. He turned, and peered through the door, expecting to see empty chairs; a television playing to a half-empty coffee cup. Instead, his face pinched as he stared into the room. There, sitting in the corner, was a young man. Quince stood in the doorway, and stared at a man reading a magazine. Feeling Quince's stare, the young veteran looked up, and nodded. Quince did not answer.

"How's it going?" asked the young veteran.

Quince was silent.

"Are you all right?" asked the young man.

Quince nodded. His brow was low, furrowed.

"You here to see Dr. Gates?" he asked.

Quince shook his head, paused, and pointed at the hall. "No. I was just passing by."

The young man nodded, and dropped his eyes into the magazine.

Quince unknowingly stepped forward. "Where did you serve?" he asked.

The young veteran looked up. "Iraq. Got back in July. Terminal leave in August. Glad to be out of there. Glad to get away from Lejeune. Glad to just get away. You?"

"Afghanistan," Quince answered. "I've been coming here for a year. You're the first young veteran I've seen in this hospital."

A smile lifted the young veteran's cheeks. He nodded.

"I ain't hardly ever seen anyone in this room before?"

"So you have seen Dr. Gates?"

Quince shook his head. "You?"

The young veteran nodded. "This makes my fourth time. I had this picture that I couldn't get out of my head. I kept seeing our patrols in Ramadi. Shit, I'd freak out every time I drove past something lying on the road–a box or a dead animal or something? Messed up shit. You know?"

Quince nodded.

"I had to come see the doctor." He nodded, before swallowing spit. "I don't know that he'll ever cure it. Doubt it. But, he's helped me, Dr. Gates. He tells me if we can control it, I can get my life back. I mean. Shit. I'm only twenty-two."

Twenty-two? Quince thought to himself. *I'm nearly thirty. He's a kid.* Quince stood, nodded to the young veteran, and said, "Good luck."

"You too," answered the young man.

With that, Quince turned and left.

Chapter 42
≈ Only Beecher ≈

One afternoon, Quince sat in the grass, reading. For hours, he sat under the maples, bathing in a soft sun and enjoying the peaceful sounds of the little knoll. When afternoon waned, he gently closed the book, tossed it away, dropped his hands behind him, into the grass, and lifted his face. His eyes were shut. The sun washed over his pale complexion, and a soft grin lifted his cheeks. Below the knoll, cars parked in an overcrowded lot. Ailing veterans limped along sidewalks and through congested hallways.

After a few minutes of sun soaking, he rose, gathered the book in his hands, and walked through the grass, down the knoll. He walked along the sidewalk, through metal doors, down a hall, up the stairs, and down another hall. Laughter escaped from the hospital room, as he opened the wooden door. "Dad," he exclaimed.

Beecher turned and offered a weary grin. He was propped against a stack of pillows. Megan stood over his bed. Martha, a middle-aged nurse, sat in a chair next to the bed; her hands lay across Beecher's arm.

"He woke two hours ago," Martha noted, smiling. Martha was short. Light brown hair lay across her neck, stopping at her shoulders. She wore glasses. She was sweet and smiled a lot. She was frumpy, but not unattractive. To a man Quince's age, she had the look of a woman who was cute twenty years ago. To Beecher Magowan, she was perfect.

"Well," Beecher interjected in a weak voice, "what man wouldn't want to wake up with two beautiful women standing over his bed?"

Martha laughed. Blush colored her cheeks, and she gently slapped Beecher's arm.

Megan smiled. Her face sank as she walked across the room, glanced at Quince, opened the door, and left.

Quince ignored her shun. A smile lifted his cheeks. And the sun he soaked in on the knoll lit a calm countenance across his pale face. "Dad," he exclaimed again. "I . . .

I can't believe you're awake."

Beecher nodded.

"Isn't it something," proclaimed Martha as she stood. "Doctor said he might grow restless, or fidget some. At best, wake up for a short time, but that he might be confused, you know. We never expected him to just wake up as the old Beecher. Only Beecher can do that!"

Quince nodded, smiling. His brow rose and fell as he walked across the room, stooped, and wrapped his arms around Beecher. Beecher chuckled, and patted Quince's shoulders.

As Quince stood over Beecher's bed, Martha proclaimed, "I tell you. Over the last few months, I've come to just adore this man." Her eyes lifted from Beecher, and settled on Quince. "I was married for twenty-five years to what I thought was the love of my life. Then, one day, he said our marriage just wasn't the same, and left. I never thought I find another man worth marrying, worth anything, until your father came here. I can honestly say, I never met another man like Beecher Magowan. God threw away the mold . . ."

Beecher chuckled. For the first time in weeks, blush colored his cheeks.

"Yeah," Quince retorted, "and with it, he threw away the good and the bad."

Beecher chuckled, "And the ugly." Beecher's weak voice rose to laughter, but it wasn't the same old explosion of laughter Quince had heard his whole life.

Martha patted Beecher's arm. "All right," she said. "I'm gonna leave you two alone."

"You're coming back, right? Before your shift ends?" he asked.

"My shift ends in an hour. I'll come back when I get off." Martha opened the door, and left the room.

Beecher's eyes followed the nurse from the room. Quince stood over the bed, and watched his father with questioning eyes. When the door closed, Beecher's eyes settled on Quince. He smiled.

Quince threw a thumb over his shoulder. "How did I miss that? I mean, I know she stops in here a lot, but . . ." he paused.

"But what?"

"It's not even her floor. She covers the first."

Beecher's thin brow rose, and sank. "Megan introduced us a while back. Thought it would help us both, I reckon."

"What about Sally? I mean, she stops in here all the time," asked Quince.

Beecher nodded, grinning. "Sally's still my girl. But, hell, can't a man flirt?"

"Well. It looks like you're feeling good," Quince noted.

The grin sank from Beecher's face. His head shook. "I feel like shit. Groggy. My thoughts are all addled, you know. I tried to let the morphine wear off some, you know, to help clear my mind, but the pain is terrible."

Quince nodded.

Beecher grimaced as he shifted in bed.

Quince's face pinched. "Can I get you anything?"

Beecher's head shook.

"Nah. Don't reckon. Let's just enjoy it while it lasts."

That afternoon, Quince and Beecher watched television. Guests popped in as word spread that Beecher was awake. Sally was there. So was Martha. The two women suspiciously watched each other, until Martha left. Moose and their old friend Gravy stopped by. A few men from the Hole in the Wall were there. Reverend Shaygrove and several deacons crowded into the room. Before leaving, they insisted on praying over Beecher. Every person in the room, Moose, Gravy, Martha, men from the bar, and the deacons, joined hands as the reverend prayed. Beecher nodded. His lips pursed, and he thanked them as they left. "Reverend?" leapt Beecher's voice over the muddled conversation. The crowded room hushed. "Could you come back tomorrow?" he asked.

Reverend Shaygrove nodded, and forced a grin. "Sure. In the afternoon, I'll be here."

Beecher nodded. That evening, Beecher sipped coffee, and managed to nibble on mashed potatoes and Jell-O. When the sun fell, Quince pushed the chairs together, lay down, and threw the blanket over his legs. The television played, as the two men slept.

"Quince," whispered Beecher's soft, weak voice. "Quince."

Quince's eyes batted. A gray light soaked through the window, and lay across the tiled floor.

"Quince," whispered the voice.

Finally, he shook off the sleep, and rose, turning to the bed. "Dad?" he asked, staring at the shadowy figure lying in bed. "Are you OK?"

Beecher grimaced. "The pain's getting worse. Started a few hours ago."

"You should have woke me up," Quince chided, pushing the cover from his legs, and standing. A dim light shown through the window. Morning was close.

"You want me to get the nurse?"

Beecher nodded, grimacing.

Quince left, and returned a few minutes later with the nurse on first shift. The nurse talked with Beecher, left, spoke to Dr. Tom, returned, and hung a new morphine bag on the stand over Beecher's bed.

Beecher turned to his son who sat in a chair next to the bed. A grimace perpetually contorted his face. "I want you to do something for me."

Moisture gathered in Quince's eyes.

"Actually, I want you to do two things for me." Grimacing, Beecher pointed to a small closet door next to the bathroom. "There's an envelope in my jacket. Bring it to me."

Quince nodded, stood, walked across the room, opened the door, scratched through Beecher's leather jacket, and returned with an envelope. He handed the envelope to Beecher, and sat.

Beecher sighed, and tore open the envelope. He removed two folded papers, quickly read through them, and handed the first one to Quince.

Quince took the paper, and quickly, eagerly, glanced over the writing. His brow lifted as he read.

"I want you to call every name on that list. Ask them to come this evening."

Quince's brow hung far above his eyes.

Beecher sighed, and nodded. His lips bunched up. "This is my last day. It's the last day I'll ever know. I'm tired. I hurt terrible. But I can feel the morphine, and I'm gonna need a lot more. When I close my eyes, it'll be the last time I go to sleep."

"Dad," Quince interjected.

Beecher waved a hand. "I want you to call those names, and ask them to come here tonight."

Quince nodded. "All right. I will call them this morning."

Beecher sucked air through his nostrils, and slowly let it escape. He nodded. He glanced at the second piece of paper, nodded, and handed it to Quince.

Quince read over the words. Wrinkles creased along his forehead.

"That's what I want," Beecher proclaimed, his voice weakening.

Quince's chest sank. His expression was disbelieving. "But we talked about this months ago. You wanted to be next to Grandma and Grandpa in the old church cemetery."

Beecher shook his head. "I've had a lot of time to think about it these past few months." He nodded. "That's what I want. I done told Moose and Gravy."

Quince sighed. "Just like this?" he asked, pointing to the paper.

Beecher nodded. A faint grin lifted his sallow cheeks. "Just like that."

Quince's lips bunched. Moisture gathered in his eyes, and he nodded. "OK," he said, folding the paper, and tucking it into his pocket.

He stood, patted Beecher's arm, and moped across the room. "I've got calls to make," he said as the door closed behind him.

That afternoon, Quince and Beecher watched television. Beecher turned to Quince during a program, and sighed. "Quince. I want to ask you one more favor. This one is more important than the other two."

Quince nodded. "Sure, Dad. What is it?"

Beecher scratched his scruffy face, grimaced, and spoke. "I want you to talk with Dr. Gates."

"Dad," Quince interjected. His voice was defensive.

Beecher sighed. Exhaustion and pain contorted his face. His dull gray eyes stared at Quince, exasperated.

Quince sighed, and nodded. His lips bunched together. He was against the idea. He hated it. But, he wouldn't dare tell Beecher no, not now. "I will," he conceded. "For you."

Beecher's head shook. "Not for me, son. I'll be gone soon. Do it for you. For your daughter. For the years you got in front of you."

Quince nodded.

Reverend Shaygrove walked through the door early that afternoon. Quince and Beecher were watching television. Beecher turned to Quince, and asked for time alone with the old reverend.

Quince nodded, turned, and left the room.

He didn't know what the two men discussed. Beecher would not tell him. But, he suspected Beecher wanted forgiveness for years of drinking and failed marriages, and a broken life held together by the thread of a strong-willed man. Now, he wanted forgiveness. It was his right to ask for it, and Quince understood.

Quince walked down the hall, and up a flight of stairs. His face was resolute. He ignored every person he passed in the congested hall. The young veteran paused, leaning over the linoleum counter. "I need to talk with Dr. Gates," he stated.

The middle-aged woman stared at him over her burgundy-framed glasses. "Name?"

"I need to see him."

"Do you have an appointment?" she asked.

"No."

"Honey, I want to get you in, but the doctor is not available now," she persisted.

Quince stooped over the counter, and lifted a receiver from its cradle. He held the receiver to the woman's face. "It's important I talk with him today, now."

The woman sighed, blowing air through her nostrils. She held the receiver to her ear, and punched numbers.

"Tell him Quince Magowan needs to speak with him."

"Quince Magowan wants to meet with you. He would like to meet now, but I understand if . . ." The woman paused and listened before laying the receiver in the cradle. "The doctor says he will see you now," she noted, staring at the young veteran over her glasses.

Quince stood straight, walked down the hall, past the crowded waiting room, filled with patients needing general care. Then, he paused at a door, sighed, formed a fist, and tapped the wooden door.

"Come in," echoed a voice.

Quince Magowan pushed open the wooden door, and stepped across the threshold. The door softly closed behind him.

Chapter 43
≈ The Best Friend I Ever Had ≈

Quince opened the wooden door, and stepped into the room. Beecher was quiet, resting in bed. Reverend Shaygrove was gone. Martha sat next to him, holding his hand. Occasionally, she rubbed his sallow cheeks. As Quince walked through the door, she smiled, but her face was sad. Her eyes, moist. "He's getting tired," she said.

Quince walked over to the bed, and whispered, "How you feeling, pal?"

Beecher drew a deep breath. "Tired."

"How was your visit with Reverend Shaygrove?" asked Quince.

A faint smile lifted Beecher's cheeks. "Overdue, I reckon."

Quince smiled, and nodded.

"Where have you been?" asked the ailing father.

"I did like you asked. I went to see Dr. Gates," he answered.

"And?" he whispered.

Quince sucked air through his nostrils. "Reckon I'll go back."

Beecher's smile lifted even higher. He nodded, and whispered, "Very good."

Beecher lifted his eyes, and proclaimed, "Gonna close my eyes for a bit," as his wrinkled eyes slowly closed.

Not long afterwards, the door swung open, and Moose and Gravy walked into the room. Sally arrived a few minutes later. Then, the room grew more crowded. First Grace, Beecher's fourth wife, arrived. Then, Karen, his fifth wife came through the door. Finally, Alice, the third wife, and Rebecca, the woman Beecher married after Quince's mother passed away, came in, having ran into each other in the hall. The only ex-wife of Beecher's who was absent in the room was Quince's mother who'd died nearly thirty years before.

Everyone stood around. The women were sad. Some whimpered, and wiped away tears. Despite the failure in each relationship Beecher had with them, they each loved the man who lay dying in the hospital bed. They were cordial to one another, except for Sally and Martha who watched the other women with suspecting eyes.

After a while, Beecher began to fidget, and everyone stood around him hoping and praying he would awake. Quince patted his father's shoulder, and spoke to him. "Dad! Dad! You have guests. You have folks here who want to see you."

Finally, Beecher's wrinkled eyelids opened, and his dull, disoriented eyes tried to focus. He was quiet, but a faint smile lifted his cheeks as his eyes scanned the faces across the room. One-by-one, each woman sat in the chair next to him, patted his arm, hugged him, and said their good-byes. One-by-one, Beecher whispered an apology to each for the pain he felt he'd caused them. Gravy sat down, and told Beecher that he loved him, and wished they could go back, and be young men again, even if it meant going back to Vietnam. Then, it was Moose's turn to say goodbye. Moose barely fit in the chair. He sat there and wept. His black beard hung over his big pooched stomach. "You're the best friend, and the greatest man I ever knew. Love you, Beech," he said.

Beecher smiled. A tear trickled down his cheek.

Moose stood, wiped his eyes, stooped, kissed Beecher's head, and stepped away.

Quince walked around the bed, and sat in the chair. "Quince," Beecher whispered. "You're the best thing I ever did. The best . . ." His faint words trailed off, and his wrinkled skin slowly pulled across his dull eyes. Quince's lips bunched up. Moisture gathered in his eyes. The women whimpered loudly. They sniffled, and wiped tears with handkerchiefs.

Megan and Martha monitored Beecher throughout the night. With each hour, his breathing grew weaker. The visitors spent the evening in the room. Most stood around the bed all night. When they tired, they rested in a lounge down the hall. Quince sat in a chair next to the bed. Early the next morning, hours before dawn, he and Moose walked across the hospital, down stairs, and into the cafeteria. Quince had not eaten since yesterday morning, and his stomach ached with hunger. Together, the two men drank coffee, and ate eggs and biscuits. They did not speak. Suddenly, the glass door flew open, and Gravy shouted, "He's going now."

Quince, Moose, and Gravy ran through the hall. Quince ran far ahead of the two older men, bouncing up the stairs, through the metal door, down the hall, and into the crowded room. Whimpers filled the room, but no one spoke as he walked to Beecher's bed, and stooped over his father. Megan and Martha stood over Beecher, and monitored his pulse. "His pulse is erratic," noted Megan, sadly. She gently moved the stethoscope over Beecher's chest. Martha wiped tears from her eyes.

Quince said nothing. He stood over the bed, and watched his father's chest slowly rise and fall. He listened as a faint breath whistled through the man's nostrils. Moose and Gravy burst through the door, paused, and watched the small man under the white blanket. Megan listened. Her lips bunched, and her head shook. "It's very faint, now." Quince patted Beecher's arm. Moisture welled in his eyes. Grace, Karen, Alice, and Rebecca stood along the wall, and wept. Sally stood behind Quince, near the window, crying. Martha stood over the bed, near Megan, and wiped away tears. Moose and Gravy pulled shirtsleeves across their eyes.

Megan sat quietly, and listened for Beecher's pulse. "I can barely hear it," she said, sighing. Quince patted Beecher's arm. The man's thin, sallow cheeks were still. Frozen. Beard stubs poked from the skin along his chin. His head was completely bald. Megan suddenly nodded, wiped her eyes, and stood, handing Martha the stethoscope. She looked at Quince, swallowed, and shook her head. Martha wept, hung the stethoscope in her ears, gently laid the chest-piece over Beecher's heart, and listened. "He's gone," she whispered, patting the man's shoulder. Megan cuffed her face with her hands, and ran from the room, crying. Quince patted Beecher's arm, stooped over, and kissed his bald head. One-by-one, Karen, Grace, Alice, Rebecca, Sally, Martha, Gravy and Moose walked to the bed, knelt, and kissed the man's head. Quince sat in the chair, and held his father's hand.

An hour passed before men from the funeral home arrived. All the guests were asked to leave. Quince stood over the bed, and stared at his father's body. He stooped, kissed his cheek, turned, and left. Folks walking through the congested hallway stared at the young veteran who wept as he passed them. His hands were buried deep in his pockets as he descended the stairs, walked down a hall, through metal doors, and out on the sidewalk. A soft red glow hung in the east. The air was cool and gray. Quince moped across the grass, up the knoll, sat beneath the maples, and wept alone. Red and yellow leaves fell like snowflakes at his feet and across his shoulders. After a while, he stood, walked down the knoll, across the compound, through the crowded parking lot, slid into the red pickup, and drove away.

≈ ≈ ≈

A few days later, a deep rumble of roaring pipes echoed in the morning air. The bike slowed as Quince's boot mashed the gearshift. He stopped near the glass doors of a fancy, brick house of Victorian design. Black shutters hung like sentries on each side of every window. The lawn was lush, manicured, and boxwoods were perfectly trimmed in squares along the porch.

Quince wore a black leather jacket, old jeans, and leather boots. Straps of a red pack hung over his shoulders. He parked the bike, dropped the kickstand, pulled his leg over the seat, and slowly walked across the porch, under a small portico. A young man, wearing a blue suit, opened the door as he approached. “Mr. Magowan,” he greeted. His words were tense, serious, and he spoke through a forced grin. Quince nodded, and walked through the door, into the old funeral home.

The young man nodded once more, but was silent as he held open the door an hour later. Quince walked by, but did not acknowledge him. His face was bland, unemotional. The red pack bulged as it lay across his back as he walked across the porch, paused at the bike, threw a leg over the seat, gripped the clutch, and jumped on the kick-start. The pipes roared as he sped away from the funeral home, through town, down the interstate, and into the eastern plateau.

Chapter 44
≈ The Lake ≈

Tom Quincy Magowan walked a narrow, rock-strewn path along the shores. Alone, he was tired. His legs moved in slow, trepid motions as if pebbles, sparsely scattered along the path, excreted glue that clung to every step. The path led him behind a cove, under a poplar, to a wood bench—old, weather-beaten, flogged by winter gales; mold painted its wood planks. Leaves and twigs crumbled and lay between the cracks. Carvings and graffiti tattooed the backrest. Quince brushed leaves from the bench, sat, and looked around.

A quiet morning was born on the lake. Waters were cool and green. Autumn's frost stuck like thick, icy sugar to maple leaves yellowing on a nearby ridge. Cold fog rose from the ground. Gray skies whispered a summons through a biting wind. Small, thin clouds soon burst from their grave and giddily swept across the lake. Fallen leaves bedded the forest floor. A large poplar threw shadows over the forest. Dawn hung a lantern over the cove while night hid in the trees.

Quince was dressed in plain worn jeans and boots. An undershirt, moist with week-old perspiration, was covered beneath a leather jacket. As he sat, Quince slid the pack into his lap, and sighed. His breath caught a touch of the morning frost as he pulled the zipper, and the pack fell limp around a white box and an envelope. Reaching for the envelope, anticipation swept through his veins like a cool saline. His pulse accelerated. Cold morning air sucked through his nostrils. His green eyes swelled. Quince pulled the envelope from the pack, and held it between his fingers. A frosty whisper twisted his lips, "So damn thin."

Holding the envelope over his knees, he carefully surveyed the tan paper, a wax seal, branded with initials, and the ornate writing fancifully spelling his name. His eyes narrowed, and stared coolly at the writing. To Quince, something was alive in the package—some spirit imprisoned beneath the paper. He looked upon the envelope like a sarcophagus that, if opened, would unleash spirits of his past.

Anger warmed him in the biting cold. Blush colored his cheeks. A temptation to scream poised his lips, but they were mute. A desire to smack his fist into the thick, gnarled bark of a nearby chestnut oak fell when courage would not close his hand. Little more than a year before, he had stood like a stone tower, each block carved from the granite walls of youth and confidence. This morning, a year later, events had chiseled the mortar from his will, and stolen blocks until all that was left of him were thin, naked beams.

Angry, he felt the urge to write his own graffiti, to carve something vulgar into the wood bench, something eternal, something for the swimmers and fishermen, something the world would see and know, something like graffiti on a thin envelope. But just days earlier, while he slept in a life of chaos, thieves carted away the last two granite stones, leaving behind a white box and a tan envelope, labeled with ornate writing. His will was gone. Light green mold, painted on wood planks, would remain undisturbed that cold morning.

He sat on the park bench until the clouds broke apart, and the sun rose and lifted darkness from the forest. Painting, coloring, sunlight gave shape and detail, life. Night could hide no more. Nearby, water pecked the rocky shore. Far away, geese cried as they lifted from green pools.

Finally, Quince sighed, and slid his finger under the seal. Just then, he heard a bustle, a shuffling of brittle leaves behind a ridge. Voices muttered. Leaves crunched. Quince watched, anxiously. Someone was coming. The envelope slowly dropped into his lap. Leaves crunched. Quince watched, nervous. His pulse accelerated. Cool air sucked through his nostrils. His eyes bulged, focused on the ridge.

Soon, a silhouette, then another, emerged. Dark figures moved swiftly along the path, toward the park bench. Quince's chest pumped as the silhouettes moved closer. Thoughts slipped across his mind, then slid slowly back to a mysterious corner of his brain, like gentle, morning waves slide over a sandstone boulder. Slowly, light took out its palette, and brushed colorful oils over the morning canvass, giving expression to the faceless silhouettes, gray to the dark hair, wrinkles and crevices to smooth complexions. Quince's face opened. His pulse slowed. His eyes settled on an elderly couple out for a morning stroll. Swiftly, they moved along the path, passed Quince, and disappeared around the cove. The crunching of leaves grew faint.

Quince's eyes, once bulged, narrowed. His chest sank and a grin lifted his cheeks. As the cove grew silent, a soft breeze danced around the poplar. Swirls lifted leaves from the forest floor, and tossed them like popcorn, until the wind just disappeared, and leaves tumbled to the ground. His thoughts were loose that way, not anchored to a particular day or person, but blown around by a turbulent wind sweeping through his life, falling randomly on a day lost in time.

Early that autumn morning, Quince lost the will to open the tan envelope; thieves had simply stolen a stone too many from the foundation he had stood on his whole life. He crammed the envelope into the pack, gently patted the white box, and zipped the pack shut.

Quince stood and walked along the path, away from the poplar shade, and the old bench. He walked slowly; hands buried deep in his pockets, and soon emerged from under the shade of poplar and birch trees. He followed the path as it wound down a steep bank, between several sandstone boulders, leaving him on a flat stone. There, he stood on the edge, and looked out over the water. Beneath his boots were stones, tan and speckled with dust. The sun rose over a distant mountain. Fish fed along the shores, their pop and splash pushed tiny waves over the surface.

It was only morning, but the day had been long for him. He was tired. Standing alone, on a great, flat boulder, he was visible to all the lake and surrounding forests. Fishermen, though, were home in warm dens, and boats docked for the winter, and swimmer's tans faded under fleece and thick cotton. He stood there, visible to everything, and to nothing, all at once. That's how it was with him, his new life. His suffering was visible, but his disease was hidden, unseen to the world just as a tall man who stood on a stone above a lake.

On that rock, tan and flat, Quince sat in the speckled dust. His legs hung over the edge. He gently slid the pack from his shoulder, set it on the rock, and watched fish feed near the shore.

Pop, splash, they fed.

Quince watched the still waters part, and ripples spread from a small circle.

Pop, splash, ripples.

Again, Quince opened the pack, paused, reached over the envelope, and with both hands, lifted the box, setting it gently in the speckled dust. A tormented grin lifted his cheeks. He sat on the stone, and stared at the water, a small, white box next to him. It was a quiet morning. Waves pecked stones along the shore. The sun rose. Clouds broke apart like gray cement beneath the strike of a hammer. A soft wind brushed Quince's face. His lips poised, and spoke in a frost-less whisper, "One last time."

His eyes settled on the water, and his pale, unshaven face washed in the morning sun. After a while, a sigh lifted his chest as he bent a wrist, and took time from a watch.

Nodding, he turned, lifted the box, gently tucked it into the pack, and pulled the zipper. Quince Magowan stood on a stone boulder, along a cove, in a mountain lake. He slid the pack over his shoulder, turned, and moped along the pebbled path.

He passed under poplar shade, around a bench, to an empty, paved lot. The summer crowds—jeeps, convertibles, family minivans—gone for the season. He was alone. Quince walked across the pavement, and stopped near a motorcycle. It was a beautiful bike. Chrome handles lay over a black-hewn gas tank, thin, shiny spokes spread between the tires like dozens of storms suddenly erupting from the sun. The bike playfully leaned onto a kickstand as a child might lean into an elbow, posing for a photograph.

Quince paused, staring at the beautiful machine. A glare twisted around the curvy gas tank, and occasionally, his reflection swept over the polished surface. An overcast sky muddied his features, but he recognized the silhouette of his dark, loose hair, the cut of his jaw, a tired expression.

He stood alone, and stared at the reflection. A gentle breeze swept over the lot, brushing hair along his temple. The sky was a soup of east-moving clouds, occasionally sliced by sunshine. As clouds swept over the lake, his reflection blurred and muddied, and the face staring back at him became unrecognizable. Soon, clouds shifted beneath his stare. From the dark, polished tank, a light flashed, and the reflection materialized like a picture on the screen of an old, 50s television. Suddenly, the reflection aged. Quince's hair, thick and black, receded and grayed. White hair sprouted from his chin. Sad, blue eyes twisted over the black tank.

Quince stared at the familiar face on the tank. His eyes swelled. His pinched lips unlocked, and poised to speak, desperately struggling to say something, communicate with the man. But, beneath his silent, muttering lips, clouds swept east, and the face changed, becoming youthful again. Dark, thick hair grew on his scalp. Hair on his chin shrank. Sad blue eyes, became green.

He anxiously waited for the face to return, reappear like the screen of his grandfather's old television set, but it was gone. Clouds swept across the lake, and the face was lost in a sun far above a soupy sky. He pulled both arms through straps of the red pack, threw a leg over the seat, and grasped the handlebars. He opened the kick start, stood and dropped his weight onto the lever. Thick, chrome cylinders roared as he lazily circled the lot, paused, and turned onto the main road. A strong wind brushed hair over his scalp as he accelerated.

Weaving around mountains, climbing, descending ridges, hugging the lakeshore, he rode for miles.

Eventually, a shack on the banks of the lake drifted into his sight, and he slowed. Quince cruised through a gravel lot, stopped near the shack, and twisted the key. Loud pipes rumbled, gasped, then abruptly fell silent. He paused. A thin cloud of dust swirled around him, temporarily veiling the small building from his view. Then, a terse smile parted Quince's lips as the dust passed by. Sitting quietly, he surveyed the shack. A portion of the building rested on pilings, sinking deep into green waters. Behind the shack, stairs slid from a deck, down to the water's surface. A wood plank, supported with buoys, reached into the harbor. Boats anchored around the harbor. Fishermen dropped lines into the waters around the marina.

Here, along these waters, years before, he and Sara had bathed in the sun, sailed and dreamt of a happy marriage. Now, years later, everything had changed.

Quince sighed, pulled his leg over the seat, walked along the dusty, gravel lot, through a door, and paused just across a threshold, on a dirty tile floor. He stood alone in a small island of light thrown over the tiles by the open door. Slowly, the door closed, and light narrowed around his boots. The smell of grease and cigarettes filled his nostrils; smoke hung like fog in the room. Noise spilled from the kitchen—clanging pots, spatulas scraping pans, running water, muddled voices. Empty booths sat in soft shadows along the wall. The room was poorly lit.

Nearby, a young waitress sat behind a counter, reading a fashion magazine. As the door slammed, her eyes jumped from the pages, and rested on the stranger. Her features, wide and startled, softened and closed like pupils shrink in the light. "Just one?" she asked in a country twang.

Quince nodded.

She smiled, tossed the magazine on the counter, gathered a menu and flatware, and swayed across the room, to a booth near a window. She spread the menu and accoutrements across the linoleum table, backed away, and asked, "This all right?"

Quince nodded, forcing a grin, "This is good."

"I'm Teri," she announced, grinning widely. "Thirsty?"

Quince nodded, and mumbled, "Coffee."

Teri's lips were spread in a generous grin. Her soft eyes poured over him, admiring the stranger. Quince offered a cold smile, and she turned and swayed into the kitchen.

Quince slipped the pack from his shoulder, and gently set it on the cushioned seat, below the window. He slid the jacket down his arms, tossed it near the pack, sat and surveyed the room with cool, uncaring eyes. The sound of plates rattled in the kitchen.

Muddled conversation escaped between the sizzle of frying bacon. An old fisherman sat alone in the corner, reading a newspaper. Smoke lifted from a cigarette resting between his dirty fingers. Occasionally he coughed and shuffled pages. Otherwise, he was quiet, and his presence was known only through a smoker's cough and choking smoke.

Quince turned and stared through a large, steam-clouded window. A stout breeze had gathered over the harbor, pulling at things. Flags fluttered atop ship masts. Fishermen anchored boats to wooden posts, pulling and wrapping thick rope as the vessels bounced in their slip. Boats in the channel rocked as waves passed. Silhouettes stood in them, casting, reeling. Waves, small but white-capped, ran up the channel as if fleeing from something. Two fishermen, old and fat, waddled toward the shack.

Teri swayed from the kitchen, across the room, and paused near Quince's booth. She gently set a cup on the table near the menu, and stepped back. Steam lifted from the coffee, washing Quince's sallow face.

"Hungry?" she asked.

A terse smile bent Quince's lips. For days, his stomach had been knotted, twisted and turned, choking his appetite. Now, days later, the medicine of time had unraveled those knots. He was starved, nodding, "Eggs. Over easy. Toast. Bacon."

Teri smiled, and her brow lifted as she scribbled on a pad. Her face rose, she winked, and swayed across the room, disappearing into the kitchen.

Two fishermen waddled through the backdoor, laughing as they entered. One used his fat fingers to comb his wind-blown hair. The other peered at the kitchen window.

'Teri?" he yelled.

"In here . . ." answered a country twang.

"We're starved."

Teri leaned through a kitchen window, quickly surveyed the corpulent old men, and snapped, "You don't look it!"

The fishermen erupted into laughter; their fat bellies rose and sank. One man slapped the other's shoulder.

Teri waited for their laughter to subside, and asked, "The regular?"

The old men waddled over to a table and sat. One mumbled, "Regular."

Quince turned and again stared at the harbor. Wind blew. Boats rocked. Waves fled.

"Here you go, honey," said Teri, setting a plate beneath Quince's nose. "Anything else?" she asked, smiling.

Quince shook his head.

Teri smiled, turned, and walked across the room, pausing to talk with the old men.

Quince was famished. He ate quickly. He sopped runny eggs with toast, drank coffee, and swallowed bacon until the plate was nearly empty. With a crust of toast, he sopped the last drip of eggs, swallowed it, pushed away the plate, turned, and again stared into the harbor. There was a peace about the water. A boat milled about. A breeze tugged at the sails, pulling it around choppy waters. Fishermen cast lines.

Quince was quiet. He sat alone, watched the harbor, and thought about days gone by.

Clouds poured over the mountains, and across the lake. Wind tugged at the water, lifting waves from the once soft, green pool. He sat in the booth, sipped coffee, and watched sailboats rock in the choppy waters. Sailors and fishermen packed into the small restaurant, seeking refuge from the storm. Laughter and muddled conversation filled the dining area. Smoke lifted from burley cigarettes.

"Honey, how about more coffee?" asked Teri. The waitress smiled, and winked at him. Quince nodded. "Sure."

"OK," she happily proclaimed, "be right back."

Quince turned, and stared through the window. He watched as wind tugged at an old man who wore black gum boots and carrying a fishing pole, as he struggled to walk across the wooden dock. The old man burst through the door, and wind swept napkins from the table.

"Shut that door!" shouted someone, teasingly.

"It's a coming, boys!" he proclaimed, water dripping from his face.

"Honey, let me get you a towel before you drip water everywhere," said Teri, disappearing into the kitchen. Quince scratched through his pocket, and pulled a cigarette from the pack. He hung the burley in his lips, lit the tip with a cheap lighter, sucked the filter, and exhaled.

Smoke hung like a cloud around the booth as Quince unzipped the red pack, and took out the envelope. He opened the envelope, and spread the papers across the table. A few days ago, before he stopped at the funeral home, Quince sat with a lawyer in town, and listened as he talked about each page, and pointed where his signature was needed. When he finished, he fastened the pages with a clip, slid them into the envelope, handed the envelope to Quince, and they shook hands. "Take your time," warned the lawyer. "Think about what you're signing." His head nodded. "If you're satisfied, sign them, and mail them back. I'll handle it from there." Quince turned to walk away. Just as he opened the door to leave, the lawyer interjected, "Mr. Magowan, I'm real sorry about your father."

Quince nodded, turned, and left.

Sitting alone in the booth, he again read each line, then leaned forward, pulled the wallet from his back pocket, opened it, and took out a picture. Wrinkled and faded from sweat, the photograph was of Sara and Lilly on a beach with the sun washing their smiling faces. Quince's jaw clenched, and muscles in his cheeks trembled. He pulled the cigarette to his lips, sucked the filter, and exhaled.

"Here you go, honey," smiled Teri, filling his cup with coffee. Her face stiffened, becoming serious. "Are you all right?" she asked, standing over the man who stared at a pile of papers scattered across the table.

His brow lifted. "Uh, yeah," he said, lifting his eyes to the flirty waitress.

"OK. Well, just let me know if you need anything else. Stay as long as you want," she smiled, turned, and started to walk away.

"That pen," Quince said.

"I'm sorry?" she answered, confused.

"I need to borrow that pen," he explained, pointing to a pen lying behind the woman's ear.

"Oh," she laughed. "Sure." Teri pulled the pen from behind her ear, and handed it to him.

Quince sighed, opened the pen, signed his name, grabbed another sheet, signed his name again, slid the signed papers into the envelope, sealed it, and handed the pen to Teri.

"She's pretty. That your wife?" asked Teri, gawking at the photograph.

Quince shook his head. "Ex."

Teri's brow lifted. "Oh really? I mean, I'm sorry."

"I need one last favor?"

"Sure," she smiled.

Quince lifted the envelope. "Can you add this to your outgoing mail? Oh, and I'll take the check, please."

"Sure thing, honey," she grinned, took the envelope, and walked away, into the kitchen.

Quince's chest sank. It was all so anticlimactic. The last decade of his life ended on pages sealed in an envelope, carried away and mailed from a cheap diner by a flirty waitress. And his happiness and his relationship with Lilly, his daughter, his only child, and all of his assets were written succinctly on those few pages—a few dimes worth of paper. Words printed with a dry, uncaring legalese that Quince wouldn't give a dime for. His future and Lilly's future was written on those few short pages. Quince was overcome by frustration and sadness while holding those documents in his hands. It was his future. It meant years to him, and it felt too thin. Hadn't his life meant more? Hadn't he given enough? It was difficult for him to comprehend. To understand. Now, sitting there, his face pinched, and blood colored his cheeks. His temples throbbed. He turned, and stared through the window. Sheets of rain sailed sideways across the lake. Sailboats, tied to the marina, rocked and jerked like angry dogs yanking at their leash.

"That's one hell-of-a storm," said a fisherman.

"No sailing today," sadly noted another man.

Quince stared through the window. The cherry red boat that he and Sara sailed years ago clung to the marina by a thick rope. Wind tugged at the helpless boat, rocking wildly in the choppy waters. Lightning snapped in the trees on a distant mountain. Thunder shook the small diner.

Quince tucked the photograph in the wallet, shoved it in his pocket, stood, walked across the diner, and struck the wooden door. The door flew open and wind swept through the diner, blowing napkins into the floor.

"Shut the door," someone yelled.

Quince bolted through the open door, into the driving rain. He ran across the dock, down the wooden planks, and stooped over a wooden pole jutting out from the water. Wind pushed him; rain stung his face as he struggled to unleash the boat.

Fishermen and sailors gathered near the windows, watching him. "What the hell's he doing?" someone asked.

"What's going on?" asked Teri, as she reappeared from the kitchen.

"Hell if I know. He just got up and ran out into the storm," pointed a fisherman.

Finally, his soaked, cold fingers untangled the dock line. He stood, yanked the boat closer, and leapt into the rocking vessel. The cherry red sloop shot out into the choppy waters.

"Is he trying to sail?" asked someone.

"He'll drown in that storm," warned another man.

Rain shot from the clouds, pelting the water. Quince grimaced as drops stung his face. He drove a paddle through the choppy waters, and wind swept the boat across the pool. Wind began to sweep in all directions, turning from east to north as the small storm twisted, and Quince fought it, struggling to raise the sail. Rain pelted him. Lightning snapped against a distant mountain. Finally, wind caught the sail; it bulged and pulled the boat across the pool, then jerked it around. Quince shouted and laughed as rain stung his face.

Fishermen and sailors and Teri and the cooks anxiously watched as the young veteran fought those sails, pulling the wheel as strong gales dragged him toward the rocks. He pushed and pulled, and the small boat swung in quick, tight circles, around the pool. After a while, clouds pushed across the lake, over the mountains. Wind died. The rain eased. The sail sank, and the boat sat in the pool. Quince dropped his head, and wept. Folks in the diner watched him; a few men trickled out onto the dock as the rain subsided. A few minutes later, Quince grabbed the paddle, and pushed it through the calming waters. The small boat slowly moved across the harbor, and into the marina. Two sailors guided in the nose of the sloop.

Quince stepped from the boat.

"Man. Are you OK?" asked one sailor.

Quince ignored him. He jumped out, and walked across the dock. His face was stiff, and his eyes were focused.

"I ain't never seen anything like that!" proclaimed another sailor.

Teri's eyes were bulged as Quince walked through the door, into the diner. He stopped at the booth, pulled the jacket over his soaked shirt, slid the red pack over his shoulders, paused, opened his wallet, tossed ten dollars on the table, and walked resolutely across the diner, through the front door.

Chapter 45
≈ Beecher Goes Home ≈

The air was crisp after the storm. It was fall. Over the last few weeks, mountains turned auburn and yellow and burned in red. The wind dried Quince's rain-soaked clothes as he rode through the mountains. He cruised down the plateau, and stopped in the parking lot of a gas station near the interstate. The pipes of his bike rumbled as he glided into the lot, and steered around the gas pumps and parked among other bikes near the small store. He twisted the ignition and the pipes rumbled, spat, and fell silent. He opened the kickstand, and stood. Stretching, he looked around, slid the pack from his shoulders, and gently set it on the seat.

A door swung open, and Moose, Gravy, and a dozen other bikers walked out of the store. Their faces were solemn, sad. Moose said nothing. He stepped in front of Quince, stooped, and wrapped his gigantic arms around him, nearly pulling the young man off his feet, before letting go. "Your dad wanted this," he proclaimed. Some of the men nodded, and grunted. His big, hairy finger pointed at the pack, "Is this . . . ?" His eyes settled on Quince.

Quince nodded. His lips bunched.

Moose paused near the bike, and gently patted the red pack. "We're here to take you home, brother."

One by one, each biker approached Quince, shook his hand, thanked him or offered condolences. Gravy hugged the young man. These were the same men who waited in the freezing night air at Cherry Point when Quince's company returned from Afghanistan. These were the same men who escorted the bus from Cherry Point to Lejeune. These were the same men who escorted Quince home from Lejeune. Now, they met Quince early that morning to escort Beecher Magowan home. They were aging veterans, wearing jeans, boots, and leather jackets. Most were unshaven, and their hair was long. Patrons stared at them as they entered the small store, but these bikers just ignored them. They didn't care. They'd gathered there to honor Beecher.

That's all that mattered.

Moose glanced at his watch, noting, "We better get going. We gotta long ride." He patted Quince's shoulder, and said, smiling, "You take us there."

The parking lot rumbled as bikes sped away, down the narrow road, before turning onto the interstate. Wind tugged at Quince's hair as he led the group. Moose and Gravy rode just behind him, and the remaining bikers followed the trio. They rode east, across the Ohio River, up into the mountains of West Virginia, turned, and cruised down into the Shenandoah Valley. In Virginia, they stopped at a rest area, ate snacks, drank sodas, stretched their legs, pissed, and rode away. They rode through the pines of middle Virginia, turned north at Richmond, and fought the congestion of I-95, passing Fredericksburg and Quantico. Each biker raised a fist as they passed the exit for Marine Corps Base Quantico. As they passed Potomac Mills, and rode into D.C., the sun began to sink. Quince grew more solemn with each mile. He ignored the pain in his legs, and his wind-chapped face, and thought of his father. The time he had with Beecher was almost gone; only a few miles lay ahead.

They turned near the river and the bikers again threw fists into the cool evening air as they passed the Iwo Jima Memorial. They swept through the gates of Arlington, and stopped near the entrance. Each bike rumbled, and fell silent. Quince opened the kickstand, pulled his stiff leg over the seat, slid the pack from his shoulder, and gently handed it to Moose.

"We'll wait here for you," said Moose, nodding.

Quince sighed. His chest began to pound, and he heard the slight rumble of thunder in his ears. He slowly walked across the parking lot, down a sidewalk, turned at a large tree, and walked through the grass. A small, white sign read, Section 60. He walked along rows of small, pristine white markers, and carefully read each name. At the end, he turned, and walked along another row, reading names chiseled into the granite. After passing along several rows, and reading hundreds of names, he paused. Moisture gathered in his eyes. He nodded as if he'd been asked something, and his face sank. His chest pounded. He approached the marker, and knelt. The grass was thick and green and cool, as he sank to his knees. He was alone. It was quiet. He swallowed spit, and nodded. "Told you I'd come. Bet you doubted me." His head shook. "Nah," he turned, and stared across the graves. "I made a promise that night, standing on the roof of that old concrete bunker." Quince chuckled. A smile lifted his face. "Remember that shit? We'd stand up there for hours, smoking, drinking stale coffee, and watch the sun fall, valley grow dark, and talk about plans. What we wanted from the future." Moisture welled in Quince's eyes, and spilled down his cheeks. He looked out across the graves. The sun was sinking. Shadows grew from trees. Quince's eyes fell across the marker. He nodded, leaned forward, and rubbed the icy granite. He sighed and whispered, "I'm sorry, Pat." As the sun sank, and a cold shadow fell over him, Quince stood, turned, and walked through the grass, down the sidewalk, across the parking lot, and paused at the bike. Moose handed him the pack, and nodded. Quince slid the pack over his shoulders, threw a leg over the seat, started the bike, and they cruised past the Iwo Jima Statue, across the bridge, and into D.C.

By now, rush hour was over. Traffic eased some. The bikers passed the Lincoln Memorial, pulled into a lot, stopped, opened their kickstands, and walked along a sidewalk. Moose and Gravy walked alongside Quince. "Ain't this illegal?" asked Quince. "I mean. How in the hell did you arrange all this?"

Moose chuckled, and pointed at Gravy. "We got a buddy who works for the park service. Fellow biker. Vet. It just so happened that tonight, he's the only ranger on duty here." Quince smiled, and nodded. As they walked over a hill, the shadowy statues of three soldiers stood in the sidewalk. The smile faded from Quince's face, and he paused. Each biker paused as Moose patted the young man's back. "It's what he wanted," whispered the giant man.

Sighing, Quince nodded, and walked forward, past The Three Soldiers statue, and down the sidewalk, pausing near the black wall. It was quiet. The sun had nearly disappeared in the west. The air was cool, and gray. A soft breeze swept along the black wall. A few visitors stood before a panel, but soon left, disappearing into the night.

Moose turned, and pointed to Chatty, a tall, pot-bellied man with a long, white beard. Chatty nodded, walked around the black wall, and stood in the grass high above Quince. He fidgeted with a string on a small, satin bag, managed to untie a knot, and slid out a brass instrument. Moose and Gravy stood a few feet behind Quince. The remaining bikers gathered behind them, and pulled hats and bandanas from their heads. Chatty licked his lips, lifted the instrument to his mouth, and began to play. His cheeks swelled. Taps echoed across the grass, around monuments, through streets. When the instrument fell silent, and the echoes stopped, and Chatty's white-bearded cheeks sank, Quince unzipped the red-pack, lifted out a white box, tossed the pack to the ground, and gently set the box at his feet. He sniffled as snot leaked from his nose. He wiped the snot, and his watering eyes with a sleeve, knelt, opened the lid, set it aside, and lifted out a small, white urn.

Quince held the urn in his hands, and wept. "Dad," he whimpered. "I know you didn't want words so I'll just say we miss you. And, I hope you find peace." Quince twisted the lid, opened it, and tilted the urn. Soft, gray granules slid over the lip, rose in the evening breeze, and swept across the black wall. He wept as Beecher's ashes fell in a steady stream from the urn, just to be blown across the black granite, until the urn was empty, and dust colored a few dark panels gray. Quince set the urn on the pavement, near the wall, stood, and wiped tears from his eyes. One by one each biker hugged the young veteran. They wiped tears, and hugged each other, and patted the wall where Beecher's ashes were scattered.

The sun had fallen. Lights ignited, illuminating the black and gray wall. As Quince, Moose, Gravy, and the bikers turned to leave, Quince saw a petite figure standing near The Three Soldiers statue. His eyes were red, bloodshot, and wet, and he squinted, struggling to see through the shadowy air. He could barely make out her soft features and long, straight hair. It was Megan. He walked along the sidewalk, toward the statues, but his eyes never left the small figure. As they drew closer, Moose turned to Quince and said, "She wanted to be here."

Quince paused. His mind raced from sadness to guilt. He knew he'd treated Megan unfairly. He knew she acted out of concern for his health. He knew she loved him.

Moose patted Quince's shoulder and said, "We're going on ahead."

Quince sighed, and slowly walked closer as Megan's wet, green eyes blinked. Her features formed a smile, and her arms fell open. Quince paused and his expression softened as he wrapped his arms over her shoulders. It was dark. Cool. The sun had fallen. The day was gone.

≈ Black Walls Turn Gray ≈

About the Author

Brad Jones is a former captain and Marine veteran of the Afghanistan War. Born in Mount Sterling, Kentucky, he grew up in Salt Lick, a small town in northeast Kentucky. He holds a bachelor's degree from Morehead State University, an M.A. in political science from the University of Louisville, and an M.B.A from Sullivan University. Joining the service in October 2000, he served in the 1st Battalion 6th Marines and in the 6th Marine Regiment, and deployed to Okinawa, South Korea, Japan, Liberia, and, in 2004, to Afghanistan. Today, Brad Jones resides in Lexington, Kentucky. He is the father of a seven-year-old daughter. He is a member of a local Marine Corps League detachment and maintains his interest in the politics of war and diplomacy.

While *Black Walls* is a work of fiction, Jones draws upon some of his life experiences in developing the narrative. The story, which is set primarily in Kentucky and Afghanistan, includes arresting descriptions of their widely differing, but remarkably beautiful, rural landscapes. Nature is a voiceless but sometimes threatening character in the novel.

Jones is available for group presentations and book-signings. He may be reached at blackwallsturngray@gmail.com.

Acknowledgments

I would like to express my gratitude to the following people for their contributions, support, and other help in creating this book.

Thanks to Alex Griffith who called upon his experience as a middle linebacker for the Campbellsville University Tigers. His valuable suggestions helped make Quince Magowan a viable college football star and added credibility to an important part of his young life.

I deeply appreciate Major Jason Johnston for the time and effort he gave to review portions of this book. His rich military experiences and expertise were crucial in verifying that the weapons and gear and conversation where typical for a Marine who served in Afghanistan in 2004. I appreciate his thoughtful comments. Above all, I am deeply grateful to his service.

This novel greatly benefited from the many conversations I've had with clinical psychologists about PTSD. For years, I have studied the disease and treatments but our conversations elevated my understanding to a higher level.

To the team at Cincinnati Book Publishing: Tony Brunsman–President & CEO, Sue Ann Painter–Vice President and Executive Editor, Mark Painter–Editor, Karen Bullock–Public Relations Manager, and Amelia Stultz–Web and Electronic Media Manager. I'm indebted to your wisdom and great experience. Without your advice, I would have been lost throughout this process. Thank you!

To my parents for years of patience as they listened to me talk about "the book."

To each Marine who, during my time as an active-duty lieutenant, I served with on deployments or in CONUS. Through the good and the bad, we laughed and complained. We learned. We grew. We were challenged. We served.

Brad Jones, June 2014